To:

Jim

:)

BLOOD TRAIL ~~~~~~~~

BLOOD
TRAIL

MICHAEL SULLIVAN

JAMESON BOOKS
Ottawa, Illinois

Jameson books are available at special discounts for bulk purchases for sales promotions, premiums, fund raising or educational use. Special condensed or excerpted paperback editions can also be created to customer specifications.

For information or other requests please write:

Jameson Books, Inc.

722 Columbus Street

Ottawa, Illinois 61350

815-434-7905 • FAX 815-434-7907

E-mail 72557.3635@compuserve.com

Jameson Books titles are distributed to the book trade by LPC Group, 1436 West Randolph Street, Chicago, IL 60607. Bookstores should call 800-243-0138. Individuals who wish to order by mail should call 800-426-1357.

Library of Congress Cataloging-in-Publication Data

Sullivan, Michael, 1953–
Blood Trail / Michael Sullivan.
p.   cm.
ISBN 0-915463-84-9
I. Title.
PS3569.U349B58   1998
813'.54—dc21   98-26673
                                CIP

Manufactured in the United States of America

First Printing July 1998

1 2 3 4 / 00 99 98

If only I had possessed the vision fifteen years ago. . . .
This book is dedicated to the victims.

~~~~~~~~~~~~~~~~

IVORY WOKE FROM THE PAIN. THE WEIGHT OF CUTTER'S HUGE BODY ON him was more than he could bear. His fever burned again

He could not open his eyes. The crud that oozed out during his restless sleep cemented them shut and he could not pry them open with his fingertips. The problem had been getting worse for weeks. Ivory fumbled for the jar of water he kept under his side of the bed and dabbed at what was left of his eyelashes. Finally he could see enough to distinguish the faint light drifting through the barred windows at the end of the barracks.

Cautiously, he slipped his body from under Cutter's sedated flab. Small chance that the big shit would stir at this early hour, but Ivory couldn't afford to take risks. Cutter was always mean and the lingering effects of the downers would make him meaner. He'd give Ivory a beating for certain if his sleep were disturbed. Cutter looked like a grossly fat black Rottweiler sprawled across the bed. His lower lip sagged and his tongue hung out. Ivory shuddered.

Ivory straightened his cramped legs and pulled his prison-issued boxers up around his bony hips. There wasn't much to hold them up these days. He shuffled across the sanded pine floor to the toilets. No one else was awake except old Slappy Joe, finishing his cleaning chores. Ivory could hear the grunts and snores of the other inmates beyond the scrim-wall that Cutter had erected across his end of the room. The divider was made of old cotton table linens stitched together, weighted with broken broom handles sewn into the hem, and hung from a rafter. This bit of privacy cost Cutter dearly with the guards and attested to his untouchable power within the prison population.

Ivory fought to control his morning nausea and squatted at the commode to expel some of the nastiness from his bowels. He cleaned himself and walked over to the sink to wash. He splashed water on his face and stared at himself in the mirror—something he almost never did any more, not like the old days. The changes in his appearance frightened him. The bony arches across his forehead, the sunken cheeks, the dark circles under his stained and weary eyes; all of this stared back at him. He was no longer beautiful.

He had always been a loving and sweet boy. His mother's sisters named him Ivory because his skin was smooth and creamy like the keys on an old piano. The women had held him close and babied him and raised him like a little girl until the street took him. He was thirteen then.

The boy found that he could turn tricks with a special class of businessmen and make enough money to buy his way out of the slums of east Little Rock.

But Ivory developed a special craving for a new form of cocaine that hit the streets in the late '70s. The dealers taught him how to pop it into his arms, then between his fingers and toes, and finally in any vein that would flow.

The drug took possession of him, heart and soul, and in short order landed him at Cummins, the huge prison-farm in South Arkansas.

No one back home would recognize him now. In one long agonizing year his teeth had yellowed and gapped. His once beautiful complexion was now rough and broken. Large dark patches formed on his neck and back and he had been plagued with recurrent chest infections.

Ivory knew he was sick. Really sick. But he had to get to the showers and get ready to walk down to the infirmary. He wasn't going for treatment this morning. The nurses said he was fine. He was going for his weekly appointment to give his blood and Cutter would kill him if he failed to bring the "yellow boys" back. Percodan. Those pills and the little bit of ass he had left were the only two things that kept him in the good graces of Cutter. There were no options.

Ivory couldn't take his eyes from the mirror. He tried to cry, but the tears had long ago dried. He reached up and touched the reflection in the mirror the way the white men used to touch him.

"Poor, sweet Ivory" he whined in his mother's voice. "Sweet baby Ivory. What's happen to you, chile?"

His hand slid down the smooth face of the mirror and his eyes caught a glimpse of the scarred veins in his arms. He rubbed them and suddenly felt as though all his energy had slipped from his emaciated body.

For the first time Ivory realized that he was dying. He realized that the remaining two years of his sentence might as well be a death warrant. Without hesitation, he reached over and grabbed the safety razor. Cutter had bought it from a guard so that Ivory could shave his legs. He twisted the razor open as he walked into the showers and removed the double-edged blade, holding it in his teeth as he slipped out of his boxers and turned on the showerhead.

When the steam began to roll off the floor he sat under the warm spray with his back against the wall and plunged the razor deep into the veins of his scrawny arms.

He was surprised at how little pain there was. He tilted his head back and enjoyed the slight buzz that began to invade his consciousness. Ivory laughed quietly. He was pulling a great joke on the prison officials who expected him this morning. He decided to do what he wanted with his blood. It was his, after all, and now it was washing across the painted floor and down through the sewers of Cummins.

He was finally his own person again. No one could touch him ... not the guards, not the doctors, and not even Cutter. With a tiny laugh and then an even smaller whimper, nineteen-year-old Ivory Watkins passed from the world and made his parole the hard way.

ONE 〜〜〜〜〜〜〜

THE NA-GIA TREES BURST THROUGH THE SEAMLESS FOREST CANOPY, towering forty to fifty feet above the roof of the jungle. In this region of Vietnam, near the Cambodian border, they stood as sentinels over the fury of combat at close quarters. On nameless paths somewhere below, young men fought and fell. But the jungle kept its secrets from David. No sight, sound or smell of battle could reach him as his O-2 passed over.

David mused on troubling reports from home, where racial unrest had sparked urban rioting and a lot of kids his age were demonstrating against the war. Assholes! Much as David disliked his situation, at least it had a decent purpose. He served ungrudgingly if not gladly, and felt he was part of something big, part of history. Most of his generation, he knew, vaguely supported the American effort, but paid little heed to the savage drama playing out half a world away. They were probably swarming the lakes and beaches right now, listening to Fifth Dimension or the Beach Boys. If he were stateside, he'd be in the cool northwoods, fishing. Even Arkansas was cool in winter. Here it was always *always* too hot.

The O-2 plodded along its sweltering route. His artillery unit was somewhere up ahead under the unending green. Occasionally he'd see some latter-day pterodactyl dive out of a raggedy buzzard's nest, bailing out ahead of the plane. Big, ugly birds. Carrion eaters. The real masters of this death-soaked land, David thought.

"Remember me kindly if we ever come face to face," he mouthed over the drone of the engines, surprised by his own voice. "Remember, I'm the one who didn't light your ass with a siggy." His plane carried the small, tube-mounted rocket clusters under each wing. David had no wish to use them.

The Cessna OS-2 was a great little plane as long as you stayed low and drew as little attention as possible. It had started life as a civilian plane, notable for having its two engines in tandem. One turned a pusher prop in the back, the other turned a tractor prop in the nose. This design allowed low-time pilots to move up to the security of a second engine without having to master all the problems of asymmetric thrust in more conventional twin-engine planes.

O-2s were easy. O-2s were true. O-2s were slow—really slow. They were just the latest in a long line of small, dependable aircraft the army had chosen to do liaison, reconnaissance and artillery spotting.

Mounting rockets on the O-2 had made David laugh out loud. It was like General Patton drawing his pearl-handled colts to blast away at a strafing Messerschmitt. Recon pilots had always considered themselves well armed with a .45 on their hip and perhaps an old M-1 rifle in the back seat.

The story was, some stateside lieutenant general was hopping over to Da Nang one morning in an O-2 and drew some fire from the corner of a rice paddy. He was outraged when the pilot failed to return fire and even more outraged when he found he was in an unarmed plane. Thus the siggys.

"Alpha charlie zero six three eight bravo inbound on x-ray beacon. Over." David double-checked his radios and coordinates as he keyed the mike.

"Roger. Advise on sighting. Over," the reply came back.

David was not overjoyed about today's mission, ambushing the Ho Chi Minh trail—the main supply artery for the Vietcong. The artillery battalion he spotted for had been combining its efforts with point patrol squads working back and forth across the border between Cambodia and Vietnam. When the point squads encountered resistance, David would assist in directing the battalion's 105mm howitzer fire to the enemy position.

"Good morning, pukes. I see you stroked your bores last night. Over," he grinned as he winged over his two batteries of 105s.

"Hey, Farr, we can see you slickin' your lizard up there. You even lookin' for VC this morning? We haven't heard shit from you. Over."

"Negative on both counts, Williams, but I've got your lizard," he shot back. "Over."

The lizard crack reminded him of home and all the summer days he'd spent catching the nimble little creatures.

In South Arkansas you made your own entertainment during the hot schoolless months between May and September. Prize lizards were kept on the screen door, secured by a tiny piece of twine carefully tied around a rear leg. The other end would be attached to a safety pin and fastened to the screen. He realized his summer pursuits had not changed.

Guiding his plane along the morning's observation pattern, he knew that there were hundreds of Vietcong within earshot of his plane, but he would never see them. And, as with the lizards, tracking them and catching them were two different things.

The area he was now working was in the sector of his patrol squads. Visibility was increased due to a massive defoliation eight weeks before. He hated flying over these areas. Nauseating traces of agent orange were being borne aloft on the steamy evaporative clouds rising from the jungle floor. But it did offer him his only real chance to observe the trail. It also offered the Vietcong their best chance of taking a quick shot at him.

The drone of the plane's push-me, pull-me engines made it difficult to hear anything outside of the headsets. If not for the special indicator on the console, it would be almost impossible to know when you lost your rear engine during take-off. The vibrations were just too loud.

Today's mission was to catch any Vietcong supply shipment that passed through one of the defoliated valleys north and west of his present position. If he sighted a shipment, he'd determine its coordinates and direction, then radio for an artillery barrage to cut it off. The point squads would then move in to try and pin it down and destroy it.

The morning haze was burning off. Thermals created in the brown barren areas buffeted his plane. Farr extended the upwind leg of his pattern a mile farther than he had planned in order to roll over a ridge in the middle of a saddle. As he made the 180 and leveled out in the steppe of the next valley, he glimpsed a small metallic flash. It came from an area that had been defoliated but was covered in new greenery about eight feet tall. He had learned to follow up on these "possibles," as he called them. He kept on his course so he wouldn't alert his prey, but immediately planned to double back from the cover of the next ridge.

"Slapstick, Slapstick, six three eight charlie. I have a possible skunk in the works. Over."

"Lead me on, Eagle Eye. Over," came the reply.

David checked his instruments and compass and gave a rough estimate of the location.

"Heading two niner zero, approximately twelve clicks. Coming around momentarily to give it the sniff test. Over."

There was a moment of silence over the headsets, then, "Uh, six three eight charlie ... Roto Rooter is set up in that area so make sure you're not sniffing their ass. Over."

"Roger that, Slapstick ... stand by."

Farr knew that Roto Rooter squad would never place themselves directly on the trail. They were led by a crafty young Texan named Ricky Hicks, and Farr knew that Hicks was salivating as he listened to the radio chatter with a "possible" in his lap. He was a fighter and he knew how to set up his ambush.

David, like many, thought that the war would already have been resolved if all squad leaders were like Hicks. Once Ricky had told him that his squad had "a 55-gallon barrel of ass-whippin' that it was fixin' ta pour all over that trail."

Then he proved it. He led from the front, knew where his men were at all times, and perfected the techniques of a guerrilla strike patrol. His men would follow him anywhere.

The O-2 strained as David came back to the ridge at top speed and pulled her over the crest. He immediately killed the power and was able to nose her over to provide a nice view of the area in question. There, directly in front of him, was an exposed section of trail with something … large … in the middle of it.

His course carried him directly toward the object. He immediately added power in order to maneuver up and over the slope where it was perched. Something looked awfully familiar about that camouflaged bulge on the side of the hill. The partially shrouded tires gave it away.

"They've got a damned Chinese road grader!" he exclaimed.

As he glided even closer, he could make out the netting draped over the frame and he could see that the engine and heavy components had been stripped and replaced with hammock-style slings full of boxes and goods. The front had been lightened to a modified tricycle design and the cockpit removed.

As David approached, he realized that this weird truck was probably able to carry objects too heavy for a cart or bicycle. Objects like missiles and rockets. He also discovered that it was probably human-powered because what appeared to be dozens of Vietcong scurried out from under its apron. When David passed over their position, he noted that the caravan was already moving toward cover in the more heavily forested part of the ridge, toward the saddle he had used on his initial approach. As he cleared the peak, he pressed his PTT switch to notify the ground support.

"Slapstick, I have a major skunk infestation. You're not going to believe this one. They are loaded and heavy, heading due south toward a significant topo depression in the ridge. Over."

"Lay some numbers on me, Eagle Eye." Williams was on the other end of the radio and David could tell he was motioning activation signals to the 105 crews as they spoke.

As David read off the coordinates, he made a slow left turn over the back side of the mountain for another look. Then, below, at the saddle area, he saw what was to be his last battle in that screwed-up little war.

He could see, only too clearly, what was happening on the ground. Clearly, the road grader with its odd cargo was the tail end of a convoy and escort much larger than he had ever heard of on the trail. The front units had overrun a position that had apparently been held by the Roto Rooter squad. Hicks's men were in full fighting retreat, scrambling for their lives. The Howitzer fire he had called in might catch the tail of the enemy convoy but it would never help the men in Roto Rooter.

Reporting by radio and begging for reinforcements made David realize that any help would be too late. He had to do something. He banked hard over the battle and caught the flash of a claymore as it mowed down several VC worming their way down a small creekbed. The smoke and stench of the cordite billowed into the air.

David was circling through the valley in order to come back on the rear of the Vietcong assault when a new noise made its way through the headset. It was a noise that he knew ... much like one from back home ... the sound of an oil spout being jabbed into a can of motor oil. A metallic slipping sound following a hollow punctuated pop.

Must have taken a hit from an AK, he thought to himself. It pissed him off. It pissed him off so badly that he lost it.

Some pissant little shit had shot his plane. Someone was going to pay. Someone was going to get hurt. And he was god damned if anyone was going to overrun his buddies down there on the ground.

David jerked the yoke around to finish his final turn. This was the first time since coming to Vietnam that he had wished he were in a Skyraider or some other heavily armed plane.

Slamming the throttles to the wall he saw the rear-engine warning indicator at the same moment he felt the loss of power. The bullet must have taken out the oil pan or the fuel line. Never mind, he was lined up on target with plenty of altitude and speed. He flipped the lock off the missile trigger-panel and dove down between the naked stumps of trees.

David fired as he neared what appeared to be the largest concentration of Vietcong. The siggys zipped into the brush, opening fiery pock holes in the midst of the assault. He was close and on them. He could see the shocked expressions on some of the VC faces as they looked over their shoulders to see him so near, to suddenly know that they had gone from being the hunters to being the prey in the flick of a switch, the flash of a rocket.

And as fate would have it, David saw the face of the man who was going to kill him. Standing astraddle what appeared to be a young marine's body, a heavily camouflaged Vietcong soldier looked up as David's rockets flanked him.

David saw the slow deliberate way he turned and raised his gun, an old American-made Thompson machine gun, and began firing at him. There was nowhere for David to maneuver. As he lost sight of the young man with the gun, he heard the first of the bullets rip into the rear fuselage of the plane.

Actually the first round hit the already ruined rear engine and ricocheted forward through the firewall. But as the attacker brought his machine gun overhead, the rounds hit home. Fat .45-caliber slugs cut through the bottom of the cabin, piercing the floor and seats and exiting though the roof. One clipped David's right thigh as it came through his seat and shattered the copilot's window. David never felt it because the next round, a millisecond later, entered just under the left rudder pedal and obliterated his left heel and tibia.

The force of the bullet shot his knee up into the underside of the dash breaking the already injured leg midshin. David was only aware of a loss of left rudder and a hot numbness below his knee. He managed to lift his plane out of the battle area and level off as he dropped down into the next valley. The last few rounds had done a number on his front engine. Smoke was rolling out of the cowlings and he knew he must put her down immediately.

This is something that every pilot rehearses repeatedly in his mind.

"Don't stall the plane," he said to himself.

His voice came to him as if from a stranger, someone guiding him. He snapped out of his battle mode and was instantly overwhelmed by the red-hot pain in his left leg. He felt faint and had to bite into his lower lip to keep from passing out. A quick glance down told him the leg would be of no use to him. He carefully used his right foot to move the left one out of the way. The pain staggered him but he knew he had to have room to swing his good foot onto either pedal in the next few seconds.

In his mind's eye he had always pictured putting his plane down in heavy, mature canopy. He had told himself that if he could slow to the minimum flying speed and fly into a thick, level forest he might be able to avoid breaking up too badly. Instinctively he was making wide S-turns as he descended the mountain slope, looking for level and heavy growth. In the distance he could hear the huge explosions that must have been the 105 howitzers pounding the enemy positions behind him.

David felt something running down the right side of his nose. As he wiped, he swept granules of plexiglas and flesh from his forehead and cheek. The shattered windscreen had nailed him, but only superficially. Suddenly, just below, he spotted a possible landing zone. It was an area near the river that was still dense with trees. The tops seemed level. His biggest problem, besides being out of ideas and engines, was that he was too high.

The flap lever that he needed to activate in order to slow and assist the plane in a rapid descent, was gone. He automatically kicked in full right rudder and initiated a radical sideslip down toward the trees, using the side of the fuselage as an enormous air brake. He had learned this trick from his grizzled old flight instructor. It wasn't even included in modern aviation training.

"It might save your ass someday," the instructor had said. "That's assuming you get your thumb out of it and fly the damned plane." Those words kept echoing inside David's mind as he planned his approach and slowed the little plane, preparing to crash into the top of the jungle.

As the lush green tops of the forest filled his view, he brought the nose of the plane up, bled off his speed, and plowed straight ahead into the branches.

〰〰〰〰〰〰〰〰

David was not sure what happened next. The initial impact spun the aircraft violently. As the right wing tip caught, his head slammed against the left window and its brace. His next recollection was of coming fully conscious as the plane lurched in the branches high above the forest floor, trapped like a fly in a huge old spider web.

The plane had flipped and was now hanging in the massive trees, upside down, with her nose aimed toward the jungle floor. The weight of his body against the shoulder harness prevented him from releasing the buckles. Besides, he probably couldn't climb around in the cabin in his condition. He had never known such pain. He wanted to cry, but there was no way. Instead he forced himself to think. To concentrate. It was like trying to focus on simple things like speech and balance and basic reasoning after having too much to drink.

"Okay, okay! Shit, shit,... shit!" he said. Even thinking hurt.

As he looked around, he realized the plane was structurally intact. The wings were still attached and the cockpit was still in one piece. He reckoned that he was about sixty to seventy feet above the jungle floor. He could see pieces of limbs and vines scattered underneath him, knocked loose by his crash. He had no clue as to how he could extricate himself from this treetop snare.

The natural sounds of the wilderness slowly started registering with him. The birds and monkeys regained their voices and protested mightily about his intrusion into their world. But there was another sound. A ticking noise that sounded like metal being dinked with a drumstick. And the popping sound of a fire somewhere behind him. This terrible sound and the smell of melting plastic focused David completely.

"I'll be damned if I'm gonna flame out like a marshmallow on a stick," he offered to the trees.

He had to get out and lower himself to the ground or else bring the entire plane down. But he knew he could never get himself out even if he had a rope, which he didn't.

David began to rock the plane as much as he could with his body in order to free it from the grasp of the branches. It wouldn't budge.

"Hell, it'll take a stick of dynamite to blow me out of these limbs," David said to himself through the panic.

For a moment he pictured the fire reaching a fuel tank and the resulting explosion cooking him high in the trees. His plane was small, but he still carried over seventy gallons of high-octane gasoline. It would be quite a flame.

But then a possibility occurred to him. The missile pylon was completely torn from the right wing but was still intact on the left. It had taken on some natural camouflage of its own and was sitting slightly askew. As far as David could see, it was still armed with one missile and pointed in the general direction of the mast of the tree that seemed to have him. Another sniff of smoke convinced him to try it, no matter how crazy the effort.

He fingered the trigger but nothing happened. He tried over and over again, each time wincing from the anticipation of the explosion ... but nothing. Finally in desperation he slammed his fist into the firing console. The siggy leapt from its cradle and pulverized the side of the tree. It began breaking under the weight of the plane. Branches snapped and popped as the surrounding trees gave up their claim on the load.

As the tree collapsed from its midsection, it carried David's plane in an arc that turned him nose-high just before it dumped him tail first for the last thirty feet. The O-2 hit on its twin tail booms and crunched into the ancient mire of the river valley soil. The plane toppled from its tail-stand, upside down and severely rearranged.

David, still conscious, looked around, amazed that he had survived the fall. He frantically tore at his shoulder harness and fell through the half-opened door on the copilot's side.

Crawling on his elbows, he avoided the flaming oil and fuel dripping from the fuselage and laboriously wormed his way over a piece of wing. Each movement of his arms promised a horrible shot of pain from his left leg as it dragged along behind him. Nearing the edge of the river and finally clear of the fire now engulfing his plane, he was able to muster enough strength to roll over onto his back.

The sound of the battle and the fire and the animals was fusing into one penetrating hum. A numbness washed over him like a warm Caribbean wave, taking his pain and drowning it. One overwhelming thought filled the area of his mind where the pain had been. He realized for the first time how ultimately insignificant he was. He thought of all the effort that had gone into rearing him to this point. The love, attention, discipline, and training that had been invested in his little life were, at this moment, worth nothing. He was of no more value than any of the forest creatures. As his mind reeled, he smiled at the ridiculous complexity of events that had led to this point ... to his death in the jungle.

~~~~~~~~~~~

It was the day before he left for boot camp. Mary Ann had finally agreed to speak to him again. She had picked him up in her old Plymouth for a final date. They had been sweethearts since their junior year in high school.

She was a typical southern girl of the time: conservative, religious, and gorgeous, with long straight auburn hair parted in the middle. She was well-read, well-bred, and very mature for her age ... almost alarmingly so.

Mary Ann and David had worked their way around her religious objections to premarital sex by solemnly pledging themselves to each other. Their marriage was planned and pending until David announced his enlistment. Then things went into a tailspin.

David tried diligently to explain his reasons to her. He knew he would be drafted soon. He would rather choose his vocation in the military by enlisting. That was much better. Besides, college was not his cup of tea. Things were too strange. This would give him a chance to try to figure out what he wanted and that would make him a better husband.

Mary Ann, and especially her family, didn't see it that way. They had never been overjoyed about the relationship. David was from the wrong side of the tracks. His family was poor and came from an ancestry of Cherokee and immigrant stock. Her parents had eventually accepted him because of the insistence of their daughter. She knew what she wanted and what she wanted was David. He was an honest, likable boy, certainly not part of the new drug culture, so her family took him in by default.

They had been the perfect school couple. Mary Ann was the over-achieving cheerleader and David was a jock. They set the standards for cool and didn't have to look to some peer group for hints of what to do. They were their own entertainment. The passion was phenomenal. What Mary Ann lacked in imagination she made up for in energy. Her body was firm and tuned and she had somehow known how to channel and train his raging teenage desire to focus blindly on her. She could arouse him with a glance, a twist of her head, a touch.

Two hours after signing his enlistment papers, David had suddenly pulled over to the side of the road and cursed himself. He couldn't believe he had just signed away at least two years of uninhibited sex with Mary Ann. Guys would die just to have a date with her. What in the hell was he doing? He must have been crazy!

She had come to essentially the same conclusion that night when he broke the news at their favorite parking place. She had cried all the way home. She left him at the front door for the first time in two and a half years and had refused to see him ... until tonight. David ran out to her car when she pulled up, and he slipped behind the wheel as she slid across the seat.

"Hey, honey," David said, looking longingly at her and reaching out his hand. "You can't believe how much I've missed you."

"David, drive down Sixth Street toward the church. I want to show you something." Mary Ann spoke matter-of-factly, no warmth in her voice.

David realized something was up, but was so relieved just to be with her again, that he didn't worry.

"Can we talk, Mary Ann?" he asked.

"Not now, I've got to show you something."

David reached over and lightly touched her shoulder. She was wearing his letter jacket, with a turtleneck sweater under it. Her short pleated red plaid skirt rode deliciously up her thigh revealing the tops of her hose and one garter. David drove down Sixth Street as she directed and turned into the parking lot of the First Methodist Church. Mary Ann pointed to the broad stairs leading up to the main entrance of the chapel.

"I want you to remember this," she said. "Now please drive down Barlow Street to Sixteenth."

David sat for a moment staring at her, trying to figure out what kind of game she was playing. But she smiled at him and nodded for him to go, and he did. When they reached the intersection of Sixteenth Street, she asked him to pull into the drive of the old Barlow Mansion, a Victorian home that sat back in a stand of magnificent oaks.

"Do you see that house?" Mary Ann asked.

"Of course, honey, but what ..."

"I want you to remember it, too," she said. Her voice softened. "Now let's go out to our ... place."

David couldn't help smiling. His heart pounded and a wave of sensation left him so aroused he could hardly drive. She was asking him to take her to their parking place, a quiet, remote stand of thick pine trees behind an old folks' home. This was more like it!

Before they got to the outskirts of town, Mary Ann removed her shoes, pulled back her skirt and rolled off her hose. Then she slowly slid her panties onto the floor. David barely stayed on the road. He watched her as if he had never known her.

Mary Ann knelt on the far side of the seat and removed his letter jacket, throwing it into the back seat. With one hand she unfastened her bra, snaking it from under her sweater and arranging it around David's neck. He knew he must be a sight, driving like a madman and grinning like an idiot.

Mary Ann rubbed her breasts for a moment, looking at him with that look that she had. Then she climbed over the seat back, hesitating just long enough for him to glimpse everything that she would be saving for him.

David was wild. He never made it to the pine grove. He braked, threw the shifter into park and jumped out, pulling off his jeans, while searching through his pockets for a Trojan.

Mary Ann was more uninhibited than she had ever been. She made love to him in ways he could only have dreamed, but she never said a word. They finished with Mary Ann draped across the back of the front seat. He was behind her, leaning forward and reaching around her to grip the steering wheel as if his life depended on it. When the last spasms roared through his exhausted groin, the two of them fell back into the rear seat. He was totally spent. He slid from the seat and lay across the hump in the floorboard, gasping for breath. There didn't seem to be enough oxygen in the car.

"David," Mary Ann said from the seat above him.

"Uh huh," he moaned.

"David, sit up," she ordered, her words all business. She showed no sign of the passion that had just possessed them.

"What is it, Mary Ann?" he asked, barely raising his head.

She stepped out the back door of the car holding her panties in one hand.

"Do you see this?" she moved her hand down her sweaty and beautifully naked body. "I want you to remember this, too."

"Why are you saying these things, honey? I think about you all the time. I couldn't forget you if I wanted to. And I don't," he finished, his voice softer.

"I want you to remember all of this because in one year I intend to walk out the door of that church a married woman. Within ten years I intend to live in the Barlow house with my husband and children.

Whoever that man turns out to be is going to have my body and my mind and this kind of love for the rest of his life . . . I hope you will finally come to your senses and do what you have to do to get out of this military trap. I cannot and will not wait for you. It is impossible. My family is already pressuring me to go out with another guy from Little Rock. I'm running out of excuses. I need you now, not two years from now."

David couldn't believe what he was hearing. He felt as if someone had dropped an anvil on his chest. He lay there, naked, barely able to breathe, an intense feeling of dread and loss holding him in its grip.

~~~~~~~~~

The screams of the monkeys snapped him back to full consciousness. David mustered his strength and pushed himself up on his elbows to assess his chances. The lower portion of his left leg lay at a grotesque angle, the foot turned radically inward. He couldn't even try to move it. Exhausted beyond belief, he fell back on his back and stared up at the intricate leaf work above him.

He lay beneath a green ocean, his life slowly oozing out on the carpet of a tropical jungle. Occasionally a break in the canopy would expose the chalky blue sky. "Haint blue" is what the old folks called it back home. It was the color of the ceiling of every porch he had ever been on. It protected against evil entering your house and "messin' with you," according to the old superstition from slave days. Haint blue, a color that greeted you on the summer mornings when you awakened on the sleeping porch under sprinkled sheets. David thought this was probably the best color he could remember. He could see it through the trees. Heaven was going to be this color . . . haint blue.

TWO ~~~~~~~~~~~~

DUBLIN IS HOT TONIGHT, AND ROBERT DAVIS PRESCOTT IS IN HIS element. His fondness for redheads with abandon on their minds had finally pulled him off the campus and through the ancient gates of Trinity College. He had mostly stayed in his dorm since arriving there five days before. The three young ladies he followed took roost in a magnificently seedy pub just off Grafton Street. He had almost lost them in the melee of bodies which was the Grafton experience, but the cutest of the three had spied him in pursuit and managed to stall her friends.

Bob ordered a Bass and stood at the end of the backbar in total amazement. He had never seen a place so packed with women, available women, women intent on partying.

There were seventy or eighty different conversations going on simultaneously and yet the group seemed to be one throbbing, smoking, laughing, drinking organism. And now was the time to dive in head first.

"Another Bass Ale," he shouted to the bartender.

"What's that?"

"Another Bass, please," he repeated, holding his mug above his head.

"You a Yank?" the bartender asked.

"Yes, I guess. I just came here from the States." He prepared himself for some comment about his southern accent. Not only was he getting used to this, he was learning to turn it to his benefit.

"Well, sir, how can you do this?"

"Do what?" Bob asked, knowing that the punch line was coming.

"How can you keep poisoning your Yank soul with this piss-yellow brew?"

"You got something better?" Bob peered over the carved mahogany bar to see what the selections were.

"I have something not even in the same league, my son. I have the wondrous dark milk of your mum. One sip and you'll be cuddling up to a warm breast in no time, and as you can see, there is no shortage of warm breasts around here tonight. How about I prepare you the only drink you need to know, a man's drink ... a Guinness." He pronounced the name, Bob would come to understand, as only the Irish can, rolling it off their tongues with love and reverence.

He was continually amazed at the Irish ability to gab, to soliloquize at the drop of a hat ... and to look into your eyes as if the bullshit they were shoveling was the most important thing you would ever hear.

"You mean that black stuff?" he laughed.

"I'll do it for you as my contribution to your education and protection, and you'll thank me when you're old and famous," the barkeep promised as he pulled the brass handles to begin the draught.

Realizing it would be foolish to argue, Bob turned to relocate the girls he had been interested in. The smoke was so thick it was obscuring his view. He needed to move. The Bass might be piss but he was feeling a hell of a buzz. He was ready to mingle.

"My beer ready?"

The barkeeper turned from his task in mock disgust.

"Firstly, my round-faced friend, this nectar I prepare for you is not in any way, shape, or form ... a beer. And firstly again, like a lovely woman, it has to be caressed in stages," he nodded to the glasses on their stands, "until with drawing and pulling it culminates in a wondrous thick head." He sighed in admiration at his handiwork. "So stand there and play with yourself a little while longer and let me do me job."

"Okay, okay, thanks for your advice," Bob laughed. "It's just that I had my eye on a girl who seems to have worked her way to the other end of the room. Didn't want to lose her."

"Well, that may be so, and God forbid that I should change your intentions, sir, but if you'll look over and behind you, standing under the far wall sconce is a mysterious young lady who has had her eye on you since you stumbled your big self in here."

Bob turned as directed and caught the girl's eyes. She turned her stare to one of the guys she was talking with. A waif of a girl with long dark hair and deep-set dark eyes. She and the small group she was with wore American counterculture get-ups ... olive drab military jackets, old jeans, black accessories. They looked serious, uninterested in the partying, and it set them apart from the rest of the revelers. The little one glanced back to Bob and this time locked his stare.

"Sure now!" hissed the bartender. "I told you, lad. Now just be careful that you lock up with only the wee girl. The others with her, they're strange ones, they are." He double-handed a pint of perfectly topped Guinness across the bar and gave Bob a raised eyebrow with a nod.

Bob didn't know what to do. He'd lost the women he was following and was not exactly sure about this new girl across the room, but then, the way she looked at him was so ... experienced. He was interested.

Before he could make a decision, it was made for him. The girl made her way across the room with three empty pints and headed directly for him. She moved nimbly through the crowd, confident and quick. He turned to face the bar so as not to seem obvious, but he could feel her presence behind him. She said nothing. After several uncomfortable moments, she spoke.

"You big drink of a Yank, you could get down on your knees so that someone else might see a way to the trough." Her voice was strong and cut through the din of the pub.

There was no way to ignore her, so he turned and tried to think of something clever to say. She had a wrenched scowl on her face. If she was acting, she was doing a great job. His response slipped out before he could avert it.

"And if you get down on your knees you might find a way to get me to buy you a round."

He regretted this almost before he said it, but he finished it with the committed look of a real smartass. He had never said anything like this to a woman. The beer had loosened his tongue more than he realized.

Before he knew what was happening the girl thrust her empties into his gut, causing him to fumble for their purchase. With the same movement, she reached down to his slacks and unfastened the waist.

"Well, let's see what you got, you big-ass bastard!" With that she jerked his trousers and boxers down to half staff before he could turn away and throw the glasses on the bar. As he recovered and lurched over to grab his pants, she was on her way up. The top of her head caught him in the face. He felt his nose let go the instant before his knees went, rolling him against the wall as all the lights went out. He slid down the wall in the sweet embrace of unconsciousness, not concerned for a moment that his most private parts were planted on the cold tile floor for everyone to see.

Bob's resurrection was slow. He became aware of sounds before he could reclaim any other functions. Everything was still dark, but he could hear voices close about him.

"Well, Colleen, what exactly were ya doing to him. Were ya screwin' or boxin'?"

"I was calling a bluff," she answered tight beside his ear. He could feel her breath on his neck.

"I think the evidence suggests she was administering a proper job on his piping when his nose blew off," the bartender announced.

All kinds of voices broke out in laughter around him. But it was the thudding sound of a bar glass that forced Bob to open his eyes.

"Colleen, he's comin' around. Why don't you give him a kiss and see if you can blow off the other end?" a red-faced punk yelled from directly above his face.

Bob was still groggy. His nose suddenly screamed with pain. He moaned and tried to sit up when her face moved in front of his eyes. Then he felt her lips on his forehead.

"Sorry, Yank," she whispered.

Bob reached with his left arm to find the floor, but there was none. A sudden fit of vertigo overwhelmed him and he jerked and twisted as if he were having a seizure. He tried to orient himself.

Hands and bodies grabbed and steadied him long enough for him to realize that he was safe. Slowly he was allowed to sit up. His gradual return to the land of the waking revealed he had been stretched out on the bar, for God knows how long. There were at least thirty people surrounding him, saluting and cheering with laughter.

"Welcome back." The barkeep slammed a Bass down beside him. "Hope the Guinness wasn't the cause of your stroke."

The girl had been kneeling on the bar and now turned and sat beside him as he slowly slid his legs around. He reached up to locate what was left of his nose only to discover some horrible material jutting from each nostril. Instinctively he grabbed at the ends to pull them out. They felt like soft plastic pencils.

The girl grabbed his hands and forced them away.

"Hold on there, friend, you don't want to make things worse," she said.

"What do you have in my nose?" he honked, eyes burning and filling with tears.

"Oh, just a little salted fat from the kitchen crammed up in there to stop the bleeding and take the swelling away. It doesn't feel too great but it can work wonders, trust me."

His embarrassment hit him like a hammer. He suddenly remembered being stripped naked in front of all these people. Retreat urged him up and off the bar.

"Yeah, well, thanks for all your help," he muttered under his breath. "See ya."

He picked his way through the crowd and headed for the door. It seemed that there was a sea of strange faces laughing at him.

Over the past week he had been warming to Ireland, even liking it a little, but now his mood turned to cold, brutal hate. He had to get out.

He knew he must look like a freak with pieces of pork hanging from his nose, but he was afraid to touch them.

Finally and mercifully, Bob cleared the entrance onto the street. He felt a hand pull at his jacket. The girl had followed him out and now attached herself under his left arm. She felt tiny and fragile against his side. As he glanced down, she peeked up at him and began marching him down the sidewalk, back toward Trinity.

"Where we going?" he asked.

"As we say over here, we're going to repair to the house, and I think in your case repair might be just the right term. We're going to Trinity, of course," she finished.

"You know the school?" he asked, glad to be moving away from the vicinity of the bar for any reason.

"Of course. I've been two years there, if not my whole life."

"A student there? What are you taking—karate, self-defense, judo?"

She laughed a deep hearty laugh, belying her size. "No, I've already finished those courses; I'm into something more dangerous ... political science."

"You're kidding." He wondered whether to admit this. "So am I."

"I know," she said, pulling up to a corner. "I know quite a bit about you, you see, but I never planned on running into you like this, literally."

He was still not in the mood to laugh and this sudden revelation took him by surprise. "Why would you know about me?"

"There's a group of us on campus who are true supporters of the civil rights movement. And the way it's spilling over into protest against the war ... Well, we just try to contact as many of the Yanks as possible. Our country has a lot to gain from more progressive thinking." She paused, realizing that she was getting too serious.

"Okay, we're protesters." She looked at him to see what response this might bring.

She continued, "We know that you're here as a Bateman scholar." Still no response. "We consider him the greatest supporter of the antiwar movement in your Senate ... so we thought you might want to join us," she finished.

Bob was shocked. He never dreamed that anyone would know about his background. After all, he was just a small-town kid from Arkansas, a small-town state. Serving as a page for Senator Bateman had been more than he ever dreamed possible, yet here were people on the other side of the ocean wanting his participation because they knew of his connection with the man. This was heady stuff.

Looking down at the girl he could feel the energy seething in her. He saw that there was fierce conviction just under her surface and wondered if he really wanted to know any more about her.

"What's your name?" he asked.

"Colleen," she said, holding his arm.

"Hum, Colleen, y'all have a marvelous way of making an impression on people over here. What did you say the name of your group was?"

"I didn't," she answered as she pulled closer under his jacket.

The trip back to the campus took only a few minutes. Along the way Bob realized there were other people joining them, faces from the bar. The mood was happy and boisterous. He began feeling better.

"We'll take you up to my room and get you cleaned up, Mr. Prescott," she said, squeezing his arm and leading him through the archway. "Look at it this way. You've already survived the initiation."

He tried a smile, but any movement of his face revived the pain around the inserts in his nose. "How about these?" He indicated his nose with a protective hand.

"Oh, I think we can do away with the packing now. We'll find a little ice. Follow me." She left him and ran up an outside staircase at the end of one of the women's dorms. He followed, slowly, unable to keep up.

〰〰〰〰〰〰〰

Bob Prescott had managed in his three years of college to climb well beyond the expectations for a poor boy from Arkansas. Thanks to his mother, he had learned to carry himself well among strangers. It was one of the things Miss Naomi required of him.

Naomi Rae struggled against poverty to bring up three sons by herself. If money was short, she made sure they had plenty of pride, and insisted that they hold their heads up and look people directly in the eye. Anyone's eye.

With Bob, the oldest, she had seen the uncanny way he had of absorbing his surroundings and feeling comfortable with any group. She saw great things for Bob and eased him into situations to achieve them. The boy was bright, but his gifts went well beyond book learning. He had a charm and a disarming wit that made all of her struggles worthwhile. Everyone liked Bob. And Bob adored his mother.

Bob had been in several girls' dorm rooms in his young life. Secretly, he was fascinated with the smells and niceties that accompanied them. Growing up as he did with a protective mother and only brothers in the house, he actually knew very little about the care and feeding of a female. He loved what little he knew. However, nothing prepared him for what he saw as he stepped through the door of Colleen's room.

Pamphlets were stacked and scattered all over. Posters of Jimi Hendrix, Janis Joplin, and Joan Baez were pinned haphazardly to the walls, with Gaelic words written across them with a bold red marker. The single bed was piled with every sort of newspaper and flier. A sleeping bag sat parked in the only clean corner.

The few sticks of furniture had been painted in the most hideous neon paint, a different color for each leg. In the farthest corner stood a mannequin painted black, with white stripes and polka dots scattered about its nude body. Clothes, clean and dirty, fought with books and notepads for positions on the floor. The overall effect on Prescott was shock.

"Pardon the mess, my friend, but as you can see this is a working girl's flat. Now come on in and let me see to your war wounds."

Bob tried to appear unconcerned as she guided him through the room into the bathroom that she shared with residents of the adjacent dorm room. Thank God, it was remarkably clean. She sat him on the commode.

"Now, you must allow me to remove the packing . . . without interference," she was holding a damp towel at his chin. "You may feel the need to gag . . . only for a moment . . . just ignore it."

Bob nodded tentatively. She grabbed the plug in his right nostril and slowly twisted and pulled it down and out. He felt his throat revolt and he swallowed hard to contain the urge to vomit. Before he could protest, she pulled the other piece out. Bob felt the beer that had been floating in wait come up and over his tongue. There was no way to stop it and the full serving of piss-poor Bass Ale struck Colleen just below the chin.

Her shock was equal to his. They looked at each other helplessly until she burst into laughter. Slowly his horror melted away, and then he could not help joining in. He took the towel and began cleaning her chest with it.

Colleen regained her control and stopped him. She reached over her head and flipped her old black sweat up and off, revealing two perfect little breasts, freckled and white, with tiny tight nipples.

"Well, I guess you got even with me, Mr. Prescott," she said without a thought about being there half-naked in front of him. Bob tried not to blush but it was impossible.

"Sorry, Colleen, I really didn't mean …"

She cut him off with a flip of her wrist and a wave of the shirt.

"If that's the worst I ever get on me, 'twill be a lovely life. Now grab that clean towel and let's get the both of us cleaned up, we've places to go," she ordered.

Bob did as commanded and she cleaned his face and neck, then he wiped hers off. He didn't think he had ever had such an erotic experience. She looked directly into him with those deep, dark, laughing eyes.

"You think we could rest for a few minutes, maybe, Colleen?" He smiled at her. His voice had changed and both recognized his intentions. His nose was still hurting like a son of a bitch, but still …

She pulled up close. Bare chest against his jacket. She spoke softly. "Mr. Prescott, my presence is demanded at an important meeting in a few minutes. In fact, so is yours. But for now, know that this is my pledge to you. The next time I remove your trousers it will not be in jest or in anger, and certainly it will not be in a pub."

With this she jumped up on the side of the bath, planted a kiss firmly on his cheek, jumped back down, and flounced away, back into her dorm room.

He stood there befuddled. He didn't know what to do or say. Once again the decision was made for him. Colleen, attired in a duplicate sweatshirt, bounded back through the door, grabbed his sleeve, and jerked him through the room.

"So we're off," she yelled. And they were, hurrying down the cobbled pathways to the courtyard of Trinity and around the gnarled trees toward the bell tower. His questions were waved away with, "Oh, you'll see!"

Bob could see a group of sixty or seventy students gathered on the north side of the bell tower. Some were sitting, some standing. Some carried signs. Two or three plunked guitars and sang. The songs tapered off as he and Colleen approached.

Bob was not surprised to see that Colleen was the leader of the gathering. She stepped around him and leaped onto a bench to speak. The group went silent. Her voice was practiced and strong.

"I see most of you made it as scheduled. I hope you brought your bedrolls and blankets. I'll remind you that our plan over this weekend, before classes resume, is to form a peaceful sit-in here in the courtyard. We speak for peace. We protest any involvement in the unjust war in Vietnam by any Irish organization or school, public or private.

"We will be heard! We will speak out and sing and encourage other students and faculty members to join us. Our convictions are sure to get attention from the media. You must stick to the prepared material we handed out yesterday. Study it, memorize it, so that you can be sincere and convincing if you are interviewed.

"We will hold our ground for the entire weekend, concluding Sunday at 5:00 P.M.

"I have food and drink coming through at different intervals, but there will not be an abundance, especially if our numbers grow, so be frugal."

Colleen took a breath and shot a wink at Bob.

"As you see, one of the Americans we've discussed in our planning is here with me tonight."

There were scattered applause and a few supportive comments from the crowd. Bob felt as if someone had just shoved him in front of a train. Gesturing to him, Colleen continued, "His name is Bob Prescott. He is from a southern state that is quite familiar with sit-ins and protests. He is on loan to us through Senator Bateman's Fellowship and is on close personal terms with the senator.

"As you may know, Bateman is one of the few United States senators still speaking with a strong voice against the war. So now I would like Mr. Prescott, from his greater experience, to say a few words to help us with the goals we share and the ways we can work together for peace."

Bob thought he might swallow his tongue. He couldn't believe she had put him in the spotlight with no clue as to what to say. Not only had he never been to a protest, he wasn't even sure what they were all about. But here were seventy faces looking at him expectantly, urging him to speak. He spoke without knowing what he was saying. He was in his survival mode.

"I think you have done an excellent job in your preparation. This, without a doubt, took a lot of work and leadership." He glanced over to Colleen with a committed look. "I hope that you will remember those poor souls who are suffering the greatest indignities imaginable in Southeast Asia.

"My country has chosen, unwisely, to commit more violations against those people . . . in the name of democracy! But, thank God, we are still allowed to speak out against aggression, and against our own countrymen when they do the wrong thing.

"Remember that these have to be peaceful demonstrations. We who oppose violence cannot be trapped into using it ourselves. That would only serve to promote more disregard for human rights."

He was on a roll now. He felt oiled and tuned. He could have talked all night. The students listened to him raptly and nodded in agreement with each point he made. Sometimes they cheered or clapped. Bob Prescott could feel what they wanted him to say and he ached to say it for them. To be their voice. But he decided not to stretch his lead. He needed a finale . . . a cap. He had it.

"One of my heroes said something we all must remember . . . just before he was cut down in another act of extreme violence. These are his exact words: 'Ask not what your country can do for you. Ask what you can do for your country.'"

He said this with the utmost sincerity. His voice even cracked a little at the ending. He wasn't sure that the quote had anything to do with their purpose, but it was a great quote and it got the response he had hoped for.

Enthusiastic young men and women swarmed around him and shook his hands. It took several moments for Colleen to regain control of the group.

"It is now 3:00 A.M.," she announced. "Take two hours for your final preparations and meet back here at 5:00 A.M. Mr. Prescott ... Bob ... will be here to talk with us and if we can get him a bedroll, I'm sure he will be with us for the duration. Thank you everyone! Peace!" she finished with a shout and jumped down from the bench to hug Bob and then engineer his introductions to those waiting to meet him.

As Bob played down his experience and expertise, she played it up as if he were only being modest. It worked well. He felt great. His injured nose was an insignificant problem in the light of all this. Bob felt that there was a special glow about him, and he occasionally looked down to see if it was showing when he shook hands.

This tiny Irish girl had moved him, in *one hour,* into a position of considerable clout among the student body. He wondered if she had planned this or just built it as it happened. Anyway, he thought, it was great. She was great. He loved Ireland again.

As the activity died down, someone produced a bedroll for Bob and Colleen retrieved hers from her room. One by one people stretched out for a short nap before morning's light. Bob found Colleen and pulled her down beside him for a brief kiss.

"You were great, Yank," she whispered in his ear.

"You were manipulating," he whispered back.

"How so?"

"You just made me into what you needed at the time."

"And you loved it."

" I guess I did ...So, how 'bout you and me?"

"That's maybe and later. Let's rest for now." With that she turned over and squirmed back against him, her body warm against his in the cool Irish night.

For the second time that night he found himself on his back. But this time instead of looking up at a tin pub ceiling, he saw a wonderful Dublin sky. The wind had shifted to the southeast and the haze of the city had blown away to bare an indigo-blue canvas, draped with the faintest orange pin lights.

Robert Davis Prescott could believe anything on a night like this. Things were falling into place as they never had before. He pondered how insignificant he had been feeling, just another student at another institution, flailing for a toehold. But now ... all of these possibilities.

And this blue, blue, deep-blue sky. He thought for a moment that heaven might be like this ... deep indigo blue.

THREE 〜〜〜〜〜〜〜〜

THE SMELL OF LYSOL PERMEATED THE CORRIDORS OF THE HOSPITAL. Everything was surprisingly clean. Gurneys were lined up in order with tightly tucked sheets covering their tops. Nurses were in full crisp uniform down to the last hair clip.

Ricky Hicks knew by their nervous glances that he was out of his element. He always felt this way in proper places. One of the old Indians he had taken instruction from in Texas had told him he had "the long-tooth look." It hadn't been a compliment. It was even worse when on rare occasions he smiled at someone. He had seen terror once in a young Vietnamese whore's face when he attempted a romantic expression. She had cried. But such was his lot. Not everyone could be beautiful.

Ricky had managed to get by the old head nurse by casting her one of those smiles. She was a leftover from the Korean conflict and was single-handedly responsible for the efficient manner in which this hospital was operated. Everyone, especially the surgeons, minded her. She created and enforced all of the schedules. She cleared all of the passes. She ruled supreme most of the time, but the look of fresh kill in Ricky's eyes stilled her normal rampage about visitors not being allowed into the intensive-care wards. When his eyes pulled back in a smile and he made his request, she simply signed the pass and nervously handed it over to him, avoiding his leer. So much for protocol.

Ricky Hicks was a curious study in movement. He was thick through the shoulders and about six feet tall, but his waist was unusually narrow. His hair was probably brown but he kept it so short that it just formed a patina over his skull. His complexion was deeply bronzed. In the jungle he moved like one of the forest animals, slightly crouched but relaxed. Flowing more than stepping. But here in this waxed corridor he moved along the walls as a rat might, hating the sound of his own footsteps.

Locating the ward, he ducked through the doorway and its curtains and stepped into a large white room with twenty beds lining each long wall. Most were occupied, each with its own accompaniment of bottles, wires, casts, and charts. It was uncannily quiet.

Ricky began a slow scrutiny of the names at the foot of each bed. Some were obvious because the nurses had taped huge posters on the ends of the beds with special instructions like, "He likes to be called Jamey ... or Bubba ... or Kiki." Some said, "He doesn't like peanut butter" or "Coca-Cola only at noon." Ricky spotted the bed he was looking for on the other side of the room.

"Hey, Eagle Eye!" He reached out and grabbed the naked foot sticking out from under the bedsheets. David's head was wrapped, and gauze covered one eye, but the other eye flashed open as a convulsive jerk sparked through his body. The hardware of the orthopedic hammock that cradled what was left of his injured leg clanked and creaked as it protested.

"Man, I'm sorry!" Ricky gasped, pulling away from the bed.

David had only begun to have periods of coherence within the last two days. As was typical in Vietnam, his doctors made prolific use of morphine. David had been under her merciful spell for over a week. Waking up was always a bitch. It took a few moments to think and by the time he could, he didn't want to anymore. He recognized Hicks and slowly reached out his hand to him.

"Hey."

That was the best he could muster. His throat was parched and he tried to roll and reach for the water glass. Ricky understood, reached over, and handed the glass to him, pushing it into his hands.

As David drank, Ricky studied all the paraphernalia surrounding his friend. A bottle of dextrose, a bottle of saline solution with antibiotics, and a unit of blood all made their way down to David's arms. Ropes and clamps with stainless-steel fittings blocked every escape route from the bed. Hicks knew at that moment that he would rather die than be in his buddy's place.

"The nurses told me what you did, man," David said at last. "I owe you my life."

"No way, José. I guess you didn't hear the right story, man." Ricky sat on the side of the bed. "It's me and my guys who owe you."

"Well, I can't remember much. The last I knew I was having a really nice dream and leaking out on the bank of the river. I don't think this leg carried me out." He pointed to his stump, bandaged about six inches below the knee.

"Oh yeah, well, that's *your* story. *Mine* is that we engaged the front end of the dragon just about the time you reported seeing the tail. We'd wired the saddle to snare a few trail gooks but we got a shitload of them. They overran us.

"The first hundred or so, we kicked their asses. My guys didn't budge. But then they started trying to flank us, and they had the numbers to do it with. I had to pull back and counter their flank, and they cut us to pieces.

"It's like they were doing speed, man. I lost three men in the first fifty yards. I was getting ready to make a last stand when you dove in on them. God, it was great! They turned to see what the fuck was on their ass and we ran. We ran like shit from a goose."

He was crying through his smile as he held David's hand.

"I looked back to see your little baby rockets zipping into their advance and cutting them up sideways." He took another slow breath, remembering the men he'd lost.

"Hey, Dave, I want you to know that I saw the motherfucker who shot you." He stopped and wiped his eyes on his sleeve. "He had just shot little black Sammy, my radio man, and I was coming back to get an angle on him. I couldn't get there fast enough, man, but I guarantee you, he never had one damn second of satisfaction from what he did to you," Ricky croaked, his voice broken.

They both sat in silence for more than a long moment, tears streaming down their faces, looking at the floor. Ricky invaded the quiet.

"Man, we wanted to kiss your puckered little butt, so imagine how we felt when we stumbled over you taking your siesta beside that river. Just threw your ass on a log and floated you and the rest of our sorry selves down the Swanee River to our pickup point. Piece of cake." He slapped the mattress. They both cracked up. It seemed so strange that either of them was there to talk about it.

David found out about all the losses in Ricky's platoon and the loss of one of the auxiliary evac choppers. It had been a bloody day for the entire unit.

"How's the leg, man?" Ricky asked.

"Oh, as they say around here, no ass-kicking contests for at least a month."

"That's a bitch, man … I hear they can fix those back like new nowadays."

"Yeah, they told me this morning, as soon as I'm stabilized they're shipping me to Germany to get my oil changed and to get one of those 1969 BMW sport-model left legs. Supposed to be slick. I've been wondering if Washington will spend as much money getting it rebuilt as they did to get it shot off." They both sat there for a moment staring at his stump.

"What can I get you, Dave?" Ricky asked in a more serious tone.

David studied the sheets for a moment, "A reason."

"What's that?"

"A reason … you know … a reason that we both had to be here, man. That you had to risk your life, lose your men, and I had to leave my leg and blood here in this sorry little country … Does anyone have a plan, Ricky?"

They looked into each other's faces, searching for a glimmer of hope, of comprehension. There was none.

"Yeah, Davey … they got a plan, but I don't think winning this war is anywhere in it." He pivoted to stare across the bed, unconsciously trying to peer out the whitewashed window. "What I figure is that the bigwigs in Washington are into spending, not winning. And they've got one hand on their balls and the other hand in the pocket of this big war machine. We're just the little army men they're playing with.

"Oh, yeah, they've got lots of speeches and a whole shitload of talk." He leaned forward with his elbows on his knees. "But you're out of here, buddy. You got your ticket home the hard way." He turned and smiled that horrible smile at David.

"And what about you?" David asked.

"I'm finishing my second tour. Don't think I'm going to hang around for another stint. They're going to have to find someone else to lead these boys out to die. Besides, there are other battles around that pay a hell of a lot better than this one. I think I'll look a few of them up ... after a nice long vacation."

"How can I find you back in the States?" David asked.

"You know where my dad hangs out, down in Grand Isle. He may be able to find me. I'll tell him to watch for you. You gonna be back slopping hogs over in Hicksville?" He laughed at the pun on his own name.

"No. I'm going to spend some time up North. I think I'll take some of my layback money and just look around for a while. Hey, you want me to relay any messages to all the conscientious objectors over there?" he asked facetiously.

"Yeah, Davey ... tell them to carry their sorry fucking asses home. Tell them to crawl back and dig the graves to bury my boys ... It's the least they can do ... don't you think? It's the least they can fucking do, man."

FOUR ~~~~~~~~~~

AUGUST 28, 1968
ROSA'S CASITA
HOT SPRINGS, ARKANSAS

"J O LYNN, WOULD YOU TELL THE DRIVER TO GET THAT LIMO CRANKED up out there? And, Sweetie, bring me and Senator Bateman another cocktail before we leave. We're gonna need some fortification against this gaahddamned sultry night." Gates had a way of cussing that could charm a Baptist preacher.

He had turned in his chair so that he could watch the girl spring into action. Fishnet hose, high-heeled shoes, and a gorgeous body helped Jo Lynn conceal the fact that she was still two years too young to be working in a place that served liquor.

She walked across the bar with a real determination to keep her miniskirt pulled down far enough to cover her "womanness." Congressman Gates was certain that this latest fashion was part of Satan's plan to corrupt the younger generation. He loved it.

Turning back to his table he caught Rosa's eye from behind the bar.

"Rosa, honey, that Jo Lynn's got promise written all over her. I want you to check with her momma about her coming up to D.C. and working for me."

Rosa nodded with one of her "shame on you" looks, and smiled her catty smile. Rosa had not become the most exclusive restaurateur in the spa city by placing her morals or principles ahead of her guests'. Rosa's Casita had been a clandestine meeting place for many years. The special club of men who brokered power in Arkansas considered her discreet, out-of-the-way lakefront place to be one of their best retreats. Most of the official state business, and a good deal that could never be officially acknowledged, had first been discussed over dinner and drinks at Rosa's.

Melvin Gates had been an important figure in Congress for over twenty-five years. His early contemporaries had made the mistake of assuming that his southern drawl and laid-back "country boy" facade were real. Time and again he ambushed their naiveté with ruthless, calculated maneuvering. Men and careers were tested and wasted against his back door political assaults. Little did they realize the quality of training he had received during his years in local Arkansas politics.

The inner club, the money people, who made it through the Depression in Arkansas were in the perfect position to benefit greatly during the war years. The state population was only one-and-a-half million and of those only a handful were at a level of substantial wealth. This made for firm friendships.

This inner club had developed the Arkansas legislature for protection against any interference, from without or within. It was their practice then to handpick the most promising and clever of the bunch to push into federal positions. These included judgeships as well as congressional offices.

Melvin Gates had been one of their men after the war. He had remained tough, inventive, and loyal to their interests. He had risen to become arguably the most powerful man in Congress, chairman of the House Ways and Means Committee. All federal spending begins in the House of Representatives, and the Ways and Means chairman controls the whole process. It was funding measures coming before his committee in the fall that had prompted tonight's meeting.

Congressman Gates cut through the chitchat at the table and took command of the conversation. "Senator, I suppose the funding request on this urban renewal project will meet with considerable flack from our friends on the East Coast. As before, your assurance of support for their Defense Department proposals, especially in Vietnam, will certainly make it easier for me to clear the funding for this urban renewal mess. Which brings up a point ... has anyone wondered whether there is truly an urban area in Arkansas outside of Little Rock?" Gates finished with a huge gulp from his vodka and tonic.

Senator J. Rison Bateman had been watching Gates play this game for three decades, drinking heavily to disarm his colleagues before making his move to the kill. He spoke with little reserve in his voice when addressing the older congressman.

"Melvin, I will remind you that several of our ... own ... constituents will expect you to use every bit of your arm-twisting ability in committee to fund this proposal. There are many large areas of our cities that will be included in this plan and those landowners are quite ... serious. I would also remind you of the great popularity of this legislation with our colored voters." Senator Bateman delivered this finishing argument like an olive in a martini, just an added come-on. He glanced at the two aides who'd accompanied them to dinner and dismissed them with a tilt of the head. Gates was slugging down the last of his cocktail. The senator was not through.

"Listen here, Melvin, my position on spending in Southeast Asia is legitimate and timely. More and more of our people are coming to understand the amount of our money going to interests outside of our state. They want their cut, but not in war bonds. They want programs ... to bring some of those federal dollars to their ... enterprises. You and I are on the same team, you know." He finished with the righteous flourish that he had developed as an orator on the Senate floor for over twenty years.

"Kiss my ass, J. R.!" Gates slurred at him. "If you want the programs for 'our people,' then you are going to have to continue to play the game with the rest of us. Who gave you a conscience? You've even got that pecker-headed Prescott kid believing that bullshit. What crawled up his hind-end? Did you see that picture from Ireland? My God, he looked like a communist, sitting there smiling with all those radical Micks."

Bateman was truly surprised. Nothing slid by Gates. The rummy old bastard had connections at absolutely every level. The picture of Bob Prescott had been released by the AP and picked up by a student newsletter published for alumni congressional pages. The newsletter editors had deemed Prescott's part in staging a sit-in at Trinity College to be a major accomplishment for an alumni page. Bateman had hoped the story might go undetected, but there was no chance of that now.

"He's just a kid, Melvin. He got caught up in one of those student things. You remember what it's like. Probably some cute Irish girl in the middle of it." Bateman tried to pass it off.

Prescott had been not only his aide and page, but also his driver and constant companion for almost eighteen months. The kid was like a bright Baby Huey, new as an egg, but soaking up policy and statistics like a sponge.

The men of the inner circle would expect Bateman to keep the kid on track and Gates knew this better than anyone. Bateman's own unpopular stance against the war was not only jeopardizing the huge, money-cranking war effort, but also endangering the legitimacy of the talent coming up through the appointed ranks. Gates would love to use the Prescott kid as an example.

"J. R., the kid ought to be glad we kept his lily-white ass out of the rice paddies over there. He needs to keep his mouth shut and his mind on pussy. I seem to recall that the pursuit of the fairer sex is the only thing that he and I might share in common."

The congressman turned as Jo Lynn sauntered back through the front door.

"I swear, Melvin, you are an incorrigible old pervert. The older we get the worse you get.

"I'll talk to Prescott this week ... Tell your people not to worry. I'll reel him in. I've still got his purse strings, you know."

"Yes, and I've still got yours. The Navy boys are gonna dig in on this one. They're adamant about having your support. It won't have to be real flashy. Just chalk it up to the fact that you have new confidence in a speedy and honorable conclusion to this conflict, and you have always supported any measure that would enhance the safety of our men in battle." He smiled a greasy smile across the table.

"They'll have my support, Gates, but I'll be god damned if I need you to tell me how to twist it. I'll issue no statement unless *I* decide to, and I want that urban renewal money in the bank. Can you deliver or not?"

"My, my, Senator, you sure don't sound like much of a dove, sir." Gates grabbed the edge of the table, pulling himself into a low crouch, face to face with Bateman. "The only doves I've seen around Arkansas lately had a load of number seven shot up their rears and a wonderful white gravy dripping off their breasts."

He stood, turned, and felt his way between the red-and-white-checked tables, and lunged into the thick summer night.

FIVE 〜〜〜〜〜〜〜〜

JULY 26, 1972
RIVER CABIN
REDFIELD, ARKANSAS

THE GREEN HERON FLEW UP THE NARROW SLOUGH WHICH DRAINED into the river. Cypress and tupelo gum had choked the water flow to a trickle, and beaver had engineered an enormous blockade preventing all access up the shoot. The heron never saw the four men sitting in old metal lawn chairs with their fingers stuck in their ears.

The bird's course carried it low over the small body of open water below the bluff where they were sitting. The dingy water was dusted with small fragments of paper and wadding and unspent gunpowder, the leftovers of a weekend's target practice. At that instant, the water erupted in front of the heron. A section of the slough roughly thirty yards wide split as if struck by God on the command of some backwoods Moses. The sudden force opened the water down to a mucky bottom that had never seen the sun. The blast caught the bird full force, snapped both its wings, and tossed its lifeless remains up into the overhanging branches. A trail of blood and feathers marked its last flight.

As the water fell back, single trees on each of the opposing banks toppled majestically toward each other and crashed into the slough, intermeshing their upper branches. It was a wonderfully orchestrated event, but the bird was an unexpected surprise.

"Holy shit!" Lamar whooped as he shot from his chair.

The blast had created a rainbow of filthy mist and bark fragments that now rained down around them. The others came out of their chairs to brush the water and debris from their clothes. All of them yelled some sort of obscene praise for the moment—except for Worley.

The blasting cord, made by DuPont, resembled a plastic shrouded clothesline. The cord had been wrapped twice around each of the huge trees and draped underwater across the slough. Worley had set it off with a timed fuse and a small blasting cap.

"Did you see that goddamned bird fly into that blast? What a bunch of fucking luck!" Henry ran down to the bank in order to check the damage to the severed tree.

"Look at the fish!" Malcolm exclaimed, running behind Henry and sliding down the mud embankment. "Throw me a net, Lamar. There must be a hunnert of the sons of bitches thrashing around down here."

Lamar ignored him and looked at Worley, who was sitting back in his chair and lighting a cigarette.

Worley was a study in bad. He was long and lean with short black hair and hollow cheeks and eyes. The veins that stood out in his arms and neck made him look even more remote and intense. He had a pair of mirrored wrap-around sunglasses propped up on his forehead. Worley smiled a nasty grin through the smoke. It gave Lamar a sudden shiver.

"That is some bad motherfucking stuff, Worley! Did you use that shit over in Nam?" Lamar asked.

"Yeah, we took out bridges with it and used it to set off bigger shit. Pretty nice, huh?" He laughed at the other two, who were running around on the bank like two kids on the Fourth of July. "I ought to wrap some around their balls and save their ole ladies some grief." He pointed at Henry and Malcolm with his cigarette.

"Man, that stuff would cut a man in two, wouldn't it?"

"Shit! Have I told you about the time we were pinned down outside a little village over in Nam? We were waiting for some evac when we got closed in. There was only six of us. We had three M-16s, one SMG and a spool of this shit. I ran it down each side of the road coming into the village and pushed it down into the ditches. We hid our scared asses in some canes at the end of the road and waited. When the wormy, slant-eyed bastards came up the road, we held our fire until about fifty of 'em were in our little trap. Then this crazy little nigger named Lucius fired one round down the middle of the road and hit one of the gooks in the foot. All the rest jumped their butts into my ditches which I had so lovingly fixed for them. I counted to three and ... ba, ba, bing!

"The blast blew every one of the motherfuckers back into the road. Those that weren't killed when their guts split open got a little steel-jacket painkiller from the machine gun. It was one of my finest days over there ... I miss that place, man." He let his voice drift off nostalgically.

"Damn, Worley, that must have been beautiful." Lamar was almost salivating. "How much of that stuff you got?"

"I got enough to cut the top dome off the state capitol if I take a notion to."

"What are we really going to do with it?"

"Oh, we just got to do a little bit of convincing. Seems as how one of our big landowners wants to fight about a little ole pipeline coming across his property. Thinks he's going to hold things up in court a while and cost my people money. So we're just gonna wire about fifty of those fine old pecan trees that line the drive to his plantation and see if we can't make them all fall down at once. All around his wife's car. I hear that she'll do the rest of the talking for us. Ought to be fun."

He rocked back in his chair and reached for his beer where it rested on the ground. "While those two idiots are down there running around chasing fish, you and I need to talk." He motioned for Lamar to sit down. "How long were you down there at Cummins?" he asked.

"Six years and eight months." Lamar hardened his stare as he spoke.

"My people tell me you was a tough trustee most of that time. Said you killed some people when you was told to. All that true?"

"Yeah, I guess so. Trustees run the place down there. It was the only way you could live through the time you had to do. I just took my orders and tried to stay alive. Not too proud of it. Who told you all that?" He leaned over and got his beer.

"Boy, you might as well wake up before you end up right back over at the old farm. There is a group of men in this state that knows just about everything that goes on. Oh, there is some small time shit that goes down every now and then that they don't care about, but nothing big.

"Did you ever talk to those other idiots that were locked up with you? Did you ever wonder how so many of them were caught before they could get out of the state? Did you wonder how they had your ass before you could get to your girlfriend's car? They are connected, man. It's the best kept secret in the South because everyone who matters is under their influence. Who do you think ordered those prison-farm accidents and executions? You gettin' my drift, man? They ain't gonna have anyone messin' with their game."

"Yeah, Worley, but why me? What about my parole?" he asked.

"Fuck! Don't you understand? They *are* your parole! They're your eyes and ears and everything, man. They're your protectors, Lamar. That is, if you come with them. Those two down there are just tools for them to waste, but I think you've got the talent to keep your mouth shut and do as you're told. Am I wrong?" He spit a piece of his cigarette into the dirt.

"You got the right man, Worley, but what's the arrangement? How do we operate? How much do we get paid?"

"How much did you get paid for shootin' some old nigger out in the field when his name came down?" Worley asked.

"A gallon of hooch and a whore for a night down at the infirmary building," Lamar mumbled.

"Okay, then. Here's the deal. I train you. We work together as a team. We stay in the shadows and don't ever draw attention. Any problems with alcohol and drugs and you're out.

"One day we might be making a delivery from the prison to a state senator's house, and the next day we might be burning that same house down so's he can collect the insurance on it. We get a job and we get protection. We have to be clean and smart. If you can't follow orders, then you're out. You get too talky, you're out. Your woman gets too nosy, you're out." He took a swig from his bottle. "Oh, and Lamar—when you're out, that means that one of us that's still in is going to take your ass out. That's a promise. A man that's no longer part of the system is a danger to the rest of us, from the top man to the bottom. You copy?"

"Loud and clear!" Lamar smiled. "Who signs the paychecks?"

"We get our orders and money from a guy they just moved in to replace my old boss, the one that took his retirement. Get this: This new guy just happens to be a district judge. How about that shit?" Worley kicked back in his chair.

"So it's kinda like we'll be government employees!" Lamar laughed. "Hell of a deal!"

"Yep! The pay is good and the benefits are better. For a guy like you who enjoys this kind of work, these people are the best. They're looking for long-time relationships." He reached over and slapped Lamar on the knee. "Welcome aboard, partner-in-crime."

"Hey, guys!" Malcolm yelled from the water's edge. "Fire up that grease. We got some fish to fry!"

"You heard him, Lamar. Get that grease ready, we got some big fish to fry."

SIX ∿∿∿∿∿∿∿∿

SEPTEMBER 1972
HARVARD LAW SCHOOL
CAMBRIDGE, MASSACHUSETTS

"H EY, BOB ... YOU NOTICED THAT STEPHANIE GIRL FROM OUR legal ethics class?" George asked.

When George stopped eating long enough to ask a question like that, Bob knew he had an ulterior motive. "Yeah, I've seen her ... Why?" Bob answered guardedly. "Well, she's been asking around about you. I think she's interested, but don't say I said so," George finished. They had both been busy with Senator John McArdle's campaign and had missed the last two days of class. The senator had arranged things with their professors at Harvard, but even then you just couldn't afford to miss that much law. It had a way of snowballing on you.

"She's kind of peculiar ... wouldn't you say?" Bob asked George in between bites of his fish and chips. "She's not pretty but she has this look about her ... like she might know more than your average female law student."

Bob wouldn't admit it but he had noticed her first week of school.

She was the most confident woman he had met since he and Colleen split up in Ireland. In fact, they reminded him of each other.

Stephanie made it her business to know about all the members of her classes, the backgrounds of all the professors, and current events from everywhere in the world. She made no effort to hide her leftist views, and in fact she spoke her first words to Bob the day she found out about his leadership in the antiwar demonstrations in Ireland.

She had said, "I'm proud of you. That's the best. Power to the people, man!" Stephanie had given him the fisted salute and threw her backpack over her shoulder as she strode off down the hall. Bob just stood there and stared. Hell, yes, he had noticed her! But it bothered him to think she had been checking up on him. He'd have to get more out of his friend "gorging George."

"So, George ...what does this Stephanie Stoddard want to know about me?" Bob asked.

George looked up momentarily from his meal, but then dropped his head again and continued stuffing his face.

"Hey, man, back off on the food before you choke. Did you hear me? What's this Stephanie girl want with me?" Bob repeated, even louder.

"She would like to know if you and your 'food-fetish' friend here would like to come to her party," a voice said from behind him.

Bob nearly broke his neck turning around so fast. Stephanie Stoddard smiled over her wire-rimmed glasses as Bob's face went through several shades of embarrassment. "How long have you been standing there?" he asked sheepishly.

"Not long enough, I'm sure." She laughed back at him. "So are you two coming? It's tomorrow night at my place. I don't think you'll want to miss it."

Bob glanced over at George who slowed long enough to grunt his approval.

"What time?" Bob asked her.

"Eight o'clock, until."

"We'll be there. Do you want me to bring anything?"

"Just your mind," she laughed again. George joined with her this time.

〰〰〰〰〰〰〰

The party was unlike any Bob had ever seen. Stephanie herself met him and George at the door. She was wearing an African mosheekoo and sandals, mismatched with her ever-present wire-rimmed glasses. She greeted George with a firm handshake, but when Bob stepped through the door, she stood on her tiptoes and gave him a kiss on the cheek.

"I'm really glad you decided to come. I think you'll enjoy the people I've invited for you." She smiled and walked back into the main room.

Invited for him? What the hell was she talking about? Bob's defenses went up immediately.

But what a party! At least sixty people milled about. Stephanie shared the spacious apartment with two other girls and they had gone all out for this event.

Bob and George wandered through the various rooms. They met people of every persuasion. Union organizers mingled with law students, who mingled with professors. Most were very hip political types who wore their radical allegiances like chips on their shoulders. There were plenty of them at Harvard Law, notwithstanding the school's ancient and well-served purpose of turning out top, blue-blooded corporate attorneys.

Stephanie and her roommates had provided not only a river of free alcohol and a hill of munchies but, at two locations in the apartment, they had baskets containing pre-rolled joints and platters of marijuana brownies.

George chimed up immediately when he realized what was in front of him. "Holy shit! 'Do you smell what I see?' said the little drummer boy!"

"Absolutely cool!" Bob answered. "These girls are more connected than I imagined!"

Grass was used surreptitiously at all the parties at the time, but Bob had never seen it set out as party-favors. These girls were brave . . . or foolhardy, one of the two.

Most people hit the food and the beer first and slowly worked their way over to the grass. The mood was mellow, really laid back. Everyone Bob saw was getting stoned . . . except for Stephanie. She was working the groups and making sure the party continued to hum.

Bob and George were halfway through their first joints and well into a very strange chat with a chesty art professor when Stephanie moved up under one of Bob's arms, excused both of them, and left poor George to his own defense.

"What's up?" he asked, not able to control a giddy smile as he looked down at her.

"No more grass for you," she said, taking his half-finished joint and handing it off to a woman who had just walked in. "I need you straight."

"Straight for what? I thought this was for everyone."

"Everyone but you and me. We're the leaders, don't you know? It's our job to give the people whatever they need to break free of the establishment. We stay above it, except in private. You must keep yourself focused. Those are the rules of the movement." She turned him back toward the kitchen.

"I want to see how well you think on your feet. I want to see if there is brain to back up that brawn. So don't let me down. I'll be very, very disappointed and I don't like being disappointed."

Bob was still trying to make his clouded brain understand what she was saying when they walked up to a group where two women were in a heated discussion.

"People, excuse me, but I would like you to meet Bob Prescott. He's in law here at Harvard, but I think you may be interested in his background. He was one of the big organizers for the movement in Europe and helped plan some of the largest anti-U.S.-government rallies we saw over there." Stephanie pulled him into the group and smiled as various members introduced themselves to him.

A Professor Long, from the anthropology department at nearby Radcliffe, said, "I think I detect a southern accent. You must be quite an abnormality back home, considering your activities." The professor's comment was condescending as only an Ivy League intellectual could make it, and he affected a fake southern drawl.

"I guess you could say that I am, but I'll remind you that it was the people from the grassroots back home who marched for civil rights and who have finally done something about this damn war. They were the ones who were losing their sons and brothers and husbands, not the wealthy classes. If we had waited on the Establishment, we'd still in Nam, so I guess there were lots of us who stepped up to be counted."

"Good comeback, kid." the professor said, friendly now and nodding.

"No comeback, only the facts, sir." And Bob let loose a big conciliatory grin for the group. Stephanie glowed.

"Mr. Prescott would never name-drop, but Senator Bateman is a very close personal friend of his, and I understand he has anointed Bob here with the sacred oil of Democratic oratorical ability." Stephanie beamed again and put his hand in hers.

"Oh, well then, maybe Mr. Prescott would hold forth for us on a subject of his choice," a diminutive female professor said, pointing her cigarette at him.

"You'll hear plenty from him in the future. Just wait. Right now we have to make the rounds. Later," Stephanie said, whisking him off.

"Stephanie, where do you come off being an expert on Bob Prescott?" He spoke to the back of her head as she dragged him along toward the rear of the apartment. She stopped abruptly and turned to him. He almost ran her over.

"Look, Bob. People do not normally excite me. Principles excite me. Potential is my passion. It will do very nicely, thank you. We found out enough about you to know that I am your perfect complement. You don't know it yet, but you have all the potential in the world. Just because of whom you know and where you've been, you have more than I will ever have ... and, my sweet friend, you have a natural gift that I can never have."

"What? A warm southern smile?" Bob was captivated by this little firebrand.

"No. Testicles ... balls ... and the stature and face to complete the ticket."

"What ticket?" Bob asked, pulling her close to him.

Stephanie stopped and smiled at him. She reached up and grabbed both sides of his face and kissed him smartly. "Any ticket we choose," she said.

For a long moment they stood and stared at each other.

"You can't see that far yet because you're full of hormones. But I can. You need me and you'll come to realize that soon. You'll see. Come on."

Stephanie pulled Bob to a small room off the back entrance of the apartment. Her roommates were loading chips into two large wooden bowls.

"Brenda, Gail, I want you to meet my future husband. He doesn't know it yet, but he ... actually ... has no choice. I chose him. We're going all the way to the White House. What do you think?"

Bob could not believe the looks on the girls' faces. They weren't surprised in the least. It was as if she had told them she found the pair of socks she'd been looking for.

"So, he's the one?" Brenda responded. "Nice to meet you, Pres." She stuck out her hand and shook Bob's seriously. "You're in for a hell of a ride, friend."

SEVEN 〰〰〰〰〰〰〰

THE RED AND WHITE OF THE 182 CAST A STRANGE REFLECTION ON the water. Small groups of mallard made their hasty retreats into the protection of the rushes along the shore. The lifting effect of warm water made the old Cessna sail much farther than she should have, but David let her. Today was one of those glorious days in the northwoods. Fall colors were at full tilt and reflected richly in the lake water. The walleye and northerns were biting, and it would be hard to imagine a more perfect trip.

Canada had turned out to be the paradise that David had always dreamed of. Vast areas of the country were unspoiled. It was full of the three things David loved most: wilderness, water, and uncluttered airspace. You could fly north for hours without seeing as much as a house, a road, or another human. It was a country made for a pilot with an amphibious plane and a sense of adventure. Every lake and river was a free, inviting runway, waiting to be investigated. The water was cold and clean and held a wonderful variety of hearty game fish. Wildlife teemed in the forests, which seemed to go on forever. The moose, elk, and caribou particularly fascinated David, who had grown up hunting the whitetail deer of Arkansas. These northern cousins of his deer were anywhere from two to ten times larger.

The waterfowl and upland game birds introduced him to a more refined type of shotgunning. He spent endless mornings walking the birch- and balsam-lined trails watching for his retriever to jump a grouse or woodcock.

Snow was never far away in the fall. A morning's dusting only made a hunt more enjoyable. It was the winters that changed everything.

The winters were bitter, yet David had found solace in the intense quiet of his snowbound northwoods. Life slowed down. One was able to focus on the small, really important things in life.

The ability to switch from floats to skis on his planes ensured that he would be able to continue exploring his adopted country and make a nice living. There was always freight to haul. The needs of the local Indian reservations kept him busy. The ski planes could often travel even when the heavy snows shut down the roads.

"Okay, Zack, you've got the pedals now. Remember tip-toe, tip-toe."

Zack was only eleven, but he knew this routine well. David had taken his son in the plane since he was a pup. When Zack was six, he let him begin steering the plane in level flight. The boy had a natural gift for flying, a soft touch on the controls and excellent coordination.

David was so proud of him that sometimes he just watched him and wondered where he'd come from. This was one of those moments now, as he watched the boy smile with the concentrated look of a kid baiting a hook, his tongue working the backs of his teeth and occasionally slipping out the corners of his mouth.

David landed the plane with Zack working the rudder for him. The hum and vibration of the pontoons in the water always reminded David of his early years as a kid riding the aluminum john-boats up and down the White River, checking his nets. But there wasn't much back there in Arkansas for him now.

～～～～～～～

By the time David had been sent home from Germany, he had a new leg and a new respect for physical therapists. His family had split. His mom transferred to Southern California with her company. His brothers were engaged in construction, and his dad was working double-time as a cop and a security officer.

True to her word, his first love, Mary Ann, had married and was carrying her first child. David thought he would die during his first months in Vietnam, no letters from her and only occasional news about her new fiancé and their plans. But after his crash he put all of that behind him. He learned to put a lot behind him after Nam. He was actually relieved that he had no one from his past that he would have to answer to.

So after a brief howdy-do to Arkansas, David had made his way to Canada and found he could make a living flying. He started with a small air-cargo company but was anxious to be on his own. By the time his first Canadian autumn blazed across the landscape, he had assessed his financial situation and given notice to his boss. At Christmastime he had driven over to Chelick Bay to check out a lead on a plane. The weather turned bad and he ended up spending the night at the community college gymnasium in Blackduck.

Suni was the lithe Chippewa girl who ushered him and the other stranded travelers into the school and handed out emergency supplies. She was a sophomore at the college and was trying to study for tests when the storm hit. David was smitten. He loved everything about her. She wore her hair long and straight with beaded barrettes clamping it back. She was fully five foot nine and had uncharacteristically long legs but still moved with that uncanny steadiness of the torso that only Indian women know, and maybe Hawaiian princesses.

David had never prayed for snow the way he prayed that night. They talked until 2:00 A.M., sipping hot tea she made on one of the radiators. She was a delight and a mystery, quiet and yet confident in herself, full of plans and dreams. He kissed her almond-colored hand that night and thanked her for talking with him. She smiled up at him like a woman who suddenly smelled a wonderful remembered fragrance. He fell into her black eyes without once looking back.

It snowed solidly for two days and by March they were married. It was a Chippewa ceremony, and David felt no desire to bring his scattered family into it. He did call Hicks's father to see if Ricky might come up, but his buddy was somewhere in Mexico.

Suni was insistent on getting pregnant immediately. Her mother had died when she was only three. The doctors said she should not have waited so long to have her big family. She died on the northern boundaries of the reservation giving birth to Suni's baby brother, quietly bleeding to death in her birthing hut.

Zack was on his way before the honeymoon was over. Suni was radiant, the most beautiful pregnant woman David had ever seen. She carried the baby proudly, and everyone commented on how special this child would be. The old women of the community knew it would be a boy as early as the third month.

After the only real argument they ever had, David persuaded Suni to have a normal battery of prenatal tests. She nevertheless insisted on a tribal midwife for the delivery. Her labor lasted all of one night. The men ... David and Suni's brothers and father ... were not allowed to know what transpired, but finally, at 5:26 A.M. on Christmas Day 1969, Zack let out his first battle cry. The men were swatted away from the birthing hut by the old women. They had things to take care of before the father could see what he had helped create.

Suni had had a tough time with the birth but was resting well by midmorning. Then David was finally allowed to hold his son in the kitchen of her father's house. The sounds of laughter and cooking and infant cries made it all perfect. The baby had a thick top patch of David's reddish hair but the coloring and wonderful nose of his mother. The tribal priest said that Zachary was the fairest Indian baby he ever called a blessing for, so he made it a special one. The baby quieted and watched the priest so seriously that everyone laughed and said that he was a little shaman, born into this family of heathens.

All of David's plans had wings. He went into partnership with a man named Tom Waters from the Twin Cities. They bought up some old Beech Eighteens and formed a small air-cargo business. Tom landed a contract to fly genetically engineered breeding chicks, only peeps, down to the Central American countries. The chicken industry was huge there, and high-quality breeders fetched from seventy-five to a hundred and fifty dollars each. David and Tom would pick up their crated cargo in New York, Ontario, or Minnesota and fly it to destinations south of the border.

The Central American trips gave David the freedom he craved. He could leave the frozen north in January and be in the tropics the next day. Doing business in the typical Central American manner let David form many strong friendships that lasted even after the business went sour. It wasn't that he and Tom weren't making money, but the hassles at the border were increasing due to the escalating drug trade. David had no intention of spending ten years in prison because some cartel goon figured out a way to slip a package onto his plane. His wife and child were more important to him than the money, so they sold out.

Afterward, David missed the long trips and the rich steamy coastlands he relished, but he still found his way down every three or four months. Necessity has its way with amputees.

The prosthetist that David came to love and depend on in Germany had moved to San Antonio after the war, where he opened a small, exclusive clinic. Klaus Koenig was probably more Polish than German but he had inherited the German gift for detail. Klaus used David as his guinea pig whenever he had a new idea. Thanks to him, David was able to lead an unusually active and pain-free life. The residual muscles of his stump had remained in excellent shape and his skin-related problems were minimal.

David loved to challenge Klaus. He wanted a leg with a different ankle and foot for flying, something that would be more sensitive to the pedals. Klaus fabricated a wonderful leg with a quick detachable shin section so that David could change it in seconds when he had to switch from flying to walking at airports.

Once, Ricky Hicks convinced David that they should brush up on their skydiving skills, so Klaus made him a prosthesis with a pneumatic shock absorber. For skin diving and swimming, David had a leg with an onboard buoyancy compensator with its own little pressure valve.

When he went to San Antonio, David would call ahead, spend three or four days in the clinic, and then a couple of days in Mexico. Often he, Suni, and Zack would stretch these trips into mini-vacations, lounging on the cheap Mexican beaches over a weekend.

They were on a beach in Baja the day that Suni told David she was pregnant again. Zack was chasing sandpipers up the beach on his stubby little three-year-old legs. She looked over at David and simply said, "Zack will have some help with those birds next year."

David was ecstatic. He kissed Suni from the top of her head to the bottom of her feet. She screamed in delight, rolling from side to side under the beach umbrella. Little Zack came running to the commotion and decided to help his father with the fun, his sandy little lips covering his mother's face with munchkin kisses.

Life was comfortable and sweet. David took his money from the air-cargo business and bought pontoon planes for the back country of Canada. For the most part his clients were sportsmen from Europe and the States who wanted to get as far away from civilization as possible. David knew how they felt. He sought out the most gloriously isolated lakes and rivers he could find for his people and many times he stayed over and guided for them.

The business grew and so did Suni. She and Zack spent the winter decorating their new cabin on Lake Winniesot. David switched his Pilatus Porter bush plane over to skis and carried caribou hunters into the north country each week. Suni's brothers helped with the details and processed the meat for the hunters' trips home.

Suni was radiantly pregnant again with absolutely no warning of a complication. But on Valentine's Day she stayed in bed most of the morning. She was not due for three more weeks, but the midwife had visited every day for the last week. David knew something must be wrong, but Suni denied that there was anything to worry about.

That day the midwife, Dona, came by at 4:00 P.M. She immediately ran back to her husband, who was waiting on the snowmobile. She whispered instructions to him and he sped back to the village. David's heart was in his throat. He forced his way past Dona as she reentered their bedroom. Suni was sitting up, holding her abdomen with both hands, her eyes wide with pain and fear. Blood had seeped into the cover sheets and she had wadded them tight to try to stop the flow. David grabbed her fevered face in his hands.

"Suni, please let me take you to the strip! We can get you in the Porter and to the hospital in less than an hour. Please, please, you've got to let me try!"

"No," she said through her pain. "I can't go anywhere. The baby has to come now. I'll be fine. Just let Dona and the other women work. I love you, but you have to understand. This is the way it has to be."

David fought with himself mightily. The old urge to charge blindly into this emergency was pushed down by Suni's words. He let Dona pull him back through the door by his shirttail. The last he saw of Suni was the sweaty smile that she forced up for him. She was gone before dusk had settled. He would never know if he might have been able to save her.

The baby lived for only a few minutes. The trauma had been too great for both of them. It was a girl, and Suni had named her Mattie after her grandmother. The old women had done everything they could. Now they took up the duties that custom dictated following such a loss. David found his way up the stairs to Zack's room and woke his son from his afternoon nap. He held him close and wept into his hair. Zack patted his father's face and they fell asleep in the boy's tiny bunk against the wall.

Had it not been for the boy, David would have died. In the mornings, it was impossible to find a reason to get out of bed. But then Zack would come bounding down the stairs with his boots on the wrong feet and his little plastic six-shooters strapped on his hips.

The boy had cried for his mother at first, but eventually seemed to accept his father's explanation of where she had gone. David told him that she would be waiting in a wonderful place for them, but until then she was in the water holding them when they swam and in the trees they sat against when they were hunting and in the snow as it fell softly against their faces and melted on their outstretched tongues. This comforted Zack, and over time it even comforted David.

〰〰〰〰〰〰〰〰〰

"Dad, can we try the fly rods again today?" Zack begged.

Today was a trip just for them. The northerns were ferocious and this little stretch of river harbored some monsters.

"Sure, Zachary, my boy, but we'll have to wade out to the edge of the weeds. It'll be cold after a few minutes without our boots," David warned. "And the current is kind of swift today ... Have to watch our step."

"Aw, Dad, we've got a friend in the water, remember? I'm not afraid. Let's use the fly rods ... please?"

David smiled an old smile as he reached for the fly-rod tubes mounted under the wings. He supposed it would be fine, just fine.

EIGHT 〰〰〰〰〰〰

PATSY HARPER HAD BEGUN THE WEEK WITH HIGH EXPECTATIONS. John Doolittle, a close personal friend of her boss's, had promised a pair of tickets to the Jockey Club at Oaklawn Park. It was racing season in Arkansas and feeding the ponies was one of Patsy's favorite weekend activities.

The racetrack was a beautiful structure set in the heart of the Hot Springs business district. It was the only legalized form of gambling that remained in Arkansas after the 1960s, and it played heavily on the city's early reputation as a mob hangout.

Patsy always looked forward to her trips to the track, not least for the interesting people a young single woman could meet there. Her usual spot with her friends was along the rail in the home stretch, to scream for her picks. But Mr. Doolittle, during one of his weekly flirting sessions, had grandly promised exclusive Jockey Club tickets for Patsy and one of her girlfriends, and free use of his condominium in Hot Springs. He said he would be there only sporadically through the weekend and they could have full run of the place.

Doolittle was one of the heavy political operatives in Arkansas. He didn't hold a political office, but he traveled freely between them. Patsy knew only the little bit that he had dropped on her desk to entice her, but his involvement in banking, real estate, and bonds was impressive. Doolittle had perfected the advanced arts of self-correcting ledgers, secret accounts, insider trading, and zoning board buyouts. To him there was always a solution. It was just a matter of how many egos he had to stroke along the way. Hard cash did a lot of the stroking.

Doolittle was not an unattractive man, but he fancied himself a southern gentleman with a little of the gigolo thrown in for good measure. He dressed accordingly—white linen suits and Panama hats, with a silver-handled cane for punctuation.

It was Thursday already and still no word from him. Patsy was afraid to broach the subject with her boss, the governor. Well, actually he wasn't the governor right *now*. Bob Prescott had been voted out of office after a miserable first term.

No one believed it possible. He had shown little skill in office, but he was young and popular and headed for bigger things. At the last minute, labor and some other heavy supporters threw their collective weight to his rival and he was defeated. The circle had spoken. Bob Prescott would learn to pay closer attention.

Patsy stuck with him through it all and was now certain of his comeback reelection in the fall. Doolittle and dozens of other very powerful people said as much during their visits. This put her in line for a top position on his staff. That's why she was hesitant to ask him about Doolittle. She didn't want him to think she would let her personal life interfere with the functioning of his office, so she decided to forget it for now.

"Patsy, have you heard from Stephanie this morning?" the intercom barked.

"No, Mr. Prescott, I haven't, but I did hear from Mr. Grant. He wanted you to contact him as soon as you were through with your conference call," she replied.

"Okay, dear. Has your old buddy Doolittle dropped by yet?"

"No, sir, but I can call him if you'd like," she added eagerly, hoping for an excuse.

"I think we should wait until I talk to Grant before we call him. I'll let you know." He cut the intercom.

～～～～～～～～～～

Bob Prescott would never have believed that political defeat could be such a wonderful thing. After the enormous embarrassment of the loss and having to answer for the disappointments to the inner circle, he had been on a year-long high. People clamored to be a "Threebie," which stood for "Bring Bob Back" and ... if you had enough money ... "Bob's Best Buddy."

The reelection campaign had a life of its own. It was as if he were being carried by a rolling wave to be deposited at the next speech or the next dinner and then swept off again, the sound of applause growing ever louder. Bob Prescott lived for the campaign trail.

Even his wife Stephanie had come around this time. In the past she had been standoffish about embracing this funny little southern state of his. To her refined big-city sensibilities, it was a crude place. She had appeared only at campaign events that demanded her presence. She much preferred to pursue her career as a law professor specializing in legal theory. She was taken very seriously in the field, had a bent for trendy feminist issues, and concealed a passion for radical politics. She had actually believed for years that the people would see this scholarly image as someone that they wanted calling the shots along with their governor.

Stephanie looked like an old rug ... a badly worn old rug. This was about what she brought to the last campaign. Thank God, the press had finally commented on it after his defeat, saving Bob the appalling task of doing so. It would have been a hell of a fight at home. Stephanie was a brilliant and strong-willed woman, and she was exerting her quest for power. She had the uncanny ability to mold herself to whatever was needed to win.

In the past two years she had borne a daughter, had a complete makeover, resigned her professorship, and accepted a job at the crustiest law firm in the state, Baylor, Harold & McConnerly. Voters love it when the first family has a baby in office. It makes them great and human at once. Bob thought it might have softened Stephanie a bit as well.

Baylor, Harold had actually helped her professional image. Through the firm she was introduced to a new coterie of Arkansans. She met the men of the inner circle and warmed to them and their ways ... at once. And they saw her in a new light, a light of ... possibilities.

It seemed that in the last few months, she had been truly happy. She didn't say so, but she liked her new look. She was almost ... pretty. She loved to think of herself as the breadwinner of the family. For years she had questioned Bob's lack of interest in converting his political receivables into bankable assets. Now *she* was in a position to make things happen. With her new-found contacts in the legal and banking worlds in one hand and the testicles of the governor in the other, the future looked very satisfying. She and her buddies at Baylor, Harold were the ones who worked out Bob's political agenda and custom-crafted his state legislative policy.

Bob was glad to let her handle business. She appeared the well-dressed concerned wife when she was asked, and she spent less time checking on him during the week. This gave him more freedom, and he couldn't get enough of that. It was funny the way things had worked out. Stephanie had always been the aggressive member of the family. He had never seen a person, man or woman, so obsessed with achievement. That was the way she was.

Stephanie was never the romantic interest in his life; he had to go elsewhere for romance. But Bob had come to realize that she *was* the passion in his life. No one cared about their next political step as much as she. She completed him, exactly as promised.

Bob would go through long periods when he lost the fire and just didn't give a shit any more. Stephanie would always pull him back up for the next big push and carry him along with her fervor. She had the vision. It lifted them both.

And now she required it of him. It had been their bargain. After their brief romance ran its course, she had realized her vulnerability and forced him to make a pact with her.

She would faithfully serve as his facilitator, but he would take her along and share the decisions and the glory with her, not vicariously, but up front and in the face. The public would see in her a new Eleanor Roosevelt, and he would stand by her or lose everything.

Bob could look back now and see that he had yielded everything to her hunger. He had given it all for one thing, the one thing that kept him in this game. The campaign. Life in a campaign was everything: adrenaline, challenge, momentum, and, best of all, sex. Risky sex, with the excitement heightened by the threat of discovery. Political groupies were just as exciting and enthusiastic as rock-and-roll groupies, but without the problems. They didn't OD or freak out and they seldom had venereal diseases. No "Sweet, Sweet Connie"s. A choicer cut of meat.

A few well-informed state troopers in his entourage procured discreet recreation for the governor. A fresh, juicy recruit in every district. His private joke was that it was his way of staying in touch with his constituency.

Stephanie knew of his activities perfectly well, but she backed away from confrontations after Nicole was born. She spent more and more time with Eric Grant and Red Wheeler and the other partners at Baylor, Harold working on contracts and banking regulations. Bob saw to it that she was appointed to as many projects and boards as possible. He made sure that she was made full partner within one year. In Arkansas, the governor always had a say.

She worked hard. Many of the meetings at the firm stretched well into the night. Hell, for all he knew she was having an affair with old Eric. If that kept her off his gubernatorial ass then it was fine by him. They deserved each other. He wondered if they called it intercourse and finished with official closing statements.

Bob supposed that Eric's call was about some legal scheme he was to sign off on for Stephanie. Grant had a brilliant mind and was always careful to check everything thoroughly before committing the signature of the soon-to-be-reelected governor.

~~~~~~~~~~~~~

"Eric, how are you? Sorry I missed your call."

"Bob, I reviewed that proposal Doolittle brought by my office. On the front end it looks like it has a hell of a lot of potential. He's getting the land at a bargain and as long as the city keeps growing in that direction, the lots should turn over well. But I see a problem in some of his peripheral ideas for generating income."

"Well, fella, I have to depend on you in cases like this. You know crazy Doolittle and I are old friends. He's made Stephanie and me some decent money in the past. I only hope you and Steph will keep us above, uh, reproach, and highlight for me the things that I might need to take care of."

"I know, Bob. Listen, it boils down to this: The land deal is a piece of cake. But Doolittle has an idea about building a microbrewery with an exclusive restaurant attached. These things are going over real big in Texas. Even his conservative numbers look good. Only one problem ..."

"What, we need more capital?"

"No, he can get his hands on the money. Remember I briefed you on the SBA loans? The problem is that this land is outside Pulaski County. It's in a dry county.

"I see. Well then, what about going on with the project without the restaurant?"

"Stephanie and Doolittle are working on an angle that just might work. There appears to be no restriction on manufacturing in Grant County. Not even for a brewery. So Stephanie feels that by rolling a clause into your Industrial Red Tape Freedom Act, we could make a state law prohibiting any county law from interfering with a manufacturer's right to sell from his place of manufacturing. In other words, if a county permits someone to make something in its jurisdiction, then the new state law will allow that person to sell, test, and advertise his product in that county, without penalty."

"There will be some pissed-off people when this goes through. I don't want the exposure. Things are just now coming together again."

"You'll be clean. You can claim that this was a commonsense clause for the bill to contain. Your names won't be on the development, and Doolittle and his company will handle the paperwork. Of course, this is assuming you can push the bill through."

"I've already got commitments for it. Should sail right on through."

"Okay. Stephanie and I will finish the preliminary work and we'll give

Doolittle the verbal go-ahead on the initial purchase. He's chomping at the bit. He'll probably be by to see whether I filled you in on how wonderful he is. Tell him he's been a good boy and I think we're set on this one. Of course, you do have to get back in office for all of this to work."

The governor chuckled. "That's as good as done! I see you've gotten to know Doolittle pretty well. Anything else? Stephanie mentioned something about some prison situation."

"Oh, yeah, our friends at the prison ... the ones funding a lot of your travel right now, the Medical Administration Associates. They want your ear on a problem. This may be a simple enough project. As you know, we installed them as the healthcare providers at the prison three years ago. It's their budget each year that's allowed us to keep the focus on raising state appropriations for our little prison machine. The owner and director, Dr. Frank Warren, has an idea and he wants our protection on it."

"I agree, we definitely need to stay tight with them. What's his idea? We can't do that slave labor thing any more," Bob joked. "The prison situation just ain't what it used to be."

"I beg to differ. It seems as though there is a big market for biological products nowadays. Most of these are made from blood and some from bone marrow. It's a growing market, too. The profits can be huge. Supply is the problem. Dr. Warren looks at our inmate population as a sea of potential.

"He is in position to harvest the blood, but there's going to be a problem: Orders have already been handed down from the Health Department to abolish the old blood-donor program at Cummins. Prisoners have a high rate of infectious diseases and that can contaminate the blood. You can imagine that our little buddies down at the prison farm have all of those bugs and probably a few of their own. Prison blood programs are being shut down all over the U.S., but Warren has a plan for keeping it low key with no paper trail."

"Sounds like there's no problem at all," Bob replied confidently.

"That's what I thought. The potential here is really awesome. Warren says he won't have to buy the blood. That's the key. He has a plan to guarantee all the volunteers he can handle without a cash outlay.

"Remember last year when a couple of the inmates lost legs?"

"Yeah, some nasty infection or something?"

"Well, what they were doing was injecting spit under their skin to get an infection started. These suckers would get so sick that they would have to have surgery ... just so they could get a few days on morphine or some other painkiller. Warren was a little slow getting to a few of them and they lost their legs. But it gave him an idea for coaxing them out of their blood."

"Damn! You've got to be kidding. Those are some screwed up sons of bitches." It made Bob feel slightly nauseated just thinking about it.

"Dr. Warren says he can cover the blood draws as research or testing, of course—no charge to the state. But it seems that his experience in the past has shown that the, uh ... anxiety of giving blood is lessened considerably by a one- or two-day supply of Percodan following the procedure," Eric explained drily.

"I see! So that's his little trick. We wouldn't want our inmates to suffer," Bob chuckled. "So what does he need us for?"

"He just wants reappointment of his contract when you get back in office, and a little leeway for his operation in the system. He's willing to be generous with his harvests."

"Just what might be our return for taking care of it? Is this his only game?" Bob asked.

"Well, no. That's the good part. Remember, during your last administration, we pushed through the funding to pay our prison healthcare contractor for every inmate? It's a lump sum whether they ever get sick or not. Somewhere around fifteen hundred dollars per inmate per year.

"Warren has ways of identifying those inmates who fit under private insurance, workman's comp, or Medicare plans, and billing separately for procedures that may not always be ... essential," Eric said, guarding his words.

"The old double-dip." Bob laughed. "How much over and above our state program does he see from this?"

"About two-and-a-half million a year."

"Have you negotiated our cut?" Bob asked.

"One third," Eric said proudly. "Maybe a little extra."

"What's the insulation?"

"He keeps it clean and padded within his own series of clinics and companies. Besides, none of those insurance groups talk to each other. It's almost all profit."

"Okay. I'm sure when I get back in, we can accommodate Dr. Warren and his pals, but I want you to let the doctor know that a Miss April Hedges is going to be on his payroll. Put her at $25,000. I'll get you her account numbers. And tell him not to expect her ever to be there." He thought for a moment. "Eric, I want to stay tight with Warren. You keep your hands in his pockets so he doesn't begin to feel like a freelancer."

"I'll take care of it, Bob."

"Let's assure Dr. Warren of our support and maybe set up a little R&R event with him. What do you think?"

"Sounds great. It's about time something good comes out of that prison."

"Hey, wait a minute. We won't be screwing with the Red Cross blood people, will we? We don't want a group like that in the middle of this."

"No, no. There's no connection. He has his own market and pathways. I checked it out. There is some big money behind him and it isn't public sector."

"Okay, then. That sounds good. I'll talk with Doolittle. In fact, I think I hear him out front right now. I better go peel the *Colonel* off Patsy before she uses that cane on him. Thanks for everything, Eric. I'll see you Saturday night at the club."

"Sure, see you then. 'Bye."

Prescott opened the wide door to his reception area. Doolittle was in the process of whispering something in Patsy's ear and they both jumped when they heard his sudden entrance. Doolittle smiled as Patsy blushed. She quickly slipped what appeared to be some tickets into her desk drawer and nonchalantly turned to face her boss.

"Well, good morning, Governor," Doolittle said with his deepest Dixie accent. "Are you ready for some of that fine barbecue I've been telling you about? It is lunchtime, you know."

"I swear, Sir John, it sounds like you might be trying to bribe me. Of course, that will depend on how much they pile on those plates. I think we should investigate." He grabbed his friend's hand and pulled him from the corner of Patsy's desk.

"Patsy, dear, if you will, call Stephanie this afternoon and remind her that I will be flying to that Threebie rally in Fort Smith this afternoon. It may be tomorrow before I get back. Oh, and tell her to kiss Nicole goodnight for me. You're a dear. See you tomorrow." He waved as he ushered Doolittle out of the door.

" 'Bye, Mr. Pres.... Goodbye, Governor," she said. Patsy pulled open the drawer and grabbed the tickets. They were paper-clipped together, and wedged between them were three one-hundred-dollar bills. She squealed with surprise and delight.

"My, my, I do believe I love politics, Mr. Governor, and I do believe it loves me!"

NINE ∿∿∿∿∿∿∿∿∿∿

APRIL 22, 1986
THE RESERVATION COUNTRY CLUB
PINE BLUFF, ARKANSAS

"**G**OD DAMN!"

Dr. Frank Warren angrily threw the newspaper across the front seat of his Cadillac. The huge platinum-colored car swerved slightly in response, then gently straightened itself out in its lane. Warren squeezed the wheel so tightly that the tips of his fingers went white from the pressure.

The eruption was completely out of character for Warren. He prided himself on his self-control. He was known for his calm demeanor and cultivated bedside manner. At fifty-five, Warren was still strikingly handsome, his dark hair tipped with gray and silver, his face fashionably bronzed. He kept his body tanned and trim and dressed impeccably.

Frank Warren was a smooth mover. He had begun his career when a doctor still had carte blanche privileges. With an M.D. at the end of your signature, you could name your own game, especially in a small town. So

Warren had played at minor surgery, obstetrics, family medicine, and now industrial and emergency-room care. But his latest endeavor was the best of all.

Moving into the business end of medicine ten years ago allowed him the leverage to hire other physicians and nurses and charge for their services. His dilemma as a doctor had always been that his income was generally capped by the number of procedures he could perform in a given week. But through his medical conglomerate, Medical Administration Associates, he could hire low-end physicians and nurses and assign them hundreds of procedures per week.

It was amazing how many physicians were in trouble with the law. Some were hiding from divorce attorneys and ex-wives; others were serving embarrassing paroles or probations for drug violations, holding onto their licenses by the skin of their teeth.

Warren loved to help them. Loved it all the way to the bank. The cooperation of his friends on the State Medical Board was no small advantage. For many of his staff doctors, MAA, Inc. was the only choice they would have. He had a substantial waiting list, but waits were short due to a high rate of turnover. The legal interests his hires had left behind had a way of catching up.

He had built his business into a multifaceted, multimillion-dollar operation. He had several large industrial accounts and he supplied emergency-room physicians to over a dozen hospitals in Arkansas. His largest account was, of course, the prison system.

In recent years liberal judicial decisions had allowed inmates to demand proper medical services. The power people in the governor's circle jumped at the opportunity. They pushed expensive appropriations through the legislature, and deftly handed control of the spending to the governor with regulatory fine print. The fox got the key to the hen house.

Warren's hand could be guessed at, if not seen, in these maneuvers. Bennie set it up. Bennie was his idea man. Bennie was always thinking, always working on an angle. That's how Bennie developed his "edge." He was about Frank's age, but they were polar opposites. Bennie had not aged well. Alcohol had not preserved him as it does biological specimens in a lab.

When Bennie was sober, he was a short, greasy, red-faced troll. When he was drunk, he was God's answer to the vibrator shortage among southern women. At least he thought he was.

Bennie loved his role in this healthcare business and often passed himself off as Dr. Benjamin Smith when interviewing practical nurse applicants. It amazed Frank how often Bennie scored, considering how bad he looked.

They got along famously, with Dr. Frank as the front man and Bennie as his trained hound, sniffing around every operation, his ear always to someone's door. That was how they'd stumbled onto the plasma scheme in the first place.

Bennie overheard a health department appointee remark that it was a shame that the prison was now off limits to blood collecting, given the enormous demand these days. The man calculated that blood revenues alone could offset the state's expenses for prisons.

Frank agreed. Bennie had intercepted a great bit of intelligence. The rest was simple. They had expanded the business to a fantastic level in only two years' time. They had cut deals with other sources of blood, built remote processing facilities, and mixed the illegal prison blood with blood from legitimate sources. Names from regional phone books were applied to the identification tags.

No one suspected a thing. Hell, blood was blood.

The inmates were wonderful donors, lining up dutifully each visit like so many of Pavlov's dogs. The FDA had signed off on the processing facilities in Arkansas, Louisiana, and Florida. The payoffs to the proper people were issued as invoiced expenses to auxiliary companies around Arkansas.

What an operation! And it all rested on the help and participation of the good governor and his circle of associates and friends. Prescott and his group were greedy bastards, but they were powerful bastards as well.

The convict blood was purchased by an East Coast entity that had enormous needs and asked very few questions, an entity connected to some major East Coast families in ways Frank didn't care to know. Whoever they were, their payments were timely and helped finance part of the start-up expense for his remote labs. The group was selling blood products everywhere. The United States was the major donor for the entire world, and other countries were desperate for anything they could get.

But it was all over now. Over, it's potential hardly touched ... what a waste! God damn! Frank could see that in the morning paper he'd tossed aside. Some time back, one too many unchecked blood lots from the prison had contaminated a much larger lot in Louisiana. Since it went in with the batches from New Orleans, it had already been diluted with hundreds of other units. A decision had had to be made: Dump the whole lot, or push it through? Frank had decided to cover it and push it through, telling himself that any diseases the blood carried would be easily treated with the fantastic new antibiotics. Besides, blood was a lifesaving commodity; disease you could worry about later. He and Bennie discussed it in depth and decided together to let it slide on through. It was a twelve-thousand-dollar decision for them.

The buyer did not have redundant testing. Regulations were in flux right now, with all the talk about AIDS, a killer disease stalking the homosexual communities in San Francisco and New York City. Other blood-borne diseases were rampant, gathering more and more attention. So it happened that MAA's bad blood went into the buyer's even larger batches in Philadelphia. The lesser part was processed into platelets, whole blood, gamma globulin, and other products that were used in the northeast corridor. The greater part went out as whole blood through an under-the-table agreement with a Canadian buyer. It wasn't until months later that the incidence of disease, mainly Hepatitis of the non-A, non-B variety, caused healthcare professionals to start the search for a common denominator.

The rest had happened quickly. Warren would never forget a late-night meeting on the tarmac at Lakeshore Airport in New Orleans. His purchaser had sent down some heavies in black suits who spelled things out for him. They let him know in no uncertain terms that he would roll over on this one. He would take the brunt of the blame and, especially, he would eliminate any chance for further investigation. They would tolerate no links through him to the prisons. He was to erase all trails.

Either Warren could take care of destroying the evidence completely or they would do it for him. If *they* did it, they would just as soon *he* be in the offices when they blew.

He took care of it. The pictures in this morning's paper confirmed it.

Frank wheeled the Caddy into the parking lot at the Country Club.

Bennie's 240Z was parked there. Bennie opened the door and stumbled out as Frank pulled up. He was already wasted and it was only 11:00 A.M. He slid into the passenger seat, crumpling the newspaper as he entered.

"Hey, Frank, how did the meeting go with the insurance guys?" he slurred.

"God damn, Bennie, how can you be drinking at a time like this? I need you fresh and on your toes. You look like hell!" He slumped over and struggled to gain his composure. "Do you realize that we will have everyone from the FBI to the FDA crawling around here for the next few days? Have you thought about that? Can you pull your head out of the bottle long enough to save your ass?"

"Frank, Frank, relax. Hey, I told you I have everything covered. I got the rest of the money to the torches. They loaded up and went back to the rock they live under. Jesus, what an intense couple of fuckers! So how about the insurance policies? Are we good?"

"The insurance won't begin to cover all we owe the buyers for contaminating their batches. I'll still have to cough up over $100,000, and our blood business is shot.

"Prescott and his people want us out, too. Completely out and no arguments. They will close out everything here but we lose the operation."

"How in the hell did Prescott's bunch find out?" Bennie asked in a subdued voice, his nose as red as a chili.

"Who do you think handles the two nice fellas who threw the barbecue for us down at our clinics? They're connected. I had to hire them. Prescott and his bunch are everything here and you know it. They just let us ride along if we kept our noses clean. Now we're back to nursing a bunch of piss-poor Dr. Kildares from one job to the next. And we're made. Do you know what that means in this state?"

"Okay, Frank, get a grip, we're going to pull out of this okay. You'll see. What's our next move?"

"You checked with our managers in New Orleans and Tampa?"

"Yeah, I called them both at home last night. They had their copies of the Klan letters. I mailed those out last week when I went to Florida. There are twenty-two labs down there. I wrote separate letters to all of them, including our two, pretending to be a grand Poo Bah or some-thing. You know, all the standard shit about how the Klan hates mixing the blood of whites and blacks. Told them I was going to fix things so that they would never do business again," Bennie finished, pleased with his little trick.

"You didn't write them in your own handwriting did you?" Frank asked.

"Of course not. I typed them and then threw the typewriter off a bridge. Both managers called me when they got them. I told them to make copies and keep one with them and give one to the local police, but not to worry. I said it was probably some harmless nut. I would come down and meet with them and the police in a couple of days. In the meantime, ka-boom! Did you see those pictures in the paper? Man, there was nothing left, and neither manager suspects a thing! They're scared of more violence," Bennie laughed.

"Good, leave them scared. The FBI will want to interview them and see those letters. A little fear will play well. You don't try to fake it with the FBI. We'll wait until after this settles a little before we tell them they're out of a job. In the meantime, our stories don't budge. Business as usual at the other clinics ... You get your ass sober, now! Do you hear me?"

"Okay, I hear you. I'm straight from here on. Hey, Frank, what about all the inmates? What if they run their mouths?"

"I've shut that down from the inside. I just have to maintain a couple of the big hitters in the system and nothing will come out. No problem. I wish it were that easy on the outside. Did you put the fear of God in our girls up here? They don't know everything but they do know enough to cause trouble."

"Yeah, Frank, you know that I know how to work the ladies. No prob-lem," he boasted.

"Yeah!" He gave Bennie a *you're-full-of-shit* look.

"How many do you think will die from that blood, Frank?" The bravado had left Bennie's face.

"None who wouldn't die without getting the blood when they needed it. How many times do we have to go over this, Bennie? When you've had a wreck and burst your spleen, you don't ask the surgeon if the blood came from some nigger junkie inmate from the swamps. You just take it and thank God when it warms your lifeless body. That's the way it works. Now drop it." He flipped on the ignition of the Cadillac.

"It's dropped, Frank. See you tomorrow." Bennie slipped out the door.

TEN 〰〰〰〰〰〰〰〰〰

ZACK FARR HAD JUST TURNED SEVENTEEN. HE WAS IN THE MIDDLE of what was shaping up to be the best Christmas vacation he could remember. He and his dad had spent the first eleven days of the holiday break down in San Antonio and Mexico visiting Klaus and Ricky. His dad had cornered Klaus for a refit and let Rick and Zack have their own kind of fun. His Uncle Rick had taken him on a wild three-day trip through the desert on motocross cycles. They had camped under the stars, wondering at the coolness of the desert when the sun departed the western sky. By day, they drove like madmen, dodging potholes and ruts and cacti. They caught rattlesnakes and cooked them on green sticks over mesquite embers, wrapping their handlebars with the skins so the rattlers would stick up and buzz in the wind when they rode.

Rick was Zack's favorite relative—or sort-of-relative. He had never analyzed the connection. Rick was special. Zack wasn't even sure exactly where he lived. They often met in Mexico or Texas. But his stories, told only to Zack, were from all over the world.

Late at night, when Rick talked about his adventures, Zack would be mesmerized by the rhythm of his uncle's voice. He could smell the acrid smoke of the elephant dung fires in Cambodia, burning through the night. He could hear the slice of the paddles as the little men from New Guinea made their way up a forbidden stream, painted from head to dirty fat foot with red ocher and daubed with white clay. He could feel the beady little globules of monkey brains sliding over his tongue at a Montagnard banquet in Vietnam. And he swayed to the songs of the Afghani mountain people that Ricky would sing for him when they had a cold night and a big fire.

David was the best father in the world. His lifestyle had created endless opportunities for Zack to learn things that most boys could only dream about. His dad had taught him how to swim like a fish. Ricky had taught him how to move silently in the water without making a ripple.

His dad taught him to hunt with a rifle and a bow. Rick taught him how to stalk and wait and plan. Fighting, for his dad, was a matter of self-defense, pure and simple. For Ricky, it was an art, conservation of movement and energy. A fire for David Farr was warmth and protection. For Ricky Hicks it was mystery—a doorway to the past or the future, a synergy between man and the powers of nature.

Ricky and Zack didn't always talk. It was a natural part of their time together just to sit quietly and gaze into the fire or the night sky or the fading sun setting over the lake. Zack often caught himself staring at the man during these moments. He thought that his uncle's face might be the most exotic he'd ever seen.

Rick looked as if he were wearing a tightly pulled human skin over his actual, hidden face. A rope of a scar bolted from the right corner of his mouth back to his ear, red and alive in the firelight. And when he smiled, his eyes, those mask eyes, pulled back with his lips in a wolf's snarl. Zack loved that face, but he noticed others didn't. He liked watching people's reactions. Zack walked differently when he and Rick were together. When he was younger, he'd imagined that he could look at people the way his uncle did and stop all of their bullshit in an instant. That was power.

The days in the desert had given way to Christmas Day in San Antonio. They celebrated with Klaus and his fat blonde family with Old World gusto—drinking, eating, and drinking again until everyone sang some really stupid German songs.

On the twenty-sixth his grandmother Farr and her new husband drove down from Costa Mesa to bring him a wonderful handmade longbow. She had hired a master bowyer to make it from California yew with ram's-horn inlays. Zack spent the rest of their time in Mexico practicing with the bow and dreaming of the northwoods again. He had a plan.

David and Zack flew all day on New Year's so that David could meet a group from Minnesota on the second. They had flown this same group into the Tonic Bay area for years. The three hunters were of Swedish descent and worked together as machinists in Duluth. Zack enjoyed being with them because they took their hunting very seriously and gave him lots of pointers.

This year, as before, they were after caribou. Zack helped his dad preflight the Otter the day before the trip. It was actually the Swedes who had given him the idea behind his plan. When they called him early in December to confirm arrangements, Bjorn, the leader of the group, had reminded him, "Hey, Zack, you said you would hunt with us this year, so how 'bout it?"

"Oh, God, I'd love to. But I'll have to see if I can clear it with my dad. You sure I wouldn't be in the way?"

"No way, son, we can always use another good hunter. Maybe you could take one with a bow."

"That's what I'm dying to do, but I usually man the radios and telephones while you guys are out. That's the week Dad covers for the Med/Rescue team's holiday break. It keeps him in the air most of the week, but I'll see." He thought ... "Maybe."

"Well if you need me to talk to ol' pegleg for you, I will, yeah ... you betcha," he laughed as he hung up.

Now it was the day before, and Zack thought he had probably waited too long to pop the question. While David topped off the wing tanks, his son worked up his courage.

"Uh, Dad, you know the Swedes and I get along real well every year," he offered.

"Yeah, Zack, I've seen that, and I'm glad. It's because you've earned their respect, I think." He screwed down the fuel cap.

"Well …you know last year they really wanted me to hunt with them. Remember their asking?"

"Sure. You know, that must explain why that bundle is in the back of the Suburban." He nodded toward the truck. "Go check it out."

Zack ran over and opened the rear cargo doors. There, wrapped in Duluth Tool and Die paper, was an Indian caribou-skin anorak, the type that native guides wore in the high north country. It was heavy and slick and smelled of oil and smoke and leather. He had his nose buried in the hood of it when his dad walked up behind him.

"Bjorn called me back before we left for Mexico and asked if you could go with them. When I said yes, he said he would be sending you a package. It's great, isn't it?"

"Oh, man!" He looked at his father. "You mean I can go?"

His dad just winked and smiled, lifting his eyebrows. Zack let out a whoop of delight and dove into the parka, pantomiming stalking and shooting to see how the garment might restrict his movements.

"I told your Uncle John what you were getting, and he said for you to come over early this evening. He'll show you how to adjust the hood for hunting and how to make your glove gauntlets work. You've still got to pack your gear and get your arrows ready."

Zack jumped into the Suburban and was gone.

He didn't sleep much that night. The Swedes spent the evening telling of their hunts in the past. They talked about how plentiful the herds were and about stalking across the frozen grounds looking for double-shovel trophies that disappear over a ridge. They spoke of guns and cartridges and entrance wounds and blood trails, but none of them had ever taken one with a bow. Zack was going to.

〰〰〰〰〰〰〰〰〰〰〰〰

The morning was pristine, cold and clear with a new dusting of snow from the night before. His dad fixed his favorite breakfast. Recipe books called it chipped venison sausage on toast, but his dad had always used the army name, SOS—shit on a shingle. Soldiers always pretended to grumble about it but couldn't get enough. It tasted creamy and soothing to your morning stomach, perfect with strong black coffee and fresh juice. David said it was a recipe his grandmother taught him back in Arkansas. The Swedes wolfed down their breakfast and then set about loading the plane and checking their gear.

Zack tried not to act too green, but he had trouble keeping a cap on his excitement. The flight up took three hours. He flew, as always, in the copilot's seat, headsets in place and clipboard on his knee.

"Zack, I . . . well, I started to go over all the things we usually cover when we're hunting, but I won't. I know you know everything I might say, maybe some I might've forgotten. I just want you to be safe and plan well when you're stalking. Keep your compass with you even when you know it will be a clear day. It'll save your butt. Over."

"Yes, sir, I will. You've made me do that since I was seven. Over."

David leaned over and grabbed Zack's neck with his free hand. "I'm leaving you the heavy radio pack so you can stay in touch. You should call each afternoon just to check in, okay? Over."

"Sure, Dad, we'll be fine. You just make room in the freezer for some fresh meat. Over." He smiled across the cockpit, catching his dad's eye. They laughed.

As they flew north, the big woods slowly gave way to the great tundra, an endless white expanse punctuated only by stunted trees and scrub brush. A frozen land, as far as the eye could see.

This was the country of the Cree, hardy natives who were pushed farther north when the white man settled the lower territory. They still watched over the caribou herds in the region and served as guides for hunters tough enough to come into their cold. It was one of their handmade anoraks that Zack had rolled and tied to his pack frame.

As Zack watched the shadow of the plane play across the contours of the land, he would occasionally catch a glimpse of a small herd of caribou. Most often they were grazing along a rift or frozen stream bed, using boulders and scrub as their camouflage. It was when they approached the Victor Lake region that he saw his first big herd of the year. The plane had surprised them crossing a frozen finger of the lake at full stride.

Zack loved to watch them run, their heads high and their tailless rumps powering them like water rushing over stones. From the plane the herd looked like one large organism, no arms, no legs, yet moving rapidly beneath them. The Swedes let out a whoop and slapped one another on the legs.

Zack enjoyed the Swedes. Even in their fifties the three guys still had a youthful enthusiasm for the hunt. They no longer needed a native guide, but they continued to hire members of one family out of friendship and respect.

Benjamin Cloud and his family kept to the seminomadic ways of his people. For a good portion of the year he and his wife and three children traveled among a series of cabins stretched across the northern boundaries of their territory. The Canadian Indian Affairs Division supplied monies for these fully equipped hunting outposts, so several of the families in the tribe checked on them throughout the year. Benjamin's sons had grown up in this country and eventually traveled off to school. They were now returning as young men, spending time with their father on the trap line and the sled, addicted to the freedom.

David buzzed the plane over their cabin, spotting the dogs and snow-mobiles parked in the clearing. By the time they circled, Benjamin was standing outside the door, waving with both arms and smiling so broadly they could see it from the plane. This was the signal for him to meet them on the lake. He would pack his gear on the sleds and then ride for an hour and a half up to their hunting area. Meanwhile, Zack and the Swedes could set up their tents and windbreaks and build a fire for coffee.

David let Zack land the plane on the lake. Cutting the power to the big radial engine took it to a rapid descent, and within seconds they were skiing across the bumpy surface of the frozen lake. Zack added power so that he could maneuver near the outcropping they would call home for the next few days. The prop kicked up whirlwinds of ice and snow particles that rattled against the tail of the plane. Everyone clapped and cheered as Zack killed the engine and the prop clicked through its final rotations.

"Well, David, from the looks of that herd we passed I'd say you could just give us a few minutes to hunt and we'll be ready to go home," Bjorn joked, climbing out the side door.

"And miss getting to freeze your butts off for a few days? No way. Besides, you wouldn't have near the stories to tell next year. It must take at least a week of thinking to come up with that much b.s." David laughed as he tossed the bags to the men.

"You know the forecast is for a warming trend during our week," Richard, the optimist of the group, broke in. "I hear we may get up close to freezing."

Everyone got a chuckle out of that. A high near thirty degrees in January was just about impossible. But they could hope.

The work of setting up camp went quickly. Each man had his job, and they laughed and joked while raising the tent. Paul, the shortest of the three, was permanently assigned to crawling inside the heavy waxed tent, attaching the stove vent to the pipe, and then propping the internal tent poles. The heavy cotton wall tent smelled of wax and mildew and the smoke of fires gone by.

When the last line had been strung and the coffee was rolling on the fire, they heard the approach of Benjamin's snowmobile. He drove to within two hundred yards of the camp and stopped his machine.

It was his custom to walk into camp. A camp was home, he explained. It just wasn't right to ride up in a noisy, smelly machine. He never did. Benjamin sang a happy song of greeting as he approached, accompanying it with majestic hand motions that told of the great hunts these men had shared in the past.

Richard had always said that this greeting alone was worth the four hundred dollars they paid him for the week. They were all expected to stand there solemnly until he had finished; then they would all laugh and slap each other and the Swedes would try to imitate his gestures. It was absolutely the best way to start a hunt.

After this greeting ritual, Zack showed Benjamin his anorak and bow. Benjamin had guided Zack when he took his first caribou with a rifle four years before.

"I can't remember the last time one of the *ghosts* was taken with a longbow. And with your anorak you will be powerful. This will be special," he said, plucking the string like a musical instrument, listening to the hum, nodding his approval.

"Do you know where some good groups are?" Zack asked.

"Oh, yes, there are many pods of ghosts all about. They are heavy this year and I think there are more good bulls than I've ever seen."

Zack and the Swedes envisioned the possibilities for the coming week, planning their postures for the perfect shot as they conjured up images of heavily antlered males flanking the cows.

"Well, guys, I'm going to have to leave this little hunting party and head back to civilization." David grabbed his thermos of coffee and shook hands all around. "If my boy gives you any trouble, do like I do," he smiled.

"And what do you do?" Bjorn asked, knowing this was a set-up.

"I sit him in the 'time out corner' for thirty minutes, just like it says in Dr. Spock."

Everyone guffawed, even Zack, though he blushed at the special attention. They followed David to the plane and watched as he climbed in and turned to hand them a pack.

"I'm leaving this repeater radio with you guys for an emergency link. Our new system is pretty good, and Zack knows how to use it. Benjamin has a similar unit at his cabin. I think you should be able to get us if you have any problems." He winked at Zack.

He leaned out and shook hands once again, wishing each of them good luck on the hunt. When he got to Zack, the boy stepped up as if to hug his neck but caught himself and stuck out his hand. David caught the look in Zack's eyes; now he was a man, one of the guys, and he wanted his dad to see that.

David beamed and shook his son's hand firmly. Yes, he was a man. Six feet tall and as solid as a tree. The kid cut a striking figure, standing there in his layers of wool sweaters, his high-cut cheekbones red from the cold and his headful of golden-tipped auburn hair blown back from his face.

He wished he could see Suni looking at her boy now. He knew she would be bursting with pride. The old priest had called up a special blessing indeed for their son.

After the hunting party lost sight of David's plane, they turned to preparing supper around the fire. Benjamin filled them in on the movements of the herds and whether some of their old hunting areas might be good choices this year.

It was decided that Bjorn and Richard would go to a familiar area and flank a position where several groups were feeding daily. Paul wanted to hunt his "honey hole" from years past, a little knoll with scrub brush surrounding it. Benjamin wanted to take Zack to a place where he thought the boy might be able to approach a herd for a bow shot.

After a dinner of heavy Swedish stew, cheese, and bread, Benjamin entertained around the campfire. He retold the stories that they requested as if it were the first time he had ever told them. He had started the story of his great-grandfather's hunt for a great silver bull when he stopped abruptly and walked into the night. The faces around the fire looked at one another as if to say, "What happened?" But no one spoke.

Moments later he returned, stopping behind the windbreak to slip on his anorak. On his legs were caribou-skin gaiters fastened like chaps, and around his hooded neck was a long caribou muffler with round black stones attached to each end. He picked up his story where he'd left off.

"And they said my great-grandfather followed the bull for six days on foot, never able to get close enough for a shot. On the sixth night a vision came to him and told him what to do. He awoke and cut one of the covers from his sled to make leggings and a muffler like these. The next morning he found the bull watching over his herd near a high knoll. My great-grandfather made himself look like a ghost, grazing. He used the wind and stepped as a ghost steps, working always closer."

Benjamin demonstrated by pulling up his hood and bending over at the waist. The stones on the muffler made the ends hang down from his neck and in the firelight it was easy to see him as a caribou walking through their camp.

"My great-grandfather took all morning to work himself near the ghost. He shot the great bull with his arrow while still bent over at his waist. He told my grandmother years later that the spirit of that bull talked to him as it left that great body. It asked, 'Are you a fellow ghost who has swallowed a man or are you a man who is eating one of us?'"

He paused for dramatic effect and turned his face to the fire.

"It is well known that you do not lie to animal spirits, so he said, 'I am a man, but I will not eat you if you say.' The great bull spirit said, 'Then you must not be hungry ... I know, you must have killed me for my skin, yours is old and tattered.'

"My great-grandfather was afraid so he said, 'Your skin is beautiful but I will not take it if you say.' The spirit was puzzled but finally said, 'Then I know, you must have killed me for my heart, for I can see that yours is weak and you need my courage and wisdom. You take it now and eat it from my chest while my strength is still in it and you will be strong.'

"This my great-grandfather did, and then he took the skin and the meat home to his village and many people told about the day he came back a changed man." As he finished Benjamin tossed the long muffler with its stone hooves to Zack.

"Tomorrow you will hunt as my great-grandfather hunted. I have a perfect place for you."

Zack jumped up and tried the muffler and leggings that Benjamin had made for him. He couldn't believe his luck. He wished that his Uncle Ricky could be here now. He would *really* get into this.

～～～～～～～～～～

Sleep didn't come easily. The dawn was still an hour away when Zack and Benjamin left the camp on foot. The dim illumination from the winter sky gave them just enough visibility to find their footing. They were working their way toward a shallow rocky gorge carved out by a great glacier thousands of years ago. It created a natural bottleneck in the surrounding terrain and provided cover for the caribou.

Benjamin spoke softly about the hunt as they turned upwind and started the slow climb. Frost formed on the light beard surrounding Zack's mouth. It was cold—probably ten below—and a slight breeze was bringing snow as it freshened from the north.

"This is good, Zack. The snow only helps. I can smell the ghosts up the draw. Do you smell them?"

Zack nodded. He could pick up the barest whiff of a musty urine smell carried by the wind.

"You will use these boulders as your cover. Wait in them until the ghosts move around you and then work your way slowly into them before they can get downwind. Never walk directly at the herd." He patted the boy on the back and retraced their steps to take a position to the south and up the side of the gorge.

Patience was the hardest thing for a young man, despite his Uncle Ricky's coaching. It was especially hard now as the sky lightened and he began to see white and gray shapes moving toward him in the blowing snow.

Zack nocked an arrow, and adjusted his gloves so that his drawing hand was free. When the first of the shapes was still thirty to forty yards upwind, he stepped out of his cover, holding his breath and praying. The adrenaline was surging through him now. His hearing and vision were crisp and vivid. He matched the caribou's steps and mimicked their movements as Benjamin had shown him. He couldn't believe they were not running from him.

Their little grunting sounds were a surprise. He guessed he had never before been close enough to hear them rattle and grunt at each other, apparently communicating reassurance. He was also amazed at how *many* were in the gorge. This was not a pod, it was a full migrating herd. He had hit the jackpot.

Zack picked out a fine young bull with broad palmated antlers only twenty yards away. Just as he raised his bow, the entire herd went silent. The bull turned away, his head high and facing back up the valley. As Zack pulled his bow in a smooth, practiced arc, he thought how strange it was that none of these animals knew that a hunter, an enemy, was in their midst. At full draw he released the arrow, watched it fly the short distance, and saw it bury itself behind the front shoulder of white-tipped fur.

It was a perfect shot. The arrow disappeared completely and he could see a fine spray of blood coming from the opposite side of the bull. But the animal only flinched slightly, his attention still focused up the valley. Zack had not moved either. He still held his bow at eye level, his release hand at his ear.

What Zack could not see was another hunter at the other end of the gorge. The relatively warm weather of the past few days had awakened the hunger of an old male bear, bedded away in the recesses of the boulder-strewn gorge. His decision to emerge for breakfast at this exact moment was what focused the attention of the herd. At the first sight of him, the caribou bolted.

With one congregational movement the mass of animals pivoted and charged down the valley, eyes wide and nostrils flared. Panic had seized them. Zack's position in the bottleneck became a rushing river of bodies and antlers and hooves. He had moved into the open bed of the gorge in order to stalk the last fifty yards for his next shot. Now cover was far too far away. Realizing his predicament he turned with the herd and ran, his bow in hand. He knew he had to make it to the larger boulders for safety, but the herd quickly engulfed him, thundering down the gorge. He ran as he had never run before.

His bow snagged the antlers of a big cow beside him. He instinctively held to it for several moments and she carried him with her, his feet only occasionally touching the ground. Looking ahead desperately, he could see the herd splitting right and left around an obstacle in its way, but he couldn't tell what it was. He hoped for a stone or a log to fall behind. The cow, still dragging him, veered to the right, dodging a narrow rift in the valley floor ... a pit a dozen feet deep and lined with sharp-edged stones that the glacier had left behind.

Zack's feet dragged helplessly along the edge for a moment until the force of his weight and the jarring of the old cow's leaps snapped the string on the bow. He fell like a trout hurling itself up a run in a stream, blind to the landing below and twisting slowly through the air. Then his young body crashed into the stones and lay still.

Zack's luck had not completely failed. He escaped a fatal landing on his back or head. Bad enough that he took the full impact on his left side. The rocky outcropping he struck broke four ribs and forced one of them into the lower lobe of his left lung. His pelvis, absorbing the most force, fractured just above the hip. His head slapped so violently against his own shoulder that he fell mercifully unconscious, neither feeling pain nor seeing the frightened herd make its escape.

Benjamin had been watching the whole scene. From his vantage point, he could see the big herd and sense its apprehension when the old bear made his appearance. He had started down the embankment immediately but there had been no time, no way to warn Zack. He saw the boy running with the herd, keeping up, looking wild as the caribou. He seemed to be laughing. Then he simply disappeared.

Benjamin sprinted across the gorge, eyes darting, searching for a sign of the boy. He found blood on the gravel and followed it a short distance to its source, a beautiful bull with a broad head and a piece of one of Zack's arrows jutting from its chest.

So much for the prey, now for the hunter.

He called out against the wind, hoping the boy would answer. Running down the valley he almost missed the narrow rift. Fearing what it held, he scrambled to the edge and found Zack's motionless body below. Benjamin clambered down and searched Zack for signs of life. He was breathing! He was still alive!

Benjamin assessed the boy's wounds as best he could. He knew Zack had sustained internal injuries and that he had to get help in a hurry. The cold was the biggest enemy for now. The old guide knew what he had to do.

Zack looked into Benjamin's face and felt the massive pain at the same instant. The shock of coming to full consciousness made him gasp for breath. He gagged. His chest hurt, and a salty, metallic taste rose in his throat. He couldn't move. He was sure he must be paralyzed. Fear engulfed him as he tried to understand what Benjamin was saying to him; a chill shot through his body.

"Zack, Zack. It's okay." The Indian pulled the boy's hood back from his ears so he could hear. "You're going to be fine, but I have to go for help."

"I'm paralyzed?" he heard Zack ask.

"No, son, of course not. You have broken some ribs and maybe your hip but you're going to be fine. I am leaving you with our friend, the ghost. He said you are a mighty hunter and he will protect you until I get back."

Benjamin had carried Zack to where the caribou lay. He opened the neck, chest, and abdomen of the great animal, spilling its entrails onto the rocks and rolling Zack inside. He used rawhide thongs to secure this strange cocoon, and propped the boy up in a semi-sitting position, using the antlers to position the huge head as a backrest. Zack was only slowly becoming aware of where he was and of how important it was that he stay there.

"Now, Zack, do not move. I will get the others and the sleds. We will be back soon, as fast as we can. You okay?"

Zack nodded.

"Hey, Benjamin?" he asked.

"Yes, boy."

"Did you save me his heart?" Zack coughed from the slight exertion.

"Yes, son. It's sewn up in there with you. We'll have it for supper, okay?"

"Yeah, okay, Ben. I'll wait here for you." He managed a weak smile.

Zack watched the Cree running down the gorge and picking his way over the boulders until he disappeared in the swirling snow.

He stuck his tongue out of his blood-tinged mouth, out of the hood of his anorak, out of the ravaged neck of this beast, and caught a snowflake on the tip of it. As it melted, he felt better somehow and dissolved with it back into the darkness.

ELEVEN ~~~~~~~~~~~~~

IT WAS A TRADITION FOR THE PRESCOTTS TO HAVE SENATOR BATEMAN and his family to the Governor's Mansion during the holidays. It was also a tradition to have Stephanie raise unmitigated hell about it, starting a week in advance.

Bob endured his wife's tirades because, ultimately, she would assume her proper role and have the staff prepare a nice small party for the two families. She would have Nicole prepped and dressed, and they would sit and make proper small talk until she was ready to scream.

Stephanie did not like holidays. She no longer liked parties. She did not like parading around like an indentured servant, making conversation and smiling sweetly, and she sure as hell didn't like Senator Bateman. In fact, as far as Bob could tell, she didn't much like anyone, but her resentment of the senator went back years.

In those days, Bateman was an inconsiderate, frequent visitor. He would drop by, disrupt the family schedule, and eventually sequester Bob in his study for hours. They would talk policy and politics, and more times than not they would end up talking about her. She came to know that within a few days following one of these visits, Bob was going to start in on her again. He'd tell her how she should try to fit the mold a little better. She should try to understand the role of a governor's wife and recognize what is expected of a woman in the South. It made her want to puke! Stephanie took it because she had to.

She had gone on taking it until last year. Bob would never forget it. The explosion.

Stephanie had bitched and sulked about Bateman and his pomposity and his archaic ideas for days. The quarrels went on until December twenty-sixth, the day before the little party. Then she had gone strangely quiet and acquiescent. The kitchen staff had suddenly become very busy, and Bob thought that all would be well.

On the twenty-seventh Bob left the mansion in the early afternoon for a little exercise and recreation, both having to do with a grad student named Mary Alice. He returned in time to shower and change in his private basement quarters and was ready to answer the announcement that the Bateman party had arrived.

Bounding up the stairs to the foyer, he was almost paralyzed to find the staff and servants—most of them black—dressed in Aunt Jemima and Uncle Tom outfits. His mouth was still jacked half open when the Batemans poured through the front door, eyes wide in amazement.

Before anyone could say anything, Stephanie appeared at the top of the stairs with Nicole, both dressed in Scarlett O'Hara ball gowns. They descended the stairs in total silence. Everyone else tried to figure out what in the hell was going on.

Suddenly the kitchen staff started applauding. They had for some reason, become overwhelmed by the moment. Certainly they had never seen the First Lady look so human, so soft, so ... so southern. Whatever the reason, the clapping broke the spell. People began to move and speak, but Bob avoided the senator's eyes. The women chatted politely and giggled nervously at Stephanie's little surprise; and, of course, Nicole was delighted by the whole affair.

It was well known that the senator was fond of beef and pork, would tolerate chicken if it was fried, but despised fish of every type. Stephanie had endured years of little speeches about this pet peeve of his. Thus she started the meal with sushi appetizers and little fish kabobs. The salad was a Shanghai vinaigrette poi-fish affair with little dried squid sprinkled over the top.

With each course, it was more and more obvious that she had orchestrated a sustained, vengeful attack on the senator. She had probably hoped that, as they rolled out the whole chinook salmon garnished with langostines, he would lose his temper completely and have a massive fish-related coronary right there on the dining room floor. But she had underrated him. His years of rising above it all in Washington had trained him in how to turn Stephanie's thinly veiled assault against her. The senator sat pleasantly at the end of the table drinking his wine and eating bread through each course, murmuring pleasantries.

The party was actually quite enjoyable. The food was excellent. The enthusiasm of the kitchen staff in the *Gone with the Wind* costumes spilled over onto the dinner guests. No one would forget the image of Aunt Jemima serving a decorated tray of sushi at a formal Christmas dinner, yet it was fun.

The dessert was perhaps a little too much, though. Stephanie had had one of the Junior League ladies make a domed, pink gelatin creation with tiny red seahorse candies and aquamarine angelfish cookies swimming in suspension. Nicole was the only one who could actually eat the dessert all the way down to its inhabitants.

After dinner the group retired to the living room for an informal chat and gift exchanging. Bob remembered wanting to put his wife in the fireplace and use her for the Yule log. Of course, he didn't. Besides, she wouldn't have fit.

Bob had to hold his peace. He didn't say a word. He had been afraid that any criticism might flip her over the edge and—if it were possible—make things even worse.

Later, at the door, Bob tried to apologize quietly to the senator. Bateman ignored him completely, stepping toward Stephanie instead and kissing her hand.

In his richest Dixie tones, he said. "Miss Stephanie, you have never looked so lovely as tonight. When the pendulum on which you ride swings back again, you might consider getting off a little bit sooner, dear." He oozed southern gallantry. "Oh, and, Miss Stephanie, most of us down here have seen fit to follow the proclamation of that president from your state and unequivocally free our darkies. It would be a marvelous Christmas gesture, don't you think? Goodnight all!"

That evening ended the traditional Christmas visit for the two families.

~~~~~~~~~~~~~~~~

Bateman had called him this year on New Year's Eve with appropriate good wishes, but in truth to arrange a meeting for the two—sans family and food and entertainment.

Bob greeted the senator himself, realizing for the first time how very frail his old mentor was becoming.

"It's been too long, senator. It's good to see you."

"Good to see you too, son. I see you're eating well these days," he kidded. "Let's find a place where we can visit."

Bob led him back to the formal library study and shut the huge doors behind them.

"Can I get you a drink?" Bob asked.

"Well, I'm not supposed to but ... a Scotch, straight up?"

"Scotch it is." He turned to the decanters. "Senator, you look like a man on a mission. Anything you care to share?"

"Yes, son, we need to talk."

"Is it about Stephanie?"

"Well ... it is and it isn't." He delivered this into his glass. "Bob, you have defined your position in this state extremely well over the past few years. Many of us feel that you have become the consummate progressive southern governor ... even a role model for many to come after you."

"That's very flattering, sir, and I really appreciate your saying so." He blushed for the first time in years. "But you know that I owe a tremendous debt to you for my chance to get here."

"Make no mistake, Bob, you owe a tremendous debt to a considerable number of powerful people in this state. The movers. The doers. The circle." He sat holding his glass quietly and let this sink in for a moment. "They are an appreciative group, as you know, and they are still very much in your corner."

"That's good to know," Bob replied sincerely.

"Bob, we need to talk about your next move," he said bluntly.

"Senator, as you know, I've always hoped for a Senate seat. There are still some things I would like to accomplish here in the state though, and with our favorable polls, I think we can build a good war chest over the next few years for the eventual Senate campaign."

"And Stephanie. What does she want?"

He sheepishly responded, "Well, she wants what I want."

"Bullshit!" Bateman roared, "That's goddamned bullshit, Bob. I know that woman better than you think, so come clean." He leaned out from his chair, more animated than Bob had seen him in years.

"Senator, you know how aggressive Stephanie can be. Downright pushy at times. She has really been doing better though. Her group at Baylor, Harold has benefited my administration tremendously and we ..."

"Quit defending her and tell me what she wants!"

"To be honest, she and many of her associates have been discussing a run for the presidency." He almost regretted admitting this. "Senator, I would never let her interfere with a proper run for the Senate. We have ..."

"Oh, yes you will! We will let her stand right squarely in the way of a Senate campaign. For the first time ever that little Yankee hellion and I agree perfectly." He laughed heartily. "And you will need her desperately on this one." He turned to Bob. "How do you feel about the presidency, son? Surely you've thought about it."

Bob couldn't quite believe the course of the conversation.

"Of course I have, Senator. I'm sure every governor and senator and congressman thinks about it. I remember when you toyed with the idea, but there are obstacles and considerations, and eventually you have to ask yourself if you could actually do the job if you ever got there."

"Don't you think that every man who has gained that office has asked himself those same questions?" Bateman asked, shifting in his chair.

"I guess they have, but the point is, how did they answer them? How did you answer them?" Bob asked.

"I answered the way my people wanted me to, Bob. That's what matters. I went to the right people and I listened to them and did what they suggested. I continue to benefit from that ... arrangement. My family will ... profit for many years to come. Things are changing, Bob. You know it, too. And now it's time for you to make some decisions."

He locked eyes with Prescott. "Our people here are thinking ... bigger. Their interests and investments are spreading outside the country; and, Bob, we are talking billions and billions of dollars." The senator let that sink in before resuming. "I have reason to believe that they are willing to take a chance on you if you are willing to commit wholeheartedly in return. The time is now. It will take time, three years, to have everyone in place."

"Senator, I am honored that they feel this way. I have an excellent organization here in Arkansas. People who can move mountains. But I would have to have a network like that in every state. How will I start? How will they have me start?"

"The beauty of ... commercial interests ... is that they naturally build their own networks of extremely powerful and connected people. Their networks create the machine for you. They even ...help ...envision platform and policy for you. Keep that in mind. If you grasp it early enough, it will appear from the outset to be your idea. You will get the credit. They'll see to that. You are in a position to build on their plans for ... growth and development."

"Senator, just what does that mean in practical terms?"

"It will take its own shape as your people's international concerns are ... expressed ... over the next few years. It will be your job to give it a human rights spin and that sort of thing. All the usual appeals. Keep it in the middle of the Democratic Party platform."

"Something visionary but undefined ... just out of reach," Bob smiled. "In fact, I worked up a cover just like that once, called 'ACT Together': the 'ACT' stands for 'Amity and Cooperation for Tomorrow.' It sounds good and means anything you want it to."

"Exactly! We Americans love things that are dangled just beyond our grasp. Both parties are working with this concept, calculating how they can slip their old ideas under its skirts. Eventually it comes down to dropping some of our old protectionist policies in favor of industrial development in the Third World. Your friends are already putting their investments in place for that. This is your kind of game, Bob. It's your move. You won't get another chance."

"It's exciting." He felt a little out of breath. "I'll have to think about this and talk it over with Stephanie."

"Bob, Stephanie and her cronies down at Baylor, Harold are some of our biggest assets. Their people are our people. Everyone is going into this thing together and you will all go up to Pennsylvania Avenue together. You are the best campaigner, the best on your feet, that I have ever seen. There is only one person you have to talk to, and that is ... you."

"So, if I were going to, what do you think my time frame would be?"

"You stay in this office, right up to '92. You expand your power in the national party issues. You work more with the Democratic Governors' Council. You make even more noise about human rights and standards, and, Bob," he paused and took another sip of his Scotch, "you keep your dick in your pants!"

"What?"

"You heard me. This is no longer an option for you. Everyone knows what goes on around here, and to a certain extent, it is acceptable. No state attorney is willing to take a woman's case against the governor, but if you make a presidential bid, the out-of-state lawyers will be lining up to hear any accusation and take any chance on sinking your little love boat. The media will want to examine every hair on your butt." He finished, looking sternly at Prescott.

"Senator, I don't know what you've heard, but ..."

"It's what I *know*, Bob. Hell! I'm not judging you, but you've earned a reputation. This kind of campaigning is enough of a bitch without having to fight stories that you've been screwing Cissy and Mary Alice and ... I could name others!"

Bob, stunned, sat silently staring out the window of the study. A light snow had begun to fall. His thoughts turned to his mother and how she would feel about his making a presidential run. She had always said that he would be there some day. She just hoped she'd live to see it. She had always been right.

"I'll want the best people money can buy," Bob said after a few moments of contemplation. "And I'll want my handpicked people in whatever capacity I choose."

"The backers will want your full attention on their issues."

"They will get it. They always have. I'll expect their consultations and cooperation on policy."

"You'll get all the schooling you can use, Bob. I'm proud of you, son. You've done so well. I just hope I can see you finish this one."

"I'll finish it, Senator, but the question still remains: Can I do the job once I get there?" Bob searched the floor for an answer.

"Well, Governor, a lot of people, including me, feel that if a man can pull off the magnificent feat of surviving the election process in this country, he is obviously qualified." He laughed, and finished his glass.

TWELVE ∿∿∿∿∿∿∿∿

JANUARY 4, 1987
ONTARIO, CANADA

DAVID SPENT THE AFTERNOON OF THE THIRD FLYING BACK FROM the camp. The weather was tolerable, but the clouds had lowered and become heavy with snow. It was almost completely dark when he made his approach at the strip and skidded up to the gas pump. He filled the plane's tanks and checked the oil and deicing fluids before heading up to the cabin for the evening.

David had just turned forty. He was beginning to feel his years after a long day in the plane. It wasn't that he was over the hill. He still considered himself a young, virile man ... Well, virile, anyway. He decided he would now think of himself as "in his prime."

He had lived a simple life since Suni's death. He didn't isolate himself, but he never actively sought another woman. For a while he'd kept company with a lady named Monette, down in Sudbury. Things had gotten pretty serious between them a couple of years ago, but David had put the brakes on when he realized that she had no intention of ever sharing his outdoors life. Over the past year they had renewed their friendship and started seeing each other again, but only about once a month.

It seemed to David that the northwoods was full of lame, long-distance relationships. That seemed particularly appropriate now as he dropped onto the sofa and pulled his stump from the socket of his prosthesis. He guessed he did pretty well for a one-legged fellow. The women he dated didn't ever seem to complain. But he was beginning to long for a special relationship that would carry him into his so-called *golden* years. A companion as well as lover, so he'd never be lonely. What he really wanted was for some wonderful, gorgeous woman to knock him completely off his feet ... well, foot. Hell, everyone wants to be madly in love and he was no exception, especially with Zack almost grown.

It was cold in the cabin. He decided to crash on the sofa where it was relatively warm. Instead of putting his prosthesis back on, he pulled himself up and hopped around the kitchen, gathering a simple supper from the fridge and throwing all of the evening's essentials onto the coffee table.

Zack used to tease him about his hopping. When Zack was little he'd hop around the house in imitation of his father. David missed his son already tonight. He wasn't sure how he would handle the boy's going off to college next year.

The emergency response rescue team, for which David substituted, was aware that he would be at home tonight and officially on duty, but he decided to call and check in before hitting the sack.

"Is this Ed? ... Hey, guy. How are you? ... Well, it looks like I'll be your backup man for the next few days ... Yeah, I should be up just before sunrise and headed over toward Bristol to load a few supplies. I'll be easy enough to reach as long as I'm in the plane. Is the weather going to hold for us? ... I hope so too. I'll call you if I get closed down tomorrow. Have a good evening and tell Lisa that I still love her even though she married that professional wrestler. Yeah ... Okay ... See ya." He hung up the phone and reached over to turn on the radio. It crackled for a moment before the automatic squelch kicked in and quieted the set.

He had almost finished his sandwich when a long beep came over the radio speaker. The suddenness of it made him jump, but it was the familiar sound of a repeater unit coming in on the local frequency.

"Farr Shores Outfitters, come in please ... Over." It was Zack making his check-in call.

David groped for the mike and answered, "This is Farr Shores, go ahead, Zack." David had taught the boy to be brief and to the point over the radio so as not to interfere with emergencies.

"Everything is fine up here, Dad. You won't believe what Benjamin fixed for me, but I'll get to show you later. Have a good night and I'll talk to you tomorrow. ... Over."

"Sounds good, son. You guys have a great hunt tomorrow ... Over and out."

David had just placed the mike back on the table when Zack's voice came through the speaker. "Hey, Dad.... Thanks.... Over and out."

He smiled, finished his iced tea, and stretched out on the couch, pulling an old elk skin cover over him. He had killed the elk in Colorado a number of years ago and he liked the way he slept when he was wrapped up tight in the hide.

That night he dreamed of his remote Mexican beaches. Antique airplanes were parked at each little palapa, and black-haired girls danced on their wings. He was sitting in the back seat of an old Stearman, taxiing up and down the beach, dodging iguanas and drinking a tall mojito from a frosted fruit jar.

～～～～～～～

The morning was spitting snow as he took off in the Otter. The weather service said that it should remain light and variable throughout the day, so David decided to follow his regular schedule and hop over to Bristol for the morning. He was circling the field there when he heard a repeater call come in over the radio.

"Mayday! Mayday! ... .Emergency Services, come in ... Over," the radio squawked.

David's heart stopped. He wasn't sure whose voice was on the radio but whoever it was was out of breath.

"This is Emergency Services. Go ahead ... Over," Ed answered from the services center.

"This is Joshua Cloud. I'm calling from a hunting camp on the Tonic

Bay section of Victor Lake. We have an emergency up here. We're ... we're going to need an air ambulance ... Over," he paused to catch his breath.

David forgot for a moment that he was flying an airplane. He thought he might still be in last night's crazy dream. He prayed that he was. Then he heard Ed's voice again.

"Josh ... we read you loud and clear. Is this the party that Dave Farr dropped off yesterday?" he asked.

"Sure is, Ed ... I'm afraid that it's Zack who's hurt. My father is ... uh ... is bringing him into camp right now. He's hurt pretty bad from what we can tell. He's going to need to get to a hospital fast. Can you let his dad know?" Joshua's voice was shaking now.

"David, did you copy all of that?" Ed asked, his voice low.

David was in shock. He supposed he had heard everything but he wasn't sure. He couldn't speak. He just keyed his mike as an affirmation.

Zack was injured! He couldn't even imagine in what way. David snapped to and suddenly felt an old anger surge through his brain. He was furious. At whom, he didn't know. Probably at himself, for allowing Zack to go, or for not staying there with him for the hunt.

He pulled the Otter out of the pattern and immediately set his navcom radio to carry him north toward Tonic Bay. He was about to get back on the radio when Ed called him back.

"Josh and David, listen up ... I've got a chopper leaving right now for the camp. The snow is getting heavy and it's going to be about fifty minutes before he can get there. Mike Langly is the pilot. He knows the region well ... David, I know you are already heading there but the snow is going to shut down your chances in the Otter. Besides, Mike can get to them at least an hour before you could ... Okay? ... You got that, David?"

David was trying to rein in his emotions. It wasn't easy, but he forced himself to concentrate and think things through. "Ed ... I copy on everything ... but I have to do something, man ... You coordinate everything, okay? Give me the plan. Over."

"Good, David, we have the plan all ready ... Okay, I want you to get to Bristol and pick up Dr. Lisfranc. I'm getting in touch with him now. You bring everything he needs for life support and possible emergency surgery. Then head due north and go as fast and as far as you can in the snow. You'll need to set down in a safe area. If you can't find a proper building then set the Otter up as our treatment facility. Radio me with your Loran coordinates and we will vector the chopper to you. We don't have a doctor up here to put on the chopper or it would be a different story … Are we clear, David?"

"Copy that … I'm putting down in Bristol in the next three minutes, Ed. We'll be out of here as soon as possible, but I've got to know how my boy is … I'm going crazy up here … Can you get me his condition? … Over." David was desperate.

"Joshua … Did you copy all of the plan? … Over," Ed asked.

"This is Bjorn … David? … Listen to me. Benjamin just brought Zack into camp in his sled. The boy is hurt, David, but it is hard to tell how badly. He had a rough fall. He is unconscious right now. Benjamin says to tell you three things … Zack is bleeding internally, coughing some blood up … We are keeping him very warm … .And Ben says that he's sure Zack's going to be okay. We will be looking for the chopper. You guys hurry … Over."

David taxied the Otter up to the Quonset hut that served as the terminal for the small airport. He ran through the building yelling for help with servicing the plane. Locals at the FBO had heard the emergency call over their scanner and were already gathering blankets and standing ready to help. By the time David had located a generator and an electric heater and lights, the doctor had arrived by Sno-Cat.

Paul Lisfranc, being an experienced northwoods hand, brought three crates of supplies and his nurse. Eighteen minutes after landing, the Otter lifted off the icy field and turned north into the thickening snow.

Lisfranc was a Frenchman who had spent the twenty years since his surgical residency taking care of loggers, Indians, and unfortunate sportsmen. He had been on many flights such as this and he fell into his role easily.

Loosening his coat and handing his scarf to Jean, his nurse, he started gently giving orders. "David, you will fly the plane, yes? And you will try not to kill us, yes? Jean will prepare some of our equipment. I will talk on the radio to the people in the camp and to the people in the chopper. *So,* you must loosen your hand from the microphone that I might do this … yes? David?"

He reached for the mike. David realized that he had been gripping it like a lifeline. He snapped to and heeded the doctor's advice to concentrate on flying.

Lisfranc radioed Bjorn about Zack's vital signs and overall appearance. Then he took the headsets off and turned to David.

"My friend, your son has probably punctured one of his lungs in the fall. That is his most serious injury. It is crucial that I get to him as soon as possible. It would be very helpful if you knew what blood type the boy is. He has lost a considerable amount and we have brought several units of different types with us. Do you happen to know?"

"AB," David replied at once.

"Are you certain?" Lisfranc asked.

"Yes, I'm certain. He and I have it written in the front of our passports. Is that good, Paul? Do you have any AB blood?"

"It is ideal. The AB group is the universal recipient. We can essentially use all the units of blood we brought. This is very good! I have them in a warmer and they will be ready." The doctor put his headsets back on and continued on the radio.

David concentrated on squeezing top speed from the Otter. He stayed low and studied visual landmarks so that he could find a suitable landing zone. He had precious lifesaving cargo on board and he planned on getting it down to his son. He decided to follow the course of the Squaw River as far as he could, then land on its frozen surface.

David heard the doctor giving instructions for starting IVs on Zack. The helicopter had made it to the camp in heavy snow and the EMTs were starting drips and warming the boy up as the chopper lifted off and headed south.

Visibility was below minimum when David decided to land and prepare the plane as a treatment quarter. He made a low pass over a straight section of the river that appeared clean. Circling back, he touched down and coasted to an area where a small bluff provided a little shelter from the snow. Before killing the engine he relayed his coordinates to the chopper so that they could dial them into their navigation system. They radioed back that their ETA would be twenty minutes. He had plenty to do.

Jean helped him set the generator outside the plane and snake the electrical cords into the cargo bay. He had thrown out the extra jump seats so that they would have sufficient room for a stretcher. He connected the lights and heater as they heard the chopper approaching. David ran out onto the frozen river with a hand flare to wave them in.

David, Jean, and the EMTs hoisted Zack out of the chopper bay and hurried with him through the snow to the Otter. It was all David could do to keep from crying as he looked at his son bundled up on the stretcher. Dried blood all over him. He thought that if his son had bled this much ...

"Mr. Farr, this blood is not from your son," said one of the EMTs, reading David's dismay. He opened the layers of blankets and clothes that covered Zack. "Benjamin had your son stitched up inside a big caribou when we got there. We cut him out and he was warm as toast. Kinda messy, but I would say it saved his life considering how cold it was up there."

David nodded his head and found new hope as he pictured Benjamin caring for his son.

All four of them worked quickly to cut the heavy hunting clothes from Zack's body and cover him with the clean warm blankets. David spoke softly to his son, as if he were fully conscious, reassuring the boy that everything was going to be fine—after all, Dr. Lisfranc had taken care of him since he was five.

The doctor thumped around on Zack's chest and side and listened intently with his stethoscope.

"David," he said, "I am going to have to do a little work on Zack's chest. I've got his blood and IVs going. We just need to insert a chest tube or two as soon as possible. You have done all you can for now so you will please leave the plane and make sure the generator keeps going for us. You can use the helicopter radio to call in to the rescue center and report where we are. Okay? ... Now you will leave. Yes?"

David bent over and kissed his son on the forehead and then slipped out the door closing it fast against the wind. It was the most difficult two hours David Farr ever spent. The short winter day evaporated and left him exhausted. He fought constantly to keep morbid thoughts away. He stayed out in the cold most of the time because he felt useless and stupid sitting in the helicopter. The wind helped keep his mind fresh and he waited for any sign from the crew working inside his plane.

Finally Dr. Lisfranc opened the copilot's door and stepped out into the snow. David hurried over to him.

"How is he, Paul?" David begged.

"He's doing well considering all that has happened to him in the last few hours. Not the least of which is that he has had me probing around in his chest. We've stabilized things as well as we can and have stopped all of the significant hemorrhaging.

"We need to get him to the medical center in Doling as soon as possible. But I think we should wait until morning and fly him out in the Otter. I don't want to risk moving him right now. I'm going to send the helicopter back." He paused and looked up at David. "He's a very strong young man and I think we're out of the woods as long as there are no complications."

David wept with relief. He fell down to his knees in the snow and cried into his hands. The snow whipped around him in the dark. He had no idea how he was going to thank all the people who had come together to save his son, but he would think of a way.

〰〰〰〰〰〰〰〰〰〰〰

Later that evening he talked to Benjamin over the radio. Benjamin never seemed in the least surprised that Zack had pulled through. "David, I spoke to the spirit of the ghost that Zack took with the bow. It told me the boy would be fine. I sewed the heart up beside Zack inside the carcass as it told me. The spirit said it would protect the boy. Zack even asked me about it when I had to leave and go for the snowmobile. I told him we would eat it tonight."

"Really? . . . Well, Ben, I'd say that you should plan on doing that as soon as Zack is able to have solid food. I'll fly up and get you. Sounds like a special ceremony to me. We'll tell him you're saving it for him, okay?"

"It's gone, David . . . I looked everywhere after Zack left on the whirlybird. I skinned the whole animal so that Zack could have the coat, but the heart was gone. I think the boy needed its power and used it up. I burned the meat on a big fire and sang a prayer to the ghost. He was a great friend."

"Yes, he was, Ben." David shivered and goosebumps popped up on his arms. "He was a great friend, and so are you. Thank you both for giving me back my son."

THIRTEEN 〰〰〰〰〰〰

"SO. HOW MUCH WILL WE BE EXPOSED?" STEPHANIE REACHED across the desk and took his hand.

"My God! Steph, where do I start? Hell, I guess the question is, where do I *stop?* We are wide open. Bob has ... flaunted his manhood in every corner of the state. For the last couple of years he has been all over the country! His state police flunkies are probably the only ones who know for sure."

Eric Grant looked haggard. He was usually the picture of propriety, in his Brooks Brothers suits and Cole-Haan loafers. He was a punctual man, who prided himself on always keeping his bases covered, but this last gubernatorial campaign had undone him, and Stephanie was worried.

"Listen, Eric, we don't have to go through this tonight. You're exhausted and ..."

"No! We have to talk now. I've got to know where we're going. Where you're going." He squeezed her hand. "He's exposed. I don't know who will be brave enough to go to the press. If you only knew how many of these ... stories I've had to deal with ... apologized and threatened and paid for over the years."

He looked up at her. "I'm sorry, honey. I know that you've had to endure much more than I, and in a more personal way. But I'm worried. No, I'm flat out scared." He paused and rubbed his temples. "Have you really thought about what this will do to you and Nicole? It won't be like anything you've faced in these state races."

"Of course I've thought about it. I've thought about it for years. I'm not naïve." She leaned back in her chair, all business now.

"I have very little in life that women normally have. I don't have a faithful husband. I don't have my own home. My family life is bizarre. My schedule is dictated by the polls. But they can't change my mind, and I'm prepared to pay the price, so long as Nicole is sheltered. I'll see to that myself. They won't kill me or Nicole so they can't hurt me. I'll do what I have to do. And in the end, I'll beat them all. This is my chance, Eric. It's what I've always dreamed of."

"How could you actually want this, Steph? It's crazy to want this."

"You don't understand. I've *always* known that I could get him into the White House. From the first time I met him, I knew we could get there." Stephanie was excited now. Her voice took on a passionate tone.

"But, Steph, you of all people, should know that Bob couldn't run a dog pound. Imagine turning Bob Prescott loose on the whole country! It's a staggering job for a brilliant person with a tough work ethic who actually gives a damn. For Bob? I can't imagine what he would be like. Hell, if it hadn't been for you, he would never have lasted his first term."

"Exactly! And, Eric, I intend to do the managing when he's in the White House, too. He owes me. I haven't put up with this shit for all these years just to be a White House hostess and sponsor the annual fucking Easter egg rolls on the fucking front lawn. I want domestic!" she said in a loud strained whisper. "I'll guaran-fucking-tee you, I get domestic!"

"You'll ... what?"

"I want all of the domestic agenda. He and his advisers can have trade and military and international and foreign affairs. I am going to run domestic policy."

"How are you going to get away with that? You won't have any real office." Eric was getting more worried by the moment. She had a manic gleam in her eyes.

"I would have agreed with you five years ago, but our generation is taking over now. The country is ready for this. They'll get two presidents for the price of one. And when they see what we're going to accomplish and who we're going to bring into this administration, they'll love it." Stephanie was leaning into her argument. "And you're forgetting something, Eric. The politics. Bob will run the politics. He is the best! He will clear the way for everything we want, and make it smell like roses. Everything we want!" she repeated.

Eric struggled to speak. "Steph, it sounds impossible or crazy or ... I don't know. I can't believe we are even talking about this. I just don't know."

"It's going forward, Eric. I just need you with me. I want this to be our next step together. It will get us out of this fucking hillbilly state and open every door we want. Your Nancy will be here, Bob will be everywhere else, and *we will be together.*"

"I know, honey, I want that too. It's just that ... this is all new to me. I need time to think. We have a house of cards, right now. That's all it is. One mistake and it all comes down. As long as we stay in the state, I can keep a wall around it. Nothing is going to blow it over. But in Washington with all the sharks ..." his voice trailed off.

"Eric, they can't crucify us over some old affair he had. I'll make a statement of undying love and stand by him and it will go by the wayside."

"It's not just the affairs. There are deals that we've done, a lot of them that won't play well in the national press. They don't know how we do business here. They'll make it look horrible."

"I know all about the deals, Eric. All of them. I've been cleaning up the paper trail. Most will hold up. We can brush off questions. There's a few that worry me, but we're tracking every scrap of paper right now. We'll be all right."

"Stephanie, that's what I'm trying to tell you. You *don't* know about all the deals. I *do*. You were kept out for your own safety. I don't want you to know everything. They haunt me enough. You're right, though; this is the price we pay for achieving the offices he wanted in this state. But I'm the one who has to walk behind the horse and clean up. If I screw anything up, we're all in big trouble. I just don't know if I can take it."

"You promised me that you would, Eric," she said, placing her hands flat on the desk. "I'm depending on you."

Eric Grant looked up with a tortured frown. He slowly placed his hands on top of hers and then slumped over until his forehead rested on the cool top of the desk.

"There will only be more deals in Washington. Bigger deals. More shit for me to hide," he murmured.

"But you'll go with me, won't you, Eric?" she asked, a chill in her voice.

"Yes, Steph. I'm with you," he answered without even raising his head from the table. "God help me, I'm with you."

FOURTEEN 〜〜〜〜〜〜〜〜〜〜〜

OCTOBER 1994
TRUCKEE, CALIFORNIA

HE TINY AIRSTRIP AT TRUCKEE WAS A PERFECT BACKDROP FOR THE old Pilatus Porter as it flared for touchdown. Ricky had first seen one of these workhorse planes when he was a nineteen-year-old grunt in Vietnam. They certainly weren't anything fancy as planes went, but pilots loved them. You could fill them full of ammunition, barrels of fuel, sky jumpers, or anything you could fit through the cargo doors and still get in and out of a short field. They weren't fast or all that economical, but with tundra tires mounted on their gear they were the perfect bush plane. He and David Farr had logged many an hour bumping around the northwoods in this old bush hopper. It brought back warm memories.

As the balloon tires squeaked on the grass and the plane taxied toward the tiedowns, Ricky shook his head and said to himself, "Just like the old man, Zack. You've definitely got the touch."

He walked over to run his hand over the tail while Zack shut the bird down. Ricky chocked the wheels with some old wooden blocks left on the field for that purpose. Zack gathered up his charts in the cockpit and stowed his headsets.

It had been months since they had seen each other. This was the first time that Zack had been able to come to Truckee to fish with Ricky. The Truckee River, which runs through the mountains and past this little California border town, has some legendary natural trout sections. The stream spills into Nevada and winds down toward Reno. It was one of Ricky's favorite haunts, and he was delighted to get Zack to break away from his northwoods and meet him for a few days of camping and fishing.

Zack climbed out and tied down the starboard wing while Ricky tied down the port. They met in front of the prop and sized each other up. Just like always.

"Man! you sho' is ugly!" Ricky said in slow, straight tones.

"You is two kindsa ugly ... uglee and ugli!" Zack said with the utmost sincerity.

"I am gonna slap it off a ya!" they yelled in unison, moving forward to hug each other and wrestle around like pups.

~~~~~~~~~~~

"How's old Hop-along?" Rick asked as they transferred gear to his truck.

"Oh, he's fine. He said to remind you that you're getting too old to be living like a gypsy and he's got a wheelchair and a hospital bed in the spare cabin up at the place."

"Yeah, well remind him that he is six-and-a-half months older than I am, one-legged, and *I* still have my original teeth." He smiled widely to show Zack. They both cracked up. "And how's my beautiful Deidra? Has she decided to leave you yet? It's been what now, two years since the wedding?" Ricky teased.

"She's great, Uncle Rick, and she sends her love. She's sorry she couldn't come but she wanted to visit her sister over in Milkee. She hinted just a bit that she wasn't ready to give up all her comforts when she knew you were the tour guide."

Ricky laughed, "Oh, she just knows how hard it is to control herself when she's around me," he laughed again. "Lots of women are like that. You tell her I said that, will you?"

"Sure ... you bet I will. Hey, where are we bunking tonight?" Zack asked as they headed out onto the highway.

"I've got a temporary camp set up downstream, toward Floriston. We'll work that area tomorrow and then decide about the next few days. You hungry?"

"Not really. You know me, I ate a bunch of junk while I was flying. Maybe by suppertime."

Ricky drove down through the mountain passes that had stalled the ill-fated Donner Party in 1846 and '47. He recited the Donner story for Zack—the missed opportunities, the bad timing, the poor information, and, worst of all, the terrific snow. Inches and feet and weeks of snow. A lifetime of white. When the supplies were gone and the sick were dying from exposure, they began eating the leather from their shoes. When the shoes were gone and no hope was in sight, they decided to waste nothing and no one.

Ricky had always considered their story a paramount example of the resiliency of mankind, the ability to adapt, innovate, and survive. It was necessity, not cannibalism. Zack sat quietly, staring out his window at the darkening day and listening to the pleasant rise and fall of his uncle's voice. Finally he turned from the window.

"Ricky, do you think the ones who survived—you know, the ones who lived after they were rescued—ever recovered? Do you think they found a reason to go on the next day considering what all had happened?"

Ricky cut his eyes carefully to pick out Zack in his peripheral vision. He heard something in his question that threw a switch somewhere deep. He and the Zack were connected in a special way, and he felt more than simple curiosity about the way Zack had said things. He could tell, too, Zack was peering intently at him.

"Well, not all of them felt like keeping on. And for sure most of them took a long time, months, years, to recover to where they gave a damn again. But that's the beauty of being human. We keep on truckin'. We live down our sorrows. We find new things to focus on, new challenges, and eventually we tend to forget the pain. Mostly. We get by until it's our turn to go, and then we go our way and leave others behind to survive us."

Zack thought for a moment and almost responded, but then turned to the steamed window and traced patterns with his finger, silent. Ricky was worried but decided not to push.

They finally bounced off the highway onto an access road and from there headed upstream along a Forest Service trail just wide enough for the four-wheel-drive pickup. The trail ended in a cul-de-sac. It was bordered by huge boulders that looked as if an enormous distracted child had dropped them in a pile, meaning to come back later and play with them again. Ricky and Zack parked the truck and helped each other shoulder the backpacks and food satchel.

Zack asked, "How far from here?"

"Oh, it's about one click up the valley, but it's kinda rough walking. Let's take the higher road." He pointed up and behind them.

"And you're sure there are trout in this place?" Zack teased.

"You just wait!"

Ricky bent into his load and was off, moving between the rocks and climbing. Zack loved to watch the man move. There was almost no noise and no wasted effort. They climbed for twenty minutes, picking their way up the riverbed, a mess of huge rock and gravel slides that had fallen into the river's course from years of erosion. It was an enormous barren sluicebox of a stream.

Zack realized after a few minutes why it felt so sterile. There was very little greenery along the banks and almost nothing in the water. He was used to pulling fish out of weed beds and rushes and from the shelter of moss-covered rocks. This seemed strange to him and he wondered how fish could live in these swift, cold-water mountain streams.

Just as the last light failed them, they rounded a cut of the river and dropped down beside a long calm pool. Ricky had set up a dome tent and vestibule against a small grove of spruce. A fire was already laid and cooking pans stacked beside it. Zack unshouldered his pack. Ricky was surprised to see him stumble slightly when he let it drop onto the gravel.

"Zack, you've been hanging around your old man too much. That's the way he walks after a brisk little hike. I used to tell him he walked like his leg had come unscrewed a little. Hey, bud, you okay?" Ricky realized that Zack was really winded.

"Yeah, okay, just out of shape. You know what they say about married life. I'll be okay in just a sec." Zack found a rock and sat with his hands on his knees.

Ricky frowned. He had watched Zack run and swim circles around him in the last few years. This hike was no more than invigorating, even though they were eight thousand feet above sea level. He puzzled over this while walking down to the river. There he located the lanyard looped around a stick he had hammered into the gravel. He could feel that the fish were still alive even before he pulled them from the water. Zack was feeding the fire as he walked back into camp.

"Hey! Nice fish!" Zack said, looking up from the cookfire. The flames lit up his face in a way that made him look much older, his eyes hollow, his cheeks bony and gaunt. Ricky dropped the four rainbow trout on a flat rock near the fire and got out his filet knife.

"Tell me again why your dad couldn't make the trip with you," Ricky said, as he began gutting and cleaning the fish.

"He headed up north in the Otter to make some deliveries . . . visit for a few days with Benjamin before everything started icing up again," Zack said.

"You mean he would rather do *that* than be with two intellectually intriguing, good-looking, and humbly expert professional fishermen in one of the best trout streams in the country?"

"Hey, I didn't say he'd gotten any smarter, Uncle Rick," Zack laughed. "He said he'd call you in the next few weeks about a run south of the border."

Rick placed a small grill over the fire and Zack started cooking the potatoes. They always had potatoes, even if they had nothing else. He cooked them in oil with small pieces of bacon and onion wedges. When they were done, Ricky threw them in a paper sack and pushed Zack off the chef's rock. He dredged the small trout through some spiced flour and deftly placed them in the iron skillet for a quick browning. After turning them once he removed them onto a plate and poured the grease from the pan to leave only the drippings and dredges. He added white wine from a hip flask, then water, along with mushrooms and dried wild cherries. These he simmered for several minutes before returning the fish to the sauce and covering the concoction with a lid. The aroma was already irresistible.

"Five minutes, my man. There's beer over in my insulated pack if you want to grab a couple," Ricky said.

Zack was pulled up close to the fire, soaking in its heat, and took a moment to respond. He got up slowly and walked over to the pack. "I think I'll pass on the beer, Uncle Rick, but here's one for you." He handed it across the fire and sat back down.

The food was excellent. Ricky served the plates and they ate in relative silence, flipping their scraps into the fire. Ricky noticed that Zack was throwing more than just crumbs into the flames. Watching from the corner of his eye, he realized his nephew had taken only a few bites of the food. After the meal they cleaned up the plates and silverware and stoked the fire with the driftwood that Rick had piled up the day before. He sat and studied Zack, who was tossing stick after stick into the flames and shivering.

"Zack, do you think that fire's big enough yet?" Rick asked.

"Yeah, I'm about to get warm." He grinned sheepishly across the fire.

"No, I mean big enough for you to be able to look into it and tell me what you need to tell me."

Zack had cut his eyes back to the fire. He couldn't face his uncle. He pushed a slender branch into the coals and ignited its end. After a long time he said, "I'm sick, Uncle Ricky."

Rick felt a stab of fear. He looked searchingly at his nephew, remembering back a few years when Zack had looked into a similar fire and told him he was in love with Deidra. Then he'd been flushed with embarrassment ... and joy. He remembered more years ago, when Zack had asked him about his mother, Suni, about things he didn't think he could ask his dad without hurting him. He remembered when Zack had asked him about God and souls and death. And now this.

Ricky's heart slid into his throat and choked him. He knew nothing about this sickness Zack was harboring, and yet he knew everything. It was serious. And this was *his kid* and he suddenly felt like crying, but he didn't remember how.

They sat silently for several minutes as the fire crackled and snapped. Finally, Ricky cleared his throat and said, "Is it something we are going to fight, Zack?"

"I've already been fighting it, Rick. I've got AIDS, full-blown."

"How?" Ricky gasped, gagging on the rest of the question.

"They say I've probably been carrying the virus since my caribou accident. My immune system kept it in check until about two months ago. I started losing energy and appetite, so I finally headed over to Dr. Lisfranc for some blood work. He freaked. He's sure he was the one who put the infected blood into me back in '87. From what he could tell, that's been my only exposure."

"How could that happen? Don't they screen all the blood?" Ricky bounced off the rock in frustration and paced around the back of the fire. Zack could see the scar on the side of his face glowing scarlet in the night and his eyes picked up the yellow of the flames.

"Something happened, Uncle Rick. They don't know what," Zack said.

"I am damned well going to find out what happened," he answered, mostly to himself. He was the soldier again, the commander who always took care of his men. Nobody hurt one of his men and got away with it.

"Some ..." he snarled back his tears, "some motherfucker is gonna pay."

Rick was on the balls of his feet looking into the dark, poised for attack, but there was no target.... Suddenly he looked completely deflated. His arms dropped to his sides and he turned back to Zack.

"Sorry, son ... I ... I'm gonna fight it with you. You're gonna be fine."

He eased over to Zack's rock and dropped on his knees, grabbing him and hugging him, gently at first and then brutally, as if both their lives depended on it. They thumped each other on the back and Rick kissed the side of his nephew's head and hair, holding him close.

"Ricky, that's not all. Deidra has just tested positive for HIV. No trace of disease yet, but she's carrying the bug," Zack said this softly into his uncle's ear.

"*No*, not Deidra."

Zack pulled away from their embrace so that he could say what he needed to say. "Look, as long as it was just me, I could handle it. My hands would be full just staying alive day to day. I didn't even think of getting mad or even. I didn't figure revenge would be anything I would be able to spend any energy on, but then I found out about Deidra. It's killing me, Uncle Ricky. She's totally innocent. She doesn't deserve any of this shit! I want the bastards who are responsible for this to pay."

"And I want to know that someone is going to look after her," he added sadly.

Zack wiped his face on his cuff and looked into his uncle's reddened eyes. Ricky blinked away the tears and reached across Zack's shoulder with one hand to cup the back of his neck.

"Your dad's gone nuts over this, hasn't he?" There was a slight tremble in his voice. "Where is he really?"

"He really is up north. He reacted like you at first. He wouldn't believe it. He went wild. He called the hospitals and health departments to try and find out anything. What, really, I don't know.

"Then a few days later we found out about Deidra and he pulled back inside himself. He hired Jeffrey Olsen to take over our flying duties and then packed off in the Otter to visit Benjamin for a while. I'm really worried about what he might do. He has a look in his eye that I've never seen before. Would you try to talk to him and maybe make some sense out of all of this?"

"I know the look in his eyes, Zack. A lot of us had that look in Vietnam, your dad included. It comes from being deeply hurt and not knowing whose ass to kick. But I'll get with him this next week. My schedule is pretty free. You guys will probably see too much of me. Don't worry for a second, hear? Your dad is a lot more levelheaded than you think. He'll get on top of this shit."

He pulled Zack forward again and put his heavy arm around his shoulder.

"I love you, son. I guess you and your dad and Deidra are the only family I've got. I don't intend to lose any of you. Have you ever known of anything I wanted that I didn't get?"

"No, sir!"

"Well, then, relax, and sit down and tell me about all the new drugs out there that we're gonna get to fuck the hell out of this little virus. God!

I love a good fight!" Ricky pulled his lips back in that evil smile of his, tears still brimming in his eyes.

"Yes, sir," Zack said. And for the first time he realized that he probably really could smile like his uncle. It felt good.

FIFTEEN ~~~~~~~~~~~~

LOCAL COMPANY LINKED TO DEADLY SHIPMENT OF CONTAMINATED BLOOD TO CANADA

Hundreds Have Died, Thousands More Infected

By Carolyn Freel, James Bander, and D. Thomas Ely

Exclusive to the *Philadelphia Sentinel*

Bad blood responsible for an outbreak of AIDS and Hepatitis C infections starting in Canada in the 1980s originated in the United States and may have been processed by a now-defunct local firm, according to Canadian investigators.

Approximately 1200 HIV (AIDS) infections and more than 10,000 cases of the potentially fatal hepatitis virus have been identified in Canada so far, according to Canadian Information Commissioner John Kernwell.

"Both figures are sure to go higher as the provinces report in," Kernwell said in an interview with the *Philadelphia Sentinel*. "We fear that Hepatitis C cases will reach at least 30,000. Some say that even this estimate is much too low. We have had hundreds of deaths, all of this apparently from one shipment of bad blood.

"Canada is reeling from this terrible tragedy," Kernwell said. "We are surprised to find that few Americans are even aware of it. We hope that anyone in your country who has information about the bad blood will come forward and assist our investigation. We are doing our utmost to make sure that this never happens again."

Kernwell is accompanying a team of investigators from Canada's federal health department, who believe a now-defunct Philadelphia blood-processing company, Valley Biological Products Corporation, played a part in the shipment of tainted blood.

The investigators are combing the company's records hoping to learn where the blood originated and how it made its way to Canada. Sources say that the files are sketchy or missing and may have been tampered with, impeding the search.

Earlier, the team uncovered a lead indicating that the blood had originated in Arkansas. Despite intense efforts to follow up there, the leads "kept coming to a dead end," says a spokesman. "We did find this link to the Philadelphia blood-processing plant so we're hoping to learn something here."

The focus of the search is now the connection between Valley Biological Products and the Canadian Blood Committee, also now defunct, which was then in charge of blood distribution nationwide. The CBC was connected to the Canadian Red Cross, which has experienced a grave financial crisis due to the tainted blood scandal.

A furor arose when the Canadian government asserted recently, "Canadian Blood Committee records were destroyed in 1989 to thwart the public right to information." The matter is now being looked into by the Royal Canadian Mounted Police, but no criminal charges have yet been filed.

A commission headed by former Ontario Appeals Court Judge Horace Krever is investigating the entire bad blood disaster in order to adjudicate claims against the government that exceed $100 million already, and to recommend ways to keep the nation's blood supply safe in the future. Future claims are expected to rise to as much as half a billion dollars.

SIXTEEN ～～～～～～～～

FEBRUARY 28, 1995
PHOENIX, ARIZONA
PINE BLUFF, ARKANSAS

D R. FRANK WARREN READ THE WIRE STORY ON THE CANADIAN AIDS patients that ran in the Phoenix *Sun-Chronicle* after a call from his pitiful old partner, Bennie Smith. Bennie's wife had read him the story from the Arkansas *Democrat* over coffee, and he wanted Frank to know what was happening.

"This won't come down too heavy on us, will it? Isn't the statute of limitations up after all these years?" Bennie asked.

Frank didn't know how to respond. He had grown confident over the years that he would be able to enjoy a carefree retirement in Phoenix, where he'd lavished money and thought on a palatial home. There had been no hint of trouble from his ... shady ... past in Arkansas. He had earned enough to be set for life. All his contacts back there had been paid off. But that was before the phone calls started.

"Bennie, just calm down, will you? All you have to do is play ignorant

and deny any problems. Stick to our original story. Don't volunteer anything. I don't think you'll hear any more about this crap unless you start
running your mouth. My name was the one on all the papers and busi-
nesses, not yours."

"Yeah, but, Frank, think about how things have changed. Prescott and
his bunch were our partners back then. They're in the goddamned White
House now. This could be bigger than that Autumn Acres nursing home
deal, and the press is killing them over that."

"My God! Bennie! Just drop it. We don't want this thing snowballing
because of Prescott's exposure on it. Then all of our butts would be
burned. You don't know anything like that ... clear? Just lie low. Stay in
that little beer joint I bought you and be careful. I'll call you in a few days,
okay? Let me say hi to Wanda."

Bennie handed the phone to his wife.

"Yeah, Frank, how are ya?" Wanda had stood by her man for thirty-
five years. This was just another bump in the road.

"Fine, Wanda. Listen, I know you can't say much with Bennie sitting
there, but how is he doing with the booze? Any better?"

"No, not really," she said.

"Okay then, you need to make sure he doesn't get too involved with
this story. It's nothing, and we'll just let it blow over. Okay, dear?"

"Sure, Frank," she responded.

"How are they kids? I haven't heard from y'all in a while."

"They're great! Ben Junior is a vice president now. Samantha's fine.
You know she's expecting again in May? This will be three now," she said
proudly.

"My goodness, that's great, dear. I'll have to send her a little gift. Are
they at the same address?"

"Yes, same address, Frank. That'd be real nice. Thanks for thinking of
us. Times have been kinda tight," she said.

"Things will be okay, honey. You just keep an eye on old Bennie and
call me if you have any problems. He's lucky to have you. 'Bye," Frank finished and hung up the phone.

Frank had an unlisted number, and very few people were able to call
him. He had a limited circle of friends and spent a considerable amount

of time in Honduras, where he had bought a ranch in the jungle high-lands. He valued his privacy.

Yet three weeks ago, a call had come from Eric Grant. Grant hadn't called him in six years but suddenly there he was, calling from his office in the White House. Frank hadn't a clue how he'd found the unlisted number, but he was sure it was easy for the chief legal counsel to the president.

Grant was obviously worried sick. His informants at the Arkansas legislature had gotten word to him about a probe conducted by the Canadian medical authorities. They were in Little Rock checking out a lead on some contaminated blood that might have originated at an Arkansas collection facility. The Canadians claimed that several hundred people had contracted hepatitis and AIDS, and they wanted answers.

Grant's voice shook when he told Frank about the deaths. He seemed almost hysterical. Frank was able to interrupt and calm him down. He finally reassured Grant that all the records were purged or gone.

This was not like Grant. He was unflappable back in Arkansas. He should be more so now in the White House, Frank thought. After the first call, Frank heard from him every couple of days, always with more questions. Clearly, however, the Arkansas people were doing a great job of discouraging the investigators, and Frank had truly thought that he would hear no more about it—until this morning's call from Bennie and the *Sun-Chronicle* story.

He knew that the full force of the Arkansas and federal operatives would be working behind the scenes to smother the investigation. He was far more concerned about the hysterics of Grant and Bennie. Loose cannons, both of them. He knew too that if certain information leaked out, those bastards from Arkansas would make him the scapegoat to cover their own rears.

There was no way to warn Bennie without freaking him out completely. For all Frank knew, the sons of bitches could already have a tap on Bennie's phone. Still ... the records had been destroyed. Who'd dream of linking something like this to his or President Prescott's past? He resolved to stay calm and call Bennie or Wanda every day to make sure nothing was getting out of hand on that end.

~~~~~~~~~~~~

"Wanda, what in the hell did Frank say to you?" Bennie asked after she hung up and walked into the kitchen, humming some unrecognizable tune. He always knew when she was keeping some little tidbit of information from him. "Wanda, did you hear me, dammit?"

"Yes, Bennie. He just asked about the kids. Wanted to know how we were doing," she said from the sink.

"Sounded to me like he was asking more questions than that." Bennie topped his orange juice off with a shot of Smirnoff's Silver Label and stirred it with his little finger.

"Frank has always been a gentleman to me, Bennie, and he cares very much about you and our family," she said.

"Frank Warren ... excuse me, *Dr.* Frank Warren ... cares about one thing. He cares about watching his own ass and maybe the asses of those cute little boyfriends of his. And you remember that, Wanda, when he goes asking about our personal business. He cares about what he has to do to protect his holier-than-thou big white butt." Bennie flipped the paper open to the article on page eight with one hand. He tossed back half of the tumbler of juice with the other.

The beer joint had seemed like a nice severance pay when they split in '88. It was located in a fringe area away from the worst part of town and had a fairly nice inventory and patronage, but under Bennie's management the business slowly dropped off so that he was opening later and closing earlier. There was almost no way he could cover the expenses, and the bills were chin-deep at home as well. Wanda's measly salary at the dress shop didn't cut it anymore.

As Bennie read the story for the third time, the old moneymaking bell went off in his brain. It was the first time in many years that this had happened, and it nearly gave him a hard-on. It struck him like a flash that he was one of the few people who knew the true story. All of it. He could tie it around the neck of the President of the United States.

From what he had seen of the newshounds and the kiss-and-tell mistresses, the tabloids might pay handsomely for this kind of information. Very handsomely! Bennie felt the juices flowing and he downed the rest of his high-octane breakfast with a single gulp.

"Hot damn!" he said to himself.

"Wanda, something's come up. I've got business in Little Rock, so the bar is officially closed. If any of the old lushes call to see what's going on, just tell them to check with me next week. Or you can tell them to go to hell, whatever." Bennie pushed away from the table and pocketed the newspaper.

"Now what do you have suddenly in Little Rock?"

"This is my business and I'll tell you when you need to know. Until then just keep your trap shut. Do you hear me?"

"Yes ... Will you be home early for supper?" she asked softly.

"I'll be home sometime tonight. Don't wait on me." Bennie threw on his coat at the door.

"Honey, does this have anything to do with those people dying up in Canada?" she asked meekly.

Bennie was halfway out the door. He spun around with a crazed look on his face and closed the distance between them in two steps. "I want you to listen to me. If you shoot your mouth off to anybody about that story—*anybody*—and I find out about it, I will kick your ass out of this house so fast you'll wonder where you went! And if Dr. Franklin Warren calls back, you tell him everything is fine ... nothing else!"

He had gotten completely in her face and looked as if he were going to have a stroke. His eyes were bulging out of their sockets and his engorged nose reminded her of the bulb on the end of an enema syringe. She braced herself for a punch, her eyes closed. He spun on his heel and was out the door before she could open them.

Wanda Smith breathed a deep sigh of relief. The last time Bennie'd hit her she had headaches for a month and missed a full week of work, too. She needed the money too badly right now to have to endure that again. She should have left him, she thought. But she couldn't.

Wanda walked to the picture window that looked out on the front yard. Bennie was just then putting his old Datsun in gear and heading down the street in a cloud of blue smoke. She noticed a man in coveralls loading what appeared to be one of those new eighteen-inch satellite dishes into a van. He jumped behind the wheel and followed Bennie up the street. That was strange ... he was parked in the Turner driveway. No one had lived in that house for over two years. She guessed he must have made a mistake and almost mounted that dish on a vacant house.

Wanda had been wanting one of those TV dishes so she could watch some of that special programming late in the evening. She thought about calling Dixie-Sat, the name on the van, to check on the price. That was all the women at work talked about these days. But Bennie would never go for that kind of expense. Besides, he was passed out by eight every night, and it would be silly to spend that much money on herself.

She turned from the window and imagined just for a moment what it would be like to be free of Bennie's control. To live her life and have to answer only to herself. She thought it might be nice, but it would also be extremely scary—and she really did love him.

She pushed the thought and her dreams and that awful story from her mind and started on the breakfast dishes, thinking of what she might cook for supper.

SEVENTEEN 〰〰〰〰〰〰〰〰

FEBRUARY 28, 1995
PINE BLUFF, ARKANSAS
WASHINGTON, D.C.

THE SCREECH OF THE CAR PHONE STOPPED WHEN THE SMALL GREEN LED light blinked on. The descrambler had to be adjusted each time they used it.

"Okay, go ahead." Worley turned down the volume on the handset to keep Lamar from blasting his eardrums.

"Hey, our man on the inside just called. We've got a big job brewing up here. Our spot is getting squirrelly and starting to look like he's going to self-destruct. He's been calling Arkansas and Arizona way too often. Everyone's worried." Lamar was calling from D.C.

"He know we're on to him?" Worley asked.

"Man, he's beyond caring about us. He actually asked the big man if our people should cooperate with the Canadian snoops. Can you believe that? I think the guy's about to spill. Ya know? I heard that he and Stephi have been duking it out in the halls of the White House. Ain't that just like a down-home, redneck love affair!"

"Shit, I never cared for the bastard anyway. Even back when he was fixin' things at the state level he was so uptight you couldn't drive a six-penny nail up his ass with a fucking sledgehammer," Worley chortled. "Here's the way it goes down ... you listening?"

"Yeah, go ahead." Lamar was always dependable when serious shit was coming off.

"Our guy on the inside is still monitoring all of old tight-ass's calls. If he attempts to contact any of the Canadians, he's toast. You and Charlie up to this?"

"Man, we've mapped him so close, we can tell you when he's going to take a shit. I thought it was going to be much tougher than this, you know, at the federal whorehouse up here, but whores are whores at any level. No prob—."

"If it comes off, the drop zone will be the one you and I picked out on my last trip over there. No drinking and no speeding. It has to be clean and look like suicide. You got the piece?" Worley asked.

"Yeah, it was dropped to us yesterday. Did you see the article in the paper this morning?"

"I'm looking at it right now. They're shooting in the dark, but it may be enough to spook your spot. I think the spot *I've* been on is seeing dollar signs. I don't think we'll have to worry about the good doctor. He's got too much to lose. But when you finish up there, we'll probably have to check into Arizona and see how his dobber is hangin'."

"You following ol' Romeo right now?" Lamar asked, referring to Bennie Smith.

"Yeah, I'm in the van right on his tail. Can you believe he's still alive?"

"Shit! I figured his liver would have given up by now."

"Well, if he's thinking what I think he's thinking, I predict that the fucker's liver is going to outlive him ... if they can transplant the son of a bitch. It's probably hard as a fuckin' rock." Worley laughed and Lamar joined him.

"Hey, W. C., I'll beep you for our next call. Could be any day now, but I'll beep you first. I'm ready to get back South. I'm craving some decent food and Charlie is so hungry he's startin' to look like a damn Ethiopian." Worley could hear Charlie laughing in the background.

"Man, you wouldn't believe the way things are running up here. I thought the clearances and security would be top-notch here at the White House and all, but this son of a bitch is run like a fucking summer camp. The staff people we see coming and going look like a bunch of dropouts from a drug rehab clinic. They wear old shitty-looking jeans and t-shirts with all kinds of strange shit plastered on them. Some of the guys got rings in their noses. Most of them got long stringy hair and backpacks that you could carry thirty pounds of plastic explosives in."

"You're kiddin', right?" Worley asked in true astonishment.

"Fuck no, I'm not kidding. According to our inside man, the big boss himself had to shut down the normal background checks because so many of Stephanie's staff had sheets on them. Drugs and shit ... From what we've seen, about three fourths are a bunch of flaming fags or lesbos. There's no telling what is going on inside. Word is that the FBI and Secret Service pukes are farting in the wind. They have only a handful of the staff officially cleared. The rest just walk in as they please."

"Then the big man is wide open! Who the hell is in charge?" Worley asked.

"Miss Precious, the First Bitch. It's going to be the new wave of government. Everybody is gonna love everybody, see. Man, from what I see, anything goes. I think if we needed to, we could walk ol' Charlie right up to the West Wing and into the Oval Office. And Charlie here looks like Satan's afterbirth. Hell, I can't even stand to look at him, but he would fit right in with this bunch." Charlie was laughing again behind Lamar.

"Maybe I need to talk to the Judge about security up there. The big man can't expect to be safe when any dildo with a fucked-up last name has access to his quarters. Shit, they may need to put us up there for protection," Worley said.

"Boy, that would be a hell of a note, wouldn't it? But I'm glad it's kinda loose right now. It'll make my job easier for the time being. Let's get this over before we set off any official alarms."

"Okay, fella. Stay tight. I wish I was with you two on this one. It ought to be more fun than most. Just watch your asses and don't tangle with the federal boys. We ain't got much protection at that level," Worley warned.

"Our man still gives us the goobers' schedules. They're so busy lookin' for ragheads or fucked-up gun-totin' militiamen that we could pick their pockets. But don't worry, we're gonna give 'em a wide berth. They've been pulled off our little rabbit ... left him open to the big bad wolves," Lamar bragged.

Worley laughed. "Ain't that sad?"

"Yeah, that's sad." Lamar howled a long howl as he turned off the descrambler and closed down his phone.

EIGHTEEN 〜〜〜〜〜〜

BOB PRESCOTT SKIMMED THROUGH THE DAILY BRIEFINGS. HE WAS alone for the moment in the Oval Office. Eric Grant was due at any moment. The second transcript he read was the wire release on the Canadian blood fiasco. He was shocked at first that this story had hit the papers. He relaxed as he read the latest. He could tell that the reporter had very little information. Nothing new at all. It would seem that operations back home had frustrated the investigation. He was certain this was why Grant had called the meeting so early. Eric had been driving him crazy over the past few weeks with predictions of doom and gloom and of national press hounds growling at the door. The fucker was paranoid. Others in his department were letting on that they were "worried" about him. Bob had even asked Stephanie if Eric didn't need to take a rest. Of course she defended him and thought he was fine.

Now this. The president decided right then that if Eric didn't snap out of it, he'd have to ... take steps.

The door opened and Eric dragged himself into the office. He shut the door and just stood there staring at the president, looking like a sack of dirty laundry.

"Did you read it?" he asked.

"You mean the Canadian story? Yeah, I did Eric. Sounds like our countermeasures back home have shut down their investigation completely. Good job," Bob said in as positive a tone as possible.

Grant had approached the desk as Bob spoke, and now he stood there with a look of total disbelief on his face. "I can't believe that you can dismiss this story. Every national reporter in the country is going to try to make the connection ... to us. Three days from now we'll be diving for cover and facing another goddamned investigation." He plopped down in the chair as he finished and bent his head into his hands.

"Listen, Eric, I value your opinion, but you're wrong on this one. The press is too occupied with the Autumn Acres deal and the administrative staff problems. The Arkansas pencil pushers can't do anything except complain. So relax." Prescott flipped one of the pages over, as if to change the subject.

"Bob ... Bob, I've given you my best. I will advise you, as I did last week, that we discreetly contact the Canadian health officers and try to answer at least some of their questions. We have to face this thing head-on instead of having some reporter hamstring us in a few days. My God, Bob! There are over a thousand people dead because of this and no telling how many are sick. This could be the biggest scandal ever associated with the American presidency. We need a good offense, so that we can put some kind of spin on it."

Grant was giving this plea his best effort and had leaned forward in his armchair.

Prescott sat propped back in his huge leather swivel chair, his hand stroking the side of his face. He spoke slowly and softly. "Eric, I have put up with you for years. You have been a trustworthy associate as a counselor, but you forget your place. I'm putting my foot down on this one. You are apparently under so much pressure that you are no longer thinking clearly. If we were not already under the magnifying glass over Autumn Acres and Red Wheeler's confession, I would put you on official administrative leave. If I did that now, you would draw even more attention to us. We don't want more attention.

"I am ordering you to keep your regular schedule for the next two weeks, but you will have no official duties except rest. You do that ... rest, and pull yourself together. Let Faulkner take over some of your work. You make absolutely *no appearances* for the press. I will think about what you've said, and if I change my mind, I will call you."

"Bob, you're acting like a f—" Grant tried to say.

"I've heard all I'm going to tolerate from you, so shut the fuck up!" Prescott stood up and towered over him, adding, "Why don't you and Stephanie take a little trip and recharge the old batteries? Might give you a new perspective on things, ol' buddy." He turned his back on Grant and walked to the window, knowing full well that Grant was about to fall out of his chair.

"Bob ... Mr. President, I ..."

"Shut up, Eric. Our discussion is over and you are out of here." Prescott stayed at the window and didn't turn around as Grant got slowly to his feet.

On his way to the door he spoke to himself, but loud enough for Prescott to hear. "I'll not go down on these terms. You're the one who's lost it." Then he was gone.

The president finally turned from the window and picked up one of the phones on his credenza. "Yeah ... you watch him. He's unofficially on leave and he is cocked. I want no leaks. You, Grant, and Wheeler are the only ones in this administration who have the information and that is the way it will stay ... Good man ... This is serious." He hung up the phone.

Bob Prescott sat back down in his official chair at his official desk and picked up his official pen. As he put on his official reading glasses, he shook his head in disbelief. Of all the things he expected to come along and try to derail his plans, this was never one of them.

"I'll be damned if something as silly as this is going to stop me. You better believe that, Eric. You better believe it!" he said to the empty room. Then he turned back to the briefing papers.

NINETEEN 〜〜〜〜〜〜〜〜〜

THE CABIN WAS AS FULL AS IT HAD EVER BEEN. HEAVY RICH SMELLS were pouring out of the kitchen when the group returned from a brisk snowmobile ride around the lake trail.

Zack and Deidra came in just behind David and Suni's niece, Martha. They began the chore of zipping out of their riding suits and jackets and stowing the gloves and mufflers on the drying racks. Martha's father, Suni's brother, was taking the rest of the guests on a sleigh ride before dinner.

David's mother, Florence, had been a lifesaver over the past few days. Widowed now, she enjoyed cooking and taking care of the cabin and spoiling Zack when Deidra was at school. She claimed she was tired of Southern California and needed a break, but David knew that she wanted to have as much time as possible with her grandson.

Zack had good days and bad ones. His T-cell count had been slipping lately, and the medicine he was taking had its own impact on his quality of life, but for the most part he was holding his own. Deidra knew the schedules and medicines backward and forward and kept Zack on a tight leash. Today was one of the good days and everyone joked and chattered as they readied for dinner.

"How's the chow comin', Gran?" Zack hugged his grandmother from behind.

"My God! Your arms are freezing, Zack. Don't you have any warmer clothes for when you go out?" she asked. Florence tilted her head back and looked up at him. He was thin as a rail but stood a full foot taller than she.

"Aw, Gran, we don't mind the cold. We don't normally even wear clothes up here as a matter of fact. We do when you're here just so we won't embarrass you. You know what the saying is up here?"

"No." His grandmother braced for the punchline.

"We have a little slogan, 'Forty-eight degrees below zero sure keeps out the riffraff.'"

Deidra came up behind Zack and bear-hugged him. She was a beautiful girl, almost as tall as Zack, with champagne-colored hair. David watched the three of them holding each other and wished he had a camera.

Deidra whispered in Zack's ear, "Gran's cooking smells good, doesn't it?"

"Yeah, it really does."

"You think you might be able to pack in a little of it?" She pinched at his sides.

"I'm sure gonna try. Just don't get in my way when the plates are served." He turned from his grandmother to tickle his wife.

"Hey, has any one seen Ricky?" David yelled from the bar. He had just dipped up a buttered rum from the big crock-pot behind the counter.

"He mumbled something about going in to the post and when I turned around he was gone. I think he gets a little nervous when a lot of people are here. He's a strange bird, isn't he?" Gran asked, turning from her pots on the stove.

David and Zack and Deidra looked at each other for a moment and then broke out in unrestrained laughter.

"You don't know, Gran," Deidra laughed, "Strange is an understatement. But he loves these two guys and I don't think there is any more sincere man in the world."

"I second that!" David said. "He'll show up after dinner and sneak some leftovers. He means no offense, that's just the way he works."

"Well, he's going to miss some real southern cooking, and I'm not talking about Southern California. If my friends out on the West Coast could see this meal, they would kick me out of Cholesterol Fighters *and* the garden club," Florence laughed. "Let's call the others in and get this show on the road. Soup's on!"

The dinner was inspiring. Florence had fixed turnip greens and cornbread. She took caribou backstrap steaks and browned them in lard, then smothered them with onions and blood gravy. The potatoes were baked in their skins with molasses rubbed into them creating a wonderful caramelized casing. One platter was completely filled with southern-fried chicken thighs and legs with just the right amount of paprika and garlic seasoning in the crust. Dessert consisted of three pecan pies, which Florence said were called 'Karo nut pies' back when David and his brothers were kids.

Everyone ate until they were truly miserable. Deidra was ecstatic about how much Zack had been able to eat and calculated his calories by asking Florence about her recipes. The evening wore down and the Indian half of the family packed up the food baskets Florence had fixed for them and headed home. Everyone else was sprawled, relaxing, on the rugs and couches in the den when the phone rang. Zack picked it up.

"Hello," he said. "Uh, sure, just a minute. Dad, it's for you, but it's a bad connection. Some woman." He lifted his eyebrows as if this could be some romantic interest. Everyone chuckled.

David took the phone, "Hello. Well, hi, Diane. Where in the world are you? The connection's horrible."

"Mr. Farr, I'm in the States right now. I really can't talk, but I just wanted you to know that we didn't know this story was going to break. I would have informed you if I had been able to, but we were under strict orders. I would have lost my job if I had told you what we were working on."

"Diane, what are you talking about?" David asked, just barely able to make out her voice.

"Sorry, I gotta go. Please don't say that I called you. There will be time for more explanation in the future. 'Bye," and she was gone.

"Weird," David said as he hung up the phone.

"What was that all about?" Zack asked.

"That was Diane Folley calling from somewhere in the States. You know, she's the one who's tried to help me with the research efforts at the Health Bureau. I really didn't understand what she was talking about. Apparently something about the blood research we've been doing."

"This is what it's about!" Everyone jumped as Ricky threw the newspaper onto the coffee table. He had let himself in through the back door and startled them. "I don't think you're gonna like it."

David grabbed the paper and read the story as it appeared in the Toronto *Globe*. He got up from the sofa and handed the paper to Deidra and Zack as he crossed to Ricky.

"You going with me, buddy?" he whispered.

"You know it. Let's play it cool though. Don't scare the kids and the old woman. I mean your mom. We've got some time." Ricky eased past him and dipped up some of the buttered rum from the crock.

David turned back. Zack was bent forward on the couch with his elbows on his knees and his head bowed. Florence's hand went to her mouth and her eyes filled with tears.

Deidra fixed on David with the most expectant look he had ever seen, as if he might be able to make some sense out of this.

"Mom, I'll need you here for a while if you can swing it," David said. His mother just nodded. He turned to his son.

"Zack, I didn't think I would be going back home to shake the trees, but at least I can find my way around and I kinda know how things work down there. You guys keep everything together up here. Let's see if I can't come up with some answers. It's something I've got to do now, more than ever." David's voice trailed off.

"We'll be fine, Dad," Deidra said. "You take the time you need and come home to us. We'll live with whatever you find out."

Zack took a deep cleansing breath. He couldn't speak, but he nodded his head, in agreement with his wife.

David watched his son and daughter-in-law with an ache that almost overwhelmed him. He vowed to himself at that moment that he would find the answers. If anyone was personally responsible for what happened to Zack and Deidra, he would find them.

David glanced at Ricky and knew instantly his buddy had made the same vow. For now he was looking into the hard eyes of "Javier," a name respected and feared south of the border. Ricky was the professional again, his vacation abruptly over. They would leave in the morning.

TWENTY 〰〰〰〰〰〰〰〰

MARCH 1, 1995
RURAL SOUTH ARKANSAS

THE ONLY CLOSE CONTACT DAVID STILL HAD IN ARKANSAS WAS HIS father, who had retired from the state police, remarried, and bought a little house on Pine Lake south of Star City. They talked every month or so by phone. David made it a point to meet his dad and the new stepmother when they traveled to one of David's brother's houses during holidays.

He didn't know whether he should let his dad know the whole story. The old man was a little nuts, and he might give away his hand if he called some of his old cronies in the police department. He decided he would tell his dad only that he was working on a business deal and would come visit while he was in the state. David's father stayed pretty much to his garden and his fishing and seldom if ever read a paper.

The old Pilatus looked like a rock among diamonds as he taxied her into the tiedown line-up at Adams Field in Little Rock. She was surrounded by sleek and shiny twin-engine business-class planes that were twenty years younger.

David had the kid who worked the tarmac top her off with fuel and take him around to the car rental office on the other side of the field. He was amazed at how Little Rock appeared to have prospered over the last few years. The airport and surrounding industrial complex were nothing like the old postwar field that he remembered from his first year in college. The familiar old Quonset huts were gone, replaced by high-dollar, high-tech modern buildings housing enterprises from around the world. There seemed to be more corporate jets on the line here than he'd seen in St. Louis when he landed there to let Ricky catch a flight to New Orleans.

During the flight south he and Rick had gone over the few solid facts they had. The blood had not been collected by the Canadian Red Cross. It was traced back to a plasma company on the East Coast which had been in the blood-products business for only a few years. By the time the investigators were able to trace the tainted shipment back to this company, it had dissolved. Its staff had dispersed and several of the people involved in running it had died. Records were sketchy and almost impossible to verify. Apparently, Diane Folley and her Canadian team had dug through enough material to link the company to some obscure Arkansas connection.

David had reread the newspaper article several times to see whether he could derive any clue to where he might start his search. It was obvious that the investigator who'd leaked the story had hit a wall. Considering that they were searching in Arkansas, David was not surprised they had come up empty.

As the oldest son of a 1950s state trooper, David had some insight into the way things worked back home. He remembered many trips with his father to pick up packages or briefcases . . . or politicians. The state police had always served as gophers for the governors, legislators, and powerful business people of the state. At times they were called on to provide for higher-ups services and protection that were not found in police manuals. Often the trooper's value was based not on what he could remember about a case, but on what he could forget.

David recalled a particular fishing trip that turned into a nightmare.

He and his father had taken the state police cruiser to a remote reservoir and rented a boat one Saturday morning. Troopers were allowed the personal use of their vehicles but had to respond to emergencies. Just as they were getting into the boat for a morning of crappie fishing, a radio call came through.

A disturbance had arisen at one of the colored juke joints about eight miles away. There were reports of a shooting. A white man there might be in trouble and need transport. David remembered that his dad knew who it was immediately.

"Stevens. That damned idiot. He just can't keep his ass out of trouble. Won't leave those colored girls alone ... David, you stay down here in the front seat. Don't get out of the car, son. This might be nasty."

It *was* nasty. The nightclub was a long rambling shack built over the edge of a bayou. It was deep summer, and the layered mist rising from the water partially obscured the dozens of people in the parking lot.

Old cars and trucks were parked at every conceivable angle around the graveled clearing. Black men and women stood in groups, gesturing wildly toward the bayou. A crowd had gathered along the bank to throw rocks down toward the water, their faces fixed with hate and anger and glistening already in the morning's heat. The mob turned as one when David's father drove slowly through the lot and stopped with his bumper hanging over the bank of the bayou, right smack dab in the middle of the rock-throwers.

David was terrified. Sweaty ebony faces turned toward him, perspiration dripping from their chins, blood-tinged eyes glaring at his whiteness. He slid to the center of the front seat as his dad stepped from the car.

"Don't worry, son. You're safe here. Some of these folks are my friends. Just stay in the car."

David's father was cool. He enjoyed this kind of situation and was able to control things just because of his reputation. He was known to be fair and extremely tough. He once killed a man with his seven-cell flashlight after warning him to drop an axe he had just used to kill a dog. It didn't hurt that his dad was six-feet-four-inches tall and weighed two hundred and sixty pounds.

As the crowd parted for his father, David could see the target of the rock throwing. Huddled against the far bank and covered with mud was a very naked, very nervous, very white state senator, Jasper Stevens.

The Honorable Senator Stevens squatted in a muddy trough that runoff water had cut into the bank. He wielded a snub-nosed pistol and a galvanized garbage can lid as a shield. All around him were bottles and rocks embedded in the mud bank. A few had scored hits. David could see bloody marks on the senator's head and shoulders. He remembered thinking how pathetic and weak the man looked, crouching there like a toy knight, with a toy shield trying to cover his privates. The senator was pitiful, but he was pointing a real pistol that, so far, had kept the crowd at bay.

"Senator, you be a good boy and put that gun down right now," David's father yelled over the jeers and threats of the crowd.

"They tried to kill me, Doug. Look what they done to me," the senator yelled, still shaking his pistol.

David's father turned to a huge black man who owned the nightclub. "Does he have any bullets in that gun, Eddie?"

"The first two he shot in the ceiling. The next two he shot in Susie Alford. She be layin' down here in the cattails. And then he shot ol' Nig, who works fo' Mista Phillips, in da leg. He may have one bullet lef'," Eddie said, shaking his head and spitting tobacco juice on the rocks.

"Senator, I'm here to take you home, so you drop that piece of a gun you've got there and come on up this bank." As he spoke he unfastened the strap across the top of his Browning High Power pistol, pulling it calmly from its holster. A sudden gasp escaped from the crowd as they backed away from the bank, anticipating fireworks.

"Senator, I told you to drop that gun and you're still waving it around, so what I'm gonna do now is count to three and then shoot you in the leg. You hear me?" David's father clicked off the safety and raised his gun as he counted. The crowd on the bank broke and ran in every direction as the two crazy white men prepared to shoot each other.

"One ... two ..." and then a loud pop as David's father fired his pistol. The senator was in an alcohol-and-fear-induced stupor. At the last possible moment he swung the pistol up slightly as if to fire at the trooper. Douglas Farr's .38 super bullet hit the bottom edge of the senator's makeshift shield about four inches below his mud-covered testicles and between his legs. The impact knocked the good senator over backward and planted him firmly in the gooey bank as if he had been pressed into a child's Play-do project.

His pistol went flying into the water. His punctured shield rolled down the incline and splashed in behind it.

The senator had passed cleanly out and showed no sign of life except for a tiny arc of urine when his bladder let go. For a minute he looked a bit like a Renaissance cherub fountain created by some demented artist.

The gunshot stopped everyone cold. When the crowd saw the senator in his compromised condition, it broke out in wild laughter and heckling.

"Is Susie dead, Eddie?" Officer Farr asked his friend.

"Yup, but she got enough alcohol in her to keep her fresh for a while yet," Eddie answered.

"Were they fighting again?"

"Sho was! Ol' Susie was a-tryin' to whack his member off with a rusty ol' butcher knife. Damn near got it from what I could see," Eddie laughed.

"Well, I got to take both of them in," David's father said. And then to the crowd, "I got five dollars apiece for four men to wrap Susie up and put her in my trunk and haul the senator up that bank."

A group of men jumped at the chance. David saw the dead woman's face as they rolled her up in a piece of VisQueen and flopped her into the trunk.

"Y'all dredge the high and mighty Senator Stevens through the water a few times before you bring him up here. I don't want that mud all over my back seat."

David's dad opened the back door as the men struggled up the bank with the unconscious legislator and stopped to catch their breath. Together, they threw him into the car like a huge sack of feed, his head bouncing off the far door. One of the men handed over the pistol they had fished from the muddy water. Doug Farr paid out the twenty dollars and the investigation was ended.

David could vividly remember the stench of the man in the back seat. It gagged him to the point he had to hold his nose.

David was dropped off at his aunt's house on the way into town with admonitions about keeping his mouth shut. He never heard any more about the incident, and he didn't see the local senator again until late in the fall when the Honorable Senator Stevens presided over the ceremonies at the annual Scout-o-Rama.

~~~~~~~~~~~~~~~~~~~~

The more things change, the more Arkansas stays Arkansas, David mused, bouncing along in the kid's airport escort jeep. Perhaps he should talk with his dad after all. Yes. The old man knew a lot of people and a lot about things those people didn't want known.

After tipping the kid, David grabbed his bag and headed into the main terminal. A sign near the entrance announced a proposed name change for the airport: The Stephanie Stoddard Prescott International Airport, in honor of the controversial First Lady. David smiled to himself to think what his old flight instructor would have had to say about that.

He rented a Chevy Blazer and turned onto the interstate headed south. David never ceased to be amazed at the beauty of his home state. Even now, at the end of winter, the rolling hills and naked hardwood forests were beautiful. Arkansas had been called "The Land of Opportunity" when David was a kid. It was on all the signs and letterheads and license plates. Some PR people with a little better sense of reality had come in a few years ago and now the label was "The Natural State." Well, that's what it was. With only two-and-a-half-million people, there was lots of room for nature.

The northern and western portions of the state were rolling hills, low forested mountains, lush valleys, and clearwater streams and lakes. Timber and poultry were the moneymakers there, with much of the timber coming off the huge tracts of federal land. The southern and easternmost portions of the state bordered the Mississippi, and the Arkansas River plains were as flat as a skillet. Cotton was still king, but gave ground to soybeans and rice. This half of the state was home to grand plantations among muddy oxbow lakes and sluggish meandering bayous.

David was reminded of the years he spent as a kid, hunting and fishing and exploring in these vast tracts of wilderness. It was a perfect place for a boy to grow and learn the tricks of survival. He was certain that his early training here had helped him survive Nam and other dangers he had faced.

His hope was that this place might now hold some answers to the mystery that was haunting him. There was no longer any room in his life for unanswered irresponsible acts of others. He had endured too much posturing during and after the war. Now a hunger for truth burned in him . . .yet his hands were tied again.

Medically, he had few answers for Zack and Deidra. The entire world of medicine was helpless before the AIDS onslaught. But morally, he was going to have answers. He was going to demand them of someone.

He knew the way things used to work down here and he had a sickening feeling that someone had profited from this blood scenario. He would need only a moment alone with that "someone" to exact a proper retribution. If this was where life had brought him, so be it.

~~~~~~~~~~~~

An hour and a half later, David pulled into Douglas Farr's driveway. It was late afternoon and the pine trees lining the drive made the lane as dark as night. An old truck was parked down near the lakefront. David knew his dad was probably down there tinkering with his boat.

A blast from his horn brought Doug out from under the boat dock. He was dressed in his ever-present overalls and an old sweatshirt, wringing wet with sweat even in the cool temperatures.

"So you finally decided to lower yourself and come down to see me," he grinned as he wiped his face with an old rag.

His blond hair had thinned considerably and his beard had gone white. The old state trooper had lost a little of his height due to age, but he still carried his full complement of weight. As he bear-hugged his son, David could feel that most of it was still muscle.

"Good to see you, Dad. Where's Elaine?"

"She's cooking. You know her. If it's five o'clock, it's time to eat. She'll be tickled to see you."

"Sorry I didn't call to tell you when I was coming. It was sort of a spur-of-the-moment decision. I've got something serious to talk to you about," David said as he tried to catch his father's eyes.

"Zack's okay, isn't he?"

"Yeah, he's doing okay. Holding his own ... It's something else, Dad," David said.

"We'll talk over supper then," his father said as he swept his son toward the house.

"No, Dad, this is serious. We'd better talk out here. I don't want Elaine to know about this. In fact, no one can know. I need your advice, but you have to promise me you will not tell a soul what I'm doing."

"God damn, David! You act like I'm an old woman blabbing around at a quilting bee. Just say what you've got to say. I'm not senile yet." Doug Farr was about to get his famous temper going.

David sat his dad down at the picnic table and told him the whole story, finishing with the recent revelation of a connection to a shadowy Arkansas business. His dad sat staring out across the lake.

"Dad, I thought you might have some ideas about where I can start looking. I want these bastards if I can find them ... if they exist," David said, breaking a stick in his fingers.

"I understand, son. I want them too. Damn, this brings back some bad old memories," he paused with his chin in his hands. "Why don't you just let me take care of this? I'll find the assholes and take them out. Ain't got much time left anyhow. This could be a good way to check out," he finished, still looking out at the lake.

"No way, Pop. If you know anything, then you tell me. This is my deal and I'm going to handle it my own way." He put his hand on his dad's leg. "Spill it."

"It's no guarantee, but it's sure got all the stench of something that was going on back in the sixties. You remember the Brubaker film that exposed some of the crap going on in the Arkansas prison system?"

"Yeah. What about it?"

"The movie showed a lot of the killings and beatings that were going on there, but what it didn't tell was how the prison was a big source of what we called 'loose money' for the politicians. There were more scams going on there than you could count. Every local had his hand in it. Except for the Arkansas highway appropriations rip-offs, the prison provided more loose money than anything else ... Hey, David, remember when you used to go with me to run those big brown envelopes to Little Rock? For those asphalt contracts?"

"Yeah, Dad. I remember, but what about the prison stuff? What does it have to do with the bad blood?" David was trying to keep his dad focused.

"Hell, blood was one of their scams. From maybe the mid fifties until the mid seventies they took blood from those boys down at Cummins. At first they'd only take it from the white boys. People down here used to think the black boys' blood was different." He laughed to himself. "I remember they used to say that if you got some of that black blood in you, your hair would get kinky and you'd crave fried chicken all the time. All that stupid stuff is gone and I say good riddance. Thinking changed. Anyway, when civil rights were reformed, they were willing to take anybody's blood. The more the merrier. You know, things have a way of not really changing down here. If there's money to be made, folks'll find a way to get around any law."

"So you think someone started the prison scam back up? Ran the same game in the eighties?" David asked.

"Sure do. Listen, son, let me talk with some of my old contacts. I know some of those people that were out at the prison and I'll bet you I can get some answers from them."

"No, Pop. You promised. I've got to keep this quiet until I can do some research. It may not be the prison connection. I sure don't want anything to alert those people. Don't contact anyone. Not until I get back to you. I want all of them that might be involved ... Anyway, this gives me a place to start. Now, how about supper?"

"Yeah, Elaine's probably got it about ready. David, there's something else you need to remember."

"What's that?"

"You remember the men we used to talk about when you were little? The men who burned down houses and scared people and made trouble-makers disappear, never to be seen again?"

"Yes, sir," David answered.

"They're still around, son. If you stir up the wrong can of shit, they wouldn't think twice about taking you out. You can trust me on that one."

"I do, Dad. I'll be careful," David said.

"Just the same, I want you to take one of my pistols and promise you will keep it with you. You do remember how to shoot, don't you?"

"I can still beat you. Remember last Thanksgiving?"

"Hell! You just got lucky ... Let's eat! ... Elaine, look who came home to feed. The prodigal son."

Doug Farr slapped his son on the back again and shoved him up the back steps of the house. Elaine welcomed David with one of her "big country woman" hugs and sat him down to a marvelous, down-home meal of fried catfish, hush puppies, french fries, and cole slaw.

They ate and visited for a while, but David felt the urgency of his mission calling him back to Little Rock. He planned to hit the government offices at first light. He piled in the Blazer and promised to call later in the week. He didn't think he would need it, but it was some comfort to know that his dad's pistol was in the glove box.

David had no indication that ex-state trooper Douglas Farr had devised a plan of his own. Shortly after David left, he told Elaine that he was going to spend the next couple of nights at the deer camp so he could cook up a surprise for David. He thought he might get some of the guys together for a little party and some poker.

When she went to finish the dishes he slipped his old Browning High Power and a box of shells into his bag. Well, he'd always believed that when you needed something done, it was best to do it yourself. The old cop smiled. He had become bored with retirement. Now it was time to renew some old acquaintances.

TWENTY-ONE ~~~~~~~~~~~~~~~~~~~~

MARCH 1, 1995

ERIC GRANT, TOP ATTORNEY FOR WHITE HOUSE, FOUND DEAD

Washington, D.C. Special to the *Gazette-Star*.

Eric Grant, White House chief counsel, was found dead early this morning.

Grant, 48, from Little Rock, Arkansas, was a long-time friend and adviser to President Robert Prescott and had served as head of the White House legal staff.

City workers discovered Grant's body in a parking area beneath the east end of Hamilton Bridge. Emergency units were immediately sent to the scene.

A police spokesman refused to comment on the cause of death or release any details until a preliminary investigation is completed. However, sources say that Grant apparently died of a self-inflicted gunshot wound to his head and that a pistol was found in his hand.

It is not known how long Grant had been dead before the body was found.

Friends cannot shed any light on how or why he would go to the spot, which is in a rundown area over three miles from the White House. His car was found in the White House lot.

President Prescott issued a brief statement expressing shock at the death and extending his sympathy to Grant's family. (See story on page A2.)

Grant had become an increasingly visible administration figure due to the President's mounting legal problems. He was the personal attorney to President and Mrs. Prescott before being appointed as the White House counsel.

In Arkansas, Grant served then-governor Prescott's administration in several advisory capacities. He was a partner at Baylor, Harold & McConnerly, the state's most prestigious law firm, where he worked closely with First Lady Stephanie Prescott, also a partner at the firm.

Grant is survived by his wife Nancy and four minor children, three sons and a daughter. He was past president of the Arkansas Bar Association and an elder of the Eternal Christ Presbyterian Church of Little Rock. Plans for memorial services have not yet been released. (*Gazette-Star* Staff)

Related stories: Text of presidential message (A1)
               City Abuzz with Rumors (A2)
               Grant Was "Insider," "Well Liked," Say Friends (A2)

TWENTY-TWO ~~~~~~~~~~

BILL FAULKNER HAD STARTED HIS DAY AT 4:00 A.M. HIS BREAKFAST of coffee and a muffin was already wearing thin and it was barely 6:00. Since his move to Washington with the Prescott adminis-tration, he had not had an easy day. His work as assistant deputy legal counsel for the White House had kept him busy enough, and now he'd been assigned temporarily to the duties of his boss, Eric Grant. Appar-ently, Eric was on forced leave of absence by order of the president. Faulkner relished his promotion, even though it meant an impossible workload for him. He was at his desk before morning rush hour and stayed long into the evening.

Eric seemed dangerously near a mental breakdown. The whole staff was talking about it. When they had a moment to talk. The scandals swirling around the White House were draining everyone. Charges that the president had had an affair back in Arkansas. Charges that the First

Lady was involved in the crooked Autumn Acres nursing home deal. A special prosecutor had been appointed to investigate. It wore you down.

Bill had known Eric Grant for many years and had worked closely with him for the past six. Grant had always been an efficient and thorough attorney, just the type of adviser that Bob Prescott needed. Over the past few weeks, however, he'd grown rattled and edgy. He had been mumbling to himself and spending inordinate amounts of time on the telephone. You would bump into him in the hall and he'd walk by as if he didn't know you.

Grant's close relationship with Stephanie Prescott was one that the insiders had known about for years. They had been ever so professional and discreet, so the affair had never leaked out as a scandal. Lately they had been seen and heard in raging discussions, even in the White House itself, where there were many eyes and ears.

"The legendary halls of the White House," Bill said out loud. "What a joke!"

He had had a vision of the way things would be when they all moved up from Little Rock and began the job of running the government. The reality wasn't even close. For openers, no one had thought about the imminent FBI investigations into their backgrounds. Such interviews were part of a forty-year tradition of security at the White House. And security had always been tight.

In Bill's opinion, the Prescotts had brought some very sharp people on board in Washington. A much larger number, however, had extremely colorful pasts. They had opened the doors to hundreds of eccentrics. Kooks. Kids! You would see them in the halls in sandals and shorts and crummy t-shirts, their hair unkempt and dirty.

Bill's job from the outset had been to loosen ... virtually dismantle ... the FBI's standard security procedures at the White House. And he had to do it without calling attention to his actions.

It seemed that everyone on the staff had something to hide. Something that might disqualify them from serving in this new administration. Many had prior drug-use arrests from their student days, and some would *still* have trouble passing a drug screen. There were those who had secret bank accounts and links to shady business deals that reeked of governmental favoritism. Several were—or had been—involved in flamboyant love affairs that would make sensational headlines if word ever leaked out. Hell, Eric and the First Lady wouldn't be able to pass that investigation. He could just see the papers. God! That was one reason that Stephanie had ridden his ass since day one about emasculating the White House FBI unit. She actually wanted them out of the place.

And Bill had his own personal reasons for dismantling the system. He had skirted some IRS problems through "interesting" accounting procedures. He sure as hell couldn't afford for that to be uncovered. That was jail time.

Even with his best efforts, though, some of Prescott's people had already fallen. Resignations, even indictments. One of his best friends from Baylor, Harold, Red Wheeler, was going to do time for a string of corruption charges. Red had been doing suspiciously well. The scene surrounding Wheeler's plea bargain to legal malpractice had taken a heavy toll on the Arkansas contingent. Those who had come with him from the firm in Little Rock took a double hit of media attention and embarrassment. Stephanie and Eric were Red's closest friends. They got no breathing room from the press or from the witch hunts of the newly elected Republicans.

Faulkner's own life had taken a severe turn for the worse as well. His wife Mary Elizabeth simply could not stand their uprooted life in Washington. She didn't like the new house, the social life, the stores, anything. It seemed to her that Bill was gone constantly, leaving her alone with their young son and infant daughter. Life here was a hell for her compared to what it had been in Little Rock. Back home the kids had full-time sitters available and the country club guaranteed Mary Elizabeth her own active and varied schedule.

Bill and Bitsi used the sitter to go out four or five nights a week, to relax at parties or to dine at one of the dozens of restaurants they enjoyed in Little Rock. What it boiled down to was that they were *somebody* back home, and they knew who that somebody was. Here they were overstressed cogs in the great wheel that is Washington, on every invitation list in town. But every invitation had an agenda—which didn't include relaxation. Bill was exhausted, and they hadn't even had sex in a couple of months.

Bill felt his marriage was falling apart. That had happened to his first marriage when he was much younger, but the feeling was the same. It was like being behind in the fourth quarter of the championship game. In *this* game, he desperately did not want to lose his wife and family.

He was afraid that Mary Elizabeth and Eric were in the same emotional boat. One more straw and it would be Prozac and a long "vacation." Faulkner was ricocheting between thoughts of his wife and the data on his computer screen when the phone startled him. He was not overjoyed about an interruption this early in the morning.

"Yeah?" he said into the mouthpiece.

"Bill, this is Beatrice."

"What's up, Beatrice? You sound out of breath." Beatrice Wilson was the First Lady's personal secretary.

"I am, Bill. Something terrible has happened to Eric. We just got word from the police that his body has been found under the Hamilton Bridge ... Eric's dead, Bill, ... he's dead," she sobbed into the phone, losing her composure.

Bill Faulkner felt as if all the air had been knocked out of him. He struggled a minute to speak loudly enough to interrupt Beatrice's sobs. "How did it ... Was it a heart attack, Beatrice? Do they know anything?"

"They think ... they think it's suicide, Bill. Can you believe that? Not Eric. No way. Somebody must have killed him! But I can't imagine *anyone* wanting to kill Eric. What are we going to do?" The sobs started again.

"How did you hear this? When?"

"The call came in about five minutes ago on the emergency line. Secret Service took it. They alerted us. Stephanie is getting dressed and the president is already in his office," she gasped.

"What did Stephanie tell you to do?" he asked.

"She wanted me to call you first and warn you about investigators coming in. I'm to come down in a few minutes and secure all of Eric's personal files and memos and you are to help me. Stephanie is devastated, Bill. I don't know how she is going to get through this. Hell ... I don't know how any of us will. He was her ... her lifeline, you know."

This last admission sent her into a new weeping spell.

"Beatrice, please, get hold of yourself. You've got to function.

Stephanie is going to need you more than ever right now. What are we supposed to do with his files?"

"Bring the files to her. Those were her explicit orders, Bill. She told me to do it first and not to ask any questions."

"Whoa up, Beatrice. That could be a no-no. They could say we're interfering with a police investigation. I'm pretty sure we would be breaking the law."

"Yes, but that's what she said to do, and for her I will. We'll figure it out later. I'll be down soon—as soon as I'm dressed. Thanks, Bill."

Bill Faulkner was suddenly aware how hauntingly quiet his office was. The White House wasn't even awake yet. His head reeled with the absurd news that his boss was dead. Just hours before, Eric had sat at his desk in the next room, shuffling papers, talking to people on his phone, maybe just looking out his window onto the lawn. He was alive, he was ... permanent. Now they were supposed to believe that he had killed himself. There was no way Bill could ever believe that. Who would want a quiet man like Eric Grant dead? Could it have been a hold-up? God knows Washington had more than its share of street violence. Some bastard may have caught him at the wrong place and time, despite Eric's habitual caution. But then, there were few places where he could possibly have been exposed for a random hit. That would mean it *wasn't* random at all.

Faulkner realized he was going in circles. He pushed back from his desk and felt a sudden surge of nausea float up from his depths. The files! The papers! It struck him like a club that there might be clues to Eric's death in his office. Something in his notes. Something in the files he was to take to the First Lady.

Trotting down the hall, Bill remembered that the personal computer at which Eric spent most of his time was almost identical to his own. They were both stand-alones, not linked into the office network. Eric was a stickler for his privacy and taught Bill to be equally fastidious. Computer networks were like a party-line telephone. No privacy at all.

Faulkner made a very crucial decision in a matter of moments. He came back to his office and quickly transferred the information on his hard drive to a backup disk. Then he purged his drive, formatting it to take no chances. He unplugged the keyboard and mouse from his computer box and disconnected the monitor and printer cables from the back. He raced into Eric's office and swiftly disconnected that computer housing in the same way. Thank God Beatrice couldn't get there for the next five minutes.

He wiped down his own computer and connected it where Eric's had just been, careful not to disturb the keypad and monitor that would certainly have Eric's fingerprints on them. The switch completed, he went back and plugged Eric's computer into his own maze of wires. Then he stepped away from the desk to observe his first act of planned lawlessness since he stole two candy bars from the neighborhood grocery store, age seven.

He was sick with guilt, but he would find a way to deal with that if he could find a clue to the mystery of his friend's death. Eric had secrets he would not have wanted investigators to uncover. A lot of secrets. He was, after all, the president's chief counsel and confidant. It could take Faulkner hours to break Eric's password; that would have to wait until some of the pressure was off.

The sound of a woman's dress shoes hurrying down the outside hall brought him back to the task at hand. Beatrice burst through the door looking for all the world like a woman who had just been released from a night in a drunk tank. Her hair was wet, as was her makeup, and her clothes looked as if she had worn them to mow the lawn.

"Please, Bill, there will be others coming. You and I have to box up all of Eric's files and clear out of here within fifteen minutes. We're supposed to meet Stephanie in her study in twenty." She swept past Faulkner waving her hands and burst through the door to Eric's office like a fullback hitting the defensive line.

"Oh, my God! We've got to get his PC out of here too. We'll never get this done in time . . . Bill! Are you going to help, for God's sake?" She turned on Faulkner in anguish.

"Yeah, I'm in, Beatrice. You disconnect his computer and I'll box the files." He caught the woman's frantic glance for only a second. "Are we going to have protection on this, Bea? We're going beyond the call of duty, you know."

"We're covered, Bill. Stephanie will take care of us. Don't worry!" she said.

Bill worried. He felt the nausea return, especially when he thought about the chance of his being set up as the scapegoat by Stephanie Prescott. Then he dumped the contents of the three horizontal file cabinets onto the floor.

TWENTY-THREE ~~~~~~~~~

MARCH 2, 1995
LITTLE ROCK, ARKANSAS

SMOKE BURNED INTO THE HIGHEST PART OF HIS SINUSES. THE ACRID heat made his eyes water so heavily that he had to turn his head in order to dump the tears from his face. The effort took all of his strength. He was lying flat on his back in one of the Ojibway sweat lodges. The snow that had been piled over the log and stick structure was slowly melting and seeping through the low roof and collecting in the pine thatch beneath him.

David was aware of others surrounding him but was unable to see their faces in the thick smoke. It lingered around him as if it were alive. He felt it palpate his body like a huge gray snake trying to engulf him. In the corner somewhere he could hear the crackling of a fire. For a moment the pop and sizzle brought back an old terror ... he was in his downed plane in Vietnam, snared in the branches of tall trees, helpless to escape the fire that was licking the flesh from his face.

He blinked and tried to clear his vision enough to see the faces above him. The smoke orbited around their heads. It spiraled slowly up from their chests, seldom parting to leave a glimpse of their faces. Down near his feet he saw Dona, Zack's old nursemaid. She had taken care of the boy from the time he was five until he graduated from high school. She died that next year, and David had mourned as if she were a member of the family. How odd that she was here, smiling down through the smoke at him.

Two other elders of the village who had recently died squatted to his left, waving feathers across his body. They, too, smiled at him. He tried to reach up to touch their faces, but he was paralyzed. It was as if the smoke were an immovable weight, pressing down on him.

Then he saw Suni. Suni. She was young and radiantly beautiful, her silken hair cascading past her cheeks and caressing his chest. Around her shoulders she wore the pale blue and white mooseskin mantle that she'd worn on their wedding day. The bead and quillwork was still fresh and perfect.

David struggled desperately to speak to her . . . to reach up and stroke her glowing face, but it was useless. Somehow, to try was to lose her again after all these years. New tears welled up into his eyes and wet his cheeks.

This time Zack was there with Deidra at his side. They peered down at him as if they didn't recognize him. David's mind screamed. They weren't supposed to be here. No! No! Go away! He tried to tell them, to warn them, but the smoke choked his cries.

~~~~~~~~~~~~

David catapulted into a sitting position on the bed, jarred from sleep by a spasm of coughing. Tears streamed from his eyes as he gasped for breath. The stench of the smoke lingered from his dream.

It took David a full minute to remember where he was. The interior of the Motel 6 room was the same as hundreds of others he had stayed in through the years. He reached sleepily for his prosthesis on the floor beside him, letting his mind clear. He played back the dream, stopping at the vision of Suni. He hardly noticed his hands going through the ritual of fitting his stump into the artificial leg.

Now wide awake, he reviewed his situation. He was in Little Rock, his dad had given him leads to check out, starting with the Medical Records Division of the State Health Department. Glancing at his watch he saw that it was only five o'clock in the morning, but he was ready for the day. He'd get breakfast somewhere, review his maps, and make an early stab at navigating the capital city.

The State Health Department Building was one of those huge cement and glass affairs with no obvious front. He could imagine the architect sweating over a design so bizarre that no one could find a way in, but the maze of sidewalks eventually ended at an obscure entrance.

David scrutinized the directory in the foyer, trying to find the office he was looking for.

The Medical Records Division was on the second floor. He wanted to search without asking any more questions than he had to. The fewer people who knew about him, the better.

David rode the elevator up and then wandered down the a long corridor until he found the right door. The room was immense. At the center, it was divided into small office cubicles. People were going about their early morning routines, greeting coworkers and making their coffee and doughnut runs.

David was just inside the entrance getting his bearings when a woman approached. He glanced at her once and then a second time. As she neared and he turned to look more closely at her, he had to catch his breath. She had a slightly oriental cast to her eyes. For a moment he thought he was looking at Suni in a high-necked, yellow ribbed sweater and a long denim skirt, her dark hair held back from her face with a tortoiseshell headband.

The woman was probably in her mid thirties and had the look of a professional, perhaps a lawyer, a doctor. David thought she was one of the most beautiful women he had ever seen.

"You're right on time, I see," she said, smiling at him and offering her hand. David certainly wasn't expecting this. Her accent was sweet and completely unlike Suni's, comfortably southern with just a hint of formality. That broke the spell he was in.

"I'm Sylvia Barrows, and I think we can get all the information you will need in just a few minutes. Did you bring your notepad and pen?"

He'd been fascinated with her looks, now he was totally confused. He just stood there looking dumbly at her, not knowing what to say and thinking he must look as if he'd fallen off a turnip truck.

Sylvia blushed slightly at his stare and said. "Oh, now, don't let all this hoopla bother you. These people are just doing their jobs. We can get most of our work done over here. Come on over ... we'll get started."

She pinched the sleeve of his jacket and guided him to a row of desks and library tables with microfilm readers mounted on them. Sylvia pulled back a pair of chairs for them and nodded for him to take one. David sat as instructed but his mind was going a thousand miles an hour. The only way this woman could know he was coming was if his father had called some officials to help him get started. He couldn't figure it out. But, if this was true, all his plans for being discreet were out the window.

"Miss Barrows, is it? Who told you that I would be here this morning?" he asked.

Now Sylvia looked puzzled. She searched his eyes to see if he was kidding. "My office did, of course," she replied.

"And what office might that be, ma'am?"

"The Arkansas Department of Corrections Work Release Office," she said slowly, still not sure whether he was kidding.

In his shock, David heard only the first part of her response ... Arkansas ... Department of Corrections. The prison! How in the hell could his old man have called the prison? My God! The old bastard had lost it after all! He was going to kill his dad.

"Ma'am ... uh, Miss Barrows ... I'm sure that I need some help here, but I don't know that your office is the group to help me. I hope you haven't ruined your morning coming over here unnecessarily."

Now it was her turn to be shocked. The sincerity in his voice made the whole situation even more confusing. "So you think you can find all the information that you will need by yourself?"

"I'm sure as heck going to try," David answered, growing more perturbed.

"And don't you have any questions about the pre-employment application forms you have to complete? They can really be confusing if it's your first time."

David was really lost now.

"Miss Barrows, do you know who I am?" he asked.

"Why, of course. You're Mick Johnson," she glanced at her folder. "ADC# 76797." She looked up at him with her gorgeous almond-shaped eyes, waiting for verification.

David wasn't sure what was going on, but relief swept over him. He broke into a wide smile and sat back in his chair.

"Ma'am, I think you've got the wrong guy," he laughed.

"You mean you're not Mr. Johnson?" she glanced around as if she thought a joke was being played on her, then she rechecked her file on the table.

"No, I'm not, but do you mind my asking why you thought I was? You seemed pretty sure of it."

"I was told you would ....I mean he ... would be here at 8:00 A.M. His caseworker told me he would be wearing a brown leather flight jacket. She said he was tall, had reddish hair and a beard, and, according to her, was extremely handsome." Sylvia was reading her notes but she blushed.

Now that his panic was gone, David was fascinated by this woman. She was one of those rare people with whom he could feel a true human connection immediately. There'd been very few of them in David's life, and only one other was a woman. Suni. He wondered for a moment if his feelings were due to her resemblance to Suni. Suddenly his personal alarm went off. He was certainly not looking for involvement.

"Well, Miss Barrows, I don't know Mr. Mick Johnson, but I would say that he should have kept his appointment. He is very lucky to have someone as gracious as you working with him. Is this your normal duty with the Department of Corrections?"

"No, actually I am not employed by them at all. I'm working on a research project for my doctoral thesis. In sociology. Part of it is tracking the work history of ex-convicts. I also meet occasionally with some of the pre-release inmates to assist them in completing all of the proper paperwork—birth certificates, health records, and applications they'll need to get back into the workforce. Many of them agree to become part of my study. So I'm officially unofficial. And thanks for the compliment," she smiled. "What's your story? This doesn't appear to be your regular assignment either."

"That's true. I'm just trying to do a little research of my own. I think I might be in the wrong department."

"Well, lucky you. It looks like I've been stood up by my eight o'clock date and I do happen to know my way around here. Will you let me help?" she asked.

He thought for a second, wondering if he dared tell her anything. She was looking expectantly at him. There was no way this face could hold any malice, he decided, as if he could have possibly turned her down. "Could you tell me the procedure for checking on a medical business that the health department might have to license? Maybe some from ten years ago?"

"That's easy. There's a whole division on the fifth floor that fits under the Regulatory and Licensing heading. They'd have all the records. Of course, you'd have to be specific in your formal requests and they would have to see your picture ID." The way she finished her sentence indicated a little suspicion on her part. Why was he so hesitant to tell her his story?

"I see," he said, more or less to himself.

"Is that a problem, Mr. . . . . I'm sorry. I didn't even ask your name. I'm Sylvia." She stuck out her hand and this time he noticed how tiny it was in his. A hint of her perfume drifted toward him, something like sandalwood. Nice. He felt an old warmth course through his body and hoped she didn't sense it in his smile.

"I'm David," he said, "and, yes, it does present a problem for me, but I appreciate your help."

"Well, Mr. David Mysterious, maybe I could be persuaded to help you out here. It'll cost you the price of a bagel and cappuccino at the coffee bar up the street." Sylvia was so natural . . . it was as if they'd known each other for years. "Sound like a deal?"

"Are you this helpful with all of us cons?" he teased.

"Just the ones who are a real challenge. You ready to go?"

"Lead the way."

He couldn't believe he was allowing himself to be diverted. He hadn't even started what he had come to do. But she obviously knew her way around, where he was bewildered by the bureaucracy. Perhaps she could help find contacts for him at that. The day was pleasantly warm for March, and they relaxed and talked about her research project on the way to the coffee shop. Sylvia had been working on it for almost two years.

She had designed the study to evaluate the effectiveness of pre-release education available to the inmates. Many chose not to attend classes before their release, so she attempted to follow up on both groups. She anticipated another year of study before she would finish.

After they ordered their coffee, she finally said, "Okay, enough about me. Let's hear about you."

"My story is *very* complicated."

"Well, let me help. You need to gather some potentially damaging information on a healthcare provider and you don't want anyone to know that you're looking. Am I close?"

"I'm afraid I'm not too good at being a private eye. Was I that obvious?" He smiled at her.

"I'm afraid so ... This is really important to you, isn't it?"

David took a quick breath and looked deep into her brown eyes. He saw something there that he had been searching for, for a very long time. Without hesitating, without even thinking, he gave her his trust. He didn't know it yet.

"Do you have any professional connections with the prison?" he asked.

"Heavens, no! I'm one of their biggest critics. My research is going to show how inadequate their educational programs are. I've also collected dozens of grievances from the convicts and passed them on to the legislature. I don't know if it does any good, but at least they know someone's watching.

"Now, what are you looking for? ... Give me an idea. Something ... somebody that has a connection to the prison system?" she asked

"Possibly ... Sylvia, I'm not sure you're going to want to help me. There are people who don't want me to poke around. They could be trouble. I don't even know you! I sure don't want you dragged into anything. Look, you've already helped me understand what this place is all about. Let's just forget this, eh?"

"You said trouble, David. This isn't just some dispute, this is serious, isn't it?"

"Yes."

"Then you can't keep me out. Don't you see? I am probably the one person you can trust the most. I have no axe to grind here. I'm also a person who knows a lot about the system. And now I'm very curious. Please let me in on the whole story. I'll help you find what you need," she pleaded.

Sylvia's sincerity pushed David's resistance aside. David knew she was being honest. For the next thirty minutes, David poured out what he knew about the contaminated blood, how it had caused such grief, how he'd come to suspect the prison.

Her heart went out to him as he relived the pain of what had happened to Zack and Deidra. There were tears in her eyes when he finished. She dabbed them and reached for her briefcase. Collecting herself, she asked, "When ... what years do you think ... the blood was collected?"

"Probably 1984 or early 1985."

She paged through her files for several minutes, finally extracting a sheet and waving it at David. "I've got a client that we must see today. Now," she said excitedly.

"Do what?" David replied, astonished.

"This man was in during those years. He knew everything that went on. According to my notes, he cleaned up in the hospital unit for at least some of his sentence. Let's get my car and go see him now. His monthly check will be there by tomorrow and he'll be drunk for the next three weeks. He'll be useless then. You ready?" She was already gathering her things and making for the door.

David hurriedly paid their tab and caught up with her in front of the cafe. Her short legs were going full speed and he had trouble keeping up with her.

"Sylvia, you're going to have to slow down a little. I've got my slow leg on today," he said.

"Your what?" She stopped and looked back curiously.

"I'll tell you later. It's another long story," he laughed.

The ride to the ex-con's home took only fifteen minutes. David, enjoying the company, wished it were all day. They stopped at a liquor store along the highway and bought a case of Miller's.

His house was an old tumble-down shack in a little black community called Sweet Home, just southeast of the capitol. The man came out the front door before Sylvia and David could get out of the car. He was about sixty-five years old, hunched at the shoulders. His face was furrowed from years of rough living, but friendly. He recognized Sylvia immediately and waved both of them onto his porch.

"My, my! Girl, ya ain't been out to see this ol' crook in a while. Where ya been a-keepin' yosef?" the old fellow said, looking from her to David.

"I'm still worrying people by asking too many questions. We brought you a little gift." She turned to David who pulled the case of beer from its sack.

"Oh, me! I can feel some mighty big questions comin' from Miss Sylvia. Prob'ly gonna make me all cotton mouff like de last time." He took the beer and slid it into the front room, returning immediately with two of the cans.

"David, this is Salvador Joseph Williams," Sylvia said ceremoniously. "Salvador, this is my friend David. We just need to ask you a few questions."

"Here, mista. Take one a dese freshments. Miss Sylvia won' drink wid me and she's de only one dat calls me by my Christian name. Evabody else calls me Slappy Joe—Slap fo' short. Les sit down hea an git comfable." He arranged some old chairs.

"Salvador, we need to know about some things that went on back in the mid eighties. Now, this is just between the three of us. We don't want any of this talked around, so we thought we'd come to you. I knew I could trust you and I'll bet you knew about this," she said, setting the stage for her question.

"You cum to da right place, girl. You start askin' an' I steady be answerin'. Now go on," Slap said, sitting straight in his old chair.

"Do you remember anyone who was buying blood from the inmates back then?" she asked. "It could have been anyone, even someone from the outside. Maybe even a doctor or a nurse."

"Yes, ma'am. Lawd, dat was really sumpin' back den." Slap didn't even hesitate with his reply. "Dem people was totin' dat blood out by de tubs full. Yes'm."

David touched Sylvia on the shoulder and they exchanged a quick glance.

"Dat was Docta Frank's op'ration. He was da head doc back den, and he run lots of bidness through dat prison."

"Did he actually draw the blood right there in the prison hospital?" she asked.

"Sho did! Three times a week, dey'd line dem boys up all da way down da hall and into da rec yard. Dat was a real popalar thing. De boys hated t'see it go. I didn' doe. I was da one had t'clean up after 'em. Big ol' mess!" He sat back and killed the rest of his beer.

David got up and brought out two more. As he handed him a fresh one, he asked, "Mr. Slap, can you remember Dr. Frank's last name or any of the others who might have worked for him?"

"Now, I can't recollect right now. We always jus call him doc, but I might can remember. Sometime my ol' brain does dat on me. Ha! I do remember dat ol' weasel dat use ta work fo him doe. He was out dere all the time. If dere was a nurse aroun, he'd be dere a-messin' wid her. He told evabody he was a docta, but he wuddn't. We call him 'Docta Love' behin' his back but his name be Bennie . . . sumpin'. Damn . . . see dere, dere go my brain again." He snapped his fingers, smiled and kicked back more of his Miller.

"Salvador, what made those inmates go along with giving the blood? Were they getting paid?" Sylvia asked.

"Shoot no! Dat's de biggest ting about da whole deal, Miss Sylvia. If you was on dere blood list, you gots two of dem Perca . . . Perco . . . oh, I can't remember der real names. We call 'em 'yella boys,' yeah. Dey was fo' da pain from given dat blood. Hell, dem niggas and honky boys all be standin' in line all day jus ta get dem pills. 'Fo' long, some of da big men start forcin' der—'scuse me, Miss Sylvia, dis ain't nice fo' a woman ta hea . . . Ya see, some of de men in da joint, had strings of pitful, sickly boys dat dey kept fo' sex. Ya know? Well, dey would like make dem boys go all da time and give dey blood so's dey could bring dem pills back to 'em. Got to be a big ol' racket. Made me sick to tink dat ol' nasty blood from dem skanky-legged hoes was goin' to real sick people. Sho did!" He shook his head as he finished.

"So they paid them with drugs!" David said, biting back the anger that was welling up within.

"Yup! Fo' about five er six years, den . . . chump! It was over. New bunch come in and no mo' 'yella boys,' no mo' blood suckin'. Nuttin'."

David and Sylvia sat looking at each other for a long moment, trying to picture it. Trying to fathom the desperation and greed that fueled it.

"Slap, you've helped a lot," David said. "If you could think of those men's full names, I'll make it worth your while to call Miss Sylvia and tell her. The sooner the better."

"Sho will! Soon as my ol' brain gits loosen' up, I'll call her. Jus' leave me yo card agin, girl, and don't you tink bout payin me . . . no, ma'am. Y'all's good folks. I'll hep a little if I can." Slap sat back in his chair and glanced back and forth between David and Sylvia. "Say, is y'all sweeties? Y'all seein' each udda?" he smiled toothlessly at them and watched as they blushed. "No? Well, ya outta be. Yep. Y'all looks real fine sittin' der. Real fine."

TWENTY-FOUR ~~~~~~~~

BILL FAULKNER'S LIFE HAD BEEN IN A SLOW, DESCENDING SPIRAL for the past two days. The death of his boss, Eric Grant, set in motion a series of wrenching events. It was impossible to see where they would lead or how they would end. The White House legal office was supposed to maintain decorum, and control, especially control. A pinnacle of professionalism. The thought of it made Bill laugh to himself, thinking how naïve he had been.

From his first day on the job, he had been nothing more than a spin doctor, using the law to keep political enemies from shooting their asses off. Just the act of getting dressed in the mornings was depressing when you knew you'd spend the day formulating absurd defenses for even more absurd accusations. It was a paranoiac's paradise.

The paranoia actually had physical attributes. It had a *sound*—Bill could hear it distinctly—a constant rumble just off in the distance. It was a combination of several different tones and pitches, some high, some low, all fighting one another. It got louder and more ominous if you let yourself think about it.

The paranoia had a *smell*, too, much like the crisp electric smell from the old "pop-in" flashbulbs. It had a *taste* like that taste that flushes your mouth just before you throw up, slick and metallic-tinged along the sides of your tongue.

Worst of all, fear wore a face that Bill could not avoid. He saw it every day in the mirror. He looked like hell. With Red Wheeler and now Eric gone from the office, Bill had inherited this precarious house of cards. Sleep, for him, was just a series of short-lived battles with the sheets. He felt even worse than he looked.

Nevertheless, investigators conducted their searches and interviews and depositions and hearings. They combed Eric's office and loaded up the files that he and Beatrice had replaced. The first round was over, but more questions loomed in the future. He wasn't sure he could invent any more answers. Especially now.

It had taken him an hour and a half to break into Eric's computer. Grant had been obsessive. Bill knew that he would find all manner of lists and schedules and agendas in the machine's files. What he didn't expect were the lengthy notes Eric had written to himself. He had used his computer as a kind of "Father Confessor," and the depth and emotion that spilled out were frightening ... sometimes beautiful, but most often terribly sad.

Bill felt like a peeping tom, peering in the window of Eric's most private life, invading all of his secrets. There were notes to his wife and kids and to Bob and Stephanie Prescott that were obviously never delivered. Bill even found notes to himself.

What he discovered about Eric Grant was that the man was capable of deep concern and passion, but haunted by his "responsibilities to an irresponsible system." As Bill read his ruminations about his legal and personal pursuits, he began to see himself in Eric's predicament: schedule and necessity taking precedence over ethics and morality.

And now on the screen in front of him Bill read what must have been the catalyst for Eric's death. He was poring over a series of notes and reports from meetings that were filed under the heading "Blood Trail." Bill had read them all. The early notes were optimistic ... excited about the revenue source for Governor Prescott's administration in the eighties. There were Eric's compulsive calculations of risk and exposure and profiles of the principals involved. One pointed to the owner of a blood business, a Dr. Frank Warren, as linchpin of the operation.

Later notes ... from 1985 ... were all but encoded. "Dangerous things" were happening related to a "stupid compromise in Dr. Warren's plasma operation." "Records [would be] destroyed," and the like, with few details. Then the entries tapered off. The next series of notes were fairly recent. Eric had scanned in an entire series of news stories and editorials, compiled by a Canadian newspaper, that traced an outbreak of Hepatitis C and HIV to a shipment of contaminated blood. The later stories told of the suffering that victims and their families had endured. There had been many hundreds of deaths.

Notes from contacts in Arkansas warned that an investigative team of Canadians was snooping around in the state and making things difficult. Canadian Health Ministry officials were looking to the Prescott administration to assist in a search for the source of the contaminated blood, but they had run into a wall of red tape and missing records.

Eric had detailed notes on his meetings with the president concerning this issue. He was livid that Prescott wouldn't take him seriously. To him, this was "the issue" ... the cancer that could take down the presidency. He was terrified by the potential exposure, but he was more devastated by the sickness and death they had loosed on the Canadians.

He obviously took it personally and his notes were full of remorse.

The final entry may have been made just hours before his death. It was a formal letter to Dr. Jacques Le Bount, director of the Canadian Ministry of Health and Medicine. It proposed to lend the full support of the Prescott administration and the federal government, limited only by security and privacy concerns, to assist in the investigation. Grant indicated a sketchy knowledge of some plasma operations "discovered" in Arkansas and offered his assurance that the White House legal staff —over which he presided—would certainly help them find answers. In closing, he alluded to the possibility of federal funds being awarded to the suffering Canadian families should American culpability be established.

Faulkner had no idea whether Eric ever mailed the letter ... surely not ... or if it had been printed for discussion purposes. He had an idea, though, that this was why Eric was dead. Eric had forced the president's hand, and someone had stopped him. Bill didn't know who had stepped in, but this reeked of Arkansas's own brand of "discussion and debate." The possibility of suicide looked more remote than before. There was no suicide note. Now Bill was the one with the information, and he knew only too well what that might mean for him.

He sat at the monitor letting his mind range over the possibilities. It struck him with breath-stopping force that Eric had been watched ... stalked! A moment later, Bill shut down the computer, his hands shaking badly.

Alone in the predawn hours, Bill forced his mind to retrace his every move and contact over the last day. He relived in fast-forward all the looks, the comments, and the reactions of the people in his office, chewing on every detail. He worked through the whole exercise the way he used to mow his lawn: he didn't miss a spot. He couldn't now. His life might very well depend on it.

TWENTY-FIVE ~~~~~~~~~~

MARCH 2, 1995
LITTLE ROCK, ARKANSAS

S YLVIA'S CHEVY MONTE CARLO SWUNG ONTO THE ON RAMP OF THE Melvin Gates Freeway which split the capital city. She and David had been riding in silence since leaving Salvador's house. Seeing David looking out his side window, she tried to study him in glances. He must be in his late forties, she thought. He had the weathered hands and face of a man who spent a lot of time outdoors. His reddish hair was long and flecked with little touches of gold. He was one of those men who wore a beard so that you couldn't really imagine them without one. David's was full and red and clipped neatly away from his lips. His eyes were stern and blue. You could tell they had seen a lot of the world. She liked everything she could see.

Sylvia felt herself falling for him. This surprised her, and she tried to control her feelings. This was not in the plan. She had never been attracted to the "outdoor type" before, either. It must be the moment, or perhaps springtime. After breaking off with a coworker two months ago, she was planning to remain uninvolved. She had plenty of work to do with her research and she thought that a couple of years without a serious romance might do her some good.

Marriage was not something Sylvia craved. She had been married once, years ago. Right out of high school. They had been class sweethearts, blind with puppy love. So young, she sighed to herself. The marriage was doomed; neither was emotionally mature enough to make it root. They struggled for a few years, and then called it quits after his first year in law school. The experience convinced her that making a marriage work took more than two nice people agreeing to live together.

Bill, her ex-husband, was extremely nice—smart, ambitious, and reliable. Maybe too reliable. But he was a sweet guy. They had remained close friends. She knew his new wife and kids and they still talked every few weeks. They had not let a bad marriage get in the way of a good friendship.

Now this man, this David Farr, suddenly had her thinking about love again. She had met him only four hours earlier, but he intrigued her. She was comfortable with him. And he needed her. She knew that the first time he looked at her, and she liked ... being needed.

"David, I know it hurt to hear Salvador talk about the prison and to ... relive ... things. I feel so sorry ... Tell me, what are your plans?" she said.

David had turned to look at her. "There's no way I can thank you enough for this help," he said, too formally. "I'll call you this afternoon, if I may, to see whether Slappy Joe remembers the names of those ... bastards."

"Of course, of course. Call or come by. I'm going to stay at my condo all afternoon expecting his call. I'm pretty sure Salvador will call."

"If you'll drop me at my Blazer? I'll go make some phone calls at the motel. At least now I know that my dad's hunch about Cummins Prison was correct. I have a friend who's working with me from another angle, and I need to let him know what we know." David was still staring, fascinated by her profile and the delicate shape of her ear. "You sure I won't be bothering you or your husband or whoever?"

She laughed, "No boyfriend, no husband either, and you sure can't bother me. I'll expect to hear from you by the middle of the afternoon, okay?"

"You're a glutton for punishment," David said, reaching for his keys, pleased.

They exchanged phone numbers. He promised he would check with her about three-thirty, and maybe they'd go back to Slappy Joe's to see whether he was still trying to come up with those names.

"Slap is quite a character, isn't he?" David asked.

"Oh, yes! He has always been a great source of inside information. Every time I've seen him, though, he starts in about 'Where's my man?' 'Who am I seeing?' and all that silly stuff. Sorry if it embarrassed you."

"No, no, quite the contrary, I was flattered. But I have to ask you the same thing," he grinned. "You're really not seeing anyone?"

She blushed. "I already told you that. No."

"Good." David shut the door a little too vigorously and watched her car pull away. This was going better than he'd ever dreamed.

TWENTY-SIX 〜〜〜〜〜〜〜〜

RICKY HAD BEEN STAKED OUT MOST OF THE NIGHT JUST OFF Jackson Square. New Orleans had been Ricky's base of operations for over twenty years. The port city offered a variety of unwatched "shipping-out points" and you could blend into the throngs of international visitors in almost any disguise. He was looking for an old contact, who'd probably pass by on the way back to his apartment. He'd almost missed him. At 4:00 A.M. two ugly and exceedingly drunk women stumbled across the square. They wore fifties-style party dresses and high heels, and had hideous floral shawls wrapped around their necks. They were giggling.

Ricky might have bought it if Ramone hadn't snorted. Ramone had a *very* distinctive snort when he laughed. Ricky knew that Ramone was gay, but he hadn't guessed that he was a cross-dresser. It didn't matter, of course. Besides, Ricky needed his help now and couldn't afford to wait for a less cluttered hour in Ramone's social calendar.

Ramone felt the slight squeeze on his shoulder and froze. His testicles, already strapped high and tight inside a latex girdle, pulled up another notch from pure, cold terror. He had surveyed the street and hadn't seen a soul.

Ramone turned slowly and saw Ricky's horrible smile, the yellow of the gaslights reflected in his eyes. The two men had known each other for a dozen years, but Ramone still could not make himself look at that smile. He caught his breath quickly and tried to steady his fright. "Javier! It ... It's you. It's good to see you. What's up? I ... I ... Is something wrong?" Ramone asked, backing away from Ricky as much as he dared.

"I need to see you ... Now ... I didn't have time to go through the regular channels. It's important! Lose your friend," Ricky ordered.

Ramone turned, hiked his dress, and ran after his partner, who never noticed that he had been walking alone. Ramone forgot his dating games and sprinted like a linebacker, catching his boyfriend in forty yards. As Rick approached he was quite sure he heard him call the other one "Alfonse." Ramone was talking a streak. "I swear I will call your mother's house tomorrow and we can reschedule. You go over to Canal and catch a taxi. Now go! For God's sake, Alfonse. Stop that. I'll talk to you later. Go!" The poor fellow kept glancing back over his shoulder while he wobbled away as fast as the booze and the spike heels would allow.

Ramone jerked the scarf from his neck and kicked off his high-heeled shoes. He strode up Napoleon Street and unlocked the steel gate outside his apartment. A moment later he was flipping on the lights in his computer room.

The room was lined with equipment. Monitors displayed their strange screen-savers, whirling and dancing as if to some unheard music. Mousepads, speakers, printers, scanners, and other peripherals crowded the surfaces in a welter of wires and cables. Ramone was nothing if not an infomaniac.

"I'm sorry that you saw me like that, Javier. That is my private ..."

"No sweat." Ricky cut him off. "I need you to do a little search for me. I need information about some people who were running bad blood out of Arkansas in the mid eighties. I don't have much more to go on than that," Ricky said, plopping in one of the swivel chairs.

"Ah, sangre. Yes, I remember a wire story about it from a few days ago

... no details though," Ramone replied, typing something into a computer. There weren't many stories he missed.

"There weren't any details. I've talked to the usual sources on the street and got zilch there, too. See what you can find through your channels. I need names and current bios on whoever was involved. Addresses, any background you can get. This is personal, but the information will be handled just like any other that has passed between us. You can charge me double your normal fee but I want it soon. *Really* soon." Ricky leaned over and tried to follow what Ramone was doing on the screen. "You have any ideas?"

"Si ... yes, yes, but this will take me a while. Come by later today, Javier. Eleven or so." Ramone finished writing a note to himself and sat back in his chair. "Are you ready for a new project, Javier? I have some people down south requesting your talents. I've been putting them off, waiting to hear from you. Their government is offering a very, very good bonus if you succeed by a certain time."

"I'm still retired, Ramone. Just do the blood thing, that's all I'm interested in." Ricky turned at the door, his voice deadly. "I want these guys, mi amigo. Bad. I want every damn one. You find 'em for me." Then he was gone, into the night.

Ramone let out a long sigh as the door closed. "Dios, los proteja!" He crossed himself and spit. "Si, God have mercy on them! Señor Javier won't!"

TWENTY-SEVEN 〜〜〜〜〜〜〜

SYLVIA FIXED HERSELF A SANDWICH AND LEAFED THROUGH A PILE of dreary paperwork. The reports could have been written in Swahili. Her eyes may have been on them, but in her mind she saw David Farr.

His ease with her had overcome her reserve and aroused her feelings. And the look in his eyes when Salvador had asked if they were an item.... She could still feel the schoolgirl tingle that shot down her spine. Sylvia went through her reasons for not wanting to get involved and found that she was arguing each one down. But this vendetta of his had her worried. She wondered what he planned to do if he found the people involved. He was planning on going to the police, wasn't he? It would be very dangerous to act on his own. And wrong. He couldn't take the law into his own hands.

She had asked him about his plans twice during the morning, but he had skillfully changed the subject. The intensity in his eyes when he talked about

Zack and Deidra made her think that he might be capable of doing something ... she didn't want to think what. Sylvia really couldn't blame him. What must he feel, with this horrible attack on his family? God, she didn't know anything about him. Except that he was real.

Sylvia jumped when the phone rang, shattering her reveries. Her hand shook picking up the receiver. "Hello?"

"Sylvia, this is David."

"Oh, hi. Salvador hasn't called yet."

"Well, I couldn't reach my partner or my father. I'll have to try later. But I was wondering whether you might know anyone who would recognize those names. Maybe someone connected with the prison in some way during those years?" he asked.

"I might, let me think."

"If you did, you might be able to ask about those people. You know, just casually so they don't suspect anything. You could say the names came up during an interview or something like that. Do you think that would work? I don't want to push anything on you, but I'm really going crazy trying to think of what to do."

"No, David, that's fine. You know ... I don't know why I didn't think of him sooner," she paused.

"Who?"

"Well, my ex-husband, Bill. Bill Faulkner. He's a lawyer. He worked in state government back then, knew everybody. In fact, I think Bill actually worked Department of Corrections stuff. I'm sure he'd know the people."

"Great! Can we call him? I mean can you call him ... without mentioning my name?" he asked.

"I'll be glad to, David. I'll try right now, but give me a while ... sometimes it takes me a few minutes to get through to him. If I can get through at all."

"Is he *that* busy? A high-dollar lawyer, huh?"

"You're not going to believe this, but Bill works at the White House. He's the assistant to the chief counsel for the president," she said. "I have his priority phone number, but generally he has to call me back," Sylvia said.

"You're kidding? Wow!"

"Bill's a sweetie. I think he's doing okay up there but he's homesick for Arkansas. He always asks about things here when we talk. He'll take time to visit with me," she said confidently. "Why don't you come by? I'll fix you a little lunch and you can make your phone calls from here. I'm still expecting Salvador to call."

"Sounds good. Thanks. I'll come over in half an hour." he said.

"Good! In the meantime, I'll call Bill ... 'Bye."

Sylvia hung up the phone and fished through her purse to find Bill's number. It was always amazing to her that she was actually calling the White House. That Bill was actually working there. He had always relished the political life, but she had no interest in those things. She purposely shut out the reports of scandals in Washington, D.C. None of it made any sense to her anyway.

The phone rang and rang. Sylvia began to worry that she had misdialed when a very tired female voice said, "Go ahead." It surprised Sylvia for a second.

"Ah, yes. This is Sylvia Barrows from Little Rock. I'm calling for Bill Faulkner. Is he in today?" she asked.

"Ma'am, he's in, but I'm almost certain that he will not be able to talk to you. Things are pretty crazy here today," she said matter-of-factly.

"Would you please try? This is rather important. Just tell him I'm on the line, please." Presently Bill answered.

"Sylvia?"

"Hey, Bill. Thanks for taking my call. How are you?" she asked.

"Ah, sweet Sylvia. Good to hear a voice from home. Are you calling about Eric?" Bill sounded as if he'd been up for three days, which was not far from fact.

"Eric Grant?" she asked. "No, just saying hello. What's with Eric?"

"He's dead, Sylvia."

"What?"

"They found his body under a bridge yesterday. We don't know what happened and I'm trying to hold this place together," he said.

"My God, Bill, I had no idea. That's terrible. I'm so sorry. Are you all right? I can call back later if you're busy now." she said.

"No, no ... believe me, I'm glad you called. I needed to talk to someone in the real world. This place is insane! Right now, I'd rather be anywhere else. But of course I can't go anywhere—I'm acting chief counsel. Hey ... how's the thesis?" he asked.

"Going great! I've been working at it full time, getting lots done. You know, that reminds me, I had a question for you," she said, seizing the opportunity.

"Fire away." Bill sounded more relaxed now.

"Um, do you remember the names of any medical people who were working at Cummins back in the mid eighties?" Sylvia tried to sound as nonchalant as possible.

Bill Faulkner stiffened in his chair, hoping she had not heard his gasp. His mind raced. Was Sylvia somehow onto this nightmare he'd inherited? He didn't know how to play it. She always knew when he was lying.

"Gosh, that's been a long time ago," he said, after too long a pause. "Why do you ask?"

"This friend of mine is doing some research. He had some questions and I thought you might remember some of those people. You know me—always bugging the prison system about something." She tried to act only indirectly concerned, but she could hear Bill's defenses going up.

"Who's your friend?"

"What, are you getting jealous? After all these years?" she said, trying to throw him off the scent!

"Sylvia, listen, I don't remember any names from back then. And I think you need to stick to your own research. In my position, I can't make comments, even if this guy is your friend." Bill tried to sound firm and official.

"Are you kidding? You never forget names *or* faces Do you know them or not, Bill?" She knew now that something was up, but had to try.

"Sylvia, I think you must be confused. I don't want to sound harsh, but this office is no place to bring your academic stuff, okay? I'm just going out the door now. I'll call you back. Please don't phone me here at the office, all right?"

"Okay, Bill ..." she started, but the line went dead. Sylvia slowly put the phone down and tried to make sense of what had just happened. Something was wrong. The way he ducked the question and cut her off, you would think he was afraid someone would overhear him. Bill sounded scared. Why? What did he know?

Sylvia was still sorting her thoughts when David rang the doorbell. She soon had him parked at the kitchen table with a spread of sandwiches, chips, and iced tea. She told David about the strange conversation. Bill would call back. Before he did, maybe they could figure out enough to make a plan.

"Then you think he knows them?" David asked.

"Well, he sure didn't want to talk about it, so I guess he does. He tried to make it sound like he couldn't be bothered, but I think he was trying to warn me not to get involved."

"So did I, remember? It's not too late. Why don't we let it drop right here?"

"Because I know too much. I know you won't drop it, so I can't either. Let's see what he calls back with. Okay?"

As they finished their lunch the phone rang. It was Salvador.

"Miss Sylvia, I think I got one a dem names you was askin' 'bout." Salvador had been enjoying his case of Miller.

"Great, Salvador, I'm glad you called."

"Ol' Docta Frank's name wus Warren. Docta Frank Warren. It come to me all of a sudden like. Jus' popped inta my ol' head. Chomp! An dere it wus. Yeup."

"Oh, that's a great help, Salvador. Remember not to mention any of this to anyone. Will you?"

"Lawdy, no! Don't no one need to know. Nope. Say, Miss Sylvia, is dere any chance dat Mr. David might be dere raht now?" he asked.

She was wise to his leading question. "Yes, Salvador, he does happen to be here. Why?"

"Dere ya go! I know'd it! See, I ain't nevva wrong about dat kinda stuff. Y'all looks right togetha. Yeup," he teased.

"Okay, I'll take that into consideration, Salvador. Thanks again ... 'Bye."

"Wait, wait! ... Miss Sylvia. If you or Mr. David wus to come back out dis a way to ask anythin' else, would you bring me some o' dat Miller Lite dis time? I'm tryin ta cut down a little. It's a health ting, ya know," he announced solemnly.

"Now that you mention it, Salvador, we do have a few more questions. We'll bring some Lite with us. 'Bye!" She hung up the phone.

David had listened to the conversation and was sitting on the edge of his chair.

"He had one name for us: Dr. Frank Warren."

"Great! Finally, we're getting somewhere. Would you please check the Little Rock phone book? I'll try information."

Neither source paid off. Oddly, for such a common-sounding name, there were no Frank or Franklin Warrens listed in the central Arkansas region.

"Sylvia, can I use your phone to call my partner and get this name to him? It's long distance. I'll pay for it."

"Sure, David, of course. But I have to ask you, what are you planning to do to these men if you find them?"

"I intend to get the truth from them. I want to know how it happened, how the blood was tainted . . . how that blood was released. There are so many questions! Was it an accident? Could it have been prevented? Who was responsible? Who covered it up? What in the hell were they doing taking blood from sick inmates?" David paused. "And I want to know how much money they made poisoning my Zack and all those other people." He paused again. "When I find out what happened, I'll decide what to do."

The phone rang before she could respond. David instinctively reached for it but backed away so that she could answer.

"Hello?"

"Sylvia, this is Bill. I only have a moment to talk so listen to me. You have no idea what you have gotten into. Stop right now. Your life and your friend's may already be in danger. In fact, I'm sure they are," he said, slightly out of breath.

"Danger? My God, Bill, what do you mean?"

"Sylvia, don't ask questions, *please* . . . You know I still love you, and I couldn't bear your getting hurt. My phone is probably tapped. I'm certain I'm being watched right now. There are people . . . probably from Arkansas . . . who intend to keep this blood business quiet. They play rough, Sylvia, believe me. That much I know. They wouldn't think twice about killing you or your friend." Bill was talking almost in a whisper now, pleading.

"Bill!—I didn't say anything about blood! But that's what it is. My friend was ... hurt, Bill. He needs to know how it happened."

"Get out, Sylvia! That's what you don't understand. They'll go to any lengths to cover it up. They are the ones who killed Eric, I'm almost certain of it. He was going to expose the story and they knew it. They shot him in the head and made it look like suicide."

"Oh, dear Lord! But ..."

"No questions," he interrupted. "Just listen. And you don't tell anyone this. The only reason I'm telling you is to make sure you drop it right now, before they find out about you, too. Sylvia ... Grant and the president were the ones who authorized the blood deal at the prison. They set it up. They got paid for it ... a lot. They've covered it up ever since. This was all back when Prescott was governor. Now Eric is dead ... You've got to drop it, Sylvia, and disappear for a while. Get out of Arkansas! I have to go." And he was gone. Sylvia was breathless.

"What did he say? He knows the whole story, doesn't he?" David asked shrewdly.

"He told me there are people who might kill us if we don't drop it. He said his boss was murdered because he was ready to talk about this whole scam. That was just days ago! He even thought that our phone conversation earlier was tapped.

"Bill is sure we're in danger, David. Believe me, he is very serious and very scared." Sylvia reached across the table and touched David's hand. She didn't mention President Prescott's involvement. Her mind was still sorting everything out.

"If your call was tapped, then I have to get you out of here. I'm afraid you threw in with trouble this morning ... I'm so sorry, Sylvia." David took her hand in his. "I'm going to call my dad to see if he know's these guys. Especially, this Dr. Frank Warren. Then we have to get out of here."

He dialed his dad's place. No one had been home a couple of hours before. Now a thin female voice answered, unfamiliar and sad.

"Hello, this is David Farr. Have I reached the Farr residence?" he asked.

"Yes, you have. Just a moment." David heard a series of muffled sounds. Another unfamiliar voice got on the line.

"Is this David?"

"Yes, it is. Is my dad there?" he said.

"Oh, my, you haven't heard . . . ?"

"Heard what? What's happened?" David thought of Zack at once. He had been out of reach all day. Fear flooded him.

"David, this is Margaret. Elaine's sister. I'm sorry to tell you this, but your daddy is dead. He was shot . . . horribly killed by some ruthless child of Satan. They don't know who did it. We are here right now to see after my sister and we are praying for all of your family."

This was absolutely the last thing that David expected to hear. He was too shocked to believe the news, to respond, to feel the pain. His dad couldn't be dead. He was too tough. Too mean. He was supposed to out-live all three of his sons. That had always been the plan and no one really doubted it.

"My . . . my dad's been *killed?*" He managed to find part of his voice. Sylvia gasped.

"I'm afraid so, son. We are also praying that the horrible person who shot him will be struck down by the righteous hand of God. The police don't know anything."

"He was shot?" The words began to register. "When? Where?" David begged.

"It must have been yesterday evening, David, down at that deer camp he loved so much. There was another man dead too. They haven't figured out who he is. Old man Dunn found both of them. It was just horrible."

"Has anyone called my brothers?" he asked.

"Yes, they're on their way. The police have talked to everyone but you. Are you coming here?" she asked.

"Right away. I'll be there in a few hours. Tell everyone. Okay, Margaret? Thank you for helping Elaine."

David was devastated. Sylvia softly rubbed his shoulder, trying to comfort him. Neither said a word. Fear had replaced the concern in her eyes. Finally she came close and gently put her arms around him. He pulled her closer and his tears came from somewhere deep inside.

The old man had been indestructible. If David hadn't involved him in this mess, he would have lived to be a hundred. It was his fault, David thought miserably. Then he started. Now Sylvia was in terrible danger, too ... this soft, wonderful creature next to him, suddenly so dear. Over his dead body! He had to clear his mind and move fast.

"Sylvia, get a bag packed. Two, if you need them. Clothes and your personal papers. ID stuff. We don't have much time. I have to get you out of here. The bastards have killed my father. I don't know if they're onto me, but we have to think they are. So you have to move to safety. Okay?" He realized he was crying and holding her tearstreaked face in his hands. She was nodding, unable to speak. He kissed her on the forehead, then stood to use the phone again. He had to get in touch with Ricky. He needed help.

Rick's distinctive drawl never sounded better.

"Ricky, we've got big trouble. The bastards killed my dad."

"*What?*"

"My dad was apparently checking around on his own. They've shot him. At the deer camp. Some other guy is dead, too, don't know who. I just heard and I'm on my way down." David felt better just talking to his old friend. Sylvia had gone into her bedroom and he could hear her slamming drawers.

"Sons of bitches! Damn, Dave! I'm sorry. You okay? Sure?" Rick thought out loud. "They must have been good to take out the old man. He's one of the toughest cops I ever knew. We're going to settle the score, what do ya say?"

"Yeah ... damn right! I've got one name, that's all so far, but I've got an idea how the whole deal went down." David related.

"That's more than I've got. Lay it on me. My man can find him within the hour." Ricky was ready.

"He was apparently the ringleader, a Dr. Frank Warren. You sure you can find him, Rick? No listings in Arkansas."

"I'll make him, Dave. Call you at your dad's place. You watch your ass. Go on down and take care of the arrangements. Then be ready to move ... Listen, buddy ... No damn doctor took out your dad, y'know? These are professionals, believe me. Y'know I know what I'm talking about, right? You be careful."

"Right. You too, Rick ...Hey, uh, Rick. I'm afraid I've gotten a woman up here involved. Too complicated to explain now. She'll be with me. Her name is Sylvia Barrows. If she calls you for me or if she answers when you call, she is good ... she knows everything—okay?"

"She know you're a sex maniac?"

"God! You never give up do you?" David had to smile despite everything.

"No, and you'll be glad of that someday," Ricky boasted.

"Hey, I already am, amigo. And ... thanks." Sylvia was beside him with a suitcase and shoulder bag as he hung up the phone.

TWENTY-EIGHT ~~~~~~~~~~

"**L**ADIES AND GENTLEMEN, YOUR ATTENTION, PLEASE! I WOULD like to welcome you all here this evening. This is a wonderful crowd for our opening activities and I think you will be thrilled and inspired by the high level of professional artistry exhibited here today."

The very fat bearded man paused at the microphone as a healthy smattering of applause ran through the crowd. "So without further ado, as president of the Arkansas Branch of Gobblers for the Future, I declare the Eighteenth Annual Southeast Regional Turkey Calling Competition to be under way!"

As the crowd joined together in cheers and applause at this announcement, a door opened on each side of the podium. Forty full-grown tom turkeys came flapping and trotting out into the crowd. The people in the front rows screeched and pushed back. But the overfed toms just slipped and slid on the glistening floor. Those in the rear of the auditorium laughed uproariously when some of the women yelled and threw their popcorn in the air. The noise was deafening by the time the smiling president of Gobblers for the Future ambled back to the microphone.

"Folks, I've just been told that if you can catch 'em, you can take 'em home! These beautiful birds have been donated by the Titus Poultry Company, which is celebrating becoming not only *the largest corporation in Arkansas history,* but now *the largest independent food production company in the en-tire world!* We salute you, Titus Poultry, and all your good people!"

~~~~~~~~~~~~~~~~

Worley and Lamar strolled through the line of booths depicting every possible use or function of turkeys—hunting them, calling them, decoying them, feeding them, urging them to fornicate for breeding purposes, or cooking them. It boggled the mind.

For hunters, every type of camouflage on the market was on display, each touting its superiority over the next. There was everything from the typical Vietnam-era "jungle tiger stripe" to an actual photomontage of acorns and corncobs transferred onto dirt-colored cloth. There were face masks, hats, gloves, boots, umbrellas, blinds, and even a portable Mylar mirror to sit behind so that the unwary bird would see only itself as it approached the hunter.

Another whole section was set up for the promotion of over six hundred and fifty different types of callers. There were wooden boxes with hinges and push rods, slates with little scratching awls that looked like ancient medical devices. There were single, double, and triple rubber diaphragms that fit in the roof of the mouth like a collapsed condom. There were calls made of wood, plastic, rubber, chalk, metal, shell, cellophane, and bone. One was even designed from an old snuff can.

"Best show they've ever had, by far." Lamar stopped with his hands on his hips, and tried to take it all in. "I'll bet they even have little plastic turkey pussies that you can put on the end of your barrel so you can bring 'em in real close."

Worley snorted. "Someone's probably working on that idea right now." He munched a piece of Turkey Jerky that a kid handed him from a mobile cart.

"How long you been here?" Lamar asked, turning to business. He was satisfied that they weren't being watched.

"I got here just a few minutes before you. I kinda slept in today. It's been a busy week." Worley was looking around for something to drink so he could finish swallowing the sample that had grown in his mouth. "Let's go over to the refreshment area. I gotta have a Coke or something. Grab a table."

They both sat at a small table against an empty wall, smoking and enjoying their fountain drinks.

Lamar fit in perfectly with this crowd. He had slipped unresisting into middle age, like many other successful businessmen, with a nice roll around his middle and a little extra flesh around his neck and face. He had learned to be as comfortable in a suit and tie as he was in jeans and a windbreaker. Such were the requirements of doing business in Arkansas.

Lamar had even managed to acquire a family while carrying out his duties around the state. His wife was quiet and loyal and never questioned his schedule. When the twin boys came along ten years ago, they had moved out to one of the nice "country estate" developments and joined the local Methodist church.

The years had played differently with Worley. His hair was no longer black, but diffused with shafts of white. He wore it long on the top and swept back on the sides. He had not gained an ounce and, if anything, was even more lean and angular than he had been as a young man. The skin stretched so tautly over his facial bones that he seemed to have no wrinkles. His eyes were deep-set. Their gray intensity complemented the arch of heavy eyebrows, still jet black and even.

Worley had acquired that "middle-aged attractive" look that younger women often found fascinating. They saw him as mysterious and sensual. He found them disposable, never staying with one for more than a season. In Arkansas that meant no more than a couple of months, sometimes the same day. It kept his life simple. He sat in his jeans and navy blazer, and never stopped assessing the crowd as they talked.

"How was Charlie when you talked to him last?" he asked Lamar.

"Oh, he's pissed about having to stay in D.C., but he'll get over it. Our contacts in the legal office up there fumbled some of the phone tapping. We missed a few calls, probably not important, but Charlie swears we've got Faulkner scared shitless.

"I made a few calls to his wife before I left. Charlie's been shadowing the new chief counsel everywhere he goes. Man, his ol' lady is a nut case! I didn't have to rattle her cage much to get her attention. There's only one problem." Lamar paused.

"Yeah?"

"Well, one of the calls he took today was from a gal here in Little Rock. We didn't get much of the conversation. He left the office right away and drove to a pay phone. We think he may have got wise to us and called her back. She's probably just a girlfriend on the side, like. But she could also know something, so we'll stay alert. I'm not too worried. He's so scared that he'll keep her quiet, for sure."

"Any, uh, problems with our friend Mr. Grant?" Worley asked, squinting through the smoke from his cigarette.

"Not really. Charlie twisted his ankle a little when we were carrying the body down the embankment, but not too bad. That idea with the heavy polyethylene bag worked great. We had him in the car with it over his head.

"He was yacking about how he needed more air and I just eased the gun up to his head and pop! Low-charge frangible bullet. No fuss, no muss!

"We just left the bag over his head till we got to the bridge. Took it off, put a big rock in it and tossed it off another bridge later, in another part of the city. That's as clean as you can do it, ya know? Practically nothing to clean up. How 'bout you?"

"Strange, strange. I'd been following Mr. Bennie for a few days. The other night he started to Little Rock in a big hurry like he was going to spill to someone. Then he stopped in at this beer joint on the outskirts for some liquid courage, I think. The little bastard must have chickened out. He drug himself home three hours later. Really bombed. I was so bored that I thought about doing a freebie on the jerk, just so I didn't have to follow his ass any more. Then last night, I'm watching him stumble across the same parking lot, going to his car and this big-ass guy pulls up in a Suburban, opens his door. They talk. Bennie starts cussing him and bam! This guy belts him with one of those black leather saps and throws him in the back of his truck. I mean it came out of nowhere! He must've had it in his back pocket. Then pow! He knew what he was doing." Worley was reliving the scene.

"Damn! Was it anyone we know?" Lamar asked.

"Wait now, that's the good part. So I follow this guy and loop south, out of town. We're going down every gravel road in two counties. Finally end up at this hunting camp. All vacant and closed up. I had to drive for miles with my lights out. Ended up walking the last half mile so I wouldn't spook him.

"Before I get up to the camp I hear Bennie begging and screaming. I ease on up through the trees with my little H&K with the twilight scope on it. This big motherfucker has Bennie handcuffed around this log post that they skin deer on. Bennie's screaming about how he didn't hurt no one and how the guy's got the wrong man and all that bullshit. This big guy is standing there with a pair of those big pruning shears, lopping off old Bennie's fingers, one by one. Never saw nothin' like it.

"Bennie stops begging and just starts screaming. Then he slides down around the post like he can't catch his breath. I figure he's having a heart attack and my job is finished. But then the big guy leans over and says, 'Blood for blood, you motherfucker. I didn't even know you had a fucking heart but I guess I was wrong,'" Worley finished.

"So this guy was after Bennie over the blood deal?" Lamar asked.

"I don't know for sure, but I couldn't take a chance. Things were getting too weird. So I popped him. Didn't make too great a shot. That nine-millimeter slug took off part of his jaw and he kind of spun around. He shook his head and headed for me, pulling out this fucking nickel-plated Browning he had under his jacket. I had to shoot him six more times before he dropped. Old bastard got off a couple of rounds at me, but he couldn't really see me too well ... Guess who he was."

"Hell, I don't know," Lamar said.

"Remember that old state cop that whipped all those drunk college boys at a Razorback game a few years ago?"

"That big old bastard?"

"Yeah. Man, I felt kinda bad. I always liked him, but shit happens."

"You think he was nosing around? Working for somebody?"

"No, not really. The more I think about it, the more I think that he was just settling an old score with Bennie. And he did, too; Bennie's dead as a rock. But when he said blood, I got nervous. Couldn't take a chance." Worley finished his Coke. "Hey, you want a hot dog or something? I'm getting hungry."

"Naw, I'm trying to get in shape. I'd hate to think I had to chase anyone right now," Lamar joked. "Hell, I might turn up with a heart attack like old Bennie. What's up now—you going to go down to Arizona to keep an eye on our doctor buddy?"

Worley stood up and stretched, slipping on the Gargoyle sunglasses. "Yeah. And I bet he's really squirrelly since Grant, uh, did himself in. And now Mr. Bennie. But I still think he'll be a real good boy. I'll go down and take his pulse. I want you to keep a check on the girl that Faulkner talked to. Did you pick up my traveling money?" Worley asked.

"Yeah, I slipped it in your trunk when I got here. Say, you know what the Judge said when I picked it up? He wanted to know if we were keeping our receipts!" Lamar laughed.

"What did you say?"

"I told him yeah, but we were having trouble getting our clients to sign 'em, har har har; he didn't think it was so funny."

They walked to the exit just as the last loose turkey was trapped and throttled in the revolving door.

TWENTY-NINE ∼∼∼∼∼∼∼∼∼∼∼∼∼

D R. FRANK WARREN WASN'T WAITING FOR ANYONE. WHEN HE read about Eric Grant's suicide, he pushed down the panic and tried to appraise his situation calmly. His gut told him that Eric had been ready to shoot off his mouth about their little secret, and somebody made sure he didn't. But his head told him that the man had snapped. The pressure had been apparent in their conversations, and Warren knew that some people just couldn't take it. And the police said there was no foul play. But then Bennie. . . .

Bennie's wife Wanda had called three times that day. The first two times she was worried because Bennie hadn't come home, and she didn't know where he was. Frank reassured her. After all, this wasn't *too* unusual for Bennie. But late that afternoon she called back in hysterics. He couldn't understand a word she was saying. Finally Wanda's daughter took the phone and told him that they had recovered Bennie's body from a deer camp. He had been *tortured to death*. Frank told the girl he would fly up immediately. Then he hung up, trembling.

With a couple of phone calls he arranged for a small twin-engine plane out of Phoenix to fly him south to La Ceiba, Honduras. He packed his bags, put a few essential files into a briefcase and closed up his home in suburban Scottsdale. It hurt to think he might not see his place for a few months—maybe even a year—but he had no choice.

The flight took much longer than he'd expected. They had to divert to Cancun because of what turned out to be a small problem with an oil-pressure gauge, but the "small problem" took hours to correct and the Mexican paperwork took even more hours.

During the endless wait, Warren tried to concentrate on the prospect of returning to his ranchero in Honduras. It was situated in the jungled highlands near the Guatemalan border. He had stumbled onto this gorgeous piece of land years before while on a tour of the Mayan ruins of Copán. The price was right, and he loved the seclusion. Through the years he had built up a nice bank account in Tegucigalpa, the capital city, and had remodeled the hacienda, stocking it with everything he could think of that he might need. He had supplies that would last for years, an array of electronic gear, and a formidable arsenal.

Manual labor was extremely cheap, and he had hired—at slightly higher than the going rate—a capable foreman to manage the place. In the last couple of years the ranch had turned the corner and actually shown a profit. Beef and coffee were its major crops, although Julio, the foreman, planned to switch some of the acreage over to tobacco this year.

Julio would be surprised to see the doctor, but that was all right—an unannounced visit helped keep these locals in line.

In Honduras he would be safe. He could play gentleman farmer and cultivate his interest in the local culture. These were an innocent people, and not at all unattractive. His visits there had featured some very pleasing encounters. Any goddamned Arkansas tough guys attempting to find him would stick out like stumps on a putting green. It took finesse to deal with the natives, but that was Warren's strong point. He'd have time to buy many loyalties. All in all, it was an ideal place to kick back for a while. Not Phoenix, but very comfortable.

It was almost midnight before they landed in La Ceiba and cleared customs. Warren paid the pilot and had his bags carried to a taxi, failing to notice the two dark-complected men sitting on the bumper of a Toyota Land Cruiser. As his taxi cleared the parking gate, one of them said, "Roberto, it is time to go to work. Will you drive, amigo?"

Roberto grinned and jumped behind the wheel. "Si, Javier. It will be my pleasure."

THIRTY 〜〜〜〜〜〜〜〜〜

**MARCH 3, 1995
THE OVAL OFFICE
THE WHITE HOUSE
WASHINGTON, D.C.**

PRESCOTT HAD BEEN ASKED TO SPEAK AT THE FUNERAL THE FIRST OF next week. His press secretary had made the official announcement that the president would be unable to accept that honor because he and the deceased were far too close, friends since boyhood. Rough translation: he would be too choked up to lay the departed properly to rest. Well, let them believe what they wished.

Bob Prescott wasn't happy about Eric's death, but the fact was that Eric really had killed himself. Bob had tried in every way to warn Eric that he could not go outside the circle. When you played this game, you were a life member. No one, including the president, could actually make his own decisions, or worse, break the code of silence—not even if his conscience made an unexpected appearance.

The circle needed his power, Prescott mused, but it wasn't helping him with the political decision at hand. His heart told him to fight for

200

increased appropriations for the battle against AIDS. It sounded good, too. People like "compassion." Besides, it might work. Throw money at the son of a bitch long enough, and maybe they'd find a cure. But Bob Prescott was not the average politician and all his political senses told him to find a way to cut the spending.

It had nothing to do with what he believed; it had to do entirely with the polls. If he catered to the Republicans and chopped some of this "big spending," good—especially for "liberal" causes like AIDS. Bob figured that the move would score considerable points with the conservative crowd, or at least confuse and weaken the opposition. This was what was required to hold onto the office, and, by God, no one could do it better than he. He'd been riding the old fence so long that he had a barbed-wire asshole—and his ass was never wrong.

Tomorrow, the afternoon papers would announce the president's proposed cutback of spending for AIDS research. All in good form, of course—eliminating duplication and waste and all that. Give it a couple of years and he'd reverse course and get more brownie points on the left for bumping it back in. *After* his reelection.

Prescott had suffered some severe disappointments in this first term. His private life had been showcased from every unflattering angle. He'd thought he was ready for it, but it was much worse in the reality. Stephanie had taken some major hits as well, which only fueled her obvious dislike for the media. At times, Bob had to avoid her carefully, just to stay in one piece. Every attempt he had made to let her handle some of the policy-making had backfired. All it did was expose her as a cold, ruthless, manipulative bitch. She gloated over her little victories and whined about the least setback. Bob smiled to himself to think how accurate the press really was at times.

Most of the circle's business and trade deals—presented to the public as "issues"—had gone flat. Potential bonanza investments in the People's Republic of China had been canned just because the poll numbers were so negative. Stupid.

The Japanese were still not willing to open their markets. The military hated him. His biggest disappointment had been his own staff. Of the people he'd brought with him from Arkansas, a full third had bailed out, many in disgrace and some with actual indictments against them. Stephanie's "youth crusaders" were still around, scores of them, completely useless. Not reliable, either, Bob mused. That was always a worry.

Now there'd be an investigation into Eric's death. Bill Faulkner would probably have to take the hit for removing the files from Grant's office, although it was on orders. Bill was a good guy, but that's the way it was.

At least this stupid blood fiasco had been squelched. All the loose ends were tied up, and the bit players had surely gotten a helluva message.

Bob amused himself with the thought that now he could send some operatives from back home to ... Japan. They could go over in their easygoing, down-home way, and kick the living shit out of those greedy little bastards. *That'd* get their attention. They could plant a few corporate presidents in the fountains of their tea gardens and paste Confederate flag stickers on their foreheads. Then maybe these negotiations would get moving. Bob chortled out loud at the image of Worley and Lamar touring Japan.

"The problem is, they just don't respect us any more. The motherfuckers aren't afraid of us anymore," he mused aloud.

He stood up, walked over to the window and peered out through the bulletproof glass. When you got right down to it, a man had to be crazy to want this office. He remembered that visit with old Senator Bateman—God rest his soul—and his doubts about being able to do this job if he ever got here. Well, he *was* here and he *was* doing the job and his next term was lining up very nicely. That's when he intended to settle accounts and even things up for his people.

He grinned. "That, my friends, is the American way."

THIRTY-ONE 〰️〰️〰️〰️〰️

MARCH 4, 1995
STAR CITY, ARKANSAS

SOMETHING ABOUT A COUNTRY FUNERAL IS SIMPLY MORE REAL THAN its urban counterpart. The music is tinny, the hymns are the old standards, the flowers are unorchestrated and often overdone, and the grief is palpable. The women cry unabashedly, hanging on their men and wiping their eyes. If the preacher is particularly good at eulogizing, even the men, caught up in the emotion, will let slip a few tears.

At the graveside, there are more hymns, *a cappella* of course, and then at least a small burst of hysterics as the body is lowered into the grave. The emotion is not just tolerated; it is expected.

Stand there and watch the coffin drop until it settles firmly in the ground. See the widow and the other loved ones touch it one final time as it is lowered. Hear their last goodbyes, and it is hard to deny the finality of death. And impossible not to imagine yourself, one day, in that coffin.

But a country funeral is like life. When it's over, it's over. From the graveyard, you head back to the house for a great big party. Everybody comes. There's food enough to choke Sherman's army and fellowship to lighten the hearts of the bereaved. Kids run everywhere, a couple of fights break out, and there's at least one official photo session. The men sneak off and set up a hard-liquor bar in the barn or a shed or behind a hedge, and the party stretches on into the night.

And that was exactly the way Doug Farr's funeral had gone, from the church service till the last bottle was raised near dawn.

~~~~~~~~~~~~

Two days before, David and Sylvia drove the seventy miles down from Little Rock in relative silence. She was badly frightened. Every now and then a shiver ran through her. She was constantly biting her lip.

David had called home to give the news to his mother and to check on Zack and Deidra. His mother was shocked and upset about Doug's murder, though she hadn't been close to him since long before the divorce. She was more concerned about David and Ricky and of course Zack, who had taken a little turn for the worse. Deidra had driven him in to the medical center and planned to stay the night and drive back the next day. They wouldn't be able to come to the funeral, and David didn't want them to. He asked his mother not to tell Zack how his grandfather had died. There would be time for that later.

When he and Sylvia got to a small town on the other side of his dad's place, David rented two motel rooms, then—because she was afraid to stay by herself—he took her with him to meet the family at the house. Elaine and her sisters and the gaggle of aunts and uncles and cousins assumed that she was his "significant other." They welcomed her with warm hugs and lots of sweets and coffee. Sylvia seemed to relax with them and fit in well.

It was late when they got back to the motel, but neither wanted to go to sleep. They sat for hours talking quietly about family and work and what the next few days might hold. Only then did Sylvia learn that David was an amputee. She was fascinated. David found that explaining the routines of a one-legged man was completely natural with her. She fell asleep on the sofa and he in the armchair in her room.

After breakfast, they met with David's brothers to make the

arrangements at the funeral parlor. Everyone, including his brothers, puzzled over the insane circumstances of Douglas Farr's death. Each had his own theories. The most popular theories had the old trooper stumbling on a dope deal, and being shot down for interfering. It didn't make any sense, but nothing else did either.

David wanted to tell his brothers the truth—that he had got Doug involved in this unbelievable mess—but of course he couldn't breathe a word of it. He couldn't tell the police either. He and Sylvia went for a brief interview at the station. David told the sheriff that he'd had a nice visit with his father the day before the murder and that everything was fine. Nothing in their conversation offered a clue to the murder.

"Did you know the man who was found dead at the scene with your father, a Mr. Smith?" the sheriff asked.

"I don't think so, Officer. I haven't heard anything about him. Do you have his full name?" David asked.

"He was from Pine Bluff. A Benjamin W. Smith," he read from his notes, "Went by 'Bennie.' Bennie Smith."

Both David and Sylvia remembered Salvador talking about a "Bennie." David struggled not to show any sign of recognition. He hoped Sylvia wouldn't say anything. "Bennie Smith, Bennie Smith," he said out loud, pretending to search his memory. Bennie Smith must have been the other man Salvador was trying to remember. The "Dr. Love" in his story.

"I'm afraid not, Sheriff. Can't say I've ever heard the name. Of course, I've been out of the state for about thirty years," David said.

"So your father didn't say anything to you? About getting even with this man over something?" The sheriff was really feeling him out.

David just shook his head.

"Look, Mr. Farr. We've all known your dad for years. We respected him. Hell, I'm a member at that hunting camp with him. He gave half my deputies their driving tests when they were kids. But none of us can figure why he used his old handcuffs to harness Mr. Smith to our cleaning post. Why he was using his loppers to cut off the man's fingers. That is real strange, you agree?" The sheriff looked David in the eyes. "If you remember something, any little clue, we might be able to figure out who killed Doug. We could put 'em away for a long time."

David shrugged and shook his head. He couldn't let anything show on his face. But now he knew the circumstances surrounding his father's death. His crazy old man was exacting a little retribution for his grandson. For Zack ... and Deidra, too. And probably trying to extract the critical information at the same time. It wasn't a stretch for David to picture it all. He could see his dad doing all of that.

"Did my dad kill this guy, Smith?" he asked.

"No. I think he scared him to death. Smith died of a heart attack." The sheriff suppressed a small smile. "I have to tell you that a number of people were glad to see Mr. Smith get his. The Pine Bluff police were real familiar with him."

"Then who do you think killed my dad?"

"Well ... the most popular theory has your dad breaking up a drug deal, but I haven't bought into that ... not yet. We really don't have much to go on. I hope you'll call me if you think of anything. It might be the lead we need. You know, Elaine said that he said he was going to the camp for a couple of days to prepare a surprise for you. You think this was it?" The sheriff pushed his chair back from his desk.

"I can't imagine it," David said. "Venison sausage is more like it." But inwardly he thought to himself, "Damn right it was!"

As soon as they were back in the car, Sylvia broke down in tears. David wasn't in much shape to help her. He was torn. He felt as if he was coming apart inside, and he didn't really know which way to go. On the one hand, he wanted to comfort Sylvia, so dear to him now, carry her away to the safety of his northwoods lair. On the other hand, he burned to know who had shot his dad and what his dad had learned before he died. He wanted to see the face of the gunman—then smash it. He wanted to hear from Ricky and get back on the course, calling these people to answer for what they had done.

That night Ricky finally called. David and Sylvia were at Elaine's house; he and his brothers were going over the final details of the funeral for the next day. Elaine answered the phone.

"David, it's Ricky," she called.

He tried not to sprint down the hall to answer. "Ricky, where in the hell are you?"

"Down in my old playgrounds south of the border, man. I've been on the good doctor for two days now," Ricky said.

"You're kidding! You've found him? Where, Rick?" David asked.

"Well, now, that would be a little hard to say. I don't think you could find your way down here, old buddy. Besides, your doctor has a lot of friends around. Seems as though he invested his *blood money* well." David realized that Ricky was watching Warren while he spoke on the phone.

"Just keep a close eye on him, pal, and tell me where to meet you. We need information from the son of a bitch. I'll fly down in the Porter tomorrow night. Hey, Rick, my old man was putting the screws to a guy named Bennie Smith, Dr. Frank Warren's partner, when he was murdered."

"I'm damned! Your old man found out about their good ol' boy operation, huh? Your old man had style, Dave. And at least he got some satisfaction before he checked out."

"Rick, listen, the people who killed him are a lot more powerful than I thought. This goes all the way to the top. I want their names. I want their asses on a spike! Warren must know. So where do I meet you?"

"Hey, Dave, I'll call you soon. Don't worry, man ... Listen, this connection's getting kind of fuzzy."

"Rick, don't you do this to me! He's *my* responsibility. Rick! Rick! ... I swear ..."

"This one's for my Zack. See ya, pal." With a soft click, he was gone.

David was so frustrated he felt faint. It took a long moment, eyes shut tight, drawing deep breaths, to clear his vision. When he could see again, Sylvia was standing in front of him, with a very worried look. She put her arm around his waist and asked, "Are you okay?"

"Yeah, just upset. I'll be fine."

"More bad news?"

"Yes—no. Not bad news. I think its time you know more about Ricky."

On the drive to the motel that night, David talked nonstop about his best ... and sometimes mysterious ... friend. He didn't tell her everything, but related plenty of the good times and how special Rick was to the Farr family.

"It sounds like you trust him completely."

"I do. I certainly do. And there may come a time when *you* have to. You will be completely safe when you're with him. I promise," David said. "Right now he's somewhere south of the border shadowing Dr. Frank Warren. We'll get some interesting information from him, but *I* should be the one down there kicking it out of him."

"What will Ricky . . . do to him, David?"

"Don't ask. I don't know. Zack is Ricky's soulmate. He's like a son to him. I'd say that the doctor has some serious paybacks coming his way."

"My God! I wish all this would stop. I hope it's just a bad dream and we'll wake up in the morning with everything back to normal." She leaned her head against David's shoulder.

"That's what Zack and Deidra and thousands of others in Canada want. They want it to be over, too. But it never will be, for them," David reminded her, kissing the top of her head.

~~~~~~~~~~~~~~~

The funeral was over; another part of David's life was gone. He stood in the twilight looking across the back yard and over the dark waters of the lake. He had nothing to do now but leave his motel number with his step-mother and wait for Ricky to call again. He had spoken to Zack earlier. The weakness and resignation in his son's voice had broken his heart in yet another way.

David held a memento from his past, idly turning it over in his hands. His Purple Heart. He had given the medal to his father after the war. Elaine had tearfully handed it to David at the funeral. He had intended to put it on the coffin, but for some reason he couldn't.

A sweet clear voice followed him, as if meant just for his listening. He turned to look back in the bright kitchen window. It framed the most beautiful woman he had ever seen. Sylvia was helping with the dishes and smiling for the first time in days. How strange it was to find her at this time in his life. David wondered if anything would be left for them.

THIRTY-TWO ~~~~~~~~~~~

SYLVIA BARROWS TURNED THIRTY-SIX YEARS OLD A DAY AFTER THE funeral, confined to a room at the Razorback Inn in Monticello, Arkansas. Her mother, father, sisters, and girlfriends were missing. The normal deluge of presents and cards and cake was missing. She loved all of that, and felt terribly lonely. There were no jokes about how old she was getting, or "What's that ringing?" "Oh, nothing. Just the alarm on Sylvia's biological clock!" Sylvia sighed. But she did have one very dear man, showering her with his undivided attention and little treats for a whole day.

Sylvia had called her parents the day of the funeral and told them she'd still be out of town for her birthday. She would call them in a few days. She didn't know that Elaine's sister Margaret overheard the call and asked David if he had remembered her birthday. He took the hint.

That night they had a heart-to-heart talk that lasted until the wee hours. He had kissed her sweetly at the door, then retired to the adjoining room. She had no sooner stretched out on her bed than the phone rang. David, of course. He wanted to thank her for being with him over the past few days and tell her how much he appreciated her kindness to his family. She knew he was feeling more that he could not express. It made her warm. She breathed a goodbye kiss into the phone and fell into a deep, peaceful sleep filled with the dreams of a sixteen-year-old girl. She was hooked.

They had breakfast at the motel coffee shop, but quickly returned to the room to stay by the phone. Near lunchtime David left, supposedly to pick up some things at the drugstore. He returned with a Black Forest cake adorned with candles and an armload of presents. He sang "Happy Birthday" to her as she blushed. They cut huge pieces of cake for each other and stuffed themselves.

The presents were an odd collection. The first was a box of Crayolas and two coloring books, farm animals in one, Barney the Dinosaur in the other. The next was a bottle of wine with a set of Rook cards taped to its neck. Then a very fashionable t-shirt marked "Monticello Mama," male size XL. The last was a Monopoly game that looked as if it had been sitting on a shelf for twenty years. David had left the price on the box—$2.75. It *had* been on the shelf that long. Sylvia was enchanted and giggled as she opened each treasure.

All afternoon they colored and played cards and went through two complete games of Monopoly. David was kind, but Sylvia was utterly ruthless as a landlord. She won both times, easily.

At six o'clock he opened the wine.

"We'll have to drink this here," he said, filling two gaudy plastic champagne stems.

"Why?"

"Because we're going to have dinner at Star City with a religious cult. They don't allow alcohol," he said seriously.

"You are kidding, right?"

"Nope, I'll pick you up at your front door at seven o'clock sharp. Dress is casual."

He turned, walked through their shared door, and locked it behind him.

Sylvia felt silly getting ready for a "date" after all they'd been through, but she fussed with her makeup and hair as if she were going to her senior prom. She put on a royal blue sweater dress that showed off her figure nicely and piled her hair up on her head, letting wispy ringlets spill off on the sides and down the back.

At seven she heard David leave his room and start the Blazer. A moment later he knocked on her front door and waited. Sylvia frantically primped for the last time at the mirror on the door. When she opened it he looked like an advertisement for men's clothing or a weekend in the Poconos. His hair was neat and brushed back from his face as if he were facing a brisk wind. He wore a pair of dark blue jeans, a hand-embroidered Indian-style turtleneck, and a forest-green cashmere jacket.

She blushed as she watched his eyes roam over her—but it was just what she'd hoped he would do. He took her hand, kissed it warmly, and said, "My dear, if you will allow me to show you to my carriage, we will be off to the cult."

He wasn't kidding. A very strange religious sect operated just south of Star City. The leader controlled every facet of believers' lives—jobs, housing, marriages and (it was whispered), even their fertility. One enterprise the cultists did collectively and extremely well was cook fish. The women worked in the kitchens and washrooms, the men wore aprons and waited on the tables. It was quite possibly the best fish fry in the South, and people from all over the state flooded the place.

Thus Sylvia finished out the most wonderful birthday she could remember. Until the meal was almost over. She excused herself and headed to the restroom, which was in a separate building. She was following some women from Little Rock. Sylvia was startled to overhear one woman ask the other if she had heard about Bill Faulkner and his wife?

"No, what happened?"

"I heard at the club that she came in from Washington, took the kids to her mother's house in Maumelle, and disappeared. She was supposed to be back in a few hours but she has never shown up."

"What do they think happened? Is something wrong?"

"We listened to a local talk radio station on the way down here tonight, and the host said it could all be connected to Eric Grant's suicide.

Can you imagine? No one's seen Bill for several days either. Word is he'll be indicted any day now, and they're afraid *she* might be . . . dead."

"My God!" the other woman said. "I hope not! How much more of this hell is our state going to have to endure? That poor family!"

Sylvia dawdled so that she could hear their whole conversation. The fear that had been diminishing rushed back on her with a vengeance. Her fairy-tale birthday crashed around her. Sylvia was trembling badly by the time she got back to the table. David saw the fear on her face before she ever sat down.

"Sylvia! What in the world happened? Are you all right?"

She couldn't answer. David frantically searched the room with his eyes, but saw nothing unusual. Then he took her hand.

"Please tell me!" he whispered.

"We have to go. There's something that I have to tell you, but not here. Please!" she begged.

They left immediately. Halfway back to the motel she finally managed to tell him about the conversation she'd overheard, and even then she had trouble remembering some of the details.

"I don't understand, Sylvia. What's the deal with Bill and Prescott's people up there? How are they involved?" He could see the trepidation on her face in the dim green light from the dashboard.

"I haven't told you all I know, David. I'm afraid this has gone way too far. You see, Bill's boss, Eric Grant, was one of the people who set up the blood deal in the first place. Bill told me he was killed—because he was ready to talk. They made it look like suicide. Bill stumbled into this in Eric's files. He wasn't involved. But now he and his poor wife are right in the middle of this mess. Those women said Bitsi is missing. Maybe they killed her too. Bill is terrified. He begged me not to tell anyone."

David pulled to the side of the country road, turned off the ignition, and thought for a minute.

"So someone is making sure that this story doesn't go any further . . . period. And that someone suspects that Bill knows too much."

"That's right, David. They'll do anything to cover it up. David—that 'someone' is now the president of the United States."

The words tasted vile in her mouth. They sat in silence for a moment, driving along the country road, wondering how it was that they had been sucked into something so ... big. So high in the government. When David finally spoke again, he had all the weight of the world on his shoulders. His voice was mechanical.

"The governor of Arkansas and some of his political cronies set up a blood-collection scam through the state prison. They used narcotics—purchased with state money—to pay off the inmates, so the ones who became the regulars of the program were mostly drug addicts or sex slaves or both. They were the highest-risk group. The last you would want for a donor program.

"Naturally the blood was contaminated. Somehow, they foisted off this tainted blood, and it got into the system. Thousands of people, *thousands,* were infected with hepatitis and AIDS. But they were outside the United States, so no one down here heard about it." David's voice had got louder and now it cracked with emotion. He finally understood the whole story as he put it in his own words.

Sylvia impulsively reached over and touched his neck.

"Hundreds, maybe thousands of these people have died. They are still dying. My son Zack could die. Deidra could die. And they cover it up! Of the men we *know* were involved, two are dead. Grant was murdered. Bennie was literally frightened to death. This Dr. Warren has escaped to Central America and probably wishes he had died in his bed. And the last one we know about is standing in the Oval Office at the White House. He's the one covering up at all costs—to save his rotten political ass!"

An almost childlike look of disbelief settled on David's face. He stared at Sylvia as if she could wake him from a nightmare.

"Just so he can ensure his reelection? Is this the truth, Sylvia? Is this why my dad was murdered? For Bob Prescott's political career?" His voice was cold with anger.

"Yes! David! Oh, I'm so sorry! It's all true. That's the only way it makes sense. What are we going to do?" she begged, gripping his arm.

David had no answer. He felt an old urge to tear into this fight like a madman and the devil take the hindmost. But he had to have a chance, and this was so big. And now there was Sylvia to care about. He squeezed her hand and forced a smile.

"I think we're safe right now. We're going to lie low and talk to Ricky. I'll be thinking this thing through. We can probably make some decisions tomorrow. We'll figure out what to do. Together. For now we're fine. Okay?"

"Okay." Sylvia let out a long sigh and he felt the tension go out of her hand. She looked away as if in some thought, but turned back and kissed him on the cheek.

"I haven't thanked you yet for my birthday party. In spite of everything, it was the best birthday I've ever had."

THIRTY-THREE 〰〰〰〰〰〰〰

MARCH 6, 1995
COPÁN RUINAS
HONDURAS

F INDING DR. FRANK WARREN WASN'T HARD, JUST A MATTER OF GIV-
ing Ramone the name, approximate dates, and a state. Within
hours, Ramone had accumulated a wealth of knowledge on the
man. By using the Internet, a couple of illegal link-ups, and some
extremely shady contacts, he had unfolded the doctor's most personal
information. Now Ricky knew his address in Arizona, his age, social security number, passport number, bank account balances and numbers,
credit card numbers, vehicle license number, and the PIN for his ATM
card. They had a list of all of his affiliations, magazine subscriptions,
parking tickets, L. L. Bean shirt size, and even his blood type.

By following up on his subscriptions to *Traguluz* and *Prisma,* both
Honduran magazines, they tapped into Warren's connection at Copán.
Telephone records showed two recent calls to a lawyer in Tegucigalpa.

Further checking found information and balances on his Honduran bank accounts, including a ranch account, with balances for that day.

The records showed that sixty thousand U.S. dollars had just been transferred from Arizona to Tegucigalpa. The physician had called that morning to cancel his subscription to the newspaper and had charged to his Visa card six months' worth of cleaning services, guaranteeing that someone would monitor and maintain his house in Phoenix. Frank Warren was getting ready to jump.

Ramone quickly found that a Dr. Frank Warren had often flown to the airport in La Ceiba on Lasca Airlines. Rick had him check all current bookings, but found no trace of him on any commercial flight. Ramone then checked for flight plans filed with the FAA from the Phoenix area to La Ceiba. These are required, for safety reasons, and Ramone found the one he wanted almost immediately. A flight plan had been filed for a Twin Beech Baron from Phoenix to La Ceiba. He would have about six hours to beat the good doctor there. Ricky boarded a commercial jet an hour later, but Javier stepped off when it landed.

A short flight from New Orleans to San Pedro Sula put Javier within forty-five minutes of the La Ceiba airport. Roberto Carrillo, an old comrade-in-arms, met him at the airport. Roberto was an unassuming man, slight of build and almost delicate, who could lose himself in any crowd. His Castilian ancestry showed in his facial structure and demeanor, but his agate-blue eyes suggested an English pirate somewhere in his Bay Island lineage. His soft voice belied the skills that commanded top fees as an international adviser, the kind of adviser who rarely attends conferences and almost never wears a business suit. Like Javier, he had been known (by a select few) to offer professional advice from the barrel of an H&K MP5 machine gun, and he had served as Javier's second lieutenant for many years. The man never seemed to tire and was as resourceful as the shrewdest quartermaster in any army.

Javier and Roberto had to wait much longer than they'd expected at the La Ceiba airport. But their vigil was rewarded. The doctor was easy to spot loading his bags and a briefcase. He seemed relaxed and not on his guard, as if he thought he had reached safety. They followed him at a respectful distance for four hours, winding their way up the poor mountain roads to the ruins at Copán. When at last the taxi turned through a huge entrance gate, they knew they had tracked him to his lair.

For days they watched him putter around his hacienda, never leaving the grounds. There was little to learn of his habits. Javier and Roberto knew he would emerge when his contacts confirmed that he was safe. They began to set their trap.

Copán is one of the best-preserved and archeologically important sites in the Western Hemisphere. It was a center of Mayan political and religious functions. Its magnificent pyramids and temples rival those found anywhere in the world. Though the forest of vines and trees had been stripped off many years ago, it was a daily battle to hold them off and keep the stonework visible. It must have been so for the Mayans, too.

Archeologists were still digging at the site, but most of it remained open to the public. When he wasn't on watch, Javier explored the whole area, climbing and crawling through the many passageways and chatting with villagers who lived nearby. Meanwhile, Roberto made contacts everywhere. He prowled as far as La Entrada, some sixty kilometers away, forever mingling with the locals. Wherever the alcohol was flowing he made friends and learned the secrets of the streets and jungle barrios. Listening was one of Roberto's special talents.

"Javier, did you know that the symbol for the city of Copán is el vampiro, the vampire bat?" asked Roberto as he poured a cerveza for his friend.

"I wondered about that. Today, in one of the ball courts, I saw those ugly bastards carved into everything. Hey, did you know they sacrificed the *winning* team when two cities competed in their ... their fucked-up style of soccer?"

"Si, muy sangriento. The Mayan religion was built around blood sacrifices to the gods. It was the only way they could ensure that the seasons would continue and the sun would keep to its path in the sky." Roberto described an arc through the air with his dripping bottle. He paused. "I guess it worked," he chuckled.

The sun was even then setting over the blue mountains. The first hint of the cool evening air slipped in through the open sides of the cantina. The two men sat under the eaves sipping slightly chilled beer.

"Do you not think it strange that our friend has come here, of all places in the world, to feel safe? Maybe he is at one with los hombres ancianos, the old ones who still haunt these temples." Javier voiced his thought quietly. His eyes, without interest, watched two completely naked toddlers play with a lizard on the dirt floor. "I heard them last night, you know."

Roberto stiffened and turned slowly to look at Javier. "You heard what?"

"I heard the ancient ones, los hombres santos ancianos. I heard them in our fire." Javier still stared at the children.

"No, Javier, don't start with this stuff. You know I don't want you to talk like that. It really makes me nervous. When you talk to spirits, I think you are having fantasies. Or worse." Roberto had heard this before and never got used to it.

Javier shrugged his shoulders and turned to finish his beer. The silence was heavy.

"What did they say?" Roberto demanded.

"Who?"

"Los hombres santos ancianos, what did they say?" Roberto was on the edge of his chair.

"I thought you didn't believe. I thought—," Javier joked, but Roberto was in no mood for it.

"Just tell me, okay? Just tell me before I go loco, Javier. I never know when you joke. Finish your story."

"I heard the ancient ones calling for a gift. I heard them calling for me to bring them an offering, a life. They said the stones of their altar cry out like a voice parched from thirst. They would honor us if we quench their thirst with blood and appease their craving." Ricky was talking with his eyes closed, his voice barely audible, not a trace of humor on his face. Roberto felt a shudder run from the skin on his head down to his buttocks. Suddenly, Ricky opened his eyes and spoke in a hush. "I have some things that I will need you to get for me. One of them may take some doing. We will need them tomorrow night. Tomorrow we will bait the trap."

"Si, mi amigo."

~~~~~~~~~

On watch, the next evening, they studied Frank Warren through binoculars. He paced about his courtyard for some while, disappeared into the house, then reemerged dressed in a khaki safari suit, with every nicety a Phoenix haberdasher could provide. He might have stepped out of a J. Peterman catalog—except for one thing. The pistol in a hip holster. He hadn't completely given up his paranoia.

Warren headed for his jeep. Javier exchanged a glance with Roberto. "It's time for you to get our bait. With that outfit we know where he is going. Do your best acting job and be damn careful. I'll be in the shadows, as close as I can get."

He patted Roberto's shoulder and headed back to the village.

~~~~~~~~~

Javier had guessed the doctor's destination correctly. A restaurant and bar just off the village square catered to the young crowd. Copán Ruinas had become a popular attraction for many worldly teenagers who wanted to backpack Central America.

The little cabana served up American-style burgers and MTV-style music for the Eurotrash, the Americans, and the few local kids.

It was jumping when Warren found a table near the back of the palapa. Kids were threshing around to the music, downing cerveza and burgers, and talking all at once in English and broken Spanish. Roberto, looking slightly uncomfortable, walked into the room just behind Warren. It was part of his act, but it was also exactly how he felt. Javier had asked him to do something he would never do for anyone else. He took a seat in the back, near Warren.

About five minutes later, a very attractive young man entered the room and began looking around, searching for someone. He was thin and striking, with large fawnlike eyes. He was nineteen but could pass for a fourteen-year-old. His full head of dark, finely styled brown hair had been streaked and lightened on the ends. Eventually he spotted Roberto, gave a quick wave, and slid through the crowd over to his table.

Back in New Orleans Ramone had discovered that Warren was a

long-time member of the MMBA, the Men Mentoring Boys Association, a group that advocated legalizing sexual relationships between men and young boys who already knew they were gay. Ramone knew all about the organization, although he swore that he was not a member. This information had given Javier the idea for his snare.

The elegant young man played his hand across Roberto's shoulder and down his arm as he took a seat opposite. Warren couldn't miss the action; it was being acted out right under his nose.

Roberto and the boy huddled and smiled, cooing secretly and hardly looking up when the waiter brought their beer and burgers. Halfway through the meal, Roberto burst into angry, rapid-fire accusations. He ranted and stormed about the boy cheating on him, then threw his french fries in his face. The young man burst into tears. Roberto threw a wad of limpera on the table and stomped out of the room.

The boy had been instructed not to warm up too quickly if Warren made a move. Warren didn't. The boy sat there as long as he could, snuffling now and then, before the beer got to his bladder. He wound his way through the crowd in search of a bathroom. He was pleased when the man in the crisp khaki outfit stepped up beside him at the long urinal trough. His fee for this acting job depended on results. The fish had taken the bait.

Warren smiled at the boy and handed him a handkerchief to dry his tears, then asked him in fumbling Spanish if he was okay.

"I speak English too, sir," the boy said.

"Oh! I see you do. Are you from this area?" Warren asked.

"Si. I go to school here in Copán Ruinas. My family lives many miles from here. I live with my aunt." The boy blew his nose into the handkerchief.

"Was that man in there your uncle?" Warren asked.

The boy acted slightly surprised, and then hurt.

"No. He was ... a friend. A cruel friend."

"I happen to know how to be a friend, a good friend. Would you let me?" Warren was almost drooling.

"Forgive me, sir, but I barely know you. Forgive me if I am a little afraid."

The boy was playing it perfectly. Warren smiled out from under his safari hat and reached over and patted his shoulder. "Maybe we can spend some time together this evening. You will see for yourself that I am indeed a good friend. It is a lovely night."

"Yes, I guess that is all right, sir."

"Would you like more beer and food now?" Warren gestured back to the cabana.

"Gracias, but I could not eat more. And I'm afraid my friend may come back ... I want to leave here. Shall we go to the ruins? I could show them to you. They are beautiful by the moonlight and I know them well." The boy reeled in his fish like a pro.

"Well then, my little friend, let me pay my bill and we'll be off to explore." Warren beamed and whistled a tune as they walked back through the cabana and then, together, left the rowdy party behind them in the night.

When they passed him on the footpath leading into the ruins, Javier slipped from his hiding place in the dark jungle and followed. He felt intensely alive. The hairs on the back of his neck and arms were bristling. He could smell everything, the heavy sweet smell of the jungle, the boy's perfume, the beer on his breath, the lust on Warren's. He was a silent liquid moonshadow.

It felt vitalizing to be back in his element, to stretch his muscles and test his senses. It had been eighteen months since Javier's last job and he realized now how much he had missed working. And then he thought of Zack. A blackness worked its way up from the root of him and he fought back the urge to spring on his prey right here and now. He had to follow his plan, to the letter.

The boy took his time and worked his way past the enormous ceiba tree that guarded the entrance to the biggest ball court. Then he started climbing the steps of the most ornate temple. Warren had a sense of climbing up through clouds as they ascended above the mist of the thick foliage that surrounded the stairs. He was amazed to feel how rapidly the temperature dropped when they broke through the canopy. Although the climb was strenuous, he was invigorated by the night and, of course, by the ... anticipation.

Occasionally the boy paused to speak softly to Warren and tell him about the Mayans who had built these structures. When they cleared the last few steps, they found themselves under the reconstructed arches at the peak, arches carved to represent in stone the jaws of a jaguar. A round stone altar was set directly under them.

"This is the temple of the highest priests. Only the holiest of all were allowed under its roof—and, of course, their slaves."

The boy was peering back into the rooms of the inner sanctum, the holy of holies for the ancient Mayans. The moon lit the room in a mysterious way. Its carved stelae, highlighted by the glow, seemed to come alive.

"I didn't realize they had slaves," Warren said. He stepped up very close to the boy and put his arm around his shoulders.

"They were slaves only for a short time—from one to three weeks. Many of them were young men kept here for the priest's personal uses until he decided it was time to sacrifice them. Then they became victims. The Mayan writings tell us that the priests treated them very badly and made them perform horrible duties."

The boy could hear Warren's breath coming faster and hotter on his neck.

"You see the holes along these walls? There are pairs at arm level and at ankle level. The young boys had to back up to them to stick their arms through these holes. The priests would then tie their hands on the backside of the wall. They were naked and helpless. Sometimes their ankles were tied as well." He pointed to a set of holes nearest them. "The experts have never understood why the holes are so far apart between the ankles and the hands. The Mayan people were short, but these are made for someone your size. Try it. I'll bet your hands will go in there without your having to strain."

The boy smiled seductively. Frank Warren smiled back, his eyes a mere slit as he slid his hands into the dark orifices.

"What did the priests do once they had their slaves in this position? Should I be naked and helpless, too?" the doctor asked in his huskiest voice. At that moment he felt the cold plastic band ratchet around his wrists, locking him to the wall. Abruptly, his raging, burning lust gave way to cold, paralyzing fear.

Roberto stepped out from behind the wall, moonlight making his eyes lighter than ever, and Warren caught his breath. "What in the—? Oh, no! ... Look, friends, I am not into threesomes. I like my privacy. So you unfasten my hands and you two can get someone else. This is a mistake."

Roberto calmly handed the boy an envelope and told him in Spanish that the two tickets to Brazil for him and his boyfriend were in the packet with his money. His employers were pleased to add a bonus for an excellent job. The boy pocketed the equivalent of two years' salary and bounded down the steps of the great temple.

Warren called after him, "Wait! Please don't leave. Tell your friend in Spanish that I don't want to play like this. This is a mistake. Please tell him, son! Please!"

"Shut up!" Roberto said, turning back to his captive.

"You speak English! Good! This has been a mistake, my friend! I don't like this bondage stuff! I—"

"I said *shut up*. Now. Or I will cut your tongue out as you stand at that wall. You have some questions to answer, but they are not for me to ask. I simply advise you to answer them truthfully. You are no longer in a good position to lie."

Roberto disappeared behind the wall, and a black silence fell over the temple. Warren could hear only the wheezing of his own breath and the pounding of his pulse. He had no idea what was going on, nothing! He didn't know whether to cry, scream, or pray.

From an identical opening in the opposite wall stepped a compact dark figure. Approaching Warren, it passed through pools of light and became a man. He could be seen to be wearing a long red sarong, fringed at the bottom. There was not a whisper of noise as this man moved across the temple pavement.

Warren felt depths of fear and panic that he had never imagined. It was as if he were held immobile in the web of a giant, hideous spider. He sensed doom the way a rabbit senses the hawk, long before it ever sees dark death streaking down from the sky.

The man before him looked like some ancient priest. His chest was thick and painted with oily red slashes and circles. His arms were strong, muscles and veins alike bulging in the dim light. He stopped with his head still shrouded in the shadows. His voice came from blackness. "Do you have any sins to confess so that I might judge you fairly?" The cold voice reverberated from the stones of the temple. Haunting echoes repeated the question a second time and a third before dying out.

Warren had to reach deep to find any voice at all, and the one he found was thin and tremulous. Was this a nightmare? But he was more awake than he had ever been in his life.

"I think there is a ... mistake," he squeaked. "I am a doctor, an American doctor. If it's money you want, I—"

"Here, you are nothing. You are the round stone balanced on the pyramid. You are fated to fall—if one way, to life. If the other, to death. Will you confess your sins?"

"Wha ... what are you going to do to me?"

"Bring forth your sins for cleansing," the voice said. "Did you sell diseased blood during your years as a doctor?"

Warren felt his throat close. He hadn't escaped at all. These were his persecutors from home. How did they find him? It was Prescott—the bastard, Bob Prescott. He never gives up.

"I ... I never sold bad blood. No. I was a doctor! I was *saving* lives!"

"The stone has tilted toward death. Now you must tell *two* truths to bring it back into balance." The priest intoned, still standing obscured in the dark. "You will name all of those who benefited with you from the sale of this blood. Do not omit anyone or the stone will tilt further!"

"My God! But ... but most of them are *gone*! There was Bennie, my partner. He was the one who screwed everything up. And ... Look, I won't say *his* name. Okay? I was just a little part of a big operation! If you'll let me explain a couple of things to you, you'll see that I'm not a problem for you! I'll never tell anyone about this shit! Just leave me alone, and I swear your boss will never hear from me again!" Warren was begging for his life now, convinced that he was dealing with the operatives who killed Grant.

"My boss?"

"Yes! I mean, we had this working arrangement with his administration when he was governor! We never meant to hurt anyone. He made a buck, we made a buck. The buyers made a good deal. Look at it this way:

If the Canadians can't get any information, *no one* has any problems. They'll never find us. It's all covered. No Americans got sick!"

A deep moan poured out of his interrogator, and Warren saw the fringes of the sarong move as if in a light breeze. "*His name!*" the man snarled.

"Okay, okay! I'll play your game ... Prescott ... President Bob Prescott! A lot of us shared in the profits, and his administration benefited too. I swear, that's the last time you'll ever hear me say his name. I'm not like Eric Grant! I *know* how to forget this shit! It doesn't mean anything to me. I hardly ever think of it!" Had he won a point with the man in the shadows?

In the long silence that followed, Warren could hardly breathe. The figure moved closer, passing through the shafts of moonlight, only to pause again some five feet away. The face was still dark but the voice was chillingly close.

"Can you name all the people who have suffered and died to bring you your profits?"

"Well, I ... no ... The blood went to—"

"Can you name *one?*"

"I ... uh ... I don't see how ..."

"I'm thinking of one. Can you name *him?* Can you tell me that *he* doesn't mean anything to you?" The figure stepped closer. "Can you tell me you did anything to save this one life? Can you? ... Tell me his name, and tell me how you are going to stand by his bed and tell him stories and hold his hand until he draws that last breath ... then I will forgive you."

The voice raged, but the form was motionless.

"I can't! I can't! But if you will take me to him, I *will* do all those things. I'll do even more. I'm a doctor. I can help him. Please, please let me try!" Warren was sobbing like a huge, heartbroken child.

"Just one more question," the figure said, suddenly stepping into the light only inches from Warren's tearstained face. "Do you know this face?"

He had to look directly at the creature, the taut skin, the jutting jaw, the blood-red scar blazing across one cheek. And the eyes. His eyes were narrowed like a wolf's, filled with the evil yellow glow of the moon, and the razor-cut of a mouth was smiling at him. It was more than he could bear!

"No, no! I don't know you!

"Well, know me now. Because this is the face of everyone who died and all those who suffered because of your sins. This is the face of your death!"

The face pulled back. Warren drew a breath in order to scream, but Javier hit him with the straightened tips of his fingers just above the notch in his neck. The scream never made it past his lips. Warren fell, partially paralyzed, hanging now by his wrists, which were twisted grotesquely behind him.

Roberto, behind the wall, snipped the plastic strap. Javier caught the sagging body and lifted its bulk, tossing the stunned man onto the Mayan altar stone. He flipped the man onto his back, knocking his breath away again. The revolver slid from Warren's custom-tooled holster and clattered across the stones.

Javier glared down into Warren's eyes while Roberto bound his hands and feet to the stone. Warren's body was draped like a cloth across the altar, so tightly strapped that his chest ached to taste another breath of air, just one more breath.

Roberto handed Javier the black obsidian knife he had purchased from a grave robber in the village. Then he turned and walked silently down the temple steps and into the darkness.

With a primal scream that shattered the night, Javier tore the sweat-soaked shirt from his victim's chest. He opened the man with a plunge of the glass blade, just below the rib cage. A spasm shook the dying body as he reached up through the mouth of the wound and ripped the pounding heart from its sack. A gush of steamy air and a spray of blood spurted into the night.

Javier held the heart above his head in bloody hands as if to show it to the moon. Then let it drop—still pounding—to hear it thud and roll down the carved steps of the temple.

Then Javier the priest ... Ricky, the father ... bent to look into the wide eyes of his still-living sacrifice. Tears came when he said it. "His name is Zack!"

THIRTY-FOUR 〜〜〜〜〜〜〜

MARCH 7, 1995
MONTICELLO, ARKANSAS

THREE DAYS AFTER HIS FATHER'S FUNERAL, DAVID AND SYLVIA WERE still at the motel in Monticello, but they had turned in the key to one of the rooms. While they waited anxiously to hear from Ricky, they allowed their romance to move forward. Their feelings for each other had grown beyond both the mutual attraction and the dependence on each other that had thrown them together. Now they were warmed by new love and found each other's arms. It was a strange sort of honeymoon, yet glorious. Their days swung wildly between periods of fear and depression and anger about the storm of events, and timeless moments of mad happiness and rapture. They comforted each other and lay for hours wrapped in each other's arms, speaking their hearts.

Sylvia had persuaded David to drive her to a pay phone in Pine Bluff so she might try Bill Faulkner's priority number again. David worried that it could be dangerous but Sylvia persisted. She was worried about Bill and couldn't bear another day's silence about the fate of Mary Elizabeth. Sylvia hit upon using the name of their favorite high school teacher, a woman who'd been dead for years. If Bill got the message, he would know who had sent it. The phone was answered on the first ring. The woman's voice was brisk and unfamiliar.

"The White House."

"Yes, hello. I'm calling for Bill Faulkner. Is he in?"

"Just a moment, please."

Sylvia waited nervously, one eye on the traffic passing the booth. A man's voice came over the line. "Hello. Who's calling?" he asked abruptly.

"This is Katherine Hardy. I'm calling from Arkansas. I would like to speak with Bill Faulkner, please," she said very naturally.

"Ms. Hardy, may I ask where you obtained this phone number?"

She made herself sound as brisk and no-nonsense as the real Miss Hardy. "Mr. Faulkner gave me this number. If you will just tell him I'm on the line, I'm sure that he will want to talk to me."

"I'm sure that he will, ma'am. If you will give me the number from which you're calling, I will see if Mr. Faulkner is free to call you right back."

The man had her. She wasn't going to get anywhere without exposing her location. "Just give him a message, please. The name, again, is Katherine Hardy. He has the number. Thank you," she said, hanging up before he could reply.

In desperation, she dialed her mother, who kept up with every story in Little Rock. Her mother indeed had news. Mary Elizabeth Faulkner had suffered a bad case of nerves and had disappeared to a friend's house in Vail, Colorado. Mary Elizabeth's parents were the only ones who knew about this at first. Now there was a trickle of news. Reports were that Bitsi was doing better and had sent for the kids. Local gossip also had Bill resigning his post at the White House in the next few days, probably in the face of charges of obstructing justice. It had to do with moving files out of Eric Grant's office.

Sylvia's mother did not miss the chance to gloat about her divorcing Bill when she did. Politicians, she said, rarely made good husbands, not since Harry Truman. She was about to launch into the Trumans' domestic bliss when Sylvia excused herself as gently as she could.

Sylvia was still lost in thought about Bill and Bitsi when she got back to the Blazer. David was glued to another pay phone, across the parking lot of the convenience store. He talked interminably. Sylvia bought them a couple of Cokes and he was still talking when she had finished hers. She was beginning to worry. Whom could he be talking to for so long? He had called his family several times from the motel, but apparently this was something private. Something he didn't want her to hear. That seemed ominous.

When David returned, she told him about her scary exchange at the White House number. They discussed the ramifications of Bill's pending resignation. Chances were, he would at least lose his license to practice law, and might face jail. The news about Mary Elizabeth was better, anyway.

"*You* sure had a nice long conversation," Sylvia finally said. "I thought maybe you got your finger stuck in the coin return."

"No, I just had to go over some technical stuff with a business associate," David said, disappointing her curiosity.

He put his hand on her knee. "I'm going to have to go home for a few days. I've got to take care of some things there and check on Zack. I'll be moving fast, so I really would like you to go to New Orleans now and I'll meet you there in a few days.

"I've got it set up. Rick will find you there. He's a great tour guide—knows all the out-of-the-way places—but you'll be safe and you'll have a blast. I'll meet the two of you there.... Honey ... we'll make some plans then, some plans for our future. Okay?" There was love in David's smile. He leaned over to kiss her.

"Well, if that's what you want, David. I really don't want to be away from you, but ... how will I get there? Where will I stay?"

"You have a room at a place an old friend of mine owns, the Corn Stalk Guest House. There'll be no name on the register. I don't expect any trouble, but there will be a watch at all times. Let's go get packed. I'll take you to El Dorado to catch a shuttle flight as soon as we hear from Ricky." David was turning onto the highway, heading back to their room. "You'll love the Corn Stalk. There are plaster cherubs as big as sumo wrestlers on the walls." He grinned. "Nice four-poster beds," he laughed.

"Sounds kind of kinky to me, if you want to know the truth. First you're sending me off to the romance city of the South to spend a few days with another man, and you're putting me up in a hotel with profane pink love gods over the bed," she giggled. "Do I get roses? A box of chocolates? A traveling salesman?"

David just rolled his eyes.

In their room, David checked for messages and Sylvia turned on the television. The talking heads on the tube were discussing a sudden shift in President Prescott's position on federal funding. There was a ruckus brewing in both parties. In a move guaranteed to garner more conservative support, the president was advocating slashing several federal programs, including one, that provided the bulk of the money for AIDS research. The chairman of Prescott's own party could not be cornered for a comment. Sylvia turned and looked across the bed to see whether David had heard.

He had just hung up the phone, and the look in his eyes frightened her. After a moment he got up, went into the bathroom and closed the door. Sylvia had no time to worry. The phone rang and she answered it as David had instructed her to: "Hola," she said in Spanish.

"Hola, como estas?" the husky voice asked back.

"I'm sorry. I've just exhausted my Spanish. This is Sylvia," she said.

"This is Rick." The perfect Latin accent switched to an East Texas drawl. "You mean my old buddy hasn't driven you crazy yet? That medicine must be working on him," Ricky joked.

"He's anxious to talk to you. Just a minute."

David was back in the room, and she handed him the phone.

"You okay?" he asked immediately.

"Yeah. Hey, Dave, I'm sorry I had to do you like that, but this is *my* game down here. You would have been a fish out of water. How's Zack?"

"He had a rough week, but I talked to him just this morning and I think he's feeling a little better. Where's Warren?" David already knew the answer.

"Let's just say he ... is permanently retired. He made a full confession before ... well, before we finished our conversation. Davey, I hate to tell you who's behind all this. I know who let the hit go out on your dad."

"I know too, Rick. We need to talk, soon, figure out our next step. But I've got to go home for a day or two," David said.

"What do you need me to do? I'll be in New Orleans tomorrow morning."

"Good. I'm sending Sylvia down there. She'll be on a morning hop-over from El Dorado. I think they still land at the old airport. She's got a room reserved with Winston at the Corn Stalk. If she doesn't see you at the airport, she'll take a taxi to the Quarter. You, by God, watch her, Rick!" David glanced down at Sylvia, who was hanging on every word and had a look in her eye that would melt any male heart. "I couldn't bear to think of some good-looking Cajun guy running off with her down there." He winked at Sylvia. "I don't know if I can trust you either, buddy, but I guess you'll do."

"Hey, I'm not responsible if she falls for me. Probably happen in the first five minutes. But how am I going to know what she looks like?"

"Oh, you'll guess which one she is. She'll be the only woman passenger who doesn't run away screaming when she sees your ugly mug," David laughed. "Or you could just look for the most gorgeous woman in the world."

"Damn, that was plain old mean! Tell her I'll be there. Sounds like I'll enjoy it, too. When are you coming down?" he asked.

"Dunno, day or two, as soon as I can. Thanks, buddy. Thanks for everything."

THIRTY-FIVE ~~~~~~~~~~~~~~~~~~~~

E DWARD MARSH THREADED HIS WAY DOWN THE MAIN CORRIDOR OF the West Wing of the White House. Since Eric Grant's suicide, the halls were a meeting place for the exchange of the latest theories explaining his death.

As he approached, the little groups in the corridor would change the subject, turn away or simply ignore him. In all the months he spent with this bizarre administration you would think that he would get used to them—but he hadn't. They still made him physically sick.

Marsh was the head of the Secret Service, having served over twenty years with the Treasury Department under four presidents. He was the typical federal agent, regulation haircut and medium starch in his shirts. There was only the slightest invasion of fat around his middle and he still walked ramrod straight. His gait was more like that of a man of thirty-five than one of fifty-five. He fought diligently to hide the slight limp caused by his hip wound.

Marsh had made his job his life. He had served presidents and their families to the best of his ability and without the slightest regard for their political views or party. He should have been proud of his position and responsibility, but he wasn't—not today. He was ashamed, frustrated, and disgusted.

Terrorism was on the increase; new drugs were debilitating every level of society; and he had to cope with an administration that discarded every reasonable protective practice ever created for the White House. The clearance passes, for instance, that identified and classified the hundreds of workers in these buildings were normally awarded after the FBI completed an interview and a deep background check. It was standard operating procedure. Most staff members had their applications filled out long before a new administration moved into office.

Once an employee received a permanent pass, he or she could enter through the Secret Service gates and have access to the specific areas for which cleared. The higher up one's rank and the closer he or she was to the president, the higher the level of clearance required.

Now it was chaos. Everyone from the legal department and the First Lady to the president himself had bullied, evaded, and torn down the system. Even now, only about 20 percent of current White House staffers had permanent clearances. Most of the younger ones refused to wear their tags at all. One young lady in a Grateful Dead t-shirt told Marsh that the clearance pass looked stupid with her outfit, so she left it in her drawer. The Youth Crusaders, some people called them.

Every attempt by his department to crack down was derailed. When some workers in the legal department balked at having their briefcases x-rayed and checked at the entry gate each morning, a call came down from the president himself. He said he would compile a list of all those who should be allowed to pass without being checked. Fifty-seven names made that list. That was no kind of control.

The people he was sworn to protect were actually Marsh's biggest problem.

First Lady Stephanie Prescott was a major headache from the first moment. She ran interference for anyone of those on the administrative staff who didn't want to be interviewed by the FBI, insisting that if she chose an employee, then no one could reject her decision. She brought in hordes of new people, often without warning, to work on her domestic programs. Her trick was to raise hell until Marsh agreed to give the newcomers full clearance, even to some of the highest security areas. The safety of the White House had not been jeopardized, it had been gang-raped. And Ed Marsh was ultimately responsible.

From the beginning Mrs. Prescott had insisted on calling the shots. She and the president had a momentous quarrel the night before the inauguration because she laid claim to the vice president's offices. It was unthinkable, except to Stephanie. In fact, she had already brought in decorators to redo the suite. The Secret Service agents who overheard the argument could not believe her profanities and her demands. But she won, hands down.

She forbade any workers to approach her in the halls. Everyone was instructed to turn away and *never* to attempt to follow or talk to her. About six months into the first year, she forbade her Secret Service detail to follow her from office to office. She said she was sick of it. If she saw them looking at her during the day, she'd see to it that they were fired with a full loss of benefits. Federal regulations, as a rule, did not permit such actions, but no one dared call Stephanie's hand. Several times when agents accompanied her to other cities, she ducked into the private car of some old friend and disappeared for two or three days. She despised Marsh's men, and it was obvious that she fomented resentment toward them in the rest of her staff.

The president, too, made their assignment impossible. He bowed to any demands made by senior staffers regarding background clearances. He loved to charge into a crowd without warning, shake hands, and give hugs. Alarmingly, he'd accept any little gift or trinket a fan would offer. Wiser heads had warned him, but he felt that this made him "a man of the people." He wasn't nasty about it as his wife was. He just chose when and how he would ignore his protectors.

About once every two or three weeks, the president indulged in a major insult to his security detail. He would dismiss his bedroom guards early in the evening. Then at 1:00 or 2:00 A.M., he would leave his room and take the stairs to the underground entrance. There he'd meet Jess Peters, a staff adviser from Little Rock, and jump in the back seat of an unmarked official car. They would leave through the security gates on the west side of the White House and then drive to the Grand Regency Hotel, entering through a certain service ramp.

Peters would wait in the car while the president took the service elevator to the eighth floor where he would visit a certain female media star for the rest of the night. He was totally unescorted and therefore totally unprotected. The next morning he and Peters would drive back through the gates, waving at the agents on duty as if they had been out for an ice cream.

The first time Prescott pulled this stunt, Ed Marsh lost four nights of sleep and all respect for the man, but he still honored the office of the presidency. So now Marsh had a special detail charged with monitoring the Grand Regency and secretly providing surveillance during those times when the boss dallied with his very attractive, very obliging lady friend. Such waste was uncalled for and dangerous, and it sure as hell wasn't security.

Marsh had been summoned this morning for a private audience with the president. A lot of outsiders thought there was room for change in the security systems of the White House, but none of them had spent twenty years in his shoes. He had served through two assassination attempts and had taken a bullet during one of them. It was a miracle that no one had made an attempt on this president. Marsh had advised and talked and begged until he was blue in the face. He had even seriously considered resigning, but now—finally—he had some clout behind him.

Eric Grant had supposedly committed suicide with a gun that he had had with him for an entire day. That meant he was carrying a pistol in the White House. He was, of course, one of the many who were allowed to enter without being checked. If the man had been in such a pitiful mental state, then he could have freaked out and turned homicidal. It would have been no trick for him to take the gun into the Oval Office.

The congressional committee in charge of security procedures at the White House had finally got wind of what was going on, and was getting ready to slap the president's hand. This was Marsh's best chance to get Prescott's attention ... please, God ... and implement some immediate changes.

"Hi, Sue Sue. You look super today. How's that little boy doing?" he asked.

Sue Sue was the boss's personal secretary. It was her burden to repair every schedule that he wrecked and to clean up after his innumerable little scrapes. This was an amazing juggling act and she excelled at it. If Sue Sue ever wrote a book about everything she knew at the White House, the president and his whole senior staff would be sunk.

"He's doing just fine, sir. He's already learning his ABCs and he's grown about two feet. Thanks for asking. I think the president is ready for you." She escorted him to the door of the Oval Office.

Marsh entered, not knowing what kind of reception awaited.

"Hi, Ed. Good to see you." Bob Prescott came around his desk to shake hands. "Pull up a chair and get comfortable. We need to talk."

This was unusual. The president didn't like to talk about the business of the Secret Service. He preferred to ignore it. Marsh seated himself and waited.

"I hear the Oversight Committee is getting ready to raise hell. That true?" he asked, his eyes fixed on something out the window instead of meeting Marsh's.

"Yes, sir. That's my take on it. That's why I brought the matter to your attention, Mr. President. Their chairman has requested a status report from the FBI, and they want some of my records as well. I'm here to warn you—again—that we have some major problems. I'm here to offer my services in helping to straighten them out, sir."

"That's good of you, my friend. I look forward to seeing your report to the committee. But I'm going to have to ask you to withhold certain materials that I classify as of a personal and private nature. I'm sure you know what I'm talking about. I'll send you a list, but I also want you to review all documents before submitting them, and to withhold any others that might provoke unnecessary controversy—if you know what I mean. Send any such documents to the legal people for review here."

"Yes, Mr. President, I understand." Marsh wearily leaned his elbows on his knees and dropped his head. His disappointment was only too visible.

"These are ... things we need to keep just between us guys, right?" Bob Prescott asked.

"Yes, sir. But that might be very difficult."

"I understand that, Ed. But I want to know that you will give it your most valiant effort. I know how good you are, at your best."

"Thank you, sir. I'll certainly try." Marsh fought down his disgust and looked at Prescott. He had to make his plea. "Mr. President. Excuse me for being forward, but I think now is the time. Sir, we could be in real trouble here. This committee is getting ready to strip your administration—and me—of the power to provide protection for the White House and the First Family. If that happens, Mr. President, it will be the first time in the history of the Secret Service that we have had to forfeit our duties. Personally, sir, I would rather die than have to live through such an embarrassment. I have devoted my life to doing this job and doing it well. I'd like to suggest that we could still turn this thing around, if you will give me the authority to demand some changes. I have to say, those changes would be drastic and severe. We simply have to be far more serious about security.

"To be painfully honest, sir, your staffers have hamstrung my office. *They* are responsible for weakened security in this house. I'm not a political man, Mr. President, but I'm willing to bet you that the Republicans would love to come in and straighten out the internal operation of your home base. I don't want to see that any more than you do." Marsh stood and walked to the edge of the president's desk. He stood at attention and awaited an answer.

Prescott turned to him, meeting his eye now.

"You don't have to try to convince me any further, Ed. I'll give you the authority you're looking for, *but* I want to know everything you're doing and when you're doing it. In detail ... is that clear? Any press releases will be handled here, by my staff, understood?"

"Yes, Mr. President. I appreciate your letting me speak openly."

"Okay, Ed. Oh, by the way ... This will sound a little silly, but I've been getting paranoid about that blowout we have scheduled down in Little

Rock. Don't go overboard, but I want you to be especially sharp on that trip. It's just kind of a gut feeling. You know?" Bob Prescott was looking out the window again.

"Sure, Mr. President. We'll be on it." He wondered what the president had heard. "I hope this means you'll help us devise a schedule you can adhere to when we're exposed."

The president nodded his head, and there was an uncomfortable silence between them. "Ed, is there anything else on your mind?" the president asked.

"Yes, sir, there is . . . It's the First Lady, Mr. President. She doesn't have to *like* us, but she must respect us and let us do our jobs. It has been very difficult working with her. We're ready to put our lives on the line for you and her and Nicole. That's got to count for something." Marsh couldn't believe he had said it.

"In the light of everything that's happened here in the last week, I think you will see a more compliant First Lady, Ed. If not, then she and I will have a talk—God forbid. I may need you there as a referee." Prescott chuckled.

"Whatever it takes, sir. Anything else for me today?" Ed Marsh was still speaking to the president's back.

"Just a personal question, Ed. Back in '81 when you took that bullet, did your opinion of your job change?"

"That is an interesting question, Mr. President. Before I was shot I thought I had the best job in the world. Afterward, when I was in the hospital recovering I saw the president of the United States meeting with Anwar Sadat on the TV news. Then I *knew* I had the best job in the world."

"That's . . . really good to hear. I want you to know I'm grateful, Ed. . . . So what's your opinion of your job now?"

"I'm ready to reclaim it, Mr. President."

Bob Prescott tapped the window with his hand and turned slightly to smile at him.

"Go to it, Director Marsh. I'll see you at the afternoon briefing."

THIRTY-SIX ∼∼∼∼∼∼∼∼

N ORDER FOR DAVID'S PLAN TO WORK, HE HAD TO GET EVERYTHING IN perfect order.

So far things had gone well. He had driven Sylvia to the airport in El Dorado early that morning. He didn't want to stop kissing her at the terminal, but he also didn't want her to suspect anything. It was harder than he had expected to lie to her and to Ricky. But at this moment, much as he longed for her love and trust, his obsession to settle the score burned hotter. He would finish what he had started.

It had become clear to him that no one else would ever be in the same position as he, both motivated and able to avenge the wrong. The mission was his alone. Sylvia was in danger and his dad was dead. This fight had already cost him dearly, and he wouldn't involve those he loved again.

David returned to Little Rock. At the airport he spent a full hour going over his Pilatus. By noon, satisfied that the plane had not been tampered with, he took off and headed west/southwest, no flight plan filed. He was flying VFR—visual flight reference—and he didn't want Ricky or anyone else to know where he was going.

He had already talked to Klaus several times, and would be expected in San Antonio. His course west had to detour around the big controlled air space zones of the larger cities and a couple of military no-fly zones. David stayed low over rolling forests of oak and pine that gradually yielded to the vast scrub country of West Texas.

He let the drone of his engine soothe his mind. His thoughts drifted back to recall all the trips he and Zack had made into the Canadian bush. No one he had ever met was as enthusiastic about the wilderness as that boy. Together they had fished and hunted and trapped for their own use, and introduced hundreds of other people to the soul-expanding beauty of the backcountry. David had dreamed, really *dreamed,* of living to teach a grandson or granddaughter about the joys of the outdoors. When Zack and Deidra got married, he knew it would be just a matter of time. Then he could grow old with his life full even though his love had been taken from him. Dear Suni. He missed her. He always would.

David could handle life alone. He had resigned himself to the fact that he was too old and contrary to attract the kind of woman he would want to have at his side.

But now life had turned upside down. His dream was dust. Zack and Deidra would never be able to have a family unless some miracle drug was found soon. Yet the same cruel stream of events now brought Sylvia into his life. He was perplexed by it all, yet renewed, as if blessed and given a fresh new life.

~~~~~~~~~~~~~

Klaus, still wearing his white lab jacket, met David at the airport in San Antonio at 6:30. He reeked of epoxy resin. To be hugged by Klaus was like being hugged by a polar bear. When David extricated himself, they strolled to the parking lot, Klaus critiquing and characteristically complaining about the way David was walking.

"I never made this prosthesis to be walked on like this. You have gotten into some very bad habits, very bad," Klaus chastised.

"My God, Klaus! I just spent six hours in a plane flying over every jackrabbit and redneck in Texas! It takes a minute to get the kinks out. Give me a break, will you?"

"I'll give you a tune up! That's what I'll give you. Hop in and we'll drive right to the lab. That's a joke, get it? Hop in? *Hop* in ... See?" Klaus's Germanic humor sometimes needed a word or two of explanation.

"Yeah, yeah. So are you and this old rust bucket going to get us to your place? I can't believe it still runs," David said, nodding at the old BMW.

"If not for German engineering, you would still be rolling around in a wheelchair. So watch your mouth." He laughed as if he had said something hilarious.

This familiar bantering with Klaus was refreshing. The man not only cultivated ideas on a daily basis, but could also create them and make them work, make them into realities. Everything seemed to work for Klaus. Right now David needed those precise and special skills. David had an idea of his own. He sketched it out at length to Klaus. After some thought, the big German announced that it would work.

"I was thinking just last night about a wonderful prosthesis I made for you about twenty years ago," Klaus said.

"According to you they're all wonderful," David countered.

"No, no, David. Do you remember that time you were flying in and out of Guatemala and you wanted a special secret compartment to hide a small pistol?"

"Hey! I still have that thing. It was one hell of a design. But now with metal detectors everywhere, they wouldn't fall for that. It would show up too easily. The metal in parts of the prosthesis and the metal of the gun would set off all the alarms."

Klaus smiled.

~~~~~~~~~~~~~~

Klaus had known Zack since he was two months old. He remembered Suni carrying the boy around the lab on a baby board, strapped to her back. He hadn't heard about that practice and it impressed him. But he liked to tease that Zack's development would be arrested because he'd always see where he'd been instead of where he was going. They'd had delicious arguments over that.

Klaus had been fascinated by the baby and all but adopted him into his family. Years later, on learning about Zack's illness, Klaus put David in touch with his closest friend at the University Medical Center in San Antonio—a German chemist doing pioneering research into the AIDS virus and the effectiveness of cutting-edge treatments. Dr. Heisman had taken a strong personal interest in the case and had samples of Zack's blood sent to him regularly for evaluation. Because of the restrictions on his clinical studies, the blood couldn't be sent directly, so Klaus acted as the go-between. The two Germans were great friends to have. David relaxed a bit knowing they were in his corner.

〰〰〰〰〰〰〰〰〰〰

"What would you say if I told you I have perfected an all-plastic-and-carbon prosthesis that will pass through the most sensitive detector?"

"I would say I'd have to wear it to see if it worked," David said skeptically.

"Then what would you say if I told you that—through the marvels of German engineering—I have developed a pistol that will pass through any detector as well?" Klaus asked.

"Are you serious? You have one?" David knew that he did, even as the question spilled out.

"I have manufactured the entire mechanism of high-tech ceramics and carbon reinforcements. The bullets are a caseless design. Caliber, 9 mm. Of course, it is a simple design capable of only two shots, but it is quite accurate," Klaus said with satisfaction.

As far as Klaus knew, David was tracking the men who had run the blood scam—the ones responsible for the agony of Deidra and Zack and thousands of others. He thought David was heading south into Mexico and would have to pass several checkpoints. Klaus was working on a special design so that David could travel without triggering any alarms.

"Are you sure you're comfortable with this, Klaus?" David wanted to know. "This is more than a man should ask of a friend."

"Don't you know about us Germans? We are ruthless men, capable of all sorts of atrocities," Klaus replied with a twinkle. "Seriously, I do this for

Zack and his lovely wife and for you, my friend. But please, never tell him. That's what I ask of you." Klaus reached over and patted David on the shoulder, sealing their secret.

"So do we have the lab to ourselves tonight?"

"Of course. You know I never pay my technicians overtime! They will run over you at five o'clock precisely. Just wait until you see what I have designed for you ... just wait! We have all night to perfect it. All night."

"Undetectable?" David asked.

"Absolutely undetectable, and absolutely deadly," Klaus replied.

THIRTY-SEVEN ~~~~~~~~~

"THIS THING DOESN'T SMELL RIGHT. THE WOMAN REALLY FLEW the coop, I'm sure of it. I've been hanging around for days now and there's no sign of her," Lamar reported into the pay phone. "And guess what her specialty is: She's some kind of expert on the prison system and is always picking fights with the state about it. Does that say it all or what?"

"How close have you checked?" Worley asked him.

"I've been all through her place. Some clothes are gone, no suitcases in the closet. She has so many files on inmates I'd have to spend a year to get anything from them. I punched the redial on her phone and got some boarding house in New Orleans. We'll have to check that out. Now get this, the second time I punched it, you won't believe where it rang."

"God-dammit, Lamar! Just tell me who she called, for Christ's sake." Worley was getting frayed.

"The wife of that old cop you took out. This girl knew them. She called her before she left. She knows, I'm telling you, she *knows*. We've got a problem."

"Fuck! Fuck! Fuck! Just let me think ... shit! Our asses could be on the line, Lamar. Did you find out where she works?"

"Well, yeah. I found some old pay stubs from a battered women's shelter, but she hasn't been there in months."

"What about a car? Did you get her license number?" Worley was trying to think of everything.

"Hell, Worley. Her car's sitting right in front of her condo. That son of a bitch hasn't been touched since I got here. I think we ought to go to New Orleans. Call in Charlie and maybe a couple of others and go down. Hang out near that boarding house and watch for her. That's the best place to start. I got some pictures of her out of her apartment. But you know, I'm pretty sure she's not alone," Lamar said.

"Shit, you don't know the half of it. I've been hanging around down here, trying to see if anyone knows where Dr. Frank went. All these damn old fucks live down here in Phoenix. It's a bitch to get any straight answers. So I'm planning on leaving today to come back and I pick up the local paper this morning and there's his name all over the place!"

"Damn! Did he spill?" Lamar asked.

"Nothing but blood. He's fuckin' dead! The paper says his body was found in Honduras at some old fucking temple back in the jungle."

"You say he's dead?"

"Well, I guess so! The story said he was tied to a rock and split open like a chicken."

"Shit!"

"And get this! They found his fuckin' heart way down the steps of this temple, a long way from his body. Some dogs were fighting over it." Worley spoke excitedly, still unable to believe the story himself. "The police down there are calling it a ritual killing. Everyone's afraid the Indians down there are going to start killing white folks again. But I don't believe that shit for a second. This is *revenge*, man."

"We got company, don't we, Worley? Bad, bad company. This little ol' girl I'm looking for didn't do that shit. If she's in this—and I think she is—then she's got some major help." Lamar was really getting worried. "We need to let the Judge know about this—that something's cooking.

And we need to head to New Orleans, on the fucking double."

"If this is revenge, Lamar," Worley shot back, "there's only one name left on the list: the big guy ... ! Man, they couldn't be dreaming of tapping *him*, could they?"

"I don't know. I don't know. If that story is right, they went all the way down to some banana country to filet Dr. Frank. And that was some job. They may be fucking crazy enough to go for the pres ... the big one. Let's get the Judge to pass this along and put the Secret Service boys on full alert, don't you think?" Lamar asked.

In all his years in his profession, Worley had never killed for revenge. He tried for a moment to imagine the passion of the avenger, the heady victory over a despised enemy, who deserves to die. How it would feel to have that heat in your hands, that power in your heart when you caused someone to draw that final breath. Then the fear struck him, for he had killed many times. He knew at some deep level that he would be the one who would know terror, and pain, and the swift dark. He shivered and pushed the thought away.

"Okay, here's the plan. You call Charlie and tell him to meet me in New Orleans. He needs to come by Little Rock first and get the pictures of the girl from you. Tell him to page me when he gets to the airport, and I'll pick him up. You give me the address and name of that boarding house the girl called. It's a long shot, but we'll watch it for a couple of days." Worley thought for a minute. "You go by and visit with the Judge at his place. Don't call him. I want him to know you're serious. It may not be anything to worry about but everyone needs to be up on it. He needs to get word to our man in the big house."

"Right. So you want me to stay here?" Lamar asked.

"Yeah, just in case," Worley responded.

"Hey, Worley, the girl's a looker. Small, slender, long dark hair, kind of oriental-looking. She'd be a sweet piece," Lamar said. "You won't have any trouble spotting her if you get close."

"Man, I just hate wasting good-looking women. Kind of takes the fun out of it," Worley mused.

"Yeah, me too. But, hey, somebody's got to do it, right?"

"Right," Worley replied absently, feeling the fear again.

THIRTY-EIGHT ~~~~~~~~~~

MARCH 9, 1995

GIANT HOMECOMING BARBECUE KICKS OFF
PRESCOTT REELECTION BID

by Nancy Tidwell

USA News. Little Rock, Arkansas

President Prescott will announce his bid for reelection at an old-fashioned, "down home," southern barbecue Saturday. And all of Little Rock, his old home town, is invited.

"The president loves Little Rock and he loves a party. What could be better?" says campaign spokesperson Martha Travis. "He might even sample a few bites of barbecue," Travis jokes, referring to the president's legendary fondness for the southern specialty.

Twelve master barbecue chefs have been invited from all over the South. The president has "solemnly" announced that he would not dream of slighting any of these great chefs and vows to visit each and every one of their booths for a "generous" sample.

"That's my first promise for the coming campaign and I will keep my word!" he says, flashing his famous grin.

The festivities will be held at Little Rock's Riverfront Park. For weeks, workmen have hurried to build grandstands, TV camera platforms, booths, and all the other needed facilities. The modest park amphitheater has been doubled in size and given a much bigger stage to handle the many stars and political dignitaries expected to attend.

There will be bands and fireworks and mountains of food and drink besides the barbecue. City police expect it will be the largest gathering in Little Rock history. Security will be tight.

"This is where the president's political career began, and this is where he wants his campaign kickoff party. The president was homesick. He wanted to see some of his friends back home, and made the decision to announce his intentions a little early," Marty Travis explains.

"He's never so relaxed and happy as when he comes home to Little Rock. These are his people. He loves to visit with old friends and acquaintances. It reminds him of why he sought high political office in the first place," she says.

Is he going to win? "You bet!" Travis exclaims.

THIRTY-NINE 〜〜〜〜〜〜

MARCH 10, 1995
NEW ORLEANS

"**I**KINDA EXPECTED TO HEAR FROM OLD PEGLEG LAST NIGHT. I WAS hoping we could pick him up today," Ricky said. "Not that I'm getting tired of your company, Sylvia."

"I know. Two days of window shopping are really showing on you," she laughed. "But I'm kind of worried about David. I thought he'd at least call. Is this like him—not to report?"

They were lingering over beignets and chickory coffee in the breakfast room at the Corn Stalk. Sylvia felt as safe with Rick as David had said she would. He was quiet and funny and protective. She thought he was one of the handsomest men she had ever seen—but it was an ... unusual handsomeness, and she could see why David said that Ricky scared some people. He was also a perfect gentleman in a bizarre sort of way, and she was amazed at his command of French and Spanish.

"Well, he's usually dependable, unless women are involved and then he kind of loses his head a little," Rick replied.

"So are there always women swarming around him?" She smiled slyly.

Ricky looked up at the ceiling then counted on his fingers. "Well, including you, that would be a total of ... one. As the old song says, 'He don't get around much anymore.'"

They both laughed.

"I could call the cabin and see if he's left yet," Ricky offered.

"Could you? I know I'm worrying more than I should be, but he scared me when he said goodbye at the airport. It was almost like ... like he might not ever see me again." Sylvia's eyes misted at the memory of their parting at the airport. She focused on her coffee, hoping Ricky didn't notice.

He did. Rick stood up noisily. "Man, I leave the two of you alone for five minutes, y'all get thick and mushy.

"Relax, kid. I'll bet he's already on his way. Be right back," he said over his shoulder, disappearing toward the lobby.

Sylvia's thoughts returned to David and the same old troubling questions. What would they do—what *could* they do against these terrible and shadowy people ... it all seemed insane. She was afraid without knowing what she feared.

She couldn't turn to Bill for advice, and he had been her source of news and good information for years. When David spoke of Prescott she heard the steel in his voice and she believed him. What was he contemplating?

At first she'd thought they'd go public with their information, but with David's father murdered and Eric Grant dead ... she knew that anyone making trouble could actually be killed ... silenced. Fortunately for her state of mind she could not relate that fact to her and David.

Still, even if they went to the press, nothing seemed to stick to this president. He could smile and apologize and slide right out of any predicament. David would never be satisfied to let that happen—but what *would* David consider adequate retribution?

In her musings, Sylvia was blissfully unaware that her name had just been put at the head of a short list of witnesses scheduled to die. Nor that a team of coldly efficient killers was at that moment converging on New Orleans with her whereabouts and photograph in hand.

Ricky was back, pulling his chair up close to the table. "Okay, sweetie, you stay with me on this. Your hotheaded boyfriend has slipped one past us. I checked with his mother up at the cabin and they haven't seen him. Zack says he talked to him this morning, but he assumed he was with me." Ricky frowned. "I'm afraid I know what he's going to do, so I need to make another phone call. You throw your things together. We're leaving."

"But, Ricky, where is—?"

"We'll talk in the car. Now you get packed. I'll be up to get your bags when I get off the phone."

Sylvia sat for a second, letting it all sink in. What did David think he could do? And how would they find him?

Javier called Ramone. He told him to check on flight plans for David's plane. None were filed. Accidents or crashes? Nothing.

"Okay, Ramone, let's see how good you are. What's the next big public appearance for President Prescott?"

"That's easy, Javier. I don't even have to check it. He'll be in Little Rock tomorrow for his reelection bash. He is announcing early. It sounds wonderful, too—fireworks, dancers, barbecue and—. Oh, Javier. You know I don't pry, but ... Porque, mi amigo?" Ramone was scared.

"Just wondered. I'm just fishing. Gotta run. Adios!"

Javier hung up and bounded up the stairs to get Sylvia and her luggage. He had to head to his place first to retrieve some hardware that he hoped he wouldn't need. But the Walther PPK that he carried with him now would be totally insufficient if everything went to shit in Little Rock.

Ricky and Sylvia talked nonstop all the way to his apartment on the outskirts of Metairie. He tried to explain some of what he was planning. He guessed that David was going to Little Rock. They would try to intercept him. She was full of questions about David's past. She realized she knew very little about him. Did he have irrational spells? Had he stalked anyone before? Did Ricky know if he had killed anyone?

"Yes," Ricky sighed, "He killed as many Vietcong as he could one morning in Vietnam. He was an artillery observer and that wasn't his job, really. He did it to save the lives of a platoon of his friends. And he kicked ass!"

Sylvia knew the answer before she asked. "You were there?"

"I was the platoon leader," Ricky replied. "He saved my men." He fell silent for a moment, then added: "He lost his leg. We just barely got him out in time."

Ricky pulled the Yukon into his parking lot and raced inside, leaving the motor running. He asked Sylvia to wait in the truck and listen to the news to see whether they could pick up any details of the campaign kick-off in Little Rock. She was searching for an all-news station on the radio when she saw a car pull up and stop just behind the Yukon. The next moment, the driver's door was jerked open.

A red-faced man with a ball cap and sunglasses hopped into the driver's seat beside her, flashing a badge and smiling. "Ma'am, I'm Sergeant Bill Macklin with the Metairie Police Department. Just sit tight."

Macklin took the wheel, glanced in the mirror, and flipped the ignition. The starter screeched and Macklin realized that the motor was already running. In his haste he turned the key too far the other way and the engine died.

Upstairs, Ricky ran to the window when he heard the truck door slam, then heard the screech. And he knew.

The "sergeant" fumbled with the keys, cursing, and finally restarted the engine.

Sylvia was too perplexed to react. She wasn't afraid of the police, so felt no great alarm. There was just no time to think.

The engine roared and the policeman reached to shift into reverse. The last thing he saw was a tiny metallic glint from a second-story window of the apartment house.

A split second later, a forty-caliber copper-jacketed hollow-point projectile shattered the windshield and fragmented into Sergeant Macklin's right lung. The next two bullets hit his chin and left eye, blowing pieces of bone and brains onto the dash and into the back seat.

Sylvia reflexed instinctively into a fetal position and slid down onto the floor, terrified but unable to scream. Paralyzed, she smelled the blood and flesh in the cab and heard a distant squeal of tires. She irrationally expected to hear sirens at any moment, but prayed Ricky would come.

In a moment, Ricky was there, helping her up. He had the uncanny vision of a marksman and he knew she hadn't been hit. The tears finally came and Sylvia fell into his arms, sobbing.

Rick did his best to comfort her but there was no time. He slipped gently from her grip, then moved like a cat. He threw his bag into the back of the truck, then grabbed Macklin's jacket and heaved the body over the seat, onto the back floorboards. All the while he spoke to Sylvia, soothing her in a ceaseless, steady, calm voice.

"Hey, sweetie, it's Rick. I'm back and everything will be fine. This bad guy here is harmless now, and the other one's gone. Everything's fine. I know you're scared, but that's okay. You just stop worrying and try to calm down. Everything is going to be fine. Just give me a minute here while I get this broken windshield out of our way."

Now Rick was perched on the console between the front seats. He leaned back and kicked with both feet, knocking the fractured windshield onto the hood. He slid into the driver's seat and idled up to the apartment house dumpster. He got out, flipped open both lids and swept the broken slab of glass into the bin. He jumped back into the truck and maneuvered out onto the road. The whole thing had taken less than a minute.

As far as he could tell, no neighbors had been near enough to see anything out of the ordinary. Nor would they have heard the three shots from a silenced H&K USP. He could ease up a little now.

Ricky extracted a roll of paper towels from the console and began wiping up the mess on the seat. Sylvia was still sobbing a little, softly to herself, and he tried again to talk her through it.

"Sylvia, Sylvia, it's really okay now. You're all right. I had to stop that guy. He was about to take you away, but he can't hurt you now."

This got through. The crying stopped. Sylvia said in a tiny voice, "Ricky, he was . . . he was a policeman."

"Is that what he told you? No, sweetie. Not a chance. He's no policeman, trust me. No real policeman would jump into your car and try to drive away with you. He'd just pull you over and do what they do. A ticket, a lecture. But they don't drive away with you in your own car."

"Where is he?" she asked.

"In the back. Forget about him. Don't look back there. I want you to sit up straight and breathe some of this cool fresh air. We've got a lot of that right now, eh? Come on now ... you'll be fine," he urged.

Sylvia straightened up and into her seat and felt better at once. At least at that moment. Ricky took a piece of his paper towel and very gently cleaned a bit of the man's blood from the left side of her chin.

"That-a-girl! You're doing great! We'll be out in the country in a minute and you'll feel even better," he said soothingly.

"I've got to throw up, Ricky. Now!" she croaked, groping for the door handle.

He pulled to the side of the road and held the back of her jeans as she leaned out and coughed up the wad of terror she had tried to digest. She fell back into her seat, her breath coming hard.

Ricky drove west and south of the Interstate, heading for Delcambre, a small fishing village on a spit of land that juts out into the Gulf. He had to drive slowly with the windshield gone.

At length, he turned the Yukon onto a dock and into the open loading doors of a seafood warehouse.

Sylvia was beyond surprises from this man. She merely followed their progress and let her eyes slowly adjust to the dark of the building. A short, bow-legged oriental man walked over and bowed to Ricky. They shook hands, and Ricky spoke animatedly to him in what sounded like an Asian dialect of French. The little man smiled and nodded rapidly. He left for a moment and returned with a plastic tub on rollers. Ricky opened the back door of the Yukon behind her. Sylvia stared straight forward. She grimaced at the horrible sighing and burbling noises from a fresh corpse being moved. More squeaks and thumps told her that the body had been dragged out and flopped into the tub.

After some further discussion, the two men bowed to each other and Ricky got back into the truck. Sylvia saw the little man push the cart into a refrigerated cooler as they drove away.

"Who was that?" Sylvia asked, glad the body was gone, whatever the means.

"That was Corporal Ding, a very old friend of mine from Vietnam. He agreed to take care of our buddy there. Ding has some of the nicest blue crab recipes you've ever tasted. That's his specialty."

Sylvia shuddered when she realized what he meant. It was good she'd thrown up all she could earlier. One thing was certain, she would never try one of Ding's crab dishes.

Ricky drove back toward the Interstate and turned the Yukon into an industrial area just west of town. He unlocked the gate and pulled up at a door in the back row. With an electronic key, Rick unlocked it and disarmed a security gadget. He parked beside a brand new Toyota Land Cruiser.

"We've got us a clean ride now, my dear, so let's transfer our gear and get out of this town," Ricky said in his best John Wayne imitation.

"Is this yours?" Sylvia, despite everything, was eyeing it admiringly. The Toyota was loaded with special lights and off-road accessories.

"I use it down in the desert. It's my reward to myself for being such a sweet guy."

They loaded their gear and headed north toward Lafayette. For many miles, the road looked out over the glistening waters of a bayou. Rick and Sylvia kept to their own thoughts. Ricky was wondering if he would be lucky enough to be wrong about David's plans. Or if not wrong, then lucky enough to find him before he did anything. He wasn't at all sure that if he found David in time, he'd be able to stop him. Hell, he wasn't sure he even *wanted* to stop him—but he didn't want to lose his buddy.

FORTY ～～～～～～～

"**G**ENTLEMEN, LET'S COME TO ORDER AND GET THIS LOGGED out." Director Marsh stood before a group of about sixty men in a hotel meeting room. He clicked on his laser pointer and the lights in the room were dimmed. On an enormous overhead projector was a diagram of the hotel, the whole Riverfront Park, and the adjoining streets and buildings.

"Other than Unit Sixteen who are watching Slab and the vehicles at this time, I think all our units are here or represented. I have already briefed Sixteen on this material, so by the end of this session we should be fully prepared for tomorrow."

Slab was their code name for the president. The Service always came up with its own moniker, and this one was derived from the president's fondness for a "slab" of ribs.

"As we've already discussed, we are more exposed at this event than we have been since we were here three years ago. You can see that the tall buildings surrounding the park have corresponding agent numbers assigned to each zone. Check them with the numbers on the packets that Levi is handing out right now. Unit Three will be on the bridge and in the Sheriff's Auxiliary Patrol boats on the river. Those agents need some special instructions so I'll brief them individually when we're finished here.

"Units One and Two will cover the usual perimeter around Slab from the get-go. Three, Four, and Seven will monitor access to the hotel, here; the stage, here; and the walkway, here." His laser indicated each area in turn. "Okay, here is our time schedule—updated from yesterday, so take note. At 1400 hours Slab will come from the nest down to this room to greet about two hundred and fifty people with the hologram clearance tags. They'll be checked by Unit Twelve. Slab will be here about an hour, and then at 1500 we'll proceed out the front door of the hotel and down this walkway to the amphitheater. We expect the walk to be lined with people, so all crowd units need to be there at least one hour early to work the crowd. Slab will walk the entire six hundred and fifty yards to the amphitheater. As usual, he insists on being 'among his constituents.'" The Chief more or less spit out these disapproving words.

"I'm told there will be numerous stops at the food booths, and that a number of his long-time local contributors are asking to walk with him. Become familiar with them *before* he gets out of the hotel. There should be about seven." He paused and shuffled through his handful of notes. "Make a note: Once he is on the stage, he remains there until 1830 when he proceeds to the gazebo—here—where the family will watch the fireworks display over the river. This will be a crucial period for obvious reasons. Duration should be twelve minutes. A wagon will pick him up at the entrance to the park and bring him back to the parking garage, then up the service elevator to the nest. That's it. Once we put him to bed, we'll meet back here at 2030 hours to go over the next day's schedule.

"There are a couple more things: Slab is adamant about being with the people—more so now than ever—so be at your personal best. He has promised to stick to our planned pathway and not disappear into the crowd on us. Also, we have been put on the highest level of alert by none other than Slab himself. Apparently, he has some kind of 'feeling.' *My* feeling is that we need more information than we're getting, so you be careful out there. Keep our mission in mind at all times and I'll see you back here tomorrow night."

Not one agent moved a muscle.

"Switch your communicators to circuit seven at 2100 tonight. Back-talk will be channel six. Night eyes will be in the sky from 1700 to 2000 hours tomorrow on the number nine circuit. Write that down. Does anyone have any questions?"

Not a hand went up.

"Okay then. Dismissed."

FORTY-ONE 〜〜〜〜〜〜〜〜〜〜〜

MARCH 10, 1995
LOUISIANA TO ARKANSAS

WORLEY DROVE THE MOST OF THE FOUR HUNDRED MILES back to Little Rock in a stupor. The day before he had arrived in New Orleans from Phoenix and found the boarding house in suburban Metairie. After lunch Charlie beeped him for a ride from the airport. They took turns sleeping in the car and stayed on post.

Suddenly, in the middle of the next morning, there she was. A blue Yukon pulled up and a guy ran inside. They went for her. They had pulled off similar pickups before without a hitch. It should have been an easy job. Then everything went to hell.

As he drove, Worley let his mind replay the scene as if it were on a VCR. It was a real fucking bad movie.

The guy moved like a player when he ran into the apartment-house. He fired with a silenced weapon from a distance of at least forty yards. From what Worley could tell he hit his mark repeatedly. If a tree hadn't blocked Worley's line of sight to the window, he might have seen the shooter's face, but then the guy might have put a round into him as well. The guy was good, damn good.

Occasionally, paranoia would get the best of him and Worley entertained thoughts that he and his men might be set up to be eliminated by another group of operatives. Maybe Prescott's people in D.C. . . . maybe even the Judge . . . had decided to have Charlie and Lamar and himself tapped out to prevent any leaks. But he shook the thought from his head. They had no reason not to trust him. Right now he needed to concentrate on the present plan.

He had written down the plate number of the blue Yukon, and he could run it to see what came up. Plus, he'd be in the crowd tomorrow with the *big guy*. He and Lamar would watch. At least now he knew roughly what the woman looked like. He thought he could recognize them, and if he did, he could pop them up close. Better yet, as far as Worley knew, they didn't have a clue what he or Lamar looked like.

The main danger for them lay in their exposure in the crowd and the swarm of agents who'd be scattered all over the area. Worley would be there to protect the president just as the agents were, but they couldn't know about him and Lamar. If he or Lamar showed any hardware or looked at all aggressive, *they'd* be the ones heading off to jail at best, to . . . a cemetery at worst.

When he crossed the Arkansas-Louisiana state line, Worley stopped at a pay phone and paged Lamar. A few minutes later, Lamar rang back.

"Where are you?" Worley asked.

"I'm still watching the girl's house. No sign of them yet. Where've you been?" Lamar was trying to suppress a yawn.

"Charlie's dead," Worley announced.

"Shit! How?" Lamar was shocked. He and Charlie had worked together a long time.

"We found the girl, but the guy she was with happened to be a shooter—a pro. I don't think they'll show up at her place, so pull off that and meet me at the warehouse at ten o'clock. We've got to go over some plans for tomorrow," Worley said.

"Okay, I'll be there. You say he's a shooter?"

"Yeah, he put three into old Charlie. Bing, bing, bing. From a good forty yards. Blew the whole back of his head off."

"Fuck, Worley, don't talk about that shit. That gives me the heebee-jeebees, thinking about one of our guys taking a hit. Man, that's sick!"

"Hey, Lamar."

"Yeah?"

"You know what was the last thing that went through Charlie's mind today?"

"No, what?" Lamar fell for it.

"A fucking hollow point!" Worley roared. Lamar slammed down the phone.

FORTY-TWO ～～～～～～～～～～～

BOB PRESCOTT, *PRESIDENT* BOB PRESCOTT, STOOD AT THE BULLET-proof window of the presidential suite, looking over the lights of the city and the sweep of the Arkansas River below. He was glad he had decided to announce early. He was once again in Arkansas and back on the campaign trail. It was always good to come back here. It reminded him of his childhood and of the good times he had had as a young governor and, of course, of his mother.

Bob really missed his mother. He didn't realize until she was gone how much strength he drew from her. Her death had drained him for months. Naomi Rae Prescott had pretty much raised herself back in the thirties, educated herself, and reared her three kids by herself. Her life had been lonely, but she kept plugging away and she usually came out on top. He liked to think that he was a lot like her—tough, resilient, a winner. But as she was dying, he saw how she faced death. It was pretty much the same way she lived. There was no fear or anger in her eyes. She stayed tough to the end.

Bob, deep down, knew he couldn't face death like that. He flatly refused to think about it. Death held the prospect of too many consequences.

"Mr. President, I'm sorry to disturb you," Sue Sue said softly from the foyer door. "Mr. Puddephat is here to see you. I will come back in five minutes."

"Oh, yes, bring him on in," Bob said, turning from the window.

James Puddephat was an old acquaintance from back in law school. They'd been drinking buddies and even roomed together for a short time. James had gone into private practice in Conway and become a very successful trial lawyer. He was also a wonderful organizer, a real asset to many of Bob's campaigns—both state and national. They hadn't seen each other since Bob moved to the White House.

"Jimmy! Terrific to see you, fella!" Bob smiled and pumped his friend's hand, giving it his now-famous two-handed grip.

"Bob, uh, Mr. President. Damn, I just can't get used to that—how are you? God, you look great!" James smiled at his old friend. "I'm glad you had a minute for me, I know your time is really stretched."

"Hell, fella, I'm still human. I've got to see my pals every now and then. I might be coming to them for a job in the next couple of years," he laughed. "Let me get you a drink, Jimmy. You want a beer?" Bob offered.

"Thanks, but no, I can't," he answered.

"Can't? That's not the Jimmy Puddephat I remember. Don't tell me you've gotten on the wagon, pal," the president joked.

"Well, I guess I've jumped on a few wagons, Bob. I have to be honest with you. I have an agenda for coming to you tonight," he confessed as they sat on the sofa.

"Don't apologize, friend. Everyone does. What can I do for you?"

"Bob, I've been elected president of the state AIDS Interfaith Support Network. They were looking for a well-connected lawyer to increase their exposure. I guess I was the best they could find."

"I see. And they wanted you to ask me to change my position on the research funding money, right?" Bob said, not looking up from his glass.

"No, they don't know I'm here. I did this on my own. I want to understand what's behind your withdrawal of support."

"You may not understand how things work at this level, Jimmy. I have to make sacrifices—hard ones sometimes—just to keep everything balanced. It has very little to do with how I might feel about it. I can promise you, in two years' time, it'll turn around again and there will be more money than ever. Tell your people to help me stay in office and in a couple of years we'll be in tall cotton." Bob peered at Jimmy to see how this news might be received.

"A lot of them don't *have* two years, Bob. And it's not just the money. It's your personal support, keeping the issue on the front burner and in front of the legislators."

"Oh, God! Here comes the sympathy pitch! I know you have to argue your case that way, Jimmy, and I don't mean to be callous, but you know as well as I, everybody's got a hard-luck story. Don't you get tired of working with people who whine and bring up morbid shit every time they open their mouths?"

"Yes. Sure I do. I get real tired sometimes. Sometimes I get downright sick.... See, I'm one of *them* now. One of the 'hard-luck stories.' I have AIDS, Bob."

The president sat up. He was caught off guard, but now that Puddephat had said it, it was obvious. He was too thin and his coloring was off.

"Damn, Jimmy! I'm sorry!"

"Yeah, me too."

"I'll keep working on this, Jimmy, but there's really just so much I can do. Tell your organization I'll guarantee a two-year reversal on this if I get back in. A major funding increase," he finished with just the right little smile.

"You'll have to tell them yourself, Bob. I don't have that long. In fact, most of my folks won't make it that long. You'll have to tell them every year, every six months. Look at it this way, you'll have a new and bigger group each time. More voters with short memories. That's a politician's dream, isn't it? Except in this case the voters' memories will be *terminally* short. They won't know if you keep your promises."

Jimmy stood and measured Bob with a tearless stare. He strode quietly past Sue Sue and out the opened door.

Bob sighed. He paced around the room. The city below his window somehow looked darker than it had a few minutes before. Meetings with the AIDS bunch always ended like this—depressing ... fucking insanely depressing. They needed some public relations people and some lobbyists who weren't so goddamned morbid.

He lifted his drink to his lips but froze. He set the glass down and hurriedly scrubbed his hands at the sink. Smiling to himself, he was remembering what his mom used to say:

"You can't be too careful."

Good advice. Especially in politics.

FORTY-THREE ~~~~~~~~~

A
T THAT SAME MOMENT DAVID FARR WAS ALSO GAZING AT THE CITY from his hotel room, but for reasons very different from Prescott's. Below his eighth-floor room at the North Little Rock Hilton, he could see the river and the lights from Riverfront Park. David loved Little Rock. It reminded him of when he was a kid. Every school kid in the state was required to take a special course in Arkansas history in the fifth grade. History was his favorite subject, and he remembered how excited he had been that entire year. It was traditional that, at the end of the course in the early spring, the entire fifth grade went to Little Rock and toured the Old State House, the Governor's Mansion, the Capitol, and the Territorial Restoration.

For the poorer school districts like his, this was usually the only field trip the kids ever made. He still remembered the thrill of boarding the bus and getting a lunch box packed by someone other than his mother and visiting the historic places he'd been studying about all year. He chuckled, thinking what the teachers and chaperones had had to go through. Only now did he realize how much it meant to them, too.

Looking back it seemed good that children could be enamored with the workings of government at an early age. The passing years would bring disillusionment enough about the glories of government and politics.

David was momentarily startled by a glimpse of himself in the darkened window. Who was *that*—? Then he laughed out loud. His "disguise" for the day was a success. The hair that he'd always worn moderately long was chopped off in a flat top like the one he'd worn till he was eleven. That was when Elvis hit it big and haircuts changed forever. The beard he had sported since the war was gone, revealing the older but oddly childlike face of a stranger. He thought how remarkable it was not to have seen his own face for almost thirty years. His hands reached up of their own volition to explore its texture and form. He liked the sensations he hadn't felt for so long.

On the hour, as arranged, he phoned his mother at the cabin.

"I'm glad you called, David," she said after pleasantries. "Did Ricky ever find you? He called here earlier looking for you," she asked.

"No. I've been doing a lot of running around but I'll get in touch with him later." So Ricky now knew. Well it couldn't be helped. He changed the subject. "How are the kids, Mom?"

"Well, I guess they're fine. To tell you the truth, David, Zack's been pretty ill the last few days, but he says he feels better. He just wasn't looking so good, and then today he looks great and he and Deidra drove all the way in to town to see a movie. Can you believe that?" she said happily.

"Yeah, that's great, Mom. I'm just sorry I missed them."

"Son, you know I don't want to get into your business, but are you taking your father's death okay? I know that must have been horrible for you and your brothers. I talked to them, and they said you didn't seem to be doing too well."

"I'm fine, Mom. I've just got a lot on my mind," David said.

"You know your dad and I had a lot of problems and neither one of us was the perfect parent, but I'll say this for him, he was a great father and he sure had a good impact on your life. He taught you early how to work and play hard. He was tough and he punished you when you deserved it. He couldn't bear to think that his boys would ever feel they were better than anyone else, and he wanted sons who'd fight for what was right and stand up for the underdog. He was kind of ... simple that way, but it sure paid off with you boys," she said proudly.

"Yes, ma'am. I miss him more than I ever thought I would."

"You know, I see that in Zack, too. I don't know what you and Ricky are up to down there, running around trying to find out who's responsible for this mess. I don't think I want to know. I just hope you don't beat anyone up. But Zack is so proud of you.

"I heard him talking to Deidra the other night, and he said that because of you and Rick, things might change so nothing this horrible would ever happen to anyone again. And then he said, 'You know, that's how my dad lost his leg in the war, by sticking his neck out for someone else.' She asked him what happened and he said, 'Dad never would talk about the war but Ricky told me that my dad saved his whole squad.'" She paused because her voice was cracking with emotion. "Is that true, David? I never knew. You never would talk with us about it."

"Only partly, Mom. But as Dad would say, 'Things just happen.'"

"Well, I want you to know your dad was proud of you and your son is proud of you and I'm very proud of you. Now—I got that off my chest and I won't bring it up again. Okay?"

"Okay. I love you, Mom," David said warmly.

"I love you, too. You and Rick hurry up and get back here. I want to hear about that girl your brothers told me you had with you. What's her name, Sylvia?"

"Yeah, Mom, Sylvia. You'll love her." He smiled.

"Okay. Call back tomorrow afternoon. Zack and Deidra should be home by then. 'Bye."

" 'Bye, Mom," David said. He hated to hang up the phone.

He leaned over and slipped down the sock on his prosthesis. He depressed a button near the top of the foot. A six-inch, hinged plastic door popped open just as Klaus had designed it to do. He snapped it shut and stretched out on his bed to dream about Sylvia. Soon he was praying with all his might. He prayed that she was safe and that she'd forgive him for what he was about to do. He prayed that he'd get a chance to see her again, but he knew his chances and he wasn't going to kid himself. He prayed for God to bless his mission and for God to forgive his mission.

When he dozed off, David dreamed that he was a kid again on a pallet on the sleeping porch at home. He was a child but he had the strange old face that he had just discovered under his beard. The night was thick and heavy. He had a sheet over him and his mother came out with a laundry bottle and sprinkled water droplets lightly over the sheet to cool him a bit. She switched on the ceiling fan on the porch and in his dream he was looking through the blades at the haint-blue ceiling, watching make-believe clouds pass by, pretending he was flying.

FORTY-FOUR 〜〜〜〜〜〜〜〜〜〜

MARCH 11, 1995
RIVERFRONT PARK
LITTLE ROCK, ARKANSAS

T HE DAY BROKE COOL AND CLEAR OVER RIVERFRONT PARK AND ITS
throngs of workers. Television crews in white coveralls spread
out their weird assortments of cables and cameras and dishes.
There were electricians, stage workers, lighting technicians, security
guards, and concession workers. Row after row of bright blue and yellow
portable toilets added to the color. The food vendors and their equipment looked like a science-fiction version of gypsy caravans. Their pots
and pans and serving trays glistening in the sun.

Secret Service agents mixed with the laborers, some dressed in black
jumpsuits and others in plainclothes with black jackets and caps. They
were all easy to spot.

Worley could smell the excitement in the air. The breeze from the river
wafted toward the truck, carrying the assorted carnival aromas of candied
apples, pretzels, hot dogs, and the rich odor of barbecue. He and Lamar

were dressed in uniforms stenciled with the logo of Peggy's Portable Potties, and they were unloading the temporary toilets and rolling them to specified locations in the park.

While Lamar did most of the work, Worley took his time, scanning the growing crowd continuously. He was memorizing the faces of the agents and keeping an eye out for the girl. The Judge had supplied the Peggy's coveralls and lightweight jackets. They were certainly embarrassing enough, but served perfectly for concealing the silenced Beretta SF 92-9mm pistols and their harnesses. The custom harness allowed them to carry the long pistols in an inverted position so they could be easily freed. One only had to reach back and unstick a small Velcro patch at his belt line. The gun would fall naturally into his hand, ready and armed.

The Judge had been able to give them a fairly firm schedule of events. Worley intended to be close to the president when he walked from the hotel to the park pavilion. But he'd have to stay back far enough to be out of the zone the Secret Service agents monitored with their portable metal detectors. It was going to be a bitch. He and Lamar had never been so exposed on an assignment.

~~~~~~~~~~~~~

Ricky and Sylvia had had a restless night. They had driven straight to the Little Rock airport, where Ricky found the old Pilatus tied down on the ramp. He went through its interior hoping to find a clue to David's whereabouts, but it was clean. Rick got cozy with some airport service people on the flight line to feel them out. He learned that David had flown in that morning and caught a cab from the terminal.

Finding a room was the biggest problem. Ricky ended up driving all the way to Conway to get Sylvia lodged where she would be safe. She'd been through so much. She was holding up well, but he didn't want to push his luck.

The night had little comfort for either. Rick spent an hour in his truck, cleaning his H&K and loading it with special bullets. These "safety slugs" were designed for close-in work. The frangible projectiles were a composite of granular lead loosely held together with an adhesive. They were designed to be extremely deadly. On impact they would dissipate their energy quickly so as not to pass completely through one body and into another. The charge was lowered just enough to keep the velocity subsonic to reduce noise. This still provided plenty of knockdown power but enhanced the effectiveness of Rick's integral silencer. A shot would make no more noise than a handclap.

He and Sylvia had worked up a simple but effective disguise and, thanks to the evening news, they had a fairly accurate schedule of the next day's events. During this planning phase Ricky gained added respect for this spunky woman. She was brave and committed, and her mind was constantly questioning. Much as he dreaded having Sylvia with him, he needed her. Her life would be in danger, but Ricky believed she was the only one who could stop David.

After a nearly sleepless night Sylvia had trouble keeping her breakfast down. Ricky ripped a five-milligram Valium from his surgical kit to steady her nerves. They picked up matching navy-blue jackets at a mall and got two ball caps with the presidential emblem emblazoned on the front. The caps were popular items in Little Rock since the hometown boy hit it big.

At 2:00 P.M. they drove downtown. They had to park a half-mile away and walk the remaining distance to the river. Ricky was certain David wouldn't show himself until he had to. The president wasn't scheduled to appear outside the hotel until 3:00. They were still early.

Ricky knew that he and Sylvia were necessarily exposed during this walk. The people who'd killed David's father and tried to make off with Sylvia were surely in this crowd. That was a guarantee. He relied on his ability to spot the movements, gestures, and look of a professional killer. It is hard for a wolf to wear sheep's clothing convincingly—no matter how expensive the design. He knew that from his own experience.

They found a concrete parking garage that would give them the best view of the crowd as it gathered. They were far enough away that the Secret Service agents would be checking only people with packages or those whose clothing could conceal a rifle. No one could score a hit from this range with a pistol.

Already the crowd was heavy, so he and Sylvia were obliged to muscle their way to the low concrete wall on the third level. Any higher and they wouldn't be able to descend the stairs quickly enough to intercept David. For now, they were tourists, watching the festivities.

President Prescott strode down the hall with his bevy of agents at the flanks. They rode the service elevator to the second floor. The Judge's discreet warning kept him from feeling as charged up or comfortable as he usually did during these events. Stephanie and Nicole were going to meet him later at the pavilion. They were also under heavy security, to the displeasure of both.

Prescott emerged to the tune of "Hail to the Chief" played by the White Hall High School Marching Band. The WHHS A Capella Choir followed with a hymn-like arrangement of "God Bless America" that moved listeners to tears.

At once Prescott was all smiles, waving to the crowd. He made a beeline to the stage and shook the hands of every one of the kids. Only then did he turn to his invited guests. Everyone whispered that it was so like him to spend time thanking the young musicians. Their faces were grinning so widely that they looked as if they might explode. It was a great entrance.

Bob felt better right away. His apprehensions melted away as soon as he started working the crowd. This was his element. He relaxed in the knowledge that he had the best legitimate—and illegitimate—protection money could buy. He grooved now, reveling in the adulation and doing what he did best. He knew what these people wanted to hear and he wanted to say it to them.

David, earlier, had strolled the wide brick pathway that President Prescott would use. He thought about using one of the portable toilets as a hideout until the entourage approached and then exiting into the crowd along the path, but he noticed that security people were already checking them on a regular basis. That would be too obvious. Try another plan.

He wasn't particularly worried about the Secret Service agents because

Klaus's design was truly undetectable. The mini metal detectors built into the agents' jackets would detect only the thirty cents in change in his front pocket.

David was getting a funny feeling that Ricky had figured out his plan and was somewhere in the crowd. A part of him ached to have Ricky at his side right now. But he just couldn't bear to implicate his friend. One of them had to survive. This was *his* game now, and his alone.

He found a concrete parking garage that would probably be full of people by three o'clock. From there he could watch the front of the hotel and see the president make his appearance. He planned to flank Prescott, working his way through the crowd to a spot on the walkway nearer the pavilion. If there were to be a getaway, he would play it by ear.

FORTY-FIVE 〜〜〜〜〜〜〜〜〜

MARCH 11, 1995
RIVERFRONT PARK
LITTLE ROCK, ARKANSAS

W ORLEY AND LAMAR HAD BEEN MONITORING THE ROWS OF johns set well back on each side of the walkway. Now it was 2:45 P.M. and they had worked their way to the ends of the rows nearest the hotel. About two hundred yards away was the door through which the president would step out into the crowd. They meant to arrive there at exactly three o'clock, then simply follow his path through the crowd.

Worley could spot Lamar through the growing mass of people as they began their slow approach to the door, one on each side of the wide walkway. He was also mindful of any citizens who looked like Secret Service agents. No problem there—they stuck out like sore thumbs. Walked too straight, dressed too straight, and shifted their eyes around like characters in a Bullwinkle cartoon.

～～～～～～～

David hurried down the block to the Old State House Museum, then into the parking garage. The first floor was not as crowded as he had feared. He found he could maneuver himself to a point where he had a good view of the pathway. He could feel the weight of Klaus's new invention pulling on his stump. The artificial leg moved perfectly naturally, but even the slight added weight played on his nerves.

He didn't have to wait long. A few minutes after the hour, the crowd thronging the hotel door became very loud and animated. Prescott was on his way. David felt a wave of nausea rush over him. He took a deep breath and walked slowly out from under the parking garage, working his way across the crowded street toward the walkway. He forced himself to be casual. Up ahead, perhaps a hundred yards, he picked out a thinning in the crowd that looked to be negotiable. His present pace would intercept the president's progress very nicely.

He could see Prescott's head above the crowd. That simple, arresting sight brought home the reality of what he was doing. His eyes fixed on the man who had infected Zack and Deidra with the lethal virus. The man who had had his father shot down. A righteous anger filled him as never before and he pushed forward to the rendezvous.

～～～～～～～

Ricky and Sylvia anxiously scanned the crowd. They tried to pluck from its myriad shapes, colors, and faces the familiar form of David Farr. Bodies moved and shifted as the roar traveled from the hotel exit along the president's path. If they thought they saw a hopeful detail one moment, it was gone the next. Sylvia was clutching Ricky's hand so tightly he was afraid her fingernails would break off in his palm. He could feel the energy pump through her, and he tasted the familiar surge of adrenaline spilling into the back of his mouth.

The president's height, advantageous to him most of the time, was a nightmare for security. Rick winced to see Prescott's head seemingly a foot above the surrounding mob. He could guess how difficult it would be to protect someone who literally stood out in a crowd. At this range any serious rifleman could have found an easy target.

The crowd was pulsing around Prescott. You could see that he loved it. Ricky took notice of that, but searched every face with increasing desperation.

~~~~~~~~~~~~

Worley and Lamar worked their way up to the hotel entrance just as Prescott emerged. Worley let himself wallow in Prescott's charisma for a moment. He'd been around him for years, pretty much watched him grow into his manhood, but he still found him fascinating. He nodded to Lamar across the way. On either side of the procession they pushed and wiggled their way through the cheering multitude, trying to stay even with the president and invisible to the agents.

~~~~~~~~~~~~

Sylvia saw David first. Ricky couldn't fathom how she did it. His old friend had butch-cut his hair and shaved off his beard. Ricky didn't recognize him at all. Later, when he thought about it, he supposed it was some metaphysical connection between lovers that allowed her to spot him. Rick wondered whether he'd ever get to experience such a bond.

Sylvia had seen David turn slightly to step onto the curb on the other side of the street. He had apparently come from just under them, at the lower level of the parking garage. So close!

Ricky grabbed her, clamping her under his arm like a bag of golf clubs, and pushed back through the crowd along the edge of the lower concrete wall. He had to descend two flights of stairs and he knew she wouldn't be able to keep up.

Sylvia clutched at Ricky as he slung her into a modified fireman's carry and ran down the stairs. She was begging him to put her down and trying to keep her head from bouncing so hard she'd pass out.

On the ground floor Ricky paused only for a moment of instruction. "Okay, we move fast ... but not *too* fast. Smile, try to look like you've had a couple of beers. Don't call out to him until I tell you. If I give an order, *don't think!* Just do it."

Ricky pushed off at once, tugging Sylvia by the hand. His own smile was genuine. This was his element, that dreadful moment before the battle when nerves were raw and fear was palpable.

David was a hundred yards ahead and Ricky was relieved to glimpse the back of David's head before he disappeared into the crowd. He trotted forward, knowing it would look natural. As they hit the bulk of the crowd, Ricky grabbed Sylvia around the waist and threaded her through the gaps. David moved slowly, showing no signs of hurry. They were quickly closing the distance. Ricky could see from the periphery that the president was paralleling them. They *might* be able to reach David just before he reached Prescott.

~~~~~~~~~~~~~~~~~~

Worley spotted Sylvia from about fifty feet away. Yes, by God, that was the one! Her hat had fallen off during the race down the stairs and her long hair spilled out. The man behind her moved like the guy he'd seen run into the apartment down in Metairie.

This was it! This was it! His signal to Lamar was the old cry that gypsies and carnies have used for centuries: "Hey, Rube!" His yell carried over the noise of the crowd.

Lamar's head jerked around in his direction. Worley pointed to the target and quickly lowered his arm, once again the Peggy's Portable Potties man.

~~~~~~~~~~~~~~~~~~

David was running on pure adrenaline. He had made it to the ropes along the path some twenty feet ahead of Prescott. It was time. His movements had to be natural and slow so as to attract no attention.

Two women stood between him and the ropes. The Secret Service agents scouting ahead of Prescott were already even with him. David flinched as if the women in front of him had stepped on his toe, bouncing on his good leg and lifting his prosthesis. As his pants leg slid up slightly, he triggered the release button. The door popped open. His eyes did not betray what he was doing. David didn't have to look down to feel the weapon fall into his hand. It felt slick and cold in his grip. It felt just the way revenge *should* feel. As he straightened up, a casual glance assured him that he hadn't been spotted. No one paid the least attention.

Now the bait.

~~~~~~~~~~~~~~

With practiced motions, Worley slid his hand under the back of his jacket and the pistol dropped into his hand. He brought it forward smoothly and now slid the long silencer of the barrel up under his left armpit so it was hidden under the jacket once again. It was ready for instant use. He was crouched low, pushing hard through the crowd. The man and the girl were at least ten feet ahead of him. That was a lot in a crowd so thick. They were still moving toward the president's path.

Worley sensed an eagerness in the woman's movements, and he saw the muscular tension of the man's shoulders and neck as he helped her along. He thought quickly. It struck him. She would be the bait. Their plan must be to use her looks to attract the attention of the president. Then the man would make the hit. That had to be it.

He wished to hell a Secret Service agent would step in. Otherwise, he'd have to act and he had only seconds now. The entire crowd's attention was directed toward the president.

~~~~~~~~~~~~~~

Ricky saw David bend over, and he knew that the time was now or never. He was still about fifteen feet from David and the wad of people between them was impenetrable. He tensed for the sound of a shot.

Then David straightened up, and Ricky heard his old friend's voice above the noise of the crowd.

"Veterans for Prescott! Veterans for Prescott!" he was shouting.

Ricky hoisted Sylvia in his arms so that she could see above the crowd. "Now, sweetie! Now, call him!"

Sylvia yelled at the top of her lungs even before she could see him. "David Farr! David, over here, honey! David!" Heads around her were turning to see what she was yelling about.

David seemed to freeze. He turned, and when their eyes met for a fleeting moment, she saw a look of horror and hurt on his face as he recognized her. Ricky put her down and continued pushing her through the crowd.

∼∼∼∼∼∼∼∼∼∼

When Worley saw the man lift the woman above the crowd he dropped the pistol close in front of his thigh and made a mad push toward them. The crowd was resisting and people were cursing but he was getting there.

Lamar was useless on the other side of the walkway. It was his game now. He had to stop them.

∼∼∼∼∼∼∼∼∼∼

David's plan was working. He had pinned the Purple Heart on his chest for the first time ever. It showed nicely on his tan jacket, and he had hoped it would catch Prescott's eye. He chanted, "Veterans for Prescott!" over and over. The group was real, a fledgling organization that had received lots of press. The media clamored for stories on each side of the old Vietnam business. Prescott had not served—had evaded the draft, some said. It was a perennial issue.

When he saw the image of Sylvia, he couldn't believe his eyes. Her face was strained and sweaty … like Suni's just before she died. Somehow Sylvia was floating above the crowd. He must be hallucinating. By raw will, David turned away and forced himself to concentrate on his task.

An aide walking with the president heard David's chant and then saw the Purple Heart on his chest. He touched Prescott's elbow and whispered in his ear. Prescott looked up, smiled, and headed in David's direction. He could never pass up a good photo opportunity.

David struggled to get Sylvia out of his mind. Now, for the climax of the act he had rehearsed. David stood tall and threw a crisp salute to his commander-in-chief. The president returned it, walking the last few feet to him.

∼∼∼∼∼∼∼∼∼∼

In his peripheral vision Worley saw the entourage's change of pace. He could no longer see the girl, but she couldn't be more than a few feet from the president. The man with her was pushing forward harder than ever. He had to stop them now. Why weren't the Secret Service guys keying in on this?

Worley brought his pistol up. The only shot he had was through a middle-aged man standing between him and Ricky. He had to drop him. Worley fired into the man's shoulder. He paid no heed to the screams around him and aimed where his target would come into view. The tourist fell forward. Worley saw Ricky's back twisting toward him. He fired again.

~~~~~~~~~~~~~~~~~

Sylvia felt Ricky give her one powerful push. She could finally see David again—he was reaching his hand out to the president. She could almost touch him. Then she heard the first screams ...

~~~~~~~~~~~~~~~~~

David dropped his salute and reached out for Prescott's handshake. As he opened his hand, a trigger mechanism released two minute plastic fangs. They were the delivery device for a minuscule amount of Zack's blood carefully stored in the palm of this silicone creation. Klaus had molded it so cleverly that it was essentially an invisible mitt.

The blood, of course, had come from one of the samples going to Dr. Heisman. A cooling chamber in David's prosthesis kept it fresh. Now it felt like icy, throbbing poison.

Prescott's huge hand grabbed David's. A scream rang out behind them. David watched the man's eyes shift momentarily just as the load popped silently in his palm. The old German had said that no one would feel the sting of the needles if the grip was firm, and he was right. In this split second, David was a human viper with death in his touch. His prey never felt the sting.

When Bob Prescott turned back to him, David looked him squarely in the eyes. Prescott felt nothing but a veteran's firm handshake. He seized the man's hand in both of his in his old routine and boomed his heart-felt thanks for his service to America.... The man was thanking him! David thought in disbelief, and said something inane in reply. In fact, Prescott was putting on an act for the cameras. He despised Vietnam vets.

The moment the men released each other's hand, a ruckus exploded in the crowd.

~~~~~~~~~~~~~

Ricky had seen Lamar moving along the other side of the walkway. He could tell that Lamar was trying to maneuver. There was one of the enemy. The man was a killer—Ricky sensed it in his every motion. But he was still at a safe distance.

Turning to scan his flank, Rick heard the silenced gunshot and saw the man directly behind him begin to drop. He had already plucked his pistol from its shoulder harness and as he spun he felt the impact of a slug hit his Kevlar vest and knock the breath from him.

Ricky stepped back, dropped to a crouch, and saw the snaky-looking man with the pistol leveled at him. He fired from the hip. The slug hit the man squarely on the tip of his long nose and flung his head backward so violently that it broke his neck just above the shoulders. Worley's sunglasses flew into the crowd as he convulsed on the pavement. Ricky slid his pistol back under his arm and turned toward Sylvia and David, still unable to breathe. Worley's body continued to writhe and thrash about the legs and feet of the screaming spectators. All attention was now on his grotesque death-dance.

~~~~~~~~~~~~~

Sylvia was so focused on David that she barely heard the screams of panic around her. With a final lunge she locked her fingers on David's sleeve and tugged fiercely, pulling him most of the way between the two women in front of her.

David was again astonished to see her. The next moment he realized that she was no illusion. Sylvia was here. She was pulling him to safety, away from the miracle that had just happened. He reached for her. Men in dark suits were rushing toward them from every direction. The crowd began to scatter and shouts rang out from all around.

~~~~~~~~~~~~~

From behind, Rick snagged Sylvia by the back of her belt. She had a death grip on David's sleeve and pulled him with her as Rick extracted them from the melee of bodies.

Secret Service agents had pushed Prescott down and fallen on top of him, ramming him onto his hands and knees. Their own bodies protected every inch of him.

One of the agents saw a man in coveralls flop backward and drop a huge pistol. He ran over, dove on the man, and wrestled with him for a few heady moments before he realized that his foe had no face.

The eyes of onlookers and the roving agents were drawn irresistibly to that gory, thrashing action. Ricky, with Sylvia and David in tow, used the moment to retreat. The crowd was now in full panic. Pools of blood spreading on the sidewalk sent them fleeing. Rick prodded David and Sylvia to start running like everyone else. They regrouped near the parking garage.

"Sylvia," Rick gasped, "you show David to the Land Cruiser. Here are the keys. From here on, walk, don't run. Wait on me for five minutes, no longer."

Suddenly Sylvia realized that Ricky was injured.

"We're not leaving you here! No! No!"

"Go now, that's an order. I'll be there. Don't worry. I'm not letting you keep my Toyota." He smiled that smile that told her he was still having fun. She kissed Ricky on the cheek and straightened his presidential hat. A last look in his eye ...

Sylvia took David's arm and at last they were together again. Their bodies drew close as they walked, forgetting what they were leaving.

~~~~~~~~~~~~~

Ricky approached the parking garage cautiously, scanning the onrush of people. Their eyes looked crazed and they glanced over their shoulders toward the scene of the shooting as if someone were pursuing. Rick stepped behind one of the concrete pillars and waited.

There he was. The one he had seen earlier, the other man in the coveralls, was circling a cluster of the panicked crowd. The man was in the open now, forty yards away on the other side of the street.

Ricky picked his moment and stepped from behind the pillar. He could tell that the other man recognized him. He calmly reached into his jacket as if he were going to draw his pistol. He moved precisely as quickly and smoothly as a shooter would, crouched and low.

The man in coveralls reacted exactly as Rick had hoped. He immediately drew his long Beretta from his back pouch and started edging for a shot.

Lamar may have had time to realize that Ricky was holding no gun. No one will ever know. A bullet from a .308 Sako sniper rifle entered his body just above the left nipple and angled down, expanding till it was a half-dollar-sized fist that ripped through his heart, lung, and right kidney. He folded up as if someone had sucker-punched him. Almost comically, Lamar sat back onto the sidewalk with his pistol still grasped in both hands. Then, slowly, he toppled over sideways, his fat cheek flat against the gutter, blood pouring from his mouth.

One of the Secret Service snipers on top of the garage had spotted Lamar waving his pistol and made a split-second decision. Conceivably he saved Rick's life, though Ricky had no intention of letting himself get hit.

Rick walked calmly in the direction of his Toyota, still scanning his escape route with an occasional furtive glance at the turmoil behind him. He would have time to catch David and Sylvia. Now to get the hell out of Dodge.

FORTY-SIX ~~~~~~~~~~

JUNE 19, 1995
NORTHERN TERRITORY
CANADA

THE OLD DE HAVILAND OTTER CIRCLED LOW OVER THE OUTPOST cabin at Victor Lake. Benjamin came out onto his front porch and flung his hands up in greeting. They could see his smile from the air. Ben called his boys to ready the Jeep for the trip to the bay.

David munched a sandwich in a jumpseat along the portside fuselage. His attention was fixed on Zack teaching Deidra how to lower the flaps in preparation for landing.

Moments later the floats sliced into the cold, pristine waters. Zack kept the plane on the steppe and powered it around to the small, sheltered bluff where they always landed, then babied it up near the shore.

They unloaded with a light heart and stretched their legs. David chose the moment to look around at his little family. The others moved about on one chore or another. Zack and Deidra walked to the shore. Zack, no doubt, was telling some Benjamin-style whopper about the biggest fish in the lakes. Well, perhaps not, David smiled. They were holding hands.

Ricky and Sylvia gathered deadwood for the fire and argued enthusiastically about what to have for dinner and who was going to cook it. From the sounds and the look on Ricky's face, Sylvia had the situation well in hand.

David heaved a sweet sigh of satisfaction. It couldn't get any better than this. Zack was responding extremely well to a new cocktail of medications concocted by Dr. Heisman. His T-cell count was higher and he had put on eighteen pounds. Deidra was finishing her degree. She had shown no signs of the disease so far. She was even pushing Zack to consider adopting an infant from the Reservation Agency.

Sylvia was enchanted with the northwoods from the first. David pretended that he wouldn't ask her to marry him until she had seen a winter here, but he was fingering a ring in his jacket pocket. His secret would come as a surprise to her.

Ricky announced with more fervor than usual that he would retire once and for all and run a boat a few days a week out of Grand Isle. This time he really meant it. His dad had left him a place, and it was only a short run from there to his jungle haunts. David took this with a whole handful of salt. The man wasn't built for retiring. He'd be back stirring up trouble before too long.

David's life had been on hold through the unbelievable events of the past year. Now his dreams blossomed with new hope and Sylvia filled his heart. It was rich. He wished he could save the sounds and smells and the scene before his eyes.

Benjamin and his sons arrived. The old friends whooped and hugged their greetings, then pitched in to prepare the camp for three days of fishing. The northern pike were voracious from a winter under the ice pack, and would bite at anything. Six of them immediately volunteered to be supper.

Ricky built up the fire against the cool evening breeze. This hour always belonged to Benjamin. He carried the northland in his blood and his voice. He sang her spirit. For the women, he had a song about the return of the sun in the springtime. For each visitor he had a tale about his people and their lives in the North.

Then he told a special story. The circle of friends listened, rapt.

"Many years ago in the land where the sun sets, the Great Spirit was trying to decide how to fill his sky. It was a great empty bowl over the land. Oh, it had the sun and moon and stars but nothing flew about. It was boring.

"He called in some of his creatures, the snakes and the birds. At that time they looked very different from they way they look now. They both had four limbs and walked upright like bears. They had full heads of hair and actually looked very much alike with soft, thick fur."

Benjamin looked slyly across the fire at his listeners. He wanted them to know that he was telling this parable just for them. He continued gesturing broadly with his arms and hands.

"He told them there would be a test to see who would be given the sky. The Great One sent them all into a dark cave and told them that he would call them out in three days. And so he did, and in three days he called them out and he stood them before him.

"'Snakes, what did you see in the cave?' he asked. The snakes said, 'Darkness.' And the spirit said, 'How is this so?' And the snakes said, 'The cave was dark and deep and cold. . . . So we covered our eyes with our hands and curled up to stay warm. We were afraid.'

"So the Great One cast a spell on the snakes and made their bodies naked and took their arms and legs and hair away and made them to curl up in the dark places forever.

"Then he asked the birds what they saw. And the birds said, 'We too saw the darkness at first and we were afraid. But then we stretched out our arms and opened our eyes widely and walked into the black. Suddenly there was light and we could see each other, and we could see a beautiful world in the cave, full of light and flowers and water.'

"So the Great Spirit was pleased by this. He cast a spell upon the birds. He changed their fur into feathers as colorful as the flowers they had seen. And because they searched with outstretched arms, he changed their arms into wonderful wings for riding the wind. And because they kept their eyes open in the dark, he gave them new, amazing eyes that can see for miles, and can even see in the night sky.

"The Great Spirit gave them the sky."

Benjamin paused.

"Many people are born in darkness and eat there and die there. Life is like waking up. It hurts and frightens so much that many people decide to sleep right through it and never wake up.

"David, you and your people, your family, have gone into darkness and found your life. Now you will receive the beautiful things. Like the birds, you have inherited the sky."

Benjamin warmed his hands over the orange-yellow flames of the fire. His face looked tender in the soft, shifting light, and his broad smile was a promise.

No one spoke. No one stirred except to wipe damp eyes and cheeks. They all knew the darkness was over.

FORTY-SEVEN ~~~~~~~~~~

FEBRUARY 3, 1997
THE OVAL OFFICE
THE WHITE HOUSE
WASHINGTON, D.C.

B OB PRESCOTT SAT BEHIND A FORMIDABLE STACK OF PAPERS THAT begged for his immediate attention. The turning of the year always increased the media's attention to governmental business, however humdrum. All through January they clamored for stories about his administration's goals. What agenda did he have that would change the world over the next twelve months? What issues would be his top priorities? Anything to pin his butt against the wall, Prescott mused darkly. Their interest was on conventional issues, but those were merely window dressing.

Unknown to the media were the deals and maneuvers that were near and dear—and very high priority—to his people back home. He would have to move soon. First came the sanitizing, the bargaining, the sweeteners. These would require all his formidable finesse and arm-twisting powers.

Even with his gift of gab and a pot full of luck, he was going to take some massive hits in the opinion polls. Those hated, ever-present opinion polls. Bob didn't like them; he merely lived them every day. The numbers had been on the old roller coaster ever since he had sided with the Republicans on the social program spending cuts.

One group from Arkansas was heavily invested in aerospace component manufacturing. It was expecting some unusually generous federal funding during the new year, and had waited, not always patiently, for him to come across.

Several other groups from back home had formed powerful conglomerates to develop complete power-generating systems. They were positioned for quick expansion and expected to land lucrative contracts in China, Russia, and Africa. These deals required certain obscure approvals and trade concessions. These would be pushed through Congress by Bob's people. They were prepared to offer quite a bit in return. Millions of dollars had been leveraged and billions more were in the balance.

Three major highway programs sought special federal approval and funding. Congressional bickering had delayed them time and again. The construction moguls had endured the disappointment of his first four years, but now they were demanding action, demanding it Arkansas-style. Now the chips were on the table, great piles of chips. As they said back home, "It was time for him to pay for his upbringing."

On top of all this, he'd found a note from Rodney O'Malley, M.D., on top of the files on his desk. Captain O'Malley was the physician based at Bethesda Naval Hospital who had performed Bob's physicals for the last four years. The note was simple and to the point. It demanded—*demanded*—a private visit today. The doctor would expect a call from the Oval Office to set up the time.

"What in the hell could that be about?" Bob muttered.

Generally Bob read about his yearly physical in the papers. Occasionally, Captain O'Malley would report by phone to fuss about his cholesterol or triglycerides or some other bullshit, and that would be the end of it for another year. So now what was *this* about? *Nobody* made demands on the president of the United States.

"Excuse me, Mr. President." Al Clark, one of his personal aides, stuck his head in. "Sir, I need to run something by you if I may." Al was a mousy little guy who never wasted time, one of those tidy, punctilious, four-eyed office dwellers who live for only one purpose—to organize things and people.

"What've you got, Al? I'm really behind this morning."

"I know, sir, but I think you may want to see this." He handed the president a neat two-page letter printed on a beautiful, crisp linen paper. "This came in yesterday. It was brought to my attention first thing this morning. I didn't know if it represented a threat the Secret Service should investigate, or if it was just some wacko who likes to write letters. The wording is strange, sir, so I want your direction on this. It doesn't seem to be related to that horrible hate mail following Mr. Puddephat's death last month."

Bob leaned back in his chair and slipped his glasses off his forehead and onto his nose. He read:

President Robert Davis Prescott
Commander-in-Chief of the Armed Forces
of the United States of America
January 30, 1997

Mr. President,

It is with a dual purpose that I write to you today. You don't know me, although we met briefly during your successful reelection campaign. I know there is a chance that you will not receive this letter. Still, I write in the belief that you will.

First, through a series of events you would find difficult to believe, a minuscule amount of my son's blood now flows through your veins. I guess then that you could say that my own blood and my father's flow in you as well.

My father, Douglas Robert Farr, would tell you, if he were alive, that it is good and proud blood. I will tell you, without hesitation, that it is the very best thing in you.

However, this brings up my second purpose. My son, Zachary Richard Farr, will, in fairness to you, confirm to you that it is also very deadly blood. Its contamination was caused by greed and disregard for human life—by you and by some of your associates.

It is my prayer that you use your every resource to save your own life, a life that up till now has been an abomination to the human spirit. If you can save yourself, you will, however grudgingly, help save the lives of millions of others who suffer from the same affliction you now carry within you.

I no longer worry about your power to hurt my family. I have compiled a significant file of evidence that condemns you and the ghosts of your partners. These allegations are provable and verifiable. But I fully expect they will go with me to my grave. You will never have to see them—because I need you.

You are now the only global leader with the proper motivation to do what has to be done to end the fear, pain, and suffering of millions of people around the world. Therefore, I need you alive and in office.

I hope that the tiny genetic code of my family, which now lives within you, will transform your heart and inspire your actions and provide you with the strength and dignity you will need to succeed. In closing, I pray that God will forgive both of us and that he will save you.

Sincerely,
David A. Farr
Arkansan

Bob Prescott, mesmerized, read the letter a second and a third time before laying it gingerly on his desk. Only then did he notice that Al Clark was still standing at the desk, awaiting his response.

He kept his voice even. "Oh, Al, I don't think this is anything. Leave it with me and I'll discuss it with the Service boys this afternoon. No worry. Just another nut. But thanks," he said curtly, with a nod of dismissal.

When Clark stepped out of the office, Bob snatched the letter up and studied it. This David Farr person had worded it with incredible care, with no great writing skill. A blunt, relentless honesty chose every word. And what it said . . . Bob grew pale and sweaty as its message sank in.

Comprehension turned into a fear that he would not acknowledge and to pain that he felt only too well, a burning tension in his neck and down his arms. He suddenly didn't feel well at all. His mind raged at him: he was actually feeling faint over a *letter*. A damn stupid letter! But the power in those words was transcendent. Unmistakable.

Everything hit Bob at once. This must be the loose end of the bloody fiasco at Riverfront Park. His two Arkansas "security men" shot to death, no suspects, no leads. The missing link in the "bad blood" affair. But what was the wacko fucker saying? That *he* was infected? With what, for God's sake?

Bob tried to stand but sat back down at once. Still too dizzy. A fist of panic clutched at his throat and he swallowed hard, lowering his head between his knees. The feeling passed.

Prescott forced himself to remain calm. It was a talent he had taken advantage of many times. Think! Get the doctor here immediately, yes, that was it. From the tone of that weird note from Captain O'Malley, he already knew something. O'Malley was a good one to keep this quiet. No one could be allowed to know about this.

"Sue Sue," he said weakly into the intercom.

"Yes, sir."

"Sue Sue, hold any other calls this morning and ask Captain O'Malley if he can come ASAP. I guess I'm going to have to listen to him preach to me about this weight I've put on. You're gonna have to hold off on those brownies you've been sneaking in to me." Bob regained a little of his composure as he spoke with her.

"Right away, sir, and I'm sorry about the brownies. I know how much you enjoy them. And I certainly enjoy baking them for you. I'll have Captain O'Malley here within the hour."

In fact it took an hour and seventeen minutes. Seventy-seven minutes that seemed an hour apiece. At last the intercom mercifully buzzed.

"Mr. President, Captain O'Malley is here."

"Sure, dear. Send him in, please." Oops, that letter was still out and he had decided not to tell the doctor about it. Bob quickly slipped it into his suitcoat pocket. He put on his best campaign face.

Captain O'Malley fairly burst through the door of the Oval Office. He was a short balding man in his mid fifties who habitually carried himself as if he were on his way to a street brawl. He clutched a manila envelope.

"I hope I haven't interrupted anything, Mr. President," O'Malley said.

"No problem, Rodney." Bob rose and shook hands, then motioned for him to take a seat. The doctor's stiff demeanor was not reassuring. "What can I do for you?"

"Bob, I have some ... sensitive test results to show you. I want you to know that I handled this information with utmost discretion as I always have. In the nature of things, I thought it was my duty to get this information to you without delay and in person. Nobody except myself will have access to this." O'Malley sat ramrod straight in his chair and looked at Prescott. "Bob, you have tested positive for HIV. I'm sorry."

Prescott could not breathe. He could not force a muscle to move. He gazed expressionless at this curious little doctor, paralyzed, and screamed silently somewhere deep inside his brain.

"H ... How d-d-did ... ah ..." Bob gave up trying to talk. His breathing steadied and he reached absently for a wad of Kleenex. For some unaccountable reason his eyes seemed to be watering.

"Bob, I always run your blood through an Elisa test when we do your physical. It's a crude test for antibodies associated with HIV. I run your tests under a fictitious name and get the results faxed directly to me. This last test flagged a positive result, but we occasionally get false positives, so I sent the remainder of your sample off for a Western Blot Test. It's far more accurate. I received the results yesterday and they were also positive."

O'Malley paused, and Bob nodded his understanding, still jabbing his eyes with the fistful of tissue.

"The chances that these results are incorrect are about 100,000 to 1, Bob. I wish to hell I was wrong, but we have to face some hard facts. Of course, I intend to repeat these tests and do others, but we have to talk first.

"Bob, HIV infection does not automatically mean that you have AIDS. AIDS does not automatically mean that you are going to die, not any more. We have new drugs that seem to slow the progression of the disease, for some people."

"Can you tell how far I've progressed?" Prescott asked at length. "Do I need medicine now?"

"That's what we need to talk about. I checked your Elisa test from *last* time around and it was negative. Because of a delay in viral growth, you may have been infected then but certainly no further back than two years ago. Chances are there was no infection. The majority of patients carry the virus for five to ten years before their CD-4 count starts dropping."

"CD-4?" Bob asked.

"Yes. The CD-4 count is a measure of the T-helper lymphocytes in the blood. These T-helpers, or white blood cells, are like field commanders during a battle. They plan an immune response to any foreign invaders in your body."

"So AIDS kills the T-helpers?"

"It attacks them until the immune response becomes disorganized and that's when we get into trouble." Dr. O'Malley sounded like a SWAT team lieutenant.

"So an HIV patient usually has five to ten good years before this T-cell count drops?"

"Yes, but unfortunately yours has already dropped a significant amount. We're not in a crisis yet, but we would have to classify you as a 'rapid progressor.' Only about 2 percent of those infected with HIV fall into that category, and they generally develop symptoms of AIDS much sooner."

Bob felt a tightening in his neck again. His chest was beginning to feel as if someone were squeezing it. "Rodney, this is too sudden. How do we slow the son of a bitch down? You must have something in your bag of tricks."

"First, you need to relax. I don't want you having a heart attack right now. I've been giving this some thought. I suggest that we bring in one other doctor. His name is Cameron Luers, and he is one of the most knowledgeable AIDS researchers in the United States. He also happens to be an old classmate of mine. We can work together on your medication and progress.

"I will draw your blood myself and get it to him for analysis. He will do the tests and prescribe the medications. I'll arrange to obtain them privately. You have to decide if you want to bring others in.

"Our goals will be to keep you healthy and functioning and to slow the progression of HIV effects. AIDS," he explained, "is not a disease in itself but what we call a syndrome, a cluster of opportunistic infections which ..."

"Please ..." Prescott stopped him, "I know all of that. What I want to know is, can you kill it at this stage? I want to kill it."

"To be honest, no. I'm sorry, Bob. We've got hundreds of people around the world working on this, but so far there is clearly no cure. It's going to take much more research and time before this one is whipped."

"My God." Bob slumped back into his chair, the wind knocked out of him. "How did this happen? How?"

"I have to ask you the same question. You're going to have to trust me and be honest with me. If there is a person out there who has infected you unwittingly, we have to find her. You have to tell me everyone you have had sex with over the last fourteen months. Don't leave anyone out, Bob. This is important."

O'Malley pulled a notepad and pen from his jacket pocket.

"No one!" Bob said. "Put the notepad away."

"What? You're going to have to do better than that," O'Malley scolded.

"Don't speak to me like a goddamned child, Rodney. I don't know what you may have heard about *sex* and the presidency, but it's not all that hot. No matter what the tabloids say. I've never been so celibate in my whole life."

Bob set his jaw and looked away. He couldn't bring himself to tell the doctor about his affair at the Grand Regency. He would deal with her in private. Besides, she had always insisted on a condom, so he couldn't have been exposed from that angle.

"Okay, Bob. Sorry. But what about Stephanie? I'm afraid that she has been exposed for almost a year now."

"No. Wrong again, Rodney. She's had no exposure. Not from me. It's been years since we tried anything like that," Bob explained, hating to have to bare his life this way.

"Then how *were* you exposed?" O'Malley was honestly puzzled. "I know you're clean on needle contamination, and you've had no surgery or transfusions, so how?"

"You're the one who's supposed to figure that out!" Bob yelled. "How else can you get it? Kissing? I kiss babies and old women sometimes."

"No, that's almost impossible." Dr. O'Malley sat for a moment, trying to remember if he had missed anything that should be obvious. Both men scoured their minds for a logical explanation. "Was there any time over the past year or two that you were cut or jabbed with a sharp instrument? Any time you found blood on your body that wasn't yours?"

Bob Prescott and Rodney O'Malley looked into each other's eyes at the same moment, but it was Bob who spoke: "Those cuts and scrapes I got from the Riverfront Park scramble!"

O'Malley frowned skeptically. "You had a cut on your chin, strawberries on each elbow and lacerations on one hand. We cleaned and dressed them daily and they healed without incident. Correct?"

"Yes ... except for a spot on the palm of my right hand. It got infected and stayed swollen for a couple of weeks. I remember because it hurt like a son of a bitch to shake hands." Bob was looking at his palm and replaying that frightening day in his mind.

~~~~~~~~~~

He had left the hotel and was working the crowd toward the riverfront when Banks Edwards tapped him on the elbow and whispered in his ear. "Bob, there's a decorated veteran up ahead who's a member of Veterans for Prescott. Looks like he was Vietnam era. This could be a great shot for the papers!"

Bob saluted the man, then approached him to shake hands. And all hell broke loose. For the first time now, Bob remembered the look on the man's face. A strong face. He looked ... honorable. And sincere. He may have been crying. Yes, he was. Bob puzzled. How could he remember that now? He didn't think he'd seen it in the first place. The handshake had been manly—firm and confident. A strong grip. He had returned that grip with his double-handed shake. Bob had been touched. Then the guy was gone. Wait a minute ... Honor ... sincerity ... My God. Oh, my God!

It was as if someone had slapped him! That man was *the one*. The one who wrote the letter. He'd been crying! The man was crying as Bob gripped his hand. My God, how did he do it?

~~~~~~~~~~

"Bob ... hey, Bob.... Take some deep, slow breaths," Dr. O'Malley ordered. He had hurried around the big desk and was holding the president's shoulder. "Deep, steady breaths, Bob. You're hyperventilating. It's okay. It's normal at a time like this. It's okay now. Your head will clear in a moment."

But the image was still vivid, consuming. He had been grasping the man's hand when the agents threw him to the sidewalk. And the cut on his hand had shown up the next morning. Naturally he'd assumed he got it falling on the sidewalk, but it wasn't a regular cut, was it? It looked like two pimples. The following day it was red and sore, and stayed that way long after his other scrapes were healed. That man had ... had somehow poisoned him.

"Damn him!" Bob said out loud. "Damn his Purple Heart and his Vietnam and his whole motherfucking family!"

"Whoa, Bob! What are you talking about?" Dr. O'Malley had dropped down on one knee to take Prescott's pulse. Now he stared up at the president's face with astonishment.

"Nothing, nothing, Rodney. I think I must be hallucinating or something. I'm okay." Bob quickly regained control. "Let me get up. I need to walk around."

Bob was angry now and hammered the desk with his fists. "Rodney, you are going to keep this in absolute confidence. And make that completely clear to Dr. Luers. But I want you and your friend to know that today, this very minute, we're going to war. We are going to whip this damn disease, whatever it takes!" Prescott smacked the desk again.

"I know it may seem self-serving, but I am going to make sure that Dr. Luers and all the scientists and support people in this battle will have all of the funds they can possibly use ... Actually, I've been planning this since Jimmy Puddephat died ... of AIDS.... He was a very dear friend of mine. By God, we'll name this whole initiative in his honor, the James Puddephat ... something. We'll think of a name. I am going to make things happen fast. You cannot let on about a thing. That's an order."

"*All* of my patients get the same confidentiality and the same concern, Bob. You don't have to make it an order. I'm your doctor. That still means something, you know?"

"Yeah, well, I wasn't yelling at you, Rodney, I'm just mad at ... the situation. We'll play these extra visits of yours off as a ... personal monitoring of my blood pressure, how's that? I will also need you to be an adviser on a new international initiative, 'Search for the Cure.' I'll need lots of information. I want a status report on current research projects around the world. I want it for a Cabinet meeting tomorrow afternoon." Prescott paced back and forth, crisscrossing the room.

"I can get you a solid picture by tomorrow, but not all the details. Bob, listen.... I know what you are doing, but remember this is a tough case. Keep your expectations reasonable. This is still going to take some time."

"Goddammit, Rodney. I don't *have* some time. Fuck, you ought to know that. If we make the reward big enough, someone will crack this case!" Bob yelled from across the room.

"Sure, Bob. I was just trying to give you some perspective."

The president gave him a long look. "The perspective is this, my friend: This disease is now a matter of national security. Did you think of that? You wouldn't *believe* how much power I have to deal with a national emergency, and I intend to fucking use it!" He glared at O'Malley. "I'll need that report by tomorrow noon, sir."

"Yes, Mr. President." O'Malley picked up his folder and paused at the door. "Sorry, Bob. I'm really sorry."

Prescott nodded but said nothing. He began thumbing the stacks of paperwork awaiting his attention, then swept them all to one side in irritation. He got out a fresh legal pad and a pen.

The president jotted an outline for the first week of his new life. At the top he listed a review of Captain O'Malley's report, followed by a meeting with the Cabinet later in the afternoon. At the bottom, he printed and underlined the opening salvo:

AIDS SUMMIT FOR CONG. LEADERS—BIPART.—CAMP DAVID

"Sue Sue, see if you can patch a call to Howie. If he is on his usual meeting schedule, he'll be on about the twelfth hole at Pelican River. The message is: the chief of staff will get his butt back here by the fastest means. Got that down? Okay, next I'm calling a Cabinet meeting for tomorrow at 6:00 p.m. You'll need to get the word out pronto."

"Yes, sir."

Bob went back over his list, scratching off all but the most pressing chores of his daily routine. Even at that, he'd hardly have a moment to breathe. He'd have to drop all his scheduled meetings. This would infuriate several of his long-time supporters and most of the conserva-tives he had been wooing. They had been bumped too often before. No matter. The ones he really had to answer to, no matter what the polls said, were back in Arkansas. They were expecting some fast, hot action on his part. They had huge bets on the table.

"Fuck 'em," he said to himself.

President Robert Davis Prescott had consciously been searching for months for that one unique achievement that would be *his* in the eyes of *history*. The thing he'd be remembered for when kids looked at his picture in their schoolbooks. Strange. Out of all the political issues he might have chosen, this one had chosen *him*.

In the silence of his office he strained to hear his mother's voice. He heard it less and less often these days, but he desperately needed to hear it now. She would know what to do. He cursed the interference of his own pulse pounding in his ears. Straining ... he could almost recognize *her* voice in the babble of noises in his head ... almost.

FORTY-EIGHT ~~~~~~~~

JULY 14, 1998
LITTLE ROCK, ARKANSAS

THE JUDGE THUMBED THE KEYLESS LOCKING BUTTON OF HIS MER-
cedes and stepped onto the sidewalk. In his mid sixties he was a
handsome figure, slim and tanned and confident in his stride.
Pleated khakis and a red "Razorback Supporter" polo shirt completed the
effect. Looking closely, one could see that he was just starting to lose a bit
of his striking white hair.

Earlier in the spring he had played Emile in the city's community the-
ater production of *South Pacific*. He hardly needed make-up. Everyone
loved his French-with-a-southern-drawl.

The temperature was already well into the nineties and would pass
one hundred by noon. The Judge always preferred to stay by his pool on a
day like this but he was on duty. Indeed, his errand was so pressing that it
took precedence over comfort and everything else.

He left his car on the east side of Broadway and threaded his way through heavy foot traffic toward the police station. Sergeant Joe Boving was loading his shotgun into the front seat rack of his police cruiser at the curb.

"Hot enough for you, Joe?" the Judge asked.

"Hi, Judge! Yeah, it's hot enough for me but it's not hot enough to run off all these crazy-assed homos that moved in this week. You ever seen such a bunch of fruits?" The sergeant started the car to cool it off before he slid in.

The Judge laughed and waved as he continued past the station house. The city was overrun by an international gathering of people attending the second annual "Living with AIDS Conference." The nature of the conference ensured a thick concentration of gay attendees and all of the high drama that seemed to follow them from place to place.

By the time he reached the small warehouse under a bridge abutment behind the police parking lot, he was soaking wet. And it was supposed to get even hotter—damn!

The warehouse was a run-down affair with the windows barred and painted black. It nestled partly under a bridge connecting Little Rock with North Little Rock. The Judge and his operations had been the sole tenant for over twenty years.

A huge, black, block-headed Rottweiler lay on the stoop. It tensed when the Judge approached. The dog had been trained to stop anyone he didn't know and ask questions later.

"Hey, Rommel! How are you, you big ugly bastard?" The Judge said, patting the dog on top of his enormous, meaty head.

Rommel changed from menacing killer guard dog into overgrown puppy. He wagged his tailless rump furiously and coated the Judge's hand with slimy drool.

"Damn, boy, I'd just as soon you go ahead and bite me as slobber my hand off. Is anybody here with you, old fella?" The Judge unlocked the door. He and Rommel stepped into the cool, dim, mostly empty building.

"Over here, Judge," a voice said. It came from a lighted lab bench at the far end of the long room. "I've just about got it ready."

"Where did you get the hat, Doc?" the Judge asked, bending down for a closer look.

"On the street, just like everyone else," Doc replied. He was carefully injecting a milky solution into the sweat brim on the inside of a ball cap. He wore Kevlar gloves and a jeweler's loupe over his regular glasses.

Doc was thirtyish and wore his hair long and blonde. He had been a PA in Desert Storm and put some special military skills to work for the Judge when he got back. The invention he was perfecting on the bench was by no means his first in these duties, but it surely was the most unusual. It had to be delivered in less than an hour. There was absolutely no room for error.

"Okay, Doc, show me how it's going to work."

"Let me finish this one last injection ... There we go ... Okay. You see the sweatband around the inside edge of the cap? Looks normal, right? Well, it's not." He held the cap up to the light and handed the Judge a large magnifying glass. "Just look, don't touch. Can you make out those tiny fibers angling from the brim toward the crown of the hat?"

The Judge peered through the glass and nodded. "I see them. They look like stiff little hairs. What are they?"

"They're called microtubes. They're tiny carbon straws about one-tenth the diameter of a small needle, hollow and extremely sharp. Our people over at Aerocomp Labs are working on these little jewels. I borrowed a few from a buddy of mine over there. They will be a big ticket as soon as his company gets the funding to finish their development. They'll be used for everything from airplane wings to fishing rods. They're hundreds of times smaller and stronger than any material known to man." Doc had done his research.

"Never heard the like," said the Judge. "But I'm afraid I don't see the point?"

"It's really pretty simple. I embedded them in a tiny polyurethane bladder inside the sweatband of the cap. It's not much bigger than a rubber band. I just finished charging that bladder with Anectine, which is a super-powerful chemical used by surgeons to stop the diaphragm during heart surgery. Its chemical name is succinyl-choline chloride.

"When someone puts this hat on, at least forty of those microtubes slip slightly under the skin of his scalp and start slowly forcing in the Anectine. They're so tiny you can't feel it—not until it's too late. Even if you did and jerked the hat off, it would just push the tube deeper and guarantee the injection of the drug.

"Three drops of the concentration I mixed today will put a grown man down in twenty seconds. Everyone will suppose he's having a heart attack. The hat'll probably get lost in the excitement." Doc smiled proudly and carefully placed the hat back on the bench.

"When you say down, do you mean … dead?" the Judge asked.

"I mean that his breathing will stop. You just can't live too long in that condition."

"I hope to God you've tested all this. This has to happen today. And it has to work!" The Judge was starting to be visibly edgy.

"Watch."

Doc picked up the syringe he had been using and walked over to Rommel. He patted him and then slipped the needle under the skin of his head. He pushed the plunger lightly then pulled the needle quickly out of the folds of loose flesh.

"Time it if you like," he said nonchalantly, putting the syringe back on the bench and crossing his arms. "Rommel couldn't stand this heat anyway."

Within seconds the dog began fidgeting and tried to stand. He licked his lips a few times and looked at the men as if to ask for help. His eyes twitched and his head lolled over to one side so far it flopped him down on the floor.

Rommel moved his legs for a moment as if he were running, then let out a soft moan. All his movements ceased. His eyes still looked up at them.

"Motherfucker! Where did you come up with that stuff?" the Judge asked.

"Man, every bow hunter in the South has known about this shit for the last twenty-five years. It's sold under the table at all of the good sporting goods stores around here. It comes in powder form packed in a rubber pod that sits behind your broadhead on the arrow shaft. Bow hunters like to use it because all you have to do is nick a deer and he won't run over sixty yards. You want to be careful not to nick yourself, though. It could really screw up a nice morning in the woods." He laughed. Doc folded the cap so that it could be safely carried.

"Damn! I'm impressed, Doc. If this comes off, I'll see to it that you get some ... uh ... special consideration. I'd better get moving now, not much time."

"Hey, Judge. How are you going to get it on his head? You got that part worked out?" Doc asked.

The Judge chuckled. "Hell, yes!" he said, exaggerating his drawl. "We still have one of our men on the inside, you know. I'm going to get this to him now and he'll see to the rest. Good work, Doc."

As he turned to go, he had to step over the rottweiler stretched out on the floor. "Shame about old Rommel, he was a damn good guard dog. You gonna get another?"

"Gotta have one. But I think I'm going to get a German shepherd this next time. I hear they're more loyal," he said, walking the Judge to the door. "You be careful in that heat out there. A man could have a heat stroke in a heartbeat on a day like today."

The Judge opened the door and plunged into the oven that is Arkansas in the summertime.

FORTY-NINE 〜〜〜〜〜〜〜〜〜〜

J AVIER PERCHED AT THE BAR IN A THATCHED-ROOF PALAPA ON THE city limits of Playa del Carmen. He was in a fine mood. The cerveza was cold and the breeze blowing in from the offshore reef had been cooled by an afternoon thundershower.

The ferry would dock at the landing just down the street. This was the one that brought all the rich Europeans from the island of Cozumel to the cheap shops of this bustling little Mexican village.

The stalls offered handcrafted jewelry and woven goods produced by the remnants of the Mayas. They also served the coldest beer in Mexico.

Roberto had gone across to the island this morning to meet with an official from Spain. Then he'd bring him here for a meeting with Javier. Things had apparently gone well or Roberto would have returned in a private ponga by the middle of the morning.

The barkeeper had the television tuned to CNN and one of the "blonde people" was on camera, standing outside the Old Statehouse in Little Rock. Javier recognized the setting from ... that day. The reporter was jabbering about President Prescott's being on his way from the helipad directly behind her. He would proceed thus and so to the stage, which faced one hundred thousand people gathered for the opening of the James Puddephat International Assembly to Find the Cure.

The cameras picked up the president making his way through the scores of state troopers who surrounded the stage. His security force was at least three times larger than it had been in '95. Around the podium was a clear, bulletproof enclosure to protect the speaker from a gunshot on three sides. Armed guards controlled the rear.

The president's speech was uncharacteristically brief, and he delivered it with a passion he'd never achieved in his campaigns. He spoke of all the AIDS research programs he had initiated around the world in the past year, and the hope they conveyed of finding the cure for this heartbreaking worldwide scourge. Whatever it took, together they would work ceaselessly for the same, great purpose. They would never rest and never falter in their quest. And a cure *would* be found and made available to all who suffered.

When he finished, the president stepped around the bulletproof enclosure to play to the madly cheering crowd. The First Lady and several gay-rights spokesmen from his administration were on the stage with him, applauding—smiling—hugging one another. It looked to Javier like a regular "circle-jerk," Washington-style.

Javier was glad the man had adopted a mission that might help Zack and Deidra. He was so convincing that if you didn't know better, you might think his life depended on it.

Ricky chuckled to himself and silently toasted his peglegged friend in Canada. His inspired act of retribution seemed to be working. Had it been left up to him, he would have made sure the son of a bitch had extra holes in his head—one for each fork in his tongue. The thought made him burst out laughing.

As Javier studied the fanfare on the screen, he observed once again how difficult it would be to guard this man from an assassin. The bastard was such an easy target!

"Can you change the channel, amigo?" he asked the bartender.

The bartender mumbled something in assent and reached to dry his hands. Javier saw Stephanie Prescott hold a red baseball cap above her head, and walk forward to show it to the crowd. Then she handed it to the president. It was emblazoned with the now famous insignia of his Humanity Against AIDS Foundation.

President Robert Prescott turned to the crowd as he unfolded the back of the cap. He held it above his head and presented it proudly to the people, a tear visible in the corner of one eye as the camera panned in for a headshot. The screen went blank.

The next image was a closed-circuit telecast of a bullfight in Mexico City.

"Thanks, amigo," Javier said. "I can only take so much of that garbage. Una mas cerveza, por favor."

~~~~~~~~~~~~~~~~

AUTHOR'S AFTERWORD

THIS IS PURELY A WORK OF FICTION. DAVID, RICKY, SYLVIA, AND THE others are the products of a fertile imagination.

All but Zack, that is. Zack is not "real" either, but his character represents real people—hundreds of real people who are suffering and dying throughout Canada after contracting AIDS and Hepatitis C from contaminated blood.

This underlying story is true. I wish it too were imaginative fiction, but it is not. David Farr's quest to avenge his son could be that of any father of an innocent child whose life is shattered or lost due to the greed of a few powerful, unscrupulous men.

I believe that thousands of Canadians today endure the agonies of incurable, blood-borne disease because of just such unconscionable greed. Hundreds have died.

It is a story that all Canada knows to its sorrow, but one that few Americans are even aware of. Its cost in treasure and lives rises every day.

This immense tragedy continues to play out in hospital rooms, courts, and graveyards in our great, quiet northern neighbor. As of this writing, there has been no closure for the victims and their families.

The tainted blood apparently originated in the state where I was born: Arkansas.

The story, as nearly as I can piece it together from numerous press reports and Canadian government documents, has two distinct parts.

The first part took place in Canada. It is alleged and widely believed among some victims' support groups that the bad blood was originally a back-door purchase from a U.S. supplier. The theory is that the deal involved kickbacks to officials of the Canadian government and of the Canadian Red Cross. The guilty persons have so far escaped punishment thanks to what appears to be a coverup. Families of victims vow that they will not rest until this terrible injustice is righted.

I do not vouch for the truth of these allegations, but I have spoken with some of those concerned and there is no doubt that they believe what they say. And they make a good, strong case.

The second part took place in the United States. Canadian investigators reportedly traced the bad blood to Arkansas. There they could get no further, possibly due to a similar coverup. In any case they were unable to obtain further answers and went back to Canada empty-handed.

The entire matter was investigated in great detail over a four-year period by a panel headed by former Canadian judge Horace Krever. The Krever Commission issued its final, 1132-page report in November 1997. It did not name specific wrongdoers who may have been involved in the alleged under-the-counter scheme that brought such tragedy to Canada. However, a special division of the RCMP has been charged with the duty of continuing the investigation and bringing those responsible to criminal prosecution.

Readers who wish to know more about the case can seek information best by computer. A website for Canadian news coverage of the story and of the Krever Commission report can be accessed at http://headlines.yahoo.com/Full-Coverage/canada/tainted_blood_scandal. The report can be purchased by mail [$75 Canadian], read in Canadian libraries, or downloaded free from the same web site.

I share the victims' hope that Canadian investigators will continue the search. If they pinpoint the perpetrators in their country, it may well lead to the identification of the Americans who had a hand in this foul business. Their despicable actions equally cry out for justice.